Standing in the Storm

The Last Brigade, Book 2

William Alan Webb

δ

Dingbat Publishing

Humble, Texas

CAST OF CHARACTERS

The Angriff family

Nicholas Trajanus Angriff—General of the Army. Nick the A to those who fear him. Idolizes George Patton's tactical genius and persona, but not as fussy as Patton about personal appearance and decorum. Like another hero of his, Winston Churchill, Angriff is sometimes accused of courting danger. As a three-star general, he led tactical missions more suited to a captain or lieutenant, usually against direct orders not to do so. His career survived because of his popularity with his men and the public, and his record of success.

Janine Marie Jackson Angriff—Nick's wife, a victim in the Lake Tahoe 'incident.'

Lieutenant Morgan Mary Randall, nee Angriff—Older of Nick's two daughters. Lieutenant in the US Army, executive officer First Platoon, Alpha Company, 1st Tank Battalion. Call sign Bulldozer One One Two. Married to Captain Joe Randall. Nicknamed Tank Girl.

Cynthia June Angriff—Nick's younger daughter, caught in the same attack as her mother.

The Americans

Lt. General Norman Vincent Fleming—Executive Officer of the 7th Cavalry, also the Brigade S-3, Operations. Norm is Nick Angriff's best friend, dating back to their days in OCS. Both men enlisted and worked their way through the ranks, an almost impossible feat. Fleming is the man Angriff trusts above all others.

Major General Dennis Tompkins—Survivor of the Collapse who did not go cold, but instead lived fifty years in post-Collapse America, leading his team of five survivors.

Captain Joseph Daniel Randall—The best helicopter pilot in the brigade. Married to Morgan Randall. Call sign Ripsaw Real.

Lieutenant George 'Bunny' Carlos—Joe Randall's best friend and co-pilot.

Lieutenant Alisa Plotz—AH-72 Comanche commander and Joe Randall's wingman.

Sergeant Andy Arnold—Alisa Plotz's co-pilot.

Sergeant Lorenzo 'Zo' Piccaldi—One of the two best snipers in the Marine battalion, friend and secret love interest of Lara Snowtiger.

John Paul Thibodeaux—best friend to Dennis Tompkins during their fifty years wandering in the wilderness.

Paul Hausser—One of Tompkins' five survivors.

Sig Zuckerman—Another member of Tompkins' final group of five.

Derek Tandy—One of Tompkins' five.

Monty Wilson—One of Tompkins' five.

PFC Lara Snowtiger—Marine sniper, a full-blooded Choctaw. Snowtiger embraced her heritage and is versed in Choctaw lore. She is considered as good as any sniper in the 7th Cavalry, including Zo Piccaldi.

Colonel Benjamin Franklin Walling—Promoted to his present rank by Angriff, he commands the headquarters staff and manages Angriff's day-to-day schedule.

Sergeant Major of the Army John Charles Schiller—Trusted subordinate who runs the day-to-day routine for Angriff's headquarters. Angriff often asks Schiller for advice.

Colonel William Emerson Schiller—Brother of Sergeant J.C. Schiller, he is the brigade's S-4, Supply Officer, and is considered a savant at supply chain organization and utilization.

Lt. Colonel Roger 'Rip' Kordibowski—Battalion S-2, Intelligence Officer.

Colonel Todd Berger—Commander of the Marine Recon Battalion.

Colonel Michael Ricci—Commander of the Tank Battalion.

Sergeant Norma Spears—Barracks Sergeant for the female Marines.

Captain Robert Malkinovich—First Company Commander, Tank Battalion. Call sign Bulldozer One One.

Major Harold 'Harry the Hat' Strickland—Executive Officer of the 1st Marine Recon Battalion.

Captain Martin S. Sully—Commander of Dog Company, 7th Marine Reconnaissance Battalion.

Lieutenant Akio Tensikaya—Commander of First Platoon, Alpha Company, Tank Battalion. Morgan Randall is his executive officer.

Major Fitzhugh Howarth Claringdon—Executive Officer of the

Tank Battalion.

Lt. Colonel Ashley Wisnewski-Smith—7th Brigade S-9, Civil-Military Cooperation.

Ian Jones—Civilian Head of Construction and Maintenance Department.

Private Howard Wilson Dupree—Communications specialist and computer whiz.

Sergeant Frances (Frame) Rossi—Crew chief for *Tank Girl.*

The crew of Joe's Junk

Staff Sergeant Joe Ootoi—Nicknamed 'Toy.' Gunner.

Corporal Tanya Marscal—Driver. Although born in the USA, Tanya has a faint Ukrainian accent because both of her parents emigrated from their homeland and she picked up traces of the way they spoke. She is also fluent in Russian and Ukrainian.

Martha 'Marty' Bright-Hu—Loader. Widowed, husband was Paul Hu, pronounced with a long 'U.'

Task Force Zombie, a/k/a 'The Nameless'

Green Ghost—Longtime subordinate of Angriff's and currently his S-5, Security. His real identity is unknown, as the Nameless only have code names. Angriff trusts him completely.

Vapor—Original member of TF Zombie. Wise-cracking member of the team. He and Green Ghost have known each other since childhood.

One Eye—Original member of TF Zombie. Nickname refers to his personality.

Wingnut—Original member of TF Zombie. Taciturn, a specialist at explosives and chemicals.

Glide—Replacement addition to TF Zombie, Glide is an ultra-dangerous computer specialist. She is gorgeous, and an 8th degree Krav Maga.

Nipple—Green Ghost's twin sister. Most think she is psychotic, but like her brother, her reflexes are off the chart.

Razor—Replacement addition, the newest member of the team.

The Sevens

Nabi Husam Allah—The Caliph of the Caliphate of the Seven Prayers of the New Prophet, self-proclaimed prophet of Allah. In truth, he is Larry Armstrong, a criminal conman. His adherents are fanatically loyal.

Abdul-Qudoos Fadil el Mofty—Emir of New Khorasan. His original name is Richard Lee Armstrong, brother of the Caliph, Larry Armstrong. He bears the title of Superior Imam, second only to the Caliph himself, who is the Supreme Imam. These titles were created by the Armstrong brothers to elevate them above all imams in Islam. He is also second in command of The Sword of the New Prophet, the military arm of the Caliphate.

Evie Armstrong, a/k/a Manahil Bashara—Sister of Larry and Richard Lee Armstrong, mother of Sati Bashara.

Ibrahim Yaseen—Counselor of Production for the Province and one of the men el Mofty suspected of being a spy for the Caliph.

Ahmednur Hussien Muhdin—The top-ranking general in New Khorasan.

Sati Bashara—Senior Aga and oldest nephew of Emir Abdul-Qudoos Fadil el Mofty, appointed head of the province of New Khorasan, a region of the larger Caliphate of the Seven Prayers of the New Prophet, encompassing parts of Arizona, New Mexico, and old Mexico. He is the second most powerful lieutenant in New Khorasan.

Haleem—Childhood friend and constant companion of Sati Bashara.

Wazid—Friend of Bashara.

Paco Mohammad—Born in old Mexico, Paco led a band of friends and relatives north looking for food and shelter. Confronted by forces of the Amir of New Khorasan, Paco decided to convert to the Amir's brand of Islam rather than be wiped out, becoming, in effect, a throwaway mercenary force.

Civilians

Richard Parfist—Lived in a village far outside of Prescott, until General Patton's Guards raided the village.

Lisa Parfist—Richard Parfist's wife.

Kayla Parfist—Richard and Lisa Parfist's 15-year-old daughter.

Rick Parfist, Jr.—Richard and Lisa Parfist's 12-year-old son.

The Apaches

Govind—Chief of the Western Apache.

Gosheven—The middle of the three brothers.

Gopan—Govind's youngest brother.

The New Republic of Arizona

Lester Earl Hull, a/k/a General George Patton V—Warlord leader of the New Republic of Arizona.

Colonel Norbert Cranston—Second in command to Lester Hull and commander of the military forces of the New Republic.

Author's Foreword

The Last Brigade series is my *homage* to the armed forces of the United States and all others fighting to keep the world free of tyranny. The world view the series presents is, at its core, pretty simple: America and those who stand with her are the good guys. There may be (and are) some bad people within those armed forces, but the vast majority do so for all the right reasons. This book and others in the series represent my ideals on patriotism, and I make no apologies for that. If you're looking for America-bashing, you won't find it here.

But this is not an essay. These books are designed to be fast, fun to read, a little over the top, and, maybe, bringing an important issue or two to the forefront. I don't know about you, but reading a thriller about average people doing average things doesn't sound very exciting to me. It might be realistic, but I read to be entertained, and I don't find that entertaining. A good thriller using average people as characters would have them doing extraordinary things, things that *are* over the top, things they would never do otherwise. Many writers have mastered the art of confronting a normal person with dangerous events, thereby forcing their characters to take actions they never dreamed they would take. Heck, it's an entire sub-genre of crime novels and thrillers.

My books take this premise a step further. I start with extraordinary people and then have them do extraordinary things. For example, few real people would carry a fifty-caliber Desert Eagle pistol into combat, like Nick Angriff does. I can think of a dozen reasons why it's a terrible idea. For one thing, seven rounds is a small magazine. For another, the recoil using such a pistol one-handed would require massive wrist strength to rip off multiple rounds quickly. And yet Nick does this and I think it's really cool, and apparently so do a lot of others. A real person could never do that... but what if they could? If someone else had written this series, I'd be all over it, because it's fun. I'm a fan of this genre. It's the kind of thing I like to read, and that's the only thing I know how to write.

Nick Angriff is the amalgamation of every hero I've ever read about, from George Patton and Erwin Rommel to Conan the Barbarian and Sergeant Nick Fury. He is able to fire his Desert Eagles with pinpoint accuracy while riding in an armored personnel carrier down a bumpy African road, because he is Nick Angriff. He can do it; others can't. Why? Because he can, that's why. Likewise, in real life, lieutenant generals don't lead tactical rescue missions into the jungles of a hostile nation. Nick did it in *Standing The Final Watch* because it was *fun*. This is, after all, science fiction, with a touch here and there of fantasy. I'm going to take liberties where I think them appropriate in the interest of telling a better story. And, just for the record, the Angriffs have physical abilities in the top 0.1% of humanity. If non-fiction is more your cuppa, then I'm with you there! I write that, too.

Early versions of this book had every technical detail you can imagine, from the precise model number of an APC (I even had a serial number in there) to how various small arms worked and why. The order of battle for the brigade was right out of the Army manual. But the book was s-l-o-w. So I've played fast and loose with the organization, the events, the way things lay out, and the dialogue of the military characters. Is it the way someone might speak in combat? Not always. But is it fun to read? I think so. And if I'm right, then I've done my job.

If you are preparing to read *Standing In The Storm* but have not yet read *The Ghost of Voodoo Village: Short Story and Bonus Chapters for Standing The Final Watch*, you might consider doing so first. There are a couple of sub-plots in *Bonus Chapters* that are mentioned in *SITS* and become significant in books three and later. Green Ghost's origin story, *The Ghost of Voodoo Village*, would also explain a number of lingering questions about him and his sister.

Standing The Final Watch has been a major success. I wish to thank all who invested their precious time and money with me. There is a trust burden on a writer to deliver the best possible story to the reader who spends the money to read it. Please know that I work hard at my craft. I want you to feel your time and money are well spent, and I will never forget that any success I may have is because of you, my readers.

May God bless you all!

William Alan Webb,
18 January 2017

In the west a storm is brewing, and another in the east,
In the south a tyrant lurks, less man than vicious beast;
Innocents cower in between, at the mercy of the swarm,
Until brave Americans shield them, by standing in the storm.
   Sergio Velazquez, "Standing In The Storm"

About me died the world I knew,
In its place a new world grew;
Where masses worked for a privileged few,
Just like the old world that I knew.
The ruling clique held tight the yoke,
Around the neck of common folk;
Ignoring the freedom of which they spoke,
Until the little men awoke.
        Sergio Velazquez, from "Yoke"

Prologue

What is the force that compels a man to risk his life day after day, to endure the constant tension, the fear of death... the steady loss of his friends? What can possess a rational man to make him act so irrationally?
    James McPherson

The Sonoran Desert
1647 hours, June 25

"What're we looking at, G.G.?" Vapor said. After a quick look, he lay on his back on the hill's reverse slope.

Green Ghost propped his elbows on the crest of the hill and adjusted his binoculars. After following the old highway for two days, he and his crew had deployed on opposite sides when a vehicle came up from the south. He focused the lenses.

One hundred yards away, three men stood around a Honda sedan. With the sun at his back, he could distinguish every detail of them and their vehicle. Dust coated the car, including the two jerry cans and spare tire tied to the roof. Painted on the driver's door was an upright crescent moon crossed by a scimitar. The meaning could not have been more obvious, even without the Arabic script below it.

"They're young, late teens or early twenties. They haven't missed any meals, either," he said. "Clothes are well made, no holes or patches. Leather shoes..."

"No split-tails?"

Green Ghost lowered the binoculars and gave Vapor a sideways look they both knew meant *knock it off.*

"Weapons?"

Green Ghost brought the binoculars back to his face. "Yeah, all three are carrying. Looks like M16s; could be M-4s, though."

"What's that gibberish on the car say?" Vapor asked.

"You know it's Arabic. At least it's supposed to be; the grammar is awful. It says *new prophet word.*"

"So it's Islamic?"

"I don't know. That's question numero uno for those three... damn!"

"Waddup, bwana?"

"They're hauling ass."

He shifted the binoculars to focus on a slight rise on the other side of the highway. Holding his left hand straight up, he extended five fingers, meaning *don't shoot unless you have to.* Two hundred yards away, Wingnut extended his own arm with his fingers making the *Okay* sign.

"If this goes to shit, aim for the tires. We need prisoners."

"What could possibly go wrong?" Vapor said.

Green Ghost ignored the sarcasm. Setting aside his M16, he stood up in full view. The driver had climbed into his seat and the other two had their doors open. Once they were inside the car, Green Ghost's crew could not stop it without gunfire.

"Hey!" he yelled, waving his arms. "Up here!"

The car emptied. Its occupants ran to the other side and brought their rifles to bear on the man who'd appeared out of nowhere. Green Ghost took a step down the hill, keeping his hands up. He took a second step, then a third.

One shot echoed across the desert and kicked up dust to his right.

"No!" he screamed. "Don't shoot, don't shoot. I'm unarmed."

More bullets whizzed past him. A round grazed his shoulder and he dove for cover in a shallow depression behind a brittlebush. Bluish petals settled in his dark hair.

Vapor returned fire on full automatic. His initial rounds chewed up both drivers' side tires. Targeting this new threat, they returned fire, pinning him down.

"Where the fuck are Wingnut and that lunatic sister of yours?"

On cue, Wingnut and Nipple opened fire behind the three men. One twisted and jerked as rounds tore into his back. The other two spun to return fire, too late. Nipple never missed and she put three rounds into the face of the man on her left. Wingnut squeezed the trigger on full automatic and four rounds hit the other man in his chest.

Even before the firing stopped, Green Ghost was running downhill. Rounding the front of the car, he smelled gasoline, and leaped over a stream pouring from under the car. The man Nipple had shot was missing half of his head, so he checked the other one. Despite blood-soaked clothes, the chest rose and fell in shallow breaths. Grabbing him by the armpits, Green Ghost dragged him off the highway.

Nipple and Wingnut approached, eyes to their scopes.

"Put dirt on that gas!" he said. "A fire could attract their butt buddies."

They immediately started heaping dust onto the puddling fuel. Wingnut popped the hood and inspected the engine for damage.

As they worked around the car, Green Ghost lifted the dying man's head and patted his cheek. "Hey, don't die on me yet. What's your name? Where are you from?"

The man's eyes flickered open, but it was obvious he could not see.

"Tell Sati I died facing my enemy," he said in a whisper. "Tell him... I prayed to the prophet... with my last breath."

"Who are you? What's your name?"

"May Allah protect our beloved new prophet." The man convulsed several times and coughed blood. Then he went rigid. After a long exhale, his body relaxed. Green Ghost wiped his bloody hands on the corpse's pants.

"The heap's shot to shit," Wingnut said. "And those cans are full. If this goes up, we need to be far away."

Green Ghost stood and inspected the damage. "We need to work on your marksmanship."

"Hey, I put him down, didn't I?"

"You put the car down with him. Do you like walking that much?"

"I didn't blow out the tires," Wingnut said. He changed the subject. "Did the burp tell you anything?"

He nudged the dead man with his boot. Flies buzzed into the corpse's open mouth.

"Yeah," Ghost said. "I'm just not sure what."

---

11 miles south
1649 hours

Wazid steered the pickup truck past another sinkhole and accelerated to twenty miles per hour. The further he drove southwest, the more broken the old highway became. So far he had seen nothing of Paco and his men. Now, five miles from his friend and leader, Sati Bashara, he pulled to the right shoulder and cut the wheel hard left to turn around. But over his left shoulder, he spotted a body lying close by in the desert. He stopped in the middle of the road and lifted the M16 off the truck's passenger seat. He chambered a round.

In a crouch, he walked across the hot pavement. He paused, twisting at the hips to ensure nobody lurked nearby. Satisfied, he walked into the desert and knelt beside the prone figure. He brushed a scorpion off the man's cheek.

The man wore the khaki-colored cotton uniform of the Caliphate. Dried blood crusted the back of his shirt. He could not have been dead long, since no scavengers had yet feasted on his corpse.

"Why did you come this way?" Wazid muttered.

A prairie falcon circled high overhead, its shadow racing over the arid landscape. Wazid ignored it.

Behind him, two figures covered in dirt and sand rose from shallow pits. They made no sound. Wazid had no warning before a sharpened iron spike struck the base of his skull, where the first cervical vertebrae joined the spine. The bones shattered with a loud *crack!* He toppled to one side, with only a rattle to mark his death.

The prone figure, no longer quite so dead, jumped up and helped the other two drag the newly dead man into a shallow, pre-dug trench. Using a shovel, they refilled the hole until it was nothing more than a flat patch of desert. Together they rolled a large boulder onto the grave.

Sweating, they turned to leave. Then they heard a voice and looked at each other.

"Wazid, where are you? Come back right away. Wazid, can you hear me?" It went on like that without stopping, faint and muffled but audible.

"Govind?" the youngest of the three said. The oldest shook his head.

They erased the blood and footprints at the kill site, careful to brush away their own tracks. One of the men inspected Wazid's still-running truck. Standing on the seat, he looked over the cab roof and nodded once. Govind pointed southwest and the man in the truck drove off in that direction. He and the remaining man then crossed over a small hill, where three horses stood tethered to a mesquite tree. Daylight faded as they rode off and vanished into the gathering darkness like ghosts of the desert.

Chapter 1

Who controls the past, controls the future.
Psalms of the New Prophet, Chapter 7, Verse 21

8 miles south of Green Ghost
1719 hours, June 25

Sati Bashara stood next to his battered Toyota pickup. He watched a prairie falcon fold its wings and dive. Skimming inches above the desert floor, its talons reached down and snatched its prey. Flapping skyward, it made for a distant ridgeline, dangling a snake in its claws.

"Where are they?" Bashara said. "Why do they not answer?"

"I don't know, Sati," said his best friend, Haleem. "Maybe their radios broke, or the batteries died. Maybe one blew a water hose, and the other hit a deep hole and turned over. How should I know?"

"We cannot wait on Wazid or Ibrahim any longer. Keep trying to get them, but the day is dying and we must move on."

Two other trucks cooled on the shoulder of the highway, turned off to save fuel. Bashara smelled death and destruction nearby, even if his companions didn't. Aside from the scent of decomposing bodies, smoldering ashes filled the air with tiny bits of carbonized rubber, like pollen. In a pristine desert, scents like charred truck tires acted as a beacon for those who could detect them. Sage, creosote, the indescribable earthiness after a rainstorm... those scents defined his childhood memories. His mind knew how the desert should smell. It didn't smell that way now.

"Death is close," he said. "There has been fighting near here."

"How do you know this?"

"I smell it."

"But where, Sati? We are low on fuel and the sun is fading. We have been gone longer than expected and your uncle awaits our return."

"My uncle awaits answers, Haleem, and we have none to give him. Would you like to be the one to tell him we failed to find Paco? Because that I will not do, even if I have to walk back."

Bashara raised his nose again like a tracking dog. He turned in slow circles, moved side to side, and walked a few paces in one direction, followed by the reverse. He did this for three minutes and stopped.

"There," he said, pointing to the ridgeline on their right. "They must have pulled off the road. Let us find their tracks."

Leaning against the second truck, arms folded, Haleem rolled his eyes when Bashara wasn't looking. He wound his finger in a circle, which meant *let's go*. Driving into the open desert in late afternoon did not seem like a great idea, but it wasn't his decision.

"Slamming into a hole could break an axle," he said.

"Then do not slam into a hole," Bashara said. "You are my dear friend, Haleem, but do not dispute me again."

Haleem drove with care as the light faded, leaving Bashara to search for fresh tracks. After a few minutes he pointed out the right window.

"There," he said. Dozens of tire imprints veered toward the ridge, following an old, crushed-stone road. They speeded up, heedless of holes, ruts, or rocks. Haleem crossed two bridges without slowing down. The rattle of the timbers made his heart race.

Deep shadows lay close to the ridge. In the twilight, Bashara saw what had happened to the missing men. He spotted dozens of blasted cars and trucks, like a sprawling graveyard of elephants. The skeletal shells lay contorted like bodies twisted by rigor mortis.

They parked on the outer edge of the killing field and crawled through the wreckage. Bodies and chunks of scorched metal lay scattered as if from a tornado. Bashara did not have to warn them to be wary of snakes and scorpions.

He knelt and inspected the first few bodies they found, turning his head from the stench. Hordes of maggots crawled in the putrefied flesh. Scavengers had gnawed many of the corpses to bare bone. Flies swarmed the noses and mouths of the living. Despite the parasitic insects, Bashara held his hands palm down over the bodies. He seemed to sense their spirits.

"Abulfazl," he said, "you and Azeez go there and see what you see." He pointed to the plateau high against the sheer rock wall of the ridge.

"As you wish, Sati," Abulfazl said, and the two men trotted off.

As the afternoon waned, Bashara stood and walked further into the carnage, picturing in his mind what had happened. His other men spread out to look for survivors. It seemed impossible anyone could still be alive after three or four days in the open desert, but they looked anyway. Some of his men climbed the rocks, while others joined Azeez and Abulfazl on the plateau. All held rifles at the ready.

Bashara picked up various bits of metal and turned over a glob of hardened meat with his boot. He had no idea what, or who, it had been. Shell casings littered the ground. Many came from much larger caliber weapons than the rifles Paco's men had carried. He leaned close to the holes in the vehicles, sniffed them, and ran a finger over the seared but smooth edges. The ripped metal was not jagged. Only high velocity rounds melted metal like that.

Abulfazl and Azeez ran back down the ramp, shirts drenched with sweat. Bending over, hands on knees, they gulped air for a few minutes before they could speak.

"Up there," Abulfazl said, still gasping for breath. "Three trucks, two of ours and another one. There's a long wall of rocks, low, about this high." He indicated a height halfway up his thigh. "Many dead men, all ours. Whatever killed them, Sati... they were ripped apart. Animals have been chewing them as well."

"The trucks," Sati said. "Can they be driven?"

Abulfazl shook his head. "Destroyed. Burned out. There is nothing to salvage."

"Sati, over here!" Haleem said.

He jumped up and followed the sound of the shouting, almost stepping on a ruined head lying crushed beside a leg and foot. Slowing down, he trudged forward until he found Haleem kneeling beside a man propped against a truck. Crusty blood covered his upper torso. The man's left leg had turned purple and swollen to twice its normal size. His head lolled to the side, but his chest rose and fell with shallow respiration.

Bashara knelt beside Haleem and raised the man's head. Ants crawled over his face and Bashara brushed them away. Lifting his water bottle, he wet the man's cracked lips. When the mouth parted, he poured a few drops into his throat. His movements were deft and efficient. His long fingers explored for wounds or broken bones, and he took care to be gentle.

"Who did this, Paco?" he whispered into the man's ear. "If you can hear me, you must tell me who did this."

Paco Mohammed tried to lift his right hand, but couldn't. "Agua," he said in a dry voice.

Bashara let him drink all he wanted.

"Monstruos voladores," he said, and this time his voice was strong

19

enough to be heard. "Monstruos voladores gigantes. Con grandes alas y una marca blanca en un círculo." *Giant flying monsters, with large wings and a white mark in a circle.* "I looked into the eyes of the monster and saw the souls of the men it had eaten."

Bashara and Haleem shared a glance, and Bashara patted Paco's cheek. "You have been through much, my friend. We will take you back, and you will heal, and there we will talk more."

But Paco reached out with his good right hand and grabbed a fistful of Bashara's shirt, pulling him closer. The rasp in his voice blurred the words. "I am not loco, Sati. This sun has burned me, but my mind is not cooked. They were monsters, I tell you. Giant monsters with wings on their heads, and a grande blanca mark on their side. And things my grandmother called letters; I don't know what they said. And hanging below the belly of the monsters were guns like I have not seen before, guns that killed my men before they could move. When the monsters flew overhead, the bullets, they fell like hail."

"Guns?" Bashara said. Paco's story began to make sense.

"Yes, big guns. And rockets. When I was just a young boy, mi abuela told me of such monsters. When she was a girl, they would come and kill the men of her village in Mexico. She said they were terrible. She called them helicopteros, and she said they had guns. They were monsters from Hell, she said."

"Helicopters?" Bashara's eyes narrowed and he drew in the sand with his finger. "This mark you saw, Paco, did it look like this?"

"Si." Paco nodded. "Pero blanca."

"Good, Paco, good. Now the letters, did they look anything like this?" Again he drew.

"That is them!" Paco said. "How did you know, Sati? What do they spell? Who killed my men?"

Bashara stood and motioned his men to load Paco into a truck. "He is close to death. We must go. Be gentle but quick. We will drive through the night."

"But Sati," Haleem said. "The night... it's very dark. The moon is new."

"Do as I say. Have we heard from Ibrahim or Wazid?"

"No, nothing."

"We cannot wait. They will have to make their own way back."

Paco's blood-caked hand grabbed Bashara's pant leg. "Please, Sati, tell me who killed my friends?"

"I do not know for certain, Paco. We know of men beyond Phoenix with such a mark on their vehicles, but they have not been our enemies in the past. I have met one of their lower-class leaders, a man they call

Slick. He is an infidel, uncouth, not schooled in the ways of the New Prophet. In the past it has been convenient to cooperate with them in certain matters. They have been reliable, but if they have found such power and become our enemies, then my uncle must know."

"What is this mark, Sati? What does it mean?"

"It is a star, Paco. These men bear the mark of an old enemy. If what you say is true, then your men were killed by helicopters of Los Estados Unidos."

"But there is no more Estados Unidos."

"I pray to our beloved New Prophet that you are right," Sati Bashara said. "But it would appear to be otherwise."

CHAPTER 2

Nothing is sinful that serves Him who alone knows the will of Allah.
        Psalms of the New Prophet, Chapter 1, Verse 2

New Khorasan (formerly Tucson, AZ)
1033 hours, June 26

Yet another golf ball soared aloft and sliced left into the rough. Richard Lee Armstrong wanted to scream, but held his back-swing long enough to regain his composure. For three decades he had suppressed his identity, and so the placid smile he wore as a permanent mask fit his persona. Instead of kicking his golf bag, he displayed the tranquility befitting the Emir of New Khorasan. But just because he had mastered his facial expressions did not mean he was happy.

The golf clubs were not the problem, nor the choppy greens or rough fairways. Improvements to the course required manpower and water he did not have anyway. The real problem was the balls; they all had nicks and cuts. No matter how much he practiced, a damaged golf ball did not go where aimed. In the early days new golf balls had been common, but those days were long gone. His followers had scoured New Khorasan, the city once called Tucson, for new ones, but found none.

The Emir of New Khorasan, Superior Imam of the Foretold Caliphate of the New Prophet, had worked hard on his golf swing over the years. His latest drive first sailed skyward in a perfect arc. Then the air aloft caught a cut in the ball's side and spun it off course, ruining his hard work. When the ball landed in a patch of scrub, he stood silent for several seconds with a serene look that hid his rage. All that practice wasted!

Standing behind the first tee, the other members of his foursome clapped. They were his most senior lieutenants. He turned and smiled, but Richard Lee Armstrong knew kissing ass when he saw it. He had trained himself to read body language and facial expressions. He believed that under the right circumstances he could read people's minds. For thirty years that talent had kept him alive at the top of a dangerous and fanatical religious cult. He did not need exotic methods to know that some within his inner circle would slit his throat if they knew the truth about him. The man known as Richard Lee Armstrong had not existed for thirty years. In his place stood Abdul-Qudoos Fadil el Mofty, Virtuous Servant of the Most Holy Who Holds the Fatwa, Superior Imam and Emir of New Khorasan.

"Thank you, my beloved friends," he said. "But that is not necessary. Muhsin, I believe it is your turn, is it not?"

Ahead, slaves tended the fairways with primitive rakes and shovels. More slaves uprooted cacti and bushes that had sprouted on the field of play, all of them watched over by guards with rifles. Behind them, a team of sun-scorched men in ragged clothes dragged a stripped-out pickup truck across the fairway. In the pseudo-wagon's bed was a perforated metal tank that rotated as the vehicle inched forward on skids. The tank dispensed wastewater from the septic system installed at the Superior Imam's villa, beside the eighteenth green.

The knot of golfers were halfway down the fairway at Hole Five when Muhsin covered his eyes and stared back in the direction of the first tee. A vehicle approached at high speed, raising a dust cloud on the gravel pathway.

"Abdul, is that not Sati's truck?" he said, pointing.

The Superior Imam shaded his eyes. Despite wearing aviator sunglasses, the glare made his eyes water. He studied the vehicle and smiled. "My nephew has returned. Let us hope he brings good news."

The truck parked in the shade of a mesquite tree. It had not stopped rolling before Sati Bashara jumped out and trotted over to his uncle. Sweat matted the khaki cotton shirt to his chest. Touching fist to breast, he bowed from the waist. His uncle lifted his chin with a finger and motioned for him to stand.

"My sister's son is a respectful man," he said, patting his nephew's cheek. "What news, Sati? Did Paco recover our stolen slaves?"

"Uncle, Paco met disaster. His men are all dead and their vehicles destroyed. Paco himself lives. We found him gravely wounded and I feared that he would not survive the trip back, but he did and is with the doctors now."

"Dead?" the Superior Imam said. "All of them? And their vehicles destroyed? This is a severe blow. Go, refresh yourself and put on clean clothes. We will discuss this matter in two hours, after prayers."

"But Uncle, I believe I know who did this!" Sati said.

The Emir laid a hand upon his nephew's shoulder and looked him in the eyes. "I do not want you to miss any details, Sati. This is of utmost importance. We must discover all that you know and decide what actions to take. These are grave matters and should be dealt with after Asr. Now, go."

As Sati drove away, the Emir turned to his companions. "Muhsin, I believe it is your turn?"

Light flooded the room through sheer window covers. With no air-conditioning, the Arizona sun could heat a room to dangerous temperatures. The great room on the ground floor of the Emir's villa was no exception. On a normal afternoon, heavy cloth drapes kept the room in deep darkness, as cool as possible. But for important meetings, the Emir preferred its bright natural light to the cooler basement rooms, where the primitive lighting necessary underground gave him a headache.

Seven people sat at a large, round wooden table. Besides Sati Bashara and the Emir of New Khorasan, Superior Imam Abdul-Qudoos el Mofty, the Five Counselors were also present. These men were his advisors and lieutenants, the Emirate's Ruling Council. In theory, they carried out his commands and helped him rule the Caliphate's western province. In practice, he suspected at least two spied for his brother, the Caliph. They all wore well-woven white cotton robes over duck cloth pants.

In a far dark corner sat another man, shadowed and silent. He was always there in the background, watching, listening, but never speaking. Few men knew his title and only one man knew his name.

"Gentlemen," the Emir said to open the meeting, "as some of you know, my nephew brings dire news about those we sent to retrieve a group of stolen female slaves. Sati, please tell us what you found."

The younger man stood and bowed to each of his six tablemates in turn, ending with his uncle. "My news is not good, blessed Superior Imam."

His uncle raised a hand. "We know you are a respectful man, Sati, but here you may dispense with such things and get on with our business. You are among friends and, I should say, admirers, and may speak freely."

"As you wish, Uncle. We found Paco near a steep ridgeline far to the northwest. His men were all dead. Some terrible weapon destroyed them.

Many had arms or legs ripped from their bodies, and some had no heads. Huge holes punctured the vehicles, like bullet holes, only larger, and the metal around the holes was smooth, as though melted. The damage appeared to be from heavy machine guns.

"Two of the vehicles, large trucks, apparently tried to escape but were blown up. Completely destroyed. This could only have been from explosives of some type. My guess would be missiles. We found no survivors other than Paco, and while he was alive when we arrived here, the doctor says he may yet die. He has many wounds and lost much blood before we found him, and there is always the danger of infection."

"Were Paco's wounds in the front, Sati?" said the Emir. "Was he facing his enemy?"

"His wounds were severe, Uncle. Dried blood covered his body. I could not tell where the bullets struck him."

"Come now, Nephew. You are an experienced soldier. You must have an opinion on this."

Bashara hesitated. "Uncle, please..."

"Answer my question, Sati. Paco has been a good and faithful servant since he accepted the true faith, but if he fled the enemy, then he has shown weakness in his belief of our beloved New Prophet."

Bashara bowed his head. "If I must answer, my guess is that Paco was struck in the back. But there may be an explanation. When we found him, Paco was awake. At first I thought him delirious, for he described being attacked by what he called giant flying monsters. But these monsters were familiar to him through stories told by his grandmother. She told him such creatures had often attacked their village, in the time before Allah's Punishment of the Great Satan and the rise of his New Prophet. She named these monsters helicopteros."

"Helicopters?" the Emir said, sitting forward and leaning on his elbows. The tips of his index fingers met in a steepling gesture and he rubbed his lips with them.

"Yes, helicopters. What is more, Paco said these helicopters had markings. One was a white five-pointed star, and the other was letters. He cannot read so he drew them for me in the dirt. They spelled U.S. Army."

"Impossible!" said Ibrahim Yaseen, Counselor of Production and one of the men the Emir suspected of being a spy for the Caliph. "There has been no U.S. Army for decades. The man is mad from his injuries."

"Esteemed Counselor," Bashara said, "I do not say he is correct. I merely report to you what he said. And yet... Paco took twenty-five trucks and cars with him, and more than one hundred eighty armed men. With my own eyes I witnessed the fact of their destruction, and I can say with certainty that something very powerful destroyed them. What that was I cannot say, but Paco had never seen a helicopter before, and does not know that we have any, so it seems unlikely he could imagine such a thing."

"He knew of them from his grandmother," Yaseen said. "You said so yourself. Is it so unreasonable that in his pain those nightmares came back to him? To me this makes much more sense than to believe the army of our mortal foe has come back to life and is attacking us with helicopters!"

There were grumbles of approval from several others, until the Emir motioned them to silence with a curt hand chop. "My nephew does not lie," he said, almost hissing.

Yaseen touched his forehead to the table. "No, Beloved Prince and Superior Imam, he does not. If I gave offense, then please forgive an old man. I meant only that we cannot blindly trust the words of a superstitious man who has lain gravely wounded in the sun. Sati is blessed of Allah, and shines like a star in the eye of the New Prophet."

"I took no offense, good counselor," said Bashara. "But if it is proof you wish, then perhaps I have it. The place where we found Paco and his vehicles was beside a sheer-sided ridgeline. Jutting from the side of this wall of stone was a flat platform two hundred feet above the desert. This was not a natural formation, but had been carved and smoothed at some time in the past. To accomplish this would have taken many men and many months, but with large machines it could have been done quickly. There was also a long ramp leading to this platform, wide, straight, and smooth, made of crushed stone. It is my guess that the army of the United States constructed it long ago, although to what purpose I cannot say."

"Go on," the Emir said.

Bashara sipped water and cleared his throat. "Atop this platform we found more of our brave warriors, most of them dead with the same terrible wounds found on the others, but not all. Some had gunshot wounds any at this table would recognize. The others... my lords, my words are not sufficient to convey what these men looked like. They had been thrown aside like a child's toy, and many had been struck on their left side. Remember, this platform is two hundred feet high. As our men went up the ramp, this would have meant that on their left was nothing but empty air. Whatever shot them, and they were shot with a very large gun, whatever it was came from something in the air. If that was not a helicopter, then I do not know what it could have been.

"Further back on the platform was a low wall of rocks, and behind it we found hundreds of shell casings. M16 shell casings." Reaching into his pocket, Sati dropped a few of the empty casings onto the table.

"Many people use the M16," Muhdin said. "That proves nothing."

"Truth," Bashara said. "But there is more. Three trucks were on the platform, the two stolen along with our workers and a third we did not recognize. All had been burned. However, the third one still had markings we could read on the door. Although faded and old, the letters definitely spelled U.S. Army."

"Bah!" Yaseen said. "This is pointless. There is no United States Army, and there has not been for more than forty years!"

Undeterred, Bashara waited until the murmuring around the table died down. His uncle did nothing to quiet his counselors. If he was ever to become a great leader, Bashara had to earn his own respect. Inspecting the faces of the Counselors for indications of their thoughts, Bashara didn't break contact whenever one of them looked him in the eye. Finally, when he judged the moment right, he spoke again in a louder voice.

"There is a little more evidence my lords might wish to see," he said. "Although the trucks were burned, we did find a few items that survived the fire. The first was this..."

He tossed a half-burned sheet of paper onto the table. Much of the typed message had faded to invisibility, but the addressee was still legible, as was the letterhead. Dated nearly fifty years before, it was a sheet of stationary from the office of the commanding general, 1st Infantry Division, United States Army, addressed to a Major Dennis Tompkins.

Next, Bashara emptied the contents of a canvas sack onto the table. Sifting through a pile of items, he hefted a faded green jacket with the outline of the name TOMPKINS on the left breast, and a square American flag stitched onto each arm.

Yaseen said nothing, nor did any of the others. They stared at the foreign objects as if Bashara had emptied a sidewinder onto the table. Nothing symbolized their hatred of infidels more than the American flag.

"My friends," the Emir said, "what we see cannot be, and yet it is. Sati, we struggle to explain this. Have you any thoughts about how the impossible might be possible?"

"I do, Uncle," he said. "And the explanation may not be as shocking as you think. In my times scouting in the desert, I have come across a band of criminals with whom we have sometimes done business. You know them as the Army of the Republic of Arizona. They claim to be successors of the Army of the United States, and are based in a small city northwest of the place infidels once called Phoenix. I believe their town is called Prescott."

"Ah, yes, *those* people... aren't they led by a man who claims to be an American Army officer?"

"A General Patton, yes," Bashara said.

The Emir smiled. "General Patton was a famous American general during the second great war. Either this man has a sense of humor, or those who follow him are stupid..."

"They are infidels," Yaseen said. "Of course they are stupid."

"Infidels are foolish to deny the word of Allah," the Emir said in a condescending tone. "But some are quite clever in their own way. Stupid and foolish are not one and the same, Yaseen. And they can be dangerous. If they attacked Paco, this means they feel powerful enough to challenge us. It is a declaration of war. We know very little about them, but we cannot be certain they are equally ignorant about us. 'The wise man overestimates the power of evil and guards himself accordingly.' Surely you do not disagree with the New Prophet?"

"No," Yaseen said, outmaneuvered. "All blessings be upon him. But why are we so certain it was them who attacked Paco? It makes no sense. If they wanted to attack us, why steal a few females? And then why use their most powerful weapons to destroy a relatively insignificant force sent in pursuit? It is madness. If they truly mean to fight us, all they have done is give us warning of their helicopters, so that we may take countermeasures."

Bashara started to respond but his uncle stopped him with a raised hand. "Yaseen makes a good point. You have had dealings with these criminals, have you not, Sati?"

"Only in passing, Uncle. They rarely move east or south of Phoenix. I have met one of their commanders, a lower ranking man, I believe. He bears the uncouth name Slick. He was not impressive, but he was with other soldiers, and they drove Humvees. They bore American M16 rifles and they wore American uniforms, like this." He held up the jacket. "It is my understanding they grow much food, and cotton for cloth, and trade slaves for fuel with others as far west as the Pacific coast. I cannot say why they would attack us now, but I am convinced that is what happened."

"Gentlemen," the Emir said, "it is obvious my nephew believes what he says is true. It is also obvious that if these infidels are leftovers from the American military, they feel strong enough to attack us now. Since they have not done so in the past, something must have changed. The loss of Paco's men and their vehicles is not a crippling blow—we are very powerful, after all—but it is worrisome. It is also insulting to us as Followers of the New Prophet. Either they have grown strong and confident, or they believe we are weak. Or they are not to blame for this."

"Uncle, I know what Paco told us he saw. He was not lying."

"I believe you, Sati, but Paco is not a learned man." He looked at his Counselors, who all nodded agreement. "And yet, for such a man to imagine seeing letters spelling out *U.S. Army*, and a white five-pointed star, on a machine he did not know existed, is impossible. Do you not agree, my trusted friends?"

Even Yaseen had no choice but to agree.

"Then if these infidels deliberately attacked members of my Emirate, who were carrying out the will of our New Prophet, we must consider them as now our sworn enemy. The might of the Western Province must be gathered and sent against them."

"What of their helicopters?" Muhdin said.

"As you each know, when this was the American city called Tucson, there were stores of United States military weapons here. Do not forget the weapon the Americans named *Stingers.* Those shoulder-fired anti-aircraft rockets can destroy any helicopter, and we have them."

"Yes, my lord, we do, but should we not have the same concern for these Stingers as we do for all of the older military equipment?"

"Muhdin, do you not think we will have alternate plans in case the rockets fail? Do you not believe in my leadership? Where is this timidity coming from?"

Muhdin leaned forward until his forehead touched the table. "I meant no insult, my prince. Your vision and leadership are an inspiration for followers of the New Prophet everywhere. If I am cautious, it is because we have so little information on our enemy."

"Lift your head, Muhdin," he said. "Your loyalty is not in question. You are my most trusted general." His tone, however, indicated Muhdin's loyalty was very much in question. "We must be aggressive, yes, but we must also be cautious. And we will. I want scouts sent forward to find out everything we can about these infidels. I want routes searched and water sources found. Avoid the city of Phoenix. If we move west, it will be with a great host and preparations must be complete within two weeks. Yaseen, I charge you with accomplishing this."

"Two weeks?" Yaseen said. "My lord, it will take more than two weeks for the scouts to return."

"Four weeks, then. Let us be prepared. I want to take every man we can spare, and every vehicle. Whether or not these infidels are responsible for the attack on Paco, the time has come for this province to move west, and to bring the truth of the New Prophet to those unfortunates who have not heard his word. We are not yet ready to seize Phoenix, but this city of Prescott will give us a western presence until we can. We must do this for our own security, if for nothing else."

"I will do my best," Yaseen said.

"I want this accomplished, Yaseen. This is my will."

The call for Sixth Prayers ended the meeting. After his nephew and Counselors filed out, he admired how the sun turned the desert red-orange as it sank in the west. Minutes passed and shadows deepened in the corners of the large room. The temperature cooled. The Emir drank some water and sat.

The silent figure wrapped in the shadows of one corner had not spoken or moved during the meeting. He was old. Even as a young man, he had been small in stature, and age had shrunk him to little more than a bent dwarf. He seldom spoke. No one on the council knew his identity, and none ever dared ask.

"You heard everything," the Emir finally said, slipping into the vernacular of Richard Lee Armstrong. "I want your opinion."

"Everyone has an opinion," the old man said. His raspy voice scratched out the words. "That doesn't mean they should be heard, or that their opinion is valid."

"Don't be a smartass. I didn't ask someone else for their opinion; I asked you. Are you saying your opinion isn't valid?"

For a long moment, the old man did not answer. His back ached from sitting in one place for so long, so he sat and stretched.

"Don't be a dickhead. My opinion's as valid as it ever was. But why are you asking me this shit? I think you know what to do. You have two choices. Clearly, the authority of the Caliphate itself has been challenged, and by extension the worthiness of Allah's New Prophet and his message. You can't let that go unanswered or this whole thing unravels. The big question is, who did it? And I think you nailed that one. It has to be a remnant of the old American Army. It can't be anything else."

"Okay, let's say you're right," the Emir said. "Why would they do such a stupid thing? Surely they must know we'll come after them."

"They think you are weak, Gift of Allah."

The Emir pointed a finger at him. "I've told you before about your smart mouth."

"So fucking shoot me. I'm too old to care any more. They don't fear the Caliphate and believe they're strong enough to challenge you, probably as a prelude for moving into Phoenix."

"You said that I had two choices. Let's assume what you say is true. What do you recommend I do?"

"Two paths split the road, but I don't see where you've got a choice. You must either do nothing, which would be monumentally stupid, or you must move against them with every man and vehicle you can muster. You must use overwhelming force to crush your enemies, to drive them before you and listen to the wailing of their women."

"You quote our beloved leader."

"I quote myself. I wrote that whole stanza for him. Some blood and fire now will mean less war in the coming years."

"War is good. It is the nature of Man to fight," the Emir said. "Did not the Most Blessed New Prophet also say that?"

"Stop it, Richard. I'm getting tired of having you repeat my words back to me."

"I've told you never to call me that."

"Like I said, shoot me."

"I might just do that."

"Good. Put me out of my misery. It's hot as hell and every muscle in my body hurts... but assuming you don't, you have to crush these people. You can't let this go unchallenged, but that doesn't mean you have to be reckless. Take some time to prepare for war, to manufacture weapons and train soldiers and gather stores of food. One should only attack when one is either ready to strike a first, decisive blow, or when one has been provoked and has no choice. Since we don't have the first option, we must settle for the second. But remember what America's last great general said about that... *if you attack, attack to destroy.*"

"Schwarzkopf?"

"Angriff."

Hands behind his back, the Emir paced the room. It had grown dimmer as the sun set, but he did not call for lamps or candles. "So I have no choice but to attack, unless I wish to be seen as a coward?"

"I can't control circumstances, but that's how I see it."

"Can't you? I wonder. All right, go. Get some dinner. Shall I send up a girl?"

"Not tonight."

The old man half stood, half fell out of his chair and slumped off down a dark hallway. The Emir watched him go, as though if he stared hard enough at the old man's back, he might be able to read his thoughts. For his part, once enveloped in the friendly embrace of darkness, the old man shook his head.

Chapter 3

I have not fled, I am not done,
Don't burn me on your pyre;
I do not fear the rising sun,
And my rage will not expire.
        Fragment from anonymous Viking saga, circa 900 A.D.

0330 hours, June 30

Joe Randall rubbed his eyes and yawned. He was still on restricted duty because of his neck injury. Not being one of the on-call air support crews for the day's lurps, he could have slept as long as he wanted. And Randall loved to sleep.

But it was impossible with all the noise in the hallway outside his quarters. Unable to go back to sleep, he slipped on his flight boots and stumbled off looking for coffee.

While waiting his turn at the coffee urn, Alisa Plotz and Andy Arnold slid in behind him, dressed for action. Alisa was his wingman, although they had not seen each other since the attack more than a week before.

"Damn, Joe, you look worse than usual," she said.

"I've missed you, too, Alisa. Why are you dressed out at such an ungodly hour?"

It struck Randall that two weeks ago time of day had been irrelevant, with no day and night to regulate their circadian rhythms. That had all changed when Overtime went active.

"We're on call," she said. "Four Apaches, two Comanches."

"Whoa... you're my wingman. Who's piloting the other Comanche? Tell me it's not Wang."

"Wang's not the pilot, but he is the co-pilot."

"And?"

"I'll let the pilot tell you himself."

She pointed to Randall's best friend and the co-pilot for *Tank Girl*, Bunny Carlos, who was in full flight gear and walking their way. When he got close enough in the noisy mess hall, right off the hangar deck, Randall blocked his way.

"No."

"Yes," Carlos said, nodding his head in confirmation.

"You're not flying *Tank Girl*, you prick."

"It wasn't my idea, Joe."

"I don't care whose idea it was. Nobody takes *Tank Girl* up except me."

Everybody within a twenty-foot radius had stopped to watch the argument. Carlos stepped back, straightened his spine, and then leaned forward at the waist. Randall knew exactly what those body movements meant: he had pissed off Carlos.

Too bad.

"You're the best pilot in the brigade," Carlos said. "Nobody's disputing that, so what are you bitching about? They gave me the mission because I've flown a combat sortie after wake-up. I fly *Tank Girl* same as you do, you know. She's not your personal property. I needed a co-pilot so I picked Wang. Simple as that."

Standing in his robe amid a crowd of squadron mates, all dressed in flight gear and mechanics' coveralls, Randall felt naked. He needed coffee.

"If you crash *Tank Girl*, make sure you die. Otherwise I'll kill you."

———

0337 hours

Nick Angriff scraped crust from the corner of his eye, blinked, and went back to shaving. Steam from his shower hung in the bathroom. He enjoyed the wet warmth and flexed his right thumb. He would never admit how much the arthritis in his hand bothered him, but the steam helped.

A knock on the outer door of his quarters prompted a sigh. He wrapped a towel around himself and cracked the bathroom door open.

"It better be important," he called out.

The door opened further and Sergeant Schiller stuck his head in. "My apologies, General, but you said any time, day or night."

"Green Ghost?"

Schiller nodded. "Came in about ten minutes ago. Looks worse for wear."

"Tell him my office in five minutes. And bring us some coffee, J.C."

With his personal quarters nearby, Angriff arrived at the Crystal Palace in less than five minutes. Green Ghost sat on the couch waiting for him.

"You look like Pigpen," Angriff said as he sat behind his desk. Schiller had a mug of coffee waiting for him.

Green Ghost sipped one of his own. "Pigpen?"

"The dirty kid in *Peanuts*. Left a cloud of dust when he walked...? Never mind. Where the hell have you been?"

Green Ghost ignored the question. "Looks like an op is launching. How long do you have?"

"Five minutes. Ten, tops."

"We trailed the stowaways and were about to move in when they vanished. Poof. Vanished into the night. We found flat-soled prints and horse tracks, but no other clues to what happened. I decided to extend the patrol and see what we could see."

"On foot?"

"The Range Rovers were being detailed. I do formally request we find some horses. We wound up north of where the gunships saved those women and kids, and followed a highway back. Four days ago... no, it's five now. Five days ago we ran up on three guys in a car."

"Living people in a running car?"

"Roger that. We tried to take prisoners, but they opened up on us with automatic weapons. M16s." He let that significance sink in. "Two died in the fight, but one guy hung on for a minute. Before he died, he said to tell some guy named Sati that he went out fighting. He also said that he *prayed to the prophet.*"

"Muslims don't pray to Mohammad. They pray to Allah."

"Right. But then he said something about the glory of the new prophet."

"Anything else?"

"I think he cried for his mama. The car door had a symbol painted on it, an upright crescent moon crossed by a scimitar, and a slogan in bad Arabic. I think it was supposed to say *word of the new prophet.*"

Schiller knocked at the door. "Sorry, sir, but they're moving out soon."

"Right," Angriff said. To Green Ghost, he added, "We're sending out recons in force and I want to be there to see them off."

"Which group do you want me in?" Green Ghost said.

"The group that stays here and sleeps for a day, and then gets to work on being my S-5."

CHAPTER 4

They hide together in ambush;
they watch my every step;
they lie in wait for my life.
      Psalms 56:7

0412 hours, June 30

Overtime Prime had eight ground-level access points large enough for vehicles, four on the western side of the mountain and four to the east. The middle two on each side were twice as large. The thick blast doors of reinforced titanium could withstand all but a direct hit by a medium-yield nuclear weapon. A veneer of stone covered the exterior, making the doors invisible from more than a hundred yards away.

The four long-range patrol groups lined up in the artificial glow of the tunnels. With engines off to save fuel, they waited for the lights to dim and the doors to open. Mess attendants walked between the Humvees and LAV-25s with carafes of coffee and MREs for anybody who wanted more breakfast.

Orders were to move out in company strength. Such a large force should not only be strong enough to shoot its way out of any trouble, but it provided the perfect live-fire training exercise. Since building unit cohesion was a priority, the more troops who could take part in such a maneuver, the better. Three companies were Army and one, taking the southwestern course, was Marine Recon. Each company had specialist troops attached, both snipers and engineers.

At exactly 0455 hours the lights went out, including flashlights and cigarettes. When the vehicles fired up, the driver's faces appeared as disembodied specters. Red, blue, and white instrument lights reflected from their helmet visors.

The doors separated at precisely 0500.

Hundreds of faces peered out of the tunnel at the eastern sky, where the first light of dawn haloed the mountaintops on the valley's far side. For most of them, it was the first fresh air they had breathed in half a century.

Nick Angriff stood by the southwestern portal, smoking his ever-present cigar and encouraging the troops. He told dirty jokes or calmed nervous drivers. Even though he'd worked past midnight and it was not yet dawn, he refused to show the effects of lack of sleep. His people were going in harm's way and he was going to be there to see them off. He did not get in the way of the commanders on the spot, did not disagree or countermand anything they said or did, even though a few times he wanted to. Instead, he was the father figure they could all come to with their fears and concerns.

Task Force Kicker would be lurping to the southwest. It comprised a company from his one and only Marine battalion. He wanted everyone to know that, although he was Army, the 7th Cavalry was one team. The message could not have been clearer; service rivalries died with the country that bred them. He cared for every man and woman under his command, regardless of service branch.

Task Force Kicker was Dog Company of the 7th Marine Reconnaissance Battalion, reinforced. Dog was the fourth of six line companies, with one headquarters company. Before the Collapse, standard Marine light reconnaissance battalions had featured one platoon designated for deep recon missions. Because of the unknown nature of what they would face, the 7th Battalion had an extra line company, with an entire company for deep recon. Dog was the specialized unit and the entire company was moving out that morning.

The company was also larger than average, with six officers and 144 other ranks. Usually commanded by a captain, Dog Company had Lieutenant Sully as commander due to a shortage of more senior officers. The company's other officers were second lieutenants, and Dog was short two sergeants and two corporals. The company had a total of twenty-six LAVs with various armament configurations. Most of the LAV-25s mounted the M-242 Bushmaster chain gun. Six Humvees supplemented them on the lurp. No trucks went out that morning.

Norman Fleming wrote the day's Rules of Engagement. Initiating combat either required for civilians to be in imminent danger, or in self-defense against hostile forces. In case of the latter, retreat was preferable if practical. Offensive action was at the commander's discretion within the ROE. If combat proved unavoidable, taking prisoners was desirable but preservation of assets took priority.

Once engaged, enemy forces must not escape to betray the presence of the brigade. In other words, if spotted by forces presumed hostile, run first, shoot second. But if you start shooting, don't stop until you've killed or captured them all.

At 0501 hours the driver of the first Humvee gunned his engine and lurched into the morning shadows. The rest of the company followed at regular invervals. The faint sunlight burned pink on a bank of high clouds, but despite the fresh, cool air, the day promised to grow hot. Angriff stood to one side and flashed thumbs-up to every Humvee or LAV-25.

"What's the word, General?" one LAV driver yelled over the roar of his engine.

"Weatherman's calling for a metal storm!"

Within a minute, dust swallowed the armored column, blotting out the red glow of tail lights in the darkness. Angriff stared after them, smoking, thinking, praying. Once finished, he wheeled and strode back inside. Colonel Walling awaited him with the day's schedule.

"That's the last of them," Walling said. "No problems here or with the other three teams, so it's a good beginning, General."

"No plan survives contact with the enemy. We're a long way from the short rows, but a good start beats a bad one. Come on, Walling, let's get to the Crystal Palace and patch into the comm."

"Sir, you've got a full schedule today, starting in the hydroponic labs."

"What's the matter with you, Walling? You're wound tighter than Dick's hat band. We'll get everything done, but there's only one first day of operations and that's today. So you do whatever you have to do, but I want to be on that comm if they find something. If we can do that from hydroponics, fine."

"General Angriff, General Fleming is in the Castle; if they find something, he will let you know immediately and will give a full report. Operations are his responsibility, sir."

Walling had been walking behind Angriff to the Emvee and almost slammed into his back when he stopped and turned around. Pinching his collar, Angriff said, "My stars say it's not going to happen that way, Colonel. Not when I had three, and definitely not now, when I've got five. I'm not going to interfere in tactical operations, but I will be patched into the comm network at all times. If you can do that, then I'll follow your schedule. If not, I'll be in my office."

0523 hours

Joe Randall leaned against a neatly organized worktable. Arms crossed, he stared at his beloved helicopter. Thirty feet away, Bunny Carlos sat in *Tank Girl*'s pilot seat, tapping his foot, looking anywhere except at Joe.

"Hey, Bunny, did I tell you—"

"Yeah, Joe, you told me. Whatever it is, you told me."

Randall scowled. Carlos tried to whistle.

"Morgan's going to be here soon," Randall said.

"Is that a threat?"

"You know it."

CHAPTER 5

Take me by the hand and take me where you go;
Show me all your wonders, show me all you know.
　　　Sergio Velazquez, "Take Me By the Hand"

1308 hours, June 30

"These people fled their home quickly," Govind said. Without aid of binoculars, he watched the tiny caravan plod across the desert from a mile away. "Someone pursues them."

"How can you know that?" said his youngest brother, Gosheven. "I can barely see them from here."

The third member of their triad, Gopan, slapped Gosheven across the back of the head. "Stop being a child and start being a warrior. You know his eyesight is better than anyone in the tribe. If your chief says it is so, it is so."

Govind stared for several more seconds without speaking. Something in his peripheral vision caused him to glance right. In the far distance, a dust cloud rolled up from the desert.

"What is that?" Gopan said. "Sand storm?"

"No." Govind shook his head. "It's a line of vehicles. A lot of vehicles."

"What do we do?"

"We watch."

1323 hours

Lieutenant Martin Sully thanked God he'd brought his own binoculars with him to Overtime. He'd purchased them for use in the Middle East, because they compensated better for shimmering heat rising from a desert floor than did the Marine issue ones.

Creosote bushes and saguaro cacti hid his target from view, but that was no problem. It moved at the slow pace of the skinny animals dragging it across the desert. Keeping it in view was no more complicated than scooting a few feet in either direction.

Lying prone on a small hill overlooking the bowl-shaped depression below, he ignored a beetle that crawled on the back of his hand. Only scorpions and giant centipedes concerned him, and while they were real dangers in the Sonoran Desert, Sergeant Meyers had the detail of keeping them away from both him and the snipers flanking him.

Most of the snipers were on his left, except for Lara Snowtiger, the only female sniper in the brigade. Nobody knew much about her, except she was Native American. Some said she'd been the best shot in the Corps before she went cold. All Sully cared about was that she'd scored second best of all the snipers, missing top score by a single point.

"Tell me what you see," he said to Sergeant Lorenzo Piccaldi, the sniper who lay in the dirt to his left.

Although the distance was only a few hundred yards, Piccaldi's M40A7 rifle had an advanced combat gunsight he'd bought himself. The scope was so powerful, Piccaldi could have read a newspaper at three hundred yards. Snowtiger used the standard issue scout sniper scope. It was a top-notch scope in its own right, but she shot better using an advanced combat scope. She'd blamed the difference in scopes for why she had come in second to Piccaldi in the shootout.

"I've got four horse-drawn vehicles, Loot. They look like pickup trucks, with improvised canopies and horses pulling them. Canopies appear to be cloth with a metal frame. Nine unknown subjects, two men, three women, four children. I've got a donkey or mule, some chickens, goats tied to the back, and a scrawny cow. No weapons I can see."

Sully had always been a stickler for military decorum and he hated the nickname *loot*. But Dog Company was new to him, and he to them. Most of them didn't know the name of the Marine beside them. The first time it had happened, he'd let it slide in the interest of morale. After a few days, he'd realized it was a term of endearment. They liked him as their commander, and they respected him. So while he still didn't like *loot*, it wasn't a battle worth fighting.

"Any pucker factor, Piccaldi?" he said.

"Nothin', Loot. Lame and tame, but the cow looks suicidal."

"Probably gets milked ten times a day," Company Sergeant Meyers said.

Piccaldi kept his sight focused on the little band below. "I'd let a chick milk me ten times a day," he said.

Sully looked back through his binoculars, ignoring the remark, but Snowtiger spoke up. "You'd have better luck with the cow," she said, her eye never leaving her scope.

"After fifty years, the cow's looking pretty good."

In a post-Collapse world where fuel was more precious than blood, functioning automobiles were a rare sight. Most cars and trucks of the late twentieth and early twenty-first centuries had on-board computers. The nuclear and EMP attacks America had endured during the Collapse had destroyed many of those. But the most damaging factor was age. Modern vehicles had lifespans measured in years, not decades. Hoses, belts, and tires dry-rotted, metal rusted, and gears wore out. And with no replacement parts any more, a simple problem could render any car or truck useless. Essential fluids such as brake, transmission, and oil sparked many fights. Wagons and draft animals became prized possessions to the surviving remnants of society.

The small group in the bowl comprised four small pickup trucks, three Toyotas and a Ford. Stripping out engines and extraneous parts saved weight. Sheets of corrugated metal covered the beds, reinforced with wood, over which a webbing of metal rods formed a frame. Various bits of cloth stretched over these provided relief from the sun. A team of horses dragged each wagon through the soft soil, staggering in the relentless heat. Women and children sat in the cabs of each truck, while the men walked alongside, one in front and one in back. The last truck sagged under chicken cages and wooden boxes.

"Radio," Sully said, extending his hand backward.

Meyer took the radio from his vest and slapped it into the lieutenant's hand, like a surgical technician passing a scalpel. The radio check earlier had been perfect, but they had only been two clicks from base then. Now they were eighty clicks out.

"Overtime Prime, this is Kicker Real. Do you light me?"

The response was immediate. "Kicker Real, this is Overtime Prime. Go ahead."

"Prime, we're at five three degrees, distance zero eight," Sully said. He used the simple radio code that transposed numbers from their true order and reversed directions. In fact they were at two-three-three degrees from the base, the exact opposite of fifty-three degrees. "We have eyes on what looks like refugees. Four horse-drawn vehicles, livestock, nine citizens in sight. No weapons visible. Am planning..." He stopped as a PFC ran his way in a crouch, waving. "Prime, please stand by."

"Lieutenant," the PFC said. Sully remembered his name was

Stazinsky. "We've got more company comin' up fast. Two Humvees and a Bradley, sir."

"Where?" Sully said. Sighting through his binoculars, he aimed them where Stazinsky pointed. "Where did they come from?"

He watched the three vehicles kick up a tower of dust as they sped over the desert, and keyed the radio mike again. "Overtime Prime, be advised, we have U.S. military vehicles on scene and closing on refugees. Two Humvees and one Bradley. Urgent you advise if friendlies are in our sector. I repeat, are these ours?"

1339 hours

Nick Angriff could not help gaping. He stood on a mid-level catwalk circling a chamber so vast he could not see the far end. From far over his head to hundreds of feet below, level upon level of long troughs were filled with nutrient-enriched water and growing plants. A combination of artificial lighting and natural sunlight lit the chamber via an intricate system of shafts and mirrors. Each level of hydroponic tanks was accessible by the ubiquitous metal walkways. As he stood on the narrow platform, Angriff could feel the warmth of the lights. Under his coat, sweat soaked his undershirt.

"Our first crop is probably five weeks away," Dr. Sharon Goldstone said. "We're really hoping to have some fresh tomatoes by then. But in the short term, everything seems to be going more smoothly than we could have imagined. We've already been able to start planning outside crops, and planting for spring could begin within a few months. That will be an exciting day."

"Dr. Goldstone, I am almost speechless," Angriff said. "And those who know me would tell you that's rare. This is the most amazing thing I've ever seen. You're going to be able to feed us all fresh produce? On a regular basis?"

She laughed, and Angriff noted how young she sounded, despite being close to his age. "Oh, yes, General Angriff. We will supply this base with more green vegetables than most of these young people have seen outside of their nightmares. Potatoes, corn, and grains do better in soil, so those will come later. We even have plans to grow barley and hops."

Angriff leaned on the railing and smiled, trying not to be too obvious about staring at her. "So tell me about yourself, Doctor. I—"

"Pardon me, sir?" Walling said.

"What is it?" Angriff said, annoyed.

"Sir, you wanted to be informed if a lurp encountered hostiles or IPs," he said, holding out a pair of headphones for Angriff to take.

"Who found something? Details, man!"

"Kicker, sir. The Marines came across a small group of refugees with some sort of wagons. They were about to investigate when three vehicles came on the scene... United States military vehicles."

"How is that possible? Who else do we have out there?"

"Nobody should be within four hundred clicks of their position."

Angriff took the headphones and listened for a few seconds. "Nobody's on the horn."

"Kicker was going to investigate, sir. They're probably off the air."

"Let's get to the Castle A-sap," Angriff said. He turned to Dr. Goldstone and shook her hand. "I'm sorry, Doctor. We'll have to finish this another time."

CHAPTER 6

My wanderings you have noted;
are my tears not stored in your flask,
recorded in your book?
Psalms 56:9

1350 hours, June 30

Slick Busson stood on the passenger seat of the lead Humvee, reveling as wind blew through his hair. It also cooled his sticky skin, one of the few pleasures of life in the desert. The yellow tint of his scratched goggles made the glare worse, but they kept dirt out of his eyes and that was the most important thing. The elbows and knees of his uniform had worn through, and the sergeant's insignia on his sleeves were more of a faded outline than an image.

Riding in a Humvee over open terrain was bumpy in the extreme. After so many years, Busson was like a sailor in a rough sea, so used to the jolts that he compensated without noticing them. Any discomfort was more than offset by the rugged machine's ability to scoot through the desert. In particular he loved hunting down refugees who wandered the wastelands in search of a mythical safe haven. That was likely the story with the small group ahead. Resistance was not a worry. His men had plenty of firepower, including the 30mm chain gun on the Bradley, although it was short of ammo. But all six carried M16s.

Busson was pretty sure he knew these people. Reports said a family lived in the foothills near Apache Junction—a mother and father, one married son, his wife and their three children, and a widowed daughter with one or two children of her own. He and his men had searched for months but hadn't found them until two days ago, when they'd happened upon a homestead hidden in the fold of a mountain. But the people were gone. Busson knew they could not have gotten far and the deep tracks left in the soft ground had made following them easy.

The family had been raising chickens, goats, horses, and maybe even cattle. The animals were also gone by the time Busson found the homestead, which meant the family had taken them. The chickens would be a nice dinner for his men. The only fresh meat they ever ate was what they killed, and chicken was a delicacy. The goats he might or might not keep for their milk, but the horses he would take back with him. The General could barter them for a lot of fuel, and he could barter the General's gratitude for a promotion. And if there were young girls in the family, as he suspected, he could name his price and the General would pay it. Even mature women brought high prices.

Within fifteen minutes of spotting them, they caught and surrounded the little wagon train. Busson's Humvee stopped beside the lead truck. A wiry man with gray hair and beard watched him with obvious hate. Busson strutted toward the weathered man with the arrogance of a triumphant Roman general. His M16 never pointed straight at the old man, but never pointed away, either. He circled the man twice, like a slaver judging his newest merchandise. For his part the man stood still, careful not to make a threatening move. He was well aware of the weapons pointed at his family.

Leaving the father, Busson moved down the line of trucks. He considered them already his and inspected his newest acquisitions. In the third one, he flipped back the curtain to reveal the grandmother huddled with three children under ten, two of them girls.

"Now here's something worth finding," he said, smiling.

"Come near these children and I'll cut the blood outa you," she said. She held a knife in both hands as her grandchildren tried to scoot behind her.

Without blinking, he leveled his M16 and fired.

The rifle shot echoed across the desert. Lieutenant Sully tried to see details, but the distance was too far.

"Piccaldi?"

"There's a few tears in that canopy, Loot. I see some little kids and an old lady; looks like she's trying to protect them. I can't see if anybody got hit. What do I do, Lieutenant?"

"Those look like our guys, Loot," Meyer said. "They're in Army drag, driving Army slag. For all we know, they're more leftovers and those are legitimate jimbangs they're hassling."

Sully slid down the hill and called the platoon together, leaving the snipers focused on their targets.

"I'm going down there to unfuck whatever this is. I'll leave my radio mike open. If I say *dragon*, snipers open fire and take out everybody except that sergeant. Start with the guy on the chain gun. Clear?"

"Clear, sir!"

"Get that *thumper—*" mortar "*—*up here, but don't fire without my order. Get the rest of the company back here pronto. Everybody thumbs-up? Good, let's go. Meyer, you drive."

"Me?"

"Yes, you. Now move it."

The grandmother trembled in shock. The bullet had struck her upper left arm and blood streamed from the wound. Even injured, she held her spot in front of the children, knife still raised.

"Big man needs a gun against an old woman," she said, grimacing.

Busson laughed. "You can't shame me, you old hag. I'd as soon put a bullet between your eyes. But I'll bet you're a damned good cook, and if you're dead I can't sell you."

She did not reply. The pain in her arm made it hard to concentrate, but her grandchildren pushed even closer against her.

Busson kept the M16 aimed at her chest with his right hand and gripped the canopy frame with his left. He intended to climb in and drag out the children, but a cry from behind stopped him.

The chain gunner, a man named Wolfeater, pointed up the hill to the west. Busson blocked the sun with his left hand and saw another Humvee headed towards them.

"Who the fuck is that?" he said. "Everybody out, form a line. Wolfeater, that Humvee looks brand new, so don't you shoot it to shit, you got me? You only shoot if they shoot first."

He forgot the refugee family. With his men spread out on either side, Busson propped the butt of his rifle on his right hip and waited. He motioned the driver of the Bradley to get out and watch the family. Satisfied, Busson aimed his M16 at the newcomer.

The Humvee bore a two-tone camouflage pattern of desert tan and canvas. It was spotless. Busson could not even see chipped paint. His own Humvees had worn to bare metal. Grime turned them a dirty gray-brown color, streaked with stains.

The intruder coasted to a stop about twenty feet from him. There were only two men in the vehicle, which seemed suspicious. Busson followed the Humvee's tracks and scanned the crest of the hill, but saw nothing in the midday glare. As a thin man in a new uniform emerged from the passenger seat, Busson realized they might be the same size.

"Is it Christmas?" he said, grinning at the idea of new clothes.

Meyer kept his hands on the steering wheel, as instructed. With three M16s and the chain gun pointed at him, it was all he could do not to run for it. Sully had ordered him not to do anything aggressive and he was happy to oblige. The whole thing was nuts anyway. If these were Army guys, or even if they were not, why not signal them from a safe distance? Their platoon had four LAV-25s and the mortars, so firepower was not an issue. But Sully was platoon commander and he wanted this recon done face to face.

As Sully walked around the front of his Humvee, two rifles followed him. He stepped in front of Busson and stopped. "What's your name, Sergeant?"

Busson almost giggled; was this some sort of joke? "You can call me Slick, Lieutenant. As in slicker than goose shit." He could not stop grinning, and his men started laughing. None of them recognized the small radio clipped to Sully's belt.

"Is that right?" Sully said. Starting at his boots, he inspected Busson as he would his own men on parade. "Well, Slicker Than Goose Shit, my name is Lieutenant Sully, USMC. If you really are a sergeant in the United States Army, then I order you to come to attention right now!" He said this as only a pissed-off Marine could say it.

Chuckling, Busson raised his rifle barrel and aimed at Sully's chest.

"The United States Army? Lieutenant, I don't know where the fuck you came from, but there ain't been a United States anything for a long time, and there sure as hell ain't no army! Now here's what we're gonna do—"

Sully interrupted him. "Are you telling me that you are not in the United States Army, Slick? Is that what you're saying?"

Busson did not like people cutting him off in mid-sentence, like he was nobody. His temper flared and he jabbed Sully with his rifle. "I was in the army, but that was a long time ago, when there was a United States to have an army to belong to. That ain't been true for decades. Now I'm in the General's army. You got that, Lieutenant Marine? I take orders from General Patton and nobody else. Now here's what's gonna happen. You and that guy in the Humvee are gonna take off those uniforms, boots, belts, everything. And then you're gonna give us that Humvee. And if you do all that without pissing me off more than you already have, then maybe I'll let you walk back to wherever you came from."

"And if we don't?" Sully said.

"Lieutenant, you don't look like a stupid man. You've got to know the only reason we ain't shot you yet is 'cause we don't wanna mess up them pretty uniforms you're wearing. But we will if we have to."

"What about the civilians?"

"Huh? Who gives a shit? They ain't your concern. Now, are you gonna do as I told you, or get shot?"

"You're a tough guy with a gun in my chest."

Busson smiled, nodded, and raised his rifle to point skyward. "There's two more aiming right at your head."

"I'm not worried about them," Sully said.

"Oh?" Busson said. "Why's that?"

"I have a dragon."

Snowtiger had a clean head shot on the chain gunner, while Piccaldi had the man to Sully's left.

"Alpha Mike Foxtrot," he said, and squeezed the trigger at the exact same instant Snowtiger fired.

The other three snipers were only fractions of a second behind. Piccaldi's target staggered backward with a hole in his throat. Snowtiger's round struck Wolfeater above the left eye, drilled through the skull, and exited the occipital bone below the lamboid suture in an explosion of blood and brain matter. He toppled to one side like a sack of flour. Less than a second later, all three remaining gunmen fell to the ground. Two required a second shot before they stopped twitching.

Busson flinched at the shots, and again when two more rang out a second later. He knew snipers only needed a moment to find a new target, and he was the only target left. Holding up his left hand in a gesture of peace, he moved the barrel of his rifle away from Sully's chest, squatted, and laid it on the ground. Straightening up, he held both hands over his head. Sully scowled and crossed his arms.

"Now, let's get back to business," he said. Behind him a LAV-25 crested the hill, following by three more and then the rest of the platoon. Scattered around them, the bodies of Busson's five men bled into the sand. "Are you in the United States Army or not?"

The armored reconnaissance company spread out and surrounded the little convoy of homemade wagons. Corporal Meyer got out of his Humvee and approached the lieutenant. "What should we do with the IPs?"

"Go see what they need. Give them water and any extra rations we have, and I'll be over there in a minute. There was a shot earlier; check the back of that third truck and see if somebody got hit. Detail two men to watch this prisoner."

"Aye, sir," Meyer said.

Sully turned his attention back to Busson. "I'm waiting."

"Look, Lieutenant, nobody's seen the fuckin' U.S. Army in forty years. My mom told me about the Collapse, but that was way before I was born. Then, yeah, I got recruited to join. They told me I'd be in the Army, they gave me somethin' to eat, a roof over my head, and a gun, so I joined up. I don't know for sure what I'm in. They told me then it was the U.S. Army but later they said it was the Army of the New Republic, so who the fuck knows what it is? And who cares? When you're tryin' to survive in this desert, you do what you gotta do. You can't hold that against me."

Sully considered Busson's words and nodded. The two privates had moved in behind Busson and aimed their weapons at his back.

"I see your point, Slick. If you're not in the U.S. Army, I don't have to haul you in for court-martial. I can just shoot you right here as a criminal... honestly, that makes my life a lot easier. But if you were in the Army, then you're a deserter and a traitor, which means I do have to take you back for trial."

"You can't do that!" Busson took half a step forward before he felt a rifle barrel touch his back. With great care, he eased his foot back in place. "I enlisted because they told me America still existed and would support us, but it was all bullshit. All that time is gone, can't nothin' bring it back, but if you are the American Army, hell, count me in."

"Count you in, huh?" Sully said. "First, I'm not in the Army. I'm a Marine. Second, I'm going over there and talk with these people. You'd better hope they like you more than I do." He gave the guards their orders. "If he moves, shoot to kill."

"Kicker Real, this is Overtime Prime. TacOff in charge is on the air."

"TacOff, this is Kicker Real. Five enemy dead, zero friendly casualties. We captured two Humvees and a Bradley, all in bad shape but driveable. Also have prisoner who claims he is U.S. Army, or once was. Request instructions on what to do with these assets, and a family of IPs. Over."

"Kicker, were the five KIAs also U.S. military?" asked the tactical officer.

"Unknown at this point, Overtime. Subjects were threatening harm to members of my platoon. Snipers acted on my command in defense of platoon commander and other personnel. Also, I've got an elderly female casualty with extensive blood loss from a gunshot wound. Corpsman says she needs medevac A-sap. Suggest sending full Dustoff team."

"Stand by, Kicker Real." As he waited, Sully watched the woman pant for breath while her grandchildren huddled close and stroked her hair. After a few seconds the radio came to life again. "Kicker Real, Dustoff heading your way, ETA twenty-eight minutes. Activate IFF. Monitor Tac Two. Acknowledge."

"Roger that, Prime. Will keep you advised of our position. Company should be Oscar Mike within fifteen minutes after Dustoff is gone. Over."

"You're going to have to hump it to get home before dark, Kicker Real. We'll leave the light on for you."

The old man pulled free and planted himself in front of Sully. Dirt and sweat streaked his leathery face, but underneath the grime was concern and anger. "You're not taking my wife anywhere until I know who you are!"

"Please calm down, sir." Sully pointed to the eagle, anchor, and globe pin on his collar. "Do you see this, sir? Don't you recognize it?"

That surprised the old man. He bent close to inspect the pin and seemed confused. "It looks familiar... but no, I can't remember what it means."

"It's been a long time, sir." Sully felt sympathy. The old man had kept his family alive through trials Sully could not even imagine. He softened his voice. "You've been through a lot and I understand why you're suspicious. But we're not your enemies. We're here to help you. We're United States Marines."

The man blinked and looked away, then moved in for another look at the gleaming gold pin. Somewhere his mind made connections and long-forgotten memories came into focus. He smiled. Several teeth had black decay, while others were missing altogether. "Thank you," he said, tears welling in his eyes. Without another word, he ran to his wife.

Sully turned to Meyer. "What's the status of those captured vehicles?"

"Good to go, Loot. Trasker says the engines look like shit, but for now they're running and he thinks they'll make it home."

"Trasker's the best grease-eater in the company. All right, help the family load everything into the Bradley. Use the Humvees, too, if you need them. Find some drivers for the captured stuff—"

"Already done, Loot."

"Blow up anything left behind."

"What about the animals?"

50

"Saddle them up."

"Sir?" Meyer said, using the rare epithet. "Nine horses, five goats, two dogs, I don't know how many chickens, a mule, and a cow. Loot, I don't how we're going to transport a whole zoo."

"You'll figure it out," Sully said. "That's why you're company sergeant."

1511 hours

When the last vehicle disappeared in the west, Govind stood and worked the kinks out of his back. From atop a distant saguaro, a prairie falcon preened itself as it watched him. Accompanied by his brothers, Govind made his way into the depression and inspected the abandoned corpses before the circling vultures landed. The men appeared well fed. Their clothing showed wear, but also repair. Hard-soled boots were a rarity.

"These look like men from Prescott," Gopan said. "Soldiers of the Republic."

Govind circled the bodies. "They *are* soldiers of the Republic. But tell me the lessons to be learned from today."

"They were all killed with one shot, perfectly aimed," Gopan said. "Whoever the newcomers are, they have many vehicles of war, they have flying machines..."

"Helicopters."

"Helicopters. And their warriors are killers."

"Good, all of that is true. But what else?"

Gopan thought for a moment. "I don't know."

"Their vehicles and their helicopter bore the white star."

"The sign of the Republic."

"Yes, but they killed men of the Republic. How would you explain this mystery?"

"I cannot."

"Long before the white star was the mark of the Republic of Arizona, it was the mark of the United States Army. I want those vehicles tracked. Wherever they came from, I want watches placed on them day and night. Gopan, send scouts in all directions. I want to know everything that happens in this desert. After the slaughter of those Sevens we found in the north, I have felt war is coming, and if it is, we must know on which side to fight. Or not fight."

"Is there a question? The Sevens are devils."

"Yes, they are. But Hell has many devils, and some are worse than others."

CHAPTER 7

In war, events of importance are the result of trivial causes.
  Julius Caesar

1512 hours, June 30

Central Command Two, a/k/a the Deuce or the Castle, was on the western-facing side of the mountain. Similar in architecture to CentCom, a/k/a the Clam Shell, it was about half the size. It served as headquarters for the brigade's S-3, the operations officer, who was also the executive officer, Lt. General Norman Colesworth Fleming. There was no Crystal Palace, and instead of five terraced levels there were three. Fleming's office was off to the right, down a ramp and a short hallway. It did not have a direct view outside. Instead, a tactical station in the main area had external cameras Fleming could use during active operations. A large platform on the same level had desks, work stations, monitors, communications gear, and anything else needed to run a military operation.

As the lurps had patrolled their assigned vectors, Fleming had sat beside Captain Netrice Thompson, the day's TacOff. He'd focused on every word from the field. As usual, he'd listened with eyes closed, visualizing the reports.

Tension and worry had varied throughout the day. More than six hundred of the brigade's ground strike forces were on long-range patrols, with a lot of irreplaceable hardware. It was not the potential danger that worried Fleming, but the incomplete unit training. In the days since deployment, there hadn't been time to shake hands with everybody in your platoon, much less your company. Unit cohesion could not develop in such minimal time. The only thing the lurps had going for them was world-class training and esprit de corps. But Fleming could at least run the show without interference. Angriff had left after an hour of breathing down his neck and gone back to the Crystal Palace.

"Overtime Prime, this is Piledriver Real."

Fleming perked up.

"Piledriver Real, go to you," Thompson said.

"Prime, we're at the site of last week's air strike and IP rescue, and we have fresh tire tracks leading toward the highway. No survivors on site."

"Understood, Piledriver. Get video for S-2. Overtime out."

1516 hours

"General, Private Dupree would like a word with you," Sergeant Schiller said. "He says you asked him about some sort of trap?"

Angriff had been staring out the picture window, lost in thought, and it took a moment to focus.

"Yeah, I did. Send him in."

Dupree snapped a sharp salute once in front of Angriff's desk.

"As you were, Private. So what have you got for me?"

"General, I think we can find out who tapped our mainframes. It would involve taking that tapline we found—"

"You found," Angriff said.

"Yes sir, I found. We take that line and connect it to a mainframe of our choosing. Then we load it with as much useless data as we can think of... movies, books, the Congressional Record, whatever we have that has no military value..."

"...or any other value..."

"...a lot of data. Computers don't know the difference between important data and junk. And within that junk, we load a trojan to infect their computers and send us all *their* data. Even if they discover it, they won't be able to hurt our system because it will be just that one mainframe."

"How hard would this be to carry out?"

"It might take a little time, but it won't be hard, sir. If they're looking for the trojan they can stop it, but I doubt they'll be expecting it. If this doesn't work, we're not harmed."

"Fine work, Dupree. Do it. Oh, and I forgot to do this before. You're a corporal now. Tell Sergeant Schiller on the way out. He's used to it by now."

"Thank you, sir!"

1526 hours

Once Dupree left, there was nothing to do but wait. All four lurps were on their way home. All OPs were out and in contact. Colonel Schiller had located the communication wire and laying it would begin in the next few days. For a brief period the day's schedule was clear. Schiller hadn't even come in with a new crisis. A cup of coffee steamed at his left elbow, a fresh cigar burned in the ashtray, and he was full from a lunch of PSB meat loaf. For the first time since he woke up, Angriff had time to lean back and reflect on everything that had happened.

He was proud of himself. Confronting Bettison had been sheer reflex. In his own mind, he'd had no choice. But even before he'd been completely awake, he had approved the strike mission that saved Tompkins, his men, and all those women and girls. Walling had ordered it, but instead of countermanding it, he'd made a snap judgment and approved. His instincts about Walling had proved good. And by that first afternoon, when the birds had returned, he'd sounded like his old self, even if it had been an act. That was the high point so far, saving those people, and he would never forget a single moment of it. The smell of hot oil and unwashed bodies, the shocked faces of the women and children, the shiny sides of Randall's Comanche... it had all happened so fast he hadn't had time to appreciate the moment. He chuckled at the memory of patting the girl's ass on the side of *Tank Girl*.

Then he realized something, and his laugh died. He had not connected it before because there had been no time to think about it. Now it rendered him speechless with anger, and just like that, Joe Randall was on Nick the A's shit list.

"Schiller," he yelled into the intercom headset, "get me Captain Randall on the horn, right now!"

"Aye, General," Schiller said, wondering what Randall had done now. With the internal network up and running, he got through to the hangar without delay.

"Ready Bay thirteen," a female voice said. Schiller did not recognize it.

"This is Sergeant Schiller, calling for General Angriff. The general wishes to speak with Captain Randall. Who am I talking to?"

"Sergeant Rossi. I'm Captain Randall's crew chief. The captain is speaking with Lieutenant Randall; hold on while I get him."

Within seconds he came on the line. "Captain Randall speaking."

"Hold for General Angriff, please," Schiller said, not giving Randall time to say anything.

Within seconds Angriff was on. "Captain Randall?"

"Yes, General?"

"I want that obscene filth on the side of your helicopter painted over immediately. Is that clear? I will not have an officer in my command made an object of derision by having a naked likeness of her, or him, displayed like a cartoon. Do you understand me, Captain? I want it gone. I don't care what you have to do. You have one hour."

"Yes, sir!" Randall said, almost shouting.

The line went dead and Angriff took off his headphones, folding back the microphone.

"It was the pat on the ass, wasn't it?" Carlos said. "Didn't I tell you?"

Still in his flight gear, Carlos walked in circles beside *Tank Girl*. Like most pilots, he was superstitious. *Tank Girl* had been good to them and changing her name and logo was bad juju.

"So what did you want me to do, Bunny? He'd already done it!" Randall said. "Should I have walked over and said *General, you probably shouldn't do that again. You just patted your daughter's ass.* Before he even knew she was alive?"

"Do you know how long I worked on that?" Carlos pointed at the three-foot-high image on the Comanche. "Can we at least keep the name? Not that it matters without an image to go with it."

"I didn't ask, okay? When a five-star general is yelling at you, you don't poke them so they'll yell louder."

Rossi had been listening to one side. When the conversation stopped for more than a few seconds, she spoke up. "Want me to get the airbrush, Captain?

"I don't see where we have any choice."

"Hold off on that for a minute, Rossi," Morgan Randall said, holding up one finger. She had been leaning against a bench listening, amused at her freaked-out husband. "First, let me make a call."

"Who are you calling?" her husband asked.

She smiled. "I'm friends with the management."

Angriff drew on his cigar and trickled the smoke from his nostrils. Thinking about Morgan's picture on the side of that helicopter angered him more the longer he thought about it. But a good cigar helped soothe the savage breast.

Schiller appeared at the doorway. "General, I have a call for you."

"Who is it?"

"It's Lieutenant Randall, sir, but she says that she's not calling for her commanding officer. She's calling to speak with her father, if he's available."

"Put her through." After fitting the headset and flipping down the mike, he said, "Morgan? Are you all right?"

"I'm fine, Daddy. Can we have a father-daughter conversation and not a lieutenant speaking with her CO?"

"Of course, sweetie. You can call me anytime."

"About anything?"

"Well, sure," he said, belatedly remembering that was how she'd manipulated him when she was younger. "Within reason."

"What does that mean?"

"I almost lost you for the second time, Morgan. I don't want to fight. Why did you call me?"

"Before I tell you, I want you to know that I was standing beside Joe when you called him. I could hear everything, and I want you to rescind your order."

"I thought this was a father-daughter call!"

"It is, Daddy. I would never call my CO like this. That's why I called my dad."

He cursed himself. How many times had he fallen into these traps of hers? He was about to get angry, the way he used to when Morgan weaseled out of being grounded as a teenager, but then he stopped himself. His daughter was alive and he was going to get mad at her?

"All right, I'm listening."

"Calmly?"

"I'm calm."

"Daddy, I want you to rescind that order to paint over *Tank Girl*."

"I'd better not find out that he put you up to this," he said, growling his anger and forgetting the decision made a few seconds before.

But his daughter had long ago learned how to get what she wanted from him. She reacted as she had during their frequent fights in her adolescence, with a calm voice.

"I just told you I was standing there and heard it. Joe asked me not to call, too, and don't you start saying that he should have tried harder. Since when do Angriffs listen to other people? How many times did Mom try to talk you out of stuff? Remember that fishing cabin in Wyoming? She begged you not to invest in that, but you did it anyway. How did that work out? When did she ever change your mind by arguing? Did it ever work?"

"Sometimes."

"What, once? Maybe twice? Should she have tried harder, then? If this was anybody else's helicopter, you wouldn't give a damn, and you know it. But it's your little girl and you don't want everybody seeing me as some sort of cartoon—"

"Naked cartoon," he said.

"Well, they're not, Dad. That's not what's going on. My husband has me on the side of his aircraft because he loves me. It's as simple as that. Would you have told the pilot of the *Memphis Belle* to take his girlfriend off the nose of his B-17?"

He wanted to say, *Yes, if she was holding a giant dildo, I would have.* But he could not bring himself to say *dildo* while speaking to his daughter, so he said nothing.

"It's also good for morale, which you already know. So I want you to rescind the order."

"And if I don't?"

"Then you're going to squander a whole lot of good will for nothing. Dad, don't you realize how many of these people joined because of you? They trust you, they believe in you, and you're really going to tell them that something as harmless as naming their machines is off limits? What about all of the other pilots? Are you going to let them keep their names? Are you going to issue regs on it, about what is okay and what's not? Are you going to make me change the name of my Abrams?"

"What's your tank called?"

"*Joe's Junk.*"

"Beg your pardon?"

"You heard me. It's named *Joe's Junk.* It means exactly what you think it means, and it has a caricature of my husband with a big bulge in a pair of tight pants." She said that last with emphasis, knowing how embarrassed he would be, hearing her speak that way.

"That's on your tank?"

"Yeah. Are you going to make me paint over that, too?"

"I should."

"Then you're going to have to make the whole battalion do it. We've got *Rita's Blowjob Factory, Vagina Warrior, High Explosive Money Shot,* and about fifty more like that. If you make them all comply, it's going to hurt morale for absolutely no military purpose. Do you really want to do that, Dad? Does that even make sense?"

"You're telling me that every vehicle in my command has an obscene nickname?"

Morgan hesitated for a slight second, which told him much. "Not all, no. One of the Marine LAVs has a commander named Laura. I met her in the mess hall. Her LAV is named *Shasta Vibes.* I have no idea why. But that's an exception."

Angriff's cigar ash was about four inches long, so he laid it in the ashtray before it spilled on his uniform. Why could he not finish just one cigar in peace?

"So what do you want me to do? Ignore that's you on that Comanche? It really is obscene, you know."

"Of course it's obscene. That's the whole point. But stop a minute and listen to yourself, Dad. I'm an Army brat. I heard worse than this every day of my childhood. You're talking about people who may be going into combat on a moment's notice, people you may have to order to their deaths. Are you really worried about what's painted on their machines? Come on, I know you better than that. And look at it this way—if we're toasting burps again, they hate seeing naked women."

Not only did he know he had lost the argument, he also knew his daughter was right. That irked him the most. Throughout her life, she usually had been when they'd argued, even if he could never admit it to her. She was wrong about her last point, though. The radical Islamists he knew loved abusing nude women, so long as they were infidels.

"Tell your husband to keep his damned nose art."

"Don't be mad at me, Daddy."

"Don't *Daddy* me," he said, sounding gruff, but since she could not see him, he let himself smile, just a little.

———⌖———

As she flipped the headset to Rossi, Morgan Randall's expression was triumphant.

"That's how you handle Nick the A," she said. "I've been doing it my whole life." She pointed at the image on the helicopter. "Now, do what I told you. Make that sword bigger and round off my ass."

Joe Randall grinned, picked up the airbrush from the work table, and handed it to Carlos. "You heard the lieutenant."

CHAPTER 8

Victorious warriors win first and then go to war, while defeated warriors go to war first and then seek to win.
    Sun Tzu

1702 hours, June 30

Behind his office in the Crystal Palace was the room Angriff had dubbed the Crystal Closet. Calling it a conference room was misleading. Sitting elbow to elbow, there was room for the four officers present and perhaps two or three more, but that was it.

"General Angriff," Fleming said, gesturing to the lean officer standing at attention, "you remember my senior adjutant, Major Olivia Descalso."

Angriff returned the salute. "Pleasure to see you again, Major. I'm sure you know Colonel Walling..." He paused, thought for a moment, then turned to Walling. "This is embarrassing, Colonel. You have been invaluable to me since wake-up and I never asked your first name."

"It's all right, General. You've had plenty of more important things on your mind. It's Benjamin, sir, and my friends call me B.F."

"B.F., huh? Is the F for Franklin?"

"It is, sir," he said.

"Well, it's a damned fine name." He turned back to Descalso. "So what's the latest from the lurps, Major?"

Descalso sipped some water. She had never briefed a five-star general before and had only heard stories about the wrath of Nick the A, but she didn't frighten easily, either. "I can give you the latest, General Angriff, but there're still some gaps in what we know—"

Fleming interrupted her. "Radio and reporting procedures will be changed after today, General. We've discovered some flaws."

Angriff patted the air in a consoling gesture. "It's the first op, people. Glitches are normal. Norm, I know you and your staff will fix whatever needs fixing. Go on, Major; just give me what we do have."

"Yes, sir," she said, wetting her lips again. She shuffled the papers on the table and found what she was looking for. "I'll start with the OPs. All are up and running, the closest being out twelve klicks and the furthest eighteen. None of them are hardwired yet, but I understand this will be done soon."

"That's correct," Walling said. "The S-4 found the wire straightaway. Nobody knows how he found it; he just did."

"That's Colonel Schiller," Angriff said. "He seems to be damned good at his job. Supply is a different animal and the great ones don't think like everybody else. So we've got wire, great, the OPs are out. What else?"

"Task Group Anvil took course three-two-zero out to one hundred klicks. No living humans encountered; evidence of post-Collapse settlements, ruins, lots more wildlife than expected, and wreckage of a foreign vehicle—"

"What do you mean, foreign vehicle?" Angriff said. "Like a Toyota?"

"My fault, sir; I wasn't specific. Anvil reported sighting wreckage of a possible Chinese AFV..."

Stunned silence fell around the table.

"...damaged. They're bringing back video. I'm not sure of the nature of this AFV. I have no more details at this time."

Angriff took a deep breath. "If we have Chinese military involvement, then we need to know A-sap. That escalates potential engagements to a new level. Walling, get this to Colonel Kordibowski in Intellgence; I need S-2 on this right away. Top priority. Tell him I want a report before 2200 hours, even if it's just best guess. Please continue, Major."

"Piledriver headed for the scene of last week's engagement," Descalso said. "Roughly zero-five-zero degrees. The Junkyard, as they call it. Fresh tracks from small motorized vehicles were observed and fresh footprints; no report on number of individuals. There may have been survivors of the air strike. Piledriver's video will need interpretation before we can say with certainty."

"These tracks," Angriff said. "Any idea what kind of vehicles we're talking about?"

"No, sir. Piledriver just said vehicles."

"Norm, we need to improve radio report content."

"Already got it, General. First thing on the list."

Angriff nodded for Descalso to continue.

"Hammer took course one-six-five to one hundred ten klicks. Found three old settlements, all destroyed by fire, no living humans. They did see a herd of wild horses and some antelope."

"More horses. Just what we need," Fleming said.

"Speaking of horses, Hammer had one anomaly. Let me find it... here it is. 'Multiple hoofprints, with apparent footprints intermingled.' It sounds like dismounted riders, but the video doesn't make it clear. There's one more piece to that..."

"Dismounted riders would make sense," Angriff said, cutting her off. "Even in this desert, you can find enough forage for a small group of horses to graze on. Survivors using horses is no surprise. Okay, we'll leave that for S-2. Any more from Hammer?"

Descalso moved on, forgetting she had not finished with Hammer. "No, sir. That brings us to the last task force, Kicker. As you know, Kicker encountered a family of nine people in four wagons made from stripped-out pickup trucks and hauled by horses. There were also a few farm animals tied to the wagons. These people were moving northwest when Kicker observed two Humvees and a Bradley intercept them.

"Instead of making contact, the officer commanding Kicker watched events from high ground, where he observed a man in the uniform of a sergeant in the U.S. Army shoot an unarmed woman while threatening some children she was protecting. Kicker's commanding officer, a Lieutenant Sully, interceded by taking one Humvee to the scene, accompanied only by a driver. Upon his attempt to assert superior rank, the sergeant made it clear that he and his command were no longer in the U.S. Army and threatened to shoot Lieutenant Sully."

"Deserters?"

"We don't know yet," Fleming said.

"Fearing for his own safety," Descalso said, "the lieutenant gave a code word via walkie-talkie and his sniper squad took out five of the six hostiles. The sergeant then surrendered. Upon investigating further, Sully discovered the shooting victim was an elderly female who needed immediate medevac, and we dispatched a full Dustoff team. Upon arrival, she was taken to surgery; there's no update on her condition yet. Kicker is returning with the family and all their possessions, including wagons and animals."

"They'll never make it before nightfall," Angriff said.

"ETA is 2300 hours, sir."

Angriff started to intervene, to order them to bring just the family and leave the livestock and wagons, but stopped himself. Norm Fleming was operations, not him, and he did not want to overrule his number two on something trivial.

"They're bringing this sergeant with them?"

"Yes, sir."

Angriff leaned over and pushed the left-hand button on the small intercom. "Schiller?"

"Aye, sir."

"Task Force Kicker is due to arrive back at base at 2300 hours. I want to be there."

"Got it, General. Wake you if you're asleep?"

"Wake me if I'm dead. I want to be waiting for them."

"Yes, sir. I'll make it happen."

Angriff leaned back and bumped the wall of the small room. "Anybody gone Elvis?"

"No sir. All hands accounted for."

"Then we're done here. Walling, talk to JAG and find out if this sergeant Kicker is bringing in is covered by the UCMJ. If he's not, I may shoot the son of a bitch right then and there. If he is, I might do it anyway."

2309 hours

Viewed from a distance of one kilometer, the mountain was a huge black shape in the night. A half moon in a clear sky highlighted rocky outcroppings in silver beneath a sea of stars. Task Force Kicker drove with blackout lights only, following tracks made when they'd left the base eighteen hours earlier. Even in the bright moonlight, it appeared their tracks ended at a sheer rock wall. But when the lead Humvee came within one hundred yards, thick steel doors slid open and the exhausted drivers drove their machines into the glare of electric lights.

At least fifty people crowded around the portal and waved, Nick Angriff chief among them. The Humvee driver who had shouted at him that morning flashed a thumbs-up. As the convoy crept forward in the cramped tunnel, Angriff climbed on the running board and stuck a cigar in the man's breast pocket.

"Goddamn, General," the startled driver said. "Where'd you get that?"

Angriff winked and patted him on the shoulder. "The Easter Bunny. One thing, son. Please don't take the Lord's name in vain. *Damn* works just as well."

The driver turned to the corporal sitting next to him. "The rest of these trench monkeys ain't worth a shit, but Nick's a jarhead at heart."

Angriff overheard the comment and smiled. Jumping off, he went back to greeting his returning Marines. As strange as it felt for an Army officer, that was how he thought of them, as his Marines.

As the long string of vehicles churned back into the mountain, Angriff stood at the threshold and greeted every one of them. At the rear limped two battered, overloaded Humvees with chickens in cages tied all over them. A Bradley came last, with a string of exhausted and filthy horses and a mule trailing behind it, while lying down in the cargo bay was a skinny cow. Behind the cow were some goats. The veterinary staff stood waiting to take care of the animals.

The tunnel leading from the outer doors was eighty feet wide and two hundred long. It emptied into an enormous parking and maintenance area, measuring three hundred yards long and four hundred feet wide, with a ceiling of more than fifty feet. Overhead lighting mounted on elaborate scaffolding provided a bright working environment. More tunnels led away from this assembly area, but Dog Company pulled to a cleared space close by on the right.

Exhaust fumes hung thick until giant fans dispelled them. The stink of unwashed bodies was not so easy to get rid of. As the company dismounted, the rest of the battalion crowded around, handing over water and energy bars, backslapping, and getting a good look at the IPs. But word spreads fast in a base like Prime and most of them wanted a look at the prisoner.

The tired Marines of Dog Company climbed out of their vehicles. Streaks of sweat trickled through the yellow dust covering their faces. They smiled as only Marines home from a successful operation could smile. The two dogs ran loose, barking, panting, and getting belly rubs.

Angriff tried to shake every hand in the company, and as many in the battalion as possible. He mingled until he wound up next to Sully's LAV-C2. This was a LAV-25 variant with no chain gun, but a high roof to accommodate antenna and electronics equipment. The lieutenant had his back to them, but when everybody around him snapped to attention, he glanced back and did likewise.

"As you were," Angriff said. "Lieutenant Sully? Great job today, son, great job. You did the Marine Corps proud. I know I'm proud of you." He pumped Sully's hand and couldn't help noticing the picture painted on the side of his LAV, a squawking duck running from a naked woman. Below it was the AFV's name in bright red letters outlined in white, *Fuck A Duck*. "How are your IPs holding up?"

Sully nodded at the family standing a few yards away, gawking at their surroundings while several nurses asked them questions. The children hid behind their grandfather and parents, terrified.

"I think they're overwhelmed, General. Some water and sleep will help, and they need some decent food."

"Don't we all? If you find any, let me know."

"Um, yes, sir," Sully said.

"But as much as we joke about them, we should be thankful we're not starving. I'd like to speak with the IPs later, but S-2 can do a better job of gathering intelligence than I can. In the meantime, they're in good hands. So, give me the short version of what happened out there—"

For the next few minutes, Sully related the events of the day, from the episode with the renegades to waiting on medevac, and then the long trip home trailing livestock in their wake. When he finished, Angriff pointed at a dejected man staring at the floor, surrounded by scowling Marines.

"That our deserter?"

"Yes, General," Sully said. "He says he's not a deserter, for what that's worth. His name is Busson, but everybody calls him Slick."

"Slick, huh? Who's that?" He indicated a slump-shouldered old man coated with dust, who glared at Slick.

"That's Joshua. His wife is the one Busson shot. He wanted to kill the guy, but I wouldn't let him."

"Good call."

"Thank you, sir. Our primary mission was gathering intel, and prisoners who talk are the gold star. I also promised Joshua we would punish Busson for shooting his wife."

"You can bet on that," Angriff said. "Oh, by the way, you're Captain Sully now. Company commanders need to at least be captains."

He started walking toward Busson, and Schiller ran in front to try and block him. "Is there anything you need, General?"

"Yeah, for you to get out of my way."

"General, sir, shouldn't we be getting back? You've got a long day tomorrow."

"Move. I'm not going to shoot the bastard, at least not until S-2 gets through with him. And make a note, Lieutenant Sully is now Captain Sully."

"I heard, General."

Walking straight to Busson, Angriff put his mouth inches from the prisoner's nose. "Do you know who I am, Sergeant?"

Busson had rarely interacted with General Patton or his men. Among his own small circle, he'd commanded respect and fear, and was not used to people getting in his face. But combined with seeing his friends gunned down, the long ride back, and the uncertainty of his future, it all left him trembling. "You're a... a general?"

"That's only one thing I am, Sergeant. Among other things, I'm a man who doesn't like pissant cowards who shoot helpless old women. I'm also a man who hates, and I do mean *hates*, deserters from the armed forces of the country I love, the United States of America. And if you think that nation no longer exists, then you have made a serious error. See that flag?" Angriff pointed to the far wall, where hung the largest American flag ever made. It measured more than one hundred feet long.

"As long as that flag flies over any part of this continent, the United States lives. And since it's flying here, that means you are now in the United States of America and governed by the laws of that nation—in this particular case, by the Uniform Code of Military Justice, which you swore to abide by when you joined the United States Army, and against which you have committed God knows how many violations."

"But General, I didn't—"

"Shut up. Did I give you permission to speak?"

Angriff paused to let the effect of his words sink in. He had decades of experience chewing out errant subordinates. In the past he'd often had to feign anger when the infractions were pranks or practical jokes he'd actually found quite funny. This time he did not have to fake it. He wanted to put a bullet in Busson's brain on the spot, and only self-discipline held him in check. But Busson's danger was palpable.

"The thing that you should be most concerned about," Angriff said, continuing in a softer, more sinister tone, "is that I am the only judge, jury, and executioner who matters in this place. When it comes to your life I am God. Unfortunately for you, I'm not the God of the New Testament, the God of forgiveness. I am the God of the Old Testament, the God of hellfire and damnation."

Angriff stopped, turned his head this way and that, and sniffed. Then he looked at Busson's pants, wet from the crotch down. "You really are a spineless piece of shit, aren't you? So listen close... you have one chance to avoid a prolonged and painful death, Sergeant, and only one chance. You are going to be interviewed by my intelligence staff. You will tell them anything and everything you can think of about whatever they ask you. You got that?"

His face a sickly white, Busson swallowed.

"If you hesitate to answer, if you try to mislead, if you give them any reason to think that you are not being one hundred percent cooperative, I will guarantee whatever time you have left on God's green Earth will be as torturous and miserable as it is humanly possible to be. Do I make myself clear?"

Busson nodded, eyes wide.

"In this army, you say 'Yes, General.'"

"Y-yes, General."

"You see, those intelligence officers play nice compared to who comes next. If they don't get what we need from you, we turn you over to a very attractive young lady. Blonde hair, blue eyes, a nice figure... no doubt your initial impression will be favorable, but that won't last. See, she's a psychopath who likes to hurt people. It's kind of a hobby with her. So you tell the nice officers what they want to hear, and we'll make sure you don't have to meet her. Do you understand?"

Busson nodded.

"Get him out of here before I shoot him."

Chapter 9

Many intelligence reports in war are contradictory; even more are false, and most are uncertain.
  Karl von Clausewitz

0800 hours, July 2

Lt. Colonel Roger 'Rip' Kordibowsky loved his job. When they'd first met, he'd explained to Angriff how puzzles fascinated him. He found the mental challenge from deciphering a message or solving a problem addictive. As a child, he'd needed to know how something functioned and why. Why were mills located beside rivers and who'd figured out how to harness water to turn the millstone? When was the breakthrough moment when someone figured out thrust produced lift by forcing air under a wing's surface? Who first brewed beer? Angriff had known right away Kordibowsky was his S-2. Their partnership had lasted more than a decade before both went cold.

Kordibowsky's mind saw intelligence questions as an evolutionary process. You started with scraps of information or details, and began to build the larger picture. Under Angriff's tutelage, he'd flourished. With no family to hold him back, he had not hesitated to follow his mentor into Long Sleep as S-2 of the 7th Cavalry Brigade.

Thus he found himself sitting near Angriff as Colonel Walling began the second full meeting of the brigade's staff. S-3 Norm Fleming gave a brief recap of operations to date, and updated the status of the eight established OPs. He also outlined preparations for the first FOB (forward operating base) at the site dubbed the Junkyard. (With its burned-out trucks and human skeletons picked clean by scavengers, Junkyard beat out Kill Zone as its nickname.)

Hardwiring connected all OPs to base, with radio backup, eliminating any chance of a surprise attack on the base itself. After sketching an outline of future lurps, Fleming wrapped up and turned it back to Walling, who introduced Kordibowsky.

"Ladies and gentlemen," Kordibowsky said. He had a slight New England accent, an underlying hint in a word here and there. "Before I start, allow me to say that I have far more questions than answers. My purpose today is to share with you a snapshot of what we know to be true, which is not much, and what we believe to be true, which is a little more. I'll keep unfounded speculation out of this.

"But if I cannot give you an answer, please understand it's because I do not have one for which there is adequate supporting evidence. Attempting to cover my whole report," and here he held up a thick sheaf of papers, "is impractical, so I will cover the high points. You will each receive a digital copy once the meeting has ended.

"This information was synthesized from the few sources we have available. General Tompkins and his men provided the only first-hand information we have on the Collapse. They gave us a broad overview of what happened west of the Mississippi during the intervening years. For events east of that river, we simply have no reliable intelligence. Of course, we have the media reports, so viewing the catastrophe from a wide angle is possible. But the further one attempts to dig into specifics and details, the less one finds. As for the current conditions, we cannot guess what those might be.

"For our purposes, we are quite fortunate. When the sequence of events collectively called the Collapse occurred, General Tompkins was here in the United States on leave. You were in Montana, I believe." He turned to Tompkins.

"That's right," he said. "Trout fishing on the Gallatin River."

"The Collapse was not one single disaster. We cannot say with certainty the exact order of events. But we do know a catastrophic earthquake along the New Madrid Fault was the triggering event. This occurred in mid-May. Rumors at the time attributed the quake to a nuclear device, but no one found conclusive evidence to support this. Geologists' predictions for seismic events along the New Madrid zone gave such a quake a high probability, so the simplest explanation is probably correct. It was a natural event.

"General Tompkins had the opportunity to watch news coverage before... well, that's getting things in the wrong order. The Center for Earthquake Research and Information, located at the University of Memphis, estimated the quake at nine point three on the Richter scale. Given the wide and total destruction, it was at least that strong. During similar events in 1811 and 1812, reports said the Mississippi River ran backward. This time, we know for a fact that it did. There were numerous aftershocks with strengths measured up to seven point zero.

"What made this catastrophe worse was the flow of the river at Memphis, the closest large city to the epicenter, which was near record levels. Typically around five hundred thousand cubic feet per second of water flow past a hypothetical point at that city. That's a huge volume of water. That year, winter and spring had seen significantly higher than average precipitation along much of the Mississippi River Valley. As it drained south, the river level at Memphis was estimated at three times the average.

"Media reports at the time claimed the quake disrupted the flow of the river for more than an hour. As impossible at that may seem, it makes sense given what followed. Record levels of water returned north, pushed by the energy released by the quake. At the same time, record levels were still flowing downstream. This created flooding in the surrounding areas and formed a giant lake. Imagine Lake Erie transported to the four corners area where Kentucky, Missouri, Arkansas, and Tennessee all come together.

"As long as the seismic energy kept driving water north, the lake continued to grow. But once the energy dissipated, the flow returned to normal and that enormous body of water moved south as a wave. It flooded everything in its path. For those of you familiar with vulcanology, think of a pyroclastic flow, such as the one that buried Pompeii. Billions of tons of volcanic material were held aloft by the force of the eruption. But when the upward pressure eased and could no longer support the material's weight, gravity sucked it back to Earth in a pyroclastic flow hundreds of feet high. It was a tidal wave of burning ash that swept everything before it.

"In a sense that is exactly what happened after the earthquake. Once the river flowed south again, it became just like the pyroclastic flow at Pompeii. Imagine a tidal wave hundreds of feet high sweeping through the valley of the Mississippi. St. Louis drowned in the backflow, and it destroyed every city downstream. Memphis was on a high bluff forty feet above the river. That didn't save the city. Flooding upstream drowned it from the north. The delta flatlands in Mississippi and Arkansas flooded for thirty miles inland, and the water levels were said to be fifty feet deep. Very little survived intact and casualties were almost total.

"As bad as it was from St. Louis south, it was much worse at New Orleans. When the inland tidal wave reached that city, it pushed a gigantic wall of debris before it. River barges, paddlewheel steamers, freighters, and all manner of private craft, trees, houses, cars, anything and everything you can imagine. The wave was choked with debris and struck the merchant and cruise ship fleet in port. It washed those giant ships downstream, eventually becoming so packed it created a giant dam across the river.

"When the water could no longer flow to the Gulf of Mexico through its normal channels, it flooded the surrounding area, which included New Orleans. If we were to compare catastrophes, Hurricane Katrina might be a four or five on a scale of one to ten. This was a ten. There was nothing left alive except snakes and gators. There were survivors, but they fled New Orleans because that city had ceased to exist."

After sipping some water, Kordibowsky turned to each person at the table in turn. "Overstating the damage from this event is not possible. Every bridge from St. Louis south to the Gulf of Mexico was swept away, but it was much worse than just losing the bridges. All functioning infrastructure was destroyed. Rebuilding those lost bridges would first mean clearing the highways on either side to allow access to rebuild. This would start with making the highways safe again, to a distance of perhaps fifty miles on both sides of the river. Then would come the massive job of restarting power in those areas. This, in turn, required rebuilding the local power grids. In the meantime, truck and rail traffic had to be routed north of the Ohio River, or to remaining ports along the Gulf Coast. In a real sense, America had been cut in two.

"Within the affected areas, there was no food, water, energy, or transportation. The total lack of roads crippled efforts to aid the survivors. Compounding what was already the greatest natural disaster in American history, we also lost huge food-producing areas.

"All this information we know with some certainty, and not only because General Tompkins watched the situation evolve on live television. We have additional reports in our databases from National Guard units, the NSA, FEMA, military bases in the region, and various government agencies. It makes for chilling reading.

"After two days, General Tompkins' unit recalled him and he could not keep up with the national picture. But we know the bombings began within days of the initial earthquake. A wave of terrorism spread across the country. Suicide bombers, truck bombs, Molotov cocktails dropped from highway overpasses, snipers, IEDs, attacks on grammar schools, all manner of attacks were launched in what appeared to be coordinated assaults. The obvious objective was to disrupt life and hamper recovery efforts.

"At one water filling station in Louisiana, more than five hundred refugees were killed by a truck bomb. These were mostly women and children, with older folks unfit for rescue duty also caught in the blast.

"Five women opened fire in Jackson, Tennessee, at a temporary aid station set up for refugees from the Memphis area. They shouted Islamic slogans and targeted children. Few people got hurt, however, because those at the station had their own weapons and returned fire, killing the terrorists. Four children were shot, but they all survived.

"In other areas, where the population was less well armed, similar attacks resulted in very high casualty rates. There were, quite literally, hundreds, and maybe thousands, of such attacks, to the point where people were afraid to gather in groups.

"This is when the news reports began to end. Military and government reports became sporadic and incomplete. We know plagues broke out, but the nature of the pathogens remains a mystery—ebola, anthrax, or bubonic plague, we don't know. The starting points appear to have been San Francisco, Los Angeles, San Diego, Phoenix, Miami, Boston, and New York. Whatever it was, the mortality rate was high, especially considering how overwhelmed the medical services had already become. We should keep this in mind before we enter those areas, since some pathogens can survive for decades, if not centuries.

"From this point, events become much less clear. There were undoubtedly electromagnetic pulse attacks. It's possible most areas of the country suffered such attacks, because reports of all kinds ended in the same time frame, many simultaneously. The only conclusion we can now draw is that terrorist cells infested the country in greater numbers than even the alarmists had dreamed.

"At what point in time the United States quit functioning as a nation is much harder to pin down. It is not impossible that a rump government exists to this day. We simply have no data. General Tompkins can tell you his own story, but he was assigned to a unit deployed to protect Lake Tahoe as a potential source of potable water. They bivouacked in the Tahoe National Forest and were isolated, which probably explains why they survived.

"That brings us to the present. We have some idea of what conditions are like west of the Mississippi, again thanks to General Tompkins and his intrepid command—small settlements dotted here and there, a hundred people, perhaps two hundred at the most. Big cities, well... some are ghost towns. The general never went into a large city if he could help it, because in some of them the criminal element existing before the Collapse was able to survive and institute a sort of warlord society. In others, if there are any survivors, they are aggressive and unreasonable.

"There is one place General Tompkins never verified as actually existing, a place called, with some sense of irony, Shangri-La. In the intervening years it became something of a legend, a Camelot, if you will, of post-Collapse America, where free men still live under the flag of the United States. Some say it's in the Lake Tahoe area, or perhaps merely in the Sierra Nevada Mountains. Others place it in Colorado, Montana, Northern California, or even here in Arizona."

When Kordibowsky paused for more water, Angriff turned to Fleming. "Before this goes any further, Norm, let's find out the truth behind this Shangri-La. If it's real, those are the very people we need. Start working out the details for some super long-range recons and we'll talk later. Please continue, Colonel."

Fleming nodded, betraying nothing of his thinking. Lake Tahoe was more than six hundred miles from Overtime Prime, and Colorado was not too much closer. Sending a slurp so far was tantamount to a suicide mission. But he said none of this. His opinion would be given in person and alone.

Kordibowsky went on. "Let us now move beyond the Collapse to intelligence collected by this command. First, let me address the issue of this so-called Caliphate. The official name, and this seems to be accurate, is the Foretold Caliphate of the Seven Prayers of the New Prophet."

"That's a mouthful," Angriff said. "Any idea what it means?"

"We have no hard information on its structure, size, or beliefs, but we do have enough to speculate on some aspects. We know, for example, it has moved as far west as Tucson, and has invested New Mexico, Old Mexico, and Texas, but with no idea of the exact boundaries.

"We suspect, although again, it's hard to know for certain at this point, that there is something radically different about the teachings of this religious state from other Islamic sects. For example, the Caliph is referred to as God's New Prophet, and while we can all guess what that *could* mean, right now it's just a guess. We also know they are called to prayer seven times a day, instead of five. For this reason they are referred to as Sevens, and two of the prayer sessions are made directly to this New Prophet. This is radically different from traditional Islam. But again, details of how this sect originated, what exactly it believes, and how it is structured internally are all unknown."

"So you're saying these aren't Muslims?"

"I cannot say exactly what they are. They are certainly not traditional Sunnis, but whether they are some splinter Shia sect or not, there is not enough evidence to form a conclusion."

"Best guess?" Angriff said.

"They are something brand new, perhaps building on Shia traditions. Someone may have taken advantage of the chaos to carve out their own little kingdom."

"All right, let us know when you have details. What's next?"

"Results of the long range patrols were mixed. Task Force Anvil searched to the northwest. They found old wreckage of a Chinese Wolf, a light multipurpose vehicle produced by Shaanxi Baoji Special Vehicles Manufacturing, similar to a Humvee. To our knowledge this was strictly a military vehicle. Close examination shows the mount for a 7.62mm machine gun on the roof, although the gun itself was missing. The obvious leap of logic is that the Chinese have, or had, a military presence somewhere in the western United States."

"Do we know the operational range of that vehicle?" Angriff asked.

"With standard fuel capacity, approximately six hundred kilometers."

"That's not enough to make it to the coast, is it?"

"The distance from the wreck to the nearest coastal city is more than three hundred fifty miles. However, there is no reason it could not have carried spare fuel tanks."

"So as far as we know, it could simply be an anomaly?"

"Yes, sir."

"Thanks. But Colonel, you need to prioritize this Wolf matter. If there are Chinese regulars in the neighborhood, we need to know A-sap. That changes everything."

"Consider it done, General."

"Carry on."

"Anvil produced no other actionable intelligence. Next, Task Force Piledriver patrolled to the northeast, in the sector of our initial air strikes. The video evidence they brought back confirmed there had to be at least one survivor. The fresh vehicle tracks were not military, and the tires were badly worn. They were probably full-sized pickup trucks or SUVs. Given the computerized vehicles of the late twentieth and twenty-first centuries, and the likelihood that EMPs were used in the area, it seems likely they were pre-1985 American pickup trucks. We have to assume the survivor, or survivors, were rescued and their superiors know we possess an air assault capability."

"Can we be sure of that?" Angriff said.

"At best we can hope the survivor died before providing intel on our gunships, but it would not be difficult to observe the battlefield and draw the correct conclusions."

Angriff nodded, so Kordibowsky continued. "Hammer reconnoitered out to one hundred twenty clicks on bearing one-two-five degrees, south-southeast. Once again they found a number of settlements abandoned or burned, but nothing of significance. The only anomaly was they felt someone might be watching them.

"Which brings us to Kicker..."

CHAPTER 10

You can use all the quantitative data you can get, but you still have to distrust it and use your own intelligence and judgment.
Alvin Toffler

0902 hours, July 2

"Kicker scouted the area north and west of Phoenix and brought back the Suggs family, their dogs and livestock. More important, they brought back Sergeant Busson, who has proved to be a real coup for intelligence. He has been most cooperative. He believed he was enlisting in the U.S. Army, and so will be covered under the UCMJ.

"Busson was born some years after the Collapse in the small city of Prescott. He is fuzzy on the details of growing up there, but his life has been dominated by some sort of renegade American officer turned warlord. The political entity controlling the area is called the New Republic of Arizona, which this warlord figure claims is a continuation of the United States and that he is therefore the legitimate government. He maintains a standing military force of considerable size. That is the force Busson joined. This warlord calls himself General Patton. He claims descent from the actual George Patton, and wears five stars on his collar."

Angriff sat up and raised his eyebrows. "Well, that's two five-stars. Two more and we can play a rubber of bridge. In all seriousness, what do we know about this guy, Rip?"

"His origins are obscure, sir, and his order of battle seems rather... haphazard. According to Busson, he has a core of trained soldiers num-

74

bering between seven hundred and one thousand. He calls them Freedom's Guards, or LifeGuards, or just Guards for short. These are his shock troops. Busson claims there are several thousand other soldiers like himself, men who have received some military training but are not really soldiers per se. Busson says they act more as a police force than a military one. They are called Security Police. In my opinion they are like the *Sturmabteilung* in Nazi Germany with only second-rate combat value.

"Busson's duties evolved from policing the Prescott area to scouring the countryside looking for new sources of food, fuel, and workers. The word *slave* is never used, but that is precisely what the populace of this town appears to be. There's one particularly chilling detail we discovered, and that's how fuel is obtained. It's an open secret that captives are traded to groups with access to gasoline. He also thinks something big is in the works. There has been a major effort to round up new captives. Young women, such as the ones rescued by Kicker, are a prized commodity, and young men are always needed for labor.

"An analysis of the fuel in Busson's vehicles shows it to be relatively fresh. We thought it would have an alcohol component, but that proved untrue. This means oil refineries are operating somewhere and this Patton trades with them."

"Did Arizona produce oil before the Collapse?" Angriff asked.

"It did, sir. There were some refineries east of Phoenix and a cluster of wells along the eastern and northeastern border. Production didn't reach Texas or California numbers, but it wasn't insignificant."

"And you said this Caliphate is in Tuscon?"

"That's correct. The Sevens may have seized the wells and refineries and put them back into production. The logical leap, therefore, is that Patton's trading with the Sevens. But we can't make that connection with absolute certainty.

"Returning now to the Republic of Arizona's organization—after the so-called Guards and the Security Police, there are also thousands of militia. As Busson describes them, they sound like a mob that does what they are told. Assigning them combat value would be overrating them. In a fight, he says they would only have hand weapons, such as shovels or hammers.

"The Guards have access to some good weaponry. He has seen them practicing with automatic weapons, which is significant. Without either a very large stock of ammunition, or the capability of replacing what they use, profligate live-fire training would use up too much ammunition. RPGs are also on hand in seemingly large numbers, and Busson thinks they may have working armor."

"Armor as in tanks?" Fleming asked. "Since we already know they have Bradleys."

"We asked Busson that question and it was clear he believes they have tanks. He has not seen them, but he has heard them and—he said this with no prompting from us—he has felt them."

"I don't like that," Angriff said. "You can feel an Abrams a hundred yards away, which means he's telling the truth. Anything else, Colonel?"

"About this warlord, no, sir. There is only one more interesting bit that we found, and this comes from Task Force Hammer. I overlooked it earlier. I believe I mentioned that Hammer found hoofprints. While videoing those, they also videoed the surrounding area.

"Corporal Sharansky found something she wasn't expecting during a routine magnification scan. There is a sheer rock face, maybe three hundred feet high, and about halfway up there's a cave with a ledge. On this ledge stands what looks like a pulley system, using ropes. She also noticed something painted on a rock, near a faint ladder of what might be handholds leading up to the cave. Under extreme magnification she saw a sequence of symbols. Without investigating in person, there's no way to know their age. But our best guess is within the past ten years, because the colors are quite bright. If true, if these are actually modern symbols, then they are very important."

"Do we know who made them, or what they say?" Angriff said.

"We think so, General, although we cannot be certain. According to the computers, the symbols read *Beware who comes in war, for it is war you shall have.* And there is no question the language is Apache."

The conference room had cleared, leaving Angriff alone with Fleming and Green Ghost. Schiller brought in coffee. Angriff inhaled the aroma of an unlit cigar and laid it on the table.

"Snatch-and-grabs in urban areas rank way up there on the scale of high-risk ops," Angriff said. "But you think the risk is worth it to get the intel we need?"

"I do, Saint," Green Ghost said. "They'll need two SEAL platoons, with a Marine recon company in support. In and out, grab prisoners, no other contact."

"None of your people?"

"They have their own mission here."

Angriff started to ask why he'd said *they* instead of *we*, but realized Green Ghost intended to lead the mission. He considered forbidding it, but stopped himself. He had agreed to let Green Ghost lead whatever missions he wanted, in return for acting as the brigade's security officer.

"Are the SEALs ready?" Angriff said. "They've barely had a week's training together, and most of them weren't actual SEALs to begin with."

"That's unfair, Nick," Fleming interjected. "The ones who washed out were all injuries; none of them rang the bell. The skill set is there but bad luck kept them from finishing, and they're all combat veterans. And you couldn't get a better mission leader than Green Ghost."

Seeing his opening, Angriff couldn't resist trying to get his way. "That's another thing. Why is the head of security leading an op?"

Before Green Ghost could say anything, Fleming surprised them all by answering. "Because we need him to. And since when has anybody stopped Green Ghost from going on a mission? Remember the Congo? And the events leading up to it? The guy is a machine."

"You sound like his lawyer. Do you put him up to this, Ghost? Okay, fine, you lead the mission. But unless somebody can tell me why it's urgent, I want more training time before we go. As for you," he pointed at Green Ghost, "don't get killed; otherwise, you're in trouble. But your sister stays here."

"I don't think he planned to take her," Fleming said, glancing up at Ghost.

Ghost nodded. "She has her own mission here."

"Good," Angriff said.

"She's your bodyguard."

"Like hell she is. I don't need a bodyguard, and I sure as hell don't need her. She scares me more than assassins."

"I'm the S-5 and this is a security decision. I'll tell her to be a shadow."

Angriff scowled. "Back to the operation. If you think they can do this, Norm—you're the S-3—it's your call. We definitely need reliable intel. And since we know this Patton is based in Prescott, it makes sense to go south first, instead of north into Flagstaff. If we can pull it off."

"They can do it, I'm sure. And they need the practice."

"Yeah, as long as we don't lose them. But truthfully, I do feel a lot better about it with Green Ghost involved."

"I'm gonna remember you said that," Ghost said.

"Several of them asked if those horses we brought in were in shape to be ridden," Fleming said. "It seems SEALs like riding horses in rough country, and many are trained riders. I had to say no on those poor nags the Marines captured, they're skin and bone, but it might be time to thaw out some of those in Long Sleep."

"We have horses?" Green Ghost said.

"We do," Angriff said, and then laughed. "They're still frozen, but what the hell? Check with... who is in charge of livestock, anyway?"

"I would assume it's the Ag people."

"Probably. Ask Dr. Goldstone; she'll know. And before we thaw them out, tell whoever is in charge to make sure we've got fodder. We can't graze them in the desert. I doubt our horses would know what to do with a cactus."

CHAPTER 11

Nothing you can do, sure as one and one is two
I'll be creepin' up on you.
        Status Quo, "Creepin' Up On You"

0136 hours, July 27

Richard Parfist prized no object more than his knife. His knuckles tightened on the haft, even though it hindered him as he crept forward in a crouch. Long blond hair fell into his eyes; he flipped it aside with a shake of his head. The dark night helped cover his approach behind the darker figure ahead.

Parfist moved with the stealth of a mountain lion. Barefoot, he inched toward the man squatting on the edge of the hill overlooking a blacked-out school.

When he was within arm's reach, he slid the knife point just under the man's left ear and hissed, "Make a sound and I'll cut your throat." A bird passing overhead would have made more noise.

The crouching figure did not move. Parfist paused, surprised. The darkness made it difficult to see any details. The guy wore something round on his head. All sorts of things stuck out of his bulky clothes and there was no mistaking the gun, which was identical to those carried by the Guards. But his silence was unnatural... he did not even seem to breathe.

Something sharp touched Parfist's own neck under his left ear and he flinched.

"Go ahead and stick him," a voice whispered from behind. "He won't care."

As every heartbeat expanded his neck, the point of the blade pushed into his carotid artery. Not enough to pierce it, but enough to render him motionless. His mind raced through possibilities of escape, but there were none.

Glancing at the darkened school gym at the bottom of the slope, he stifled a cry. "I won't resist. Just let me see my family again."

"Sssh!' the voice whispered. "Shut up and drop the knife."

"But—"

"Shut the fuck up."

He let the knife fall and a hand picked it up. Shadows moved in his peripheral vision, some coming up the hill, others on either side. They moved out of sight behind him. In the darkness he could barely see more shapes moving near the building below.

"Here's what's going to happen," the soft voice said. "We're going to stand up, and then we're going back up the hill. You are not going to make a sound or attempt to escape. If you do, I will kill you. If you think you can get away, you're wrong. Got it?"

Parfist nodded, but the man wanted to hear him say it. "Yes, I've got it," he said. "But my family is down there."

"Shut up."

Dark shapes lifted the crouching man, whose limbs stayed rigid. Then he stood and they were off. Once behind the crest of the hill, Parfist was pushed, pulled, and dragged through the open desert for what seemed like hours. In reality it was less than thirty minutes. The rough ground ripped at his bare feet. His soles had toughened after years of walking over rocky terrain, but several times he and his captors ran through cacti and thorns. By the time they paused, his feet were a bloody mess.

None of it made sense. He'd first assumed they were Patton's men, but that had to be wrong. His captors spoke and looked like the General's men, as much as they looked like anything in the dark night. Yet Prescott was well to the southwest now, so why were they taking him northeast? Unless they *didn't* work for the General. But if that was true, then who were they? Were they after captives for themselves? If so, why settle for just him?

Resting in the sand, he huffed for breath. His captors seemed none the worse for their sprint. One of them handed him a cloth and pointed to his feet. Parfist could not see his own feet in the darkness.

"Where are your shoes?"

"Where would I get shoes? I'm not one of the General's men." Using the strip of cloth, he dabbed at his torn feet, blotting blood and picking out thorns. With his thickened foot pads there was no real damage, aside from the pain of walking.

"Here," said one of his captors, handing him a pair of thick boots. "Try these on."

He had only worn shoes a few times in his life, so it took a few minutes to get into them. He had no idea how to tie the laces, so the man who had given him the boots had to do it. Two others trained their rifles on him. With the laces tightened, he stood.

"My feet slide in them."

"Best we can do. Let's shove off; we've still got a long way to go."

"Where are we going?" he said.

One of the men grabbed him by the arm and dragged him. "You'll find out."

"No!" He twisted his arm so fast his captor lost his grip. But he did not run, because they had guns. Plus, blundering about on the night of a dark moon was suicidal. Even forgetting snakes, spiders, and scorpions, the Sonoran Desert's apex predator was a nocturnal hunter that sometimes hunted in packs—the cougar. So instead of running, he raised his hands. "If you're the General's men, then take me back to my family. At least have the decency to let us go into slavery together!"

For a moment silence fell. Then a strange song broke the silence. Close by, an uncanny, aspirated question, sung with the intensity of a phantom, punctuated Parfist's plea. Each weird stanza ended time with a rising tone.

"What the fuck is that?"

"Billy owl," Parfist said, surprise in his voice. "They do it all night." *Why don't you know that?* he wondered.

Then a new voice in the darkness spoke up, the voice of someone in charge. "Quit dicking around. Carry him if you have to, but we need to getfooh."

Rough hands grabbed Parfist by the arms.

"What is getfooh?" he said.

"Get the fuck out of here."

"I beg you! My family is the other way! Just let me go to them, please!"

His captors ignored his pleas. Crying, struggling, yelling, none of it caused them an instant's hesitation. They dragged him until he ran to keep from falling. Parfist felt desperate to do something, but what? Every step took him farther away from his wife and children. As he trotted, tongue lolling like a tired coyote, he tried to think of some way to escape, but there was none. Although they were only vague shadows in the blackness, he knew men surrounded him, men who seemed to see in the dark. And so he plodded onward, northeast across the desert, toward the distant mountains.

No clouds obscured the constellations. The stars gleamed like polished diamonds sprinkled against the vastness of the cobalt sky. Giant saguaro cacti glowed luminescent green along the edges. Like silent sentinels, they stood glowing in the darkness, their long fingers reaching for the heavens. Parfist inhaled the smell of creosote, so much like rain, and heard the growl of a distant cougar. He loved the desert at a level so fundamental outsiders could never understand it.

They ran, and ran, and ran some more. At first the boots helped, protecting his punctured soles from further injury. But as his feet slid around in them, blisters formed and then burst. The leaking blood made him slip more, until his best gait was a stumbling walk. The effort to keep moving left him exhausted and parched. It became hard to concentrate. Mosquitoes attacked his face and arms. He swatted a few, leaving streaks of sweaty blood running down his forearms and cheeks.

As dawn tinged the eastern horizon pink, the mountains became outlines against a sky of iridescent blue. On the desert floor, Parfist could make out shapes ahead. Larger than a man, and soon it became obvious they were vehicles. Many vehicles. Sleek, angular vehicles.

Salt stung his eyes. Wiping them with the backs of his hands did not help much, but soon enough he could make out details. Most of the vehicles had four wheels on each side and some sort of gun on top, mounted in a turret. A few varied in shape, being longer and wider, and with a different configuration on top.

They slogged to a stop next to the vehicles and he leaned against one of the wider ones, panting, as sweat dripped from the tip of his nose. One of his captors handed him a bottle and he drank immediately, without worrying about what it was. He was too thirsty to care. The liquid tasted like water, but with a sweet flavor he liked. Its effect was immediate. His mind cleared and he had enough energy to stand and shake sweat from his hair.

The men surrounding him all wore uniforms like the General's men. Except they looked new, with no holes or patches, and the colors were brighter, more vivid. The men carried a lot of equipment, too. Not just rifles and pistols, but knives, packs, and bulging things he did not recognize. They even wore helmets, with large and strangely shaped goggles hanging from their necks. Their boots were dusty but showed no wear. General Patton's men looked similar but much shabbier, with old and worn-out equipment and uniforms. When he asked yet again who they were, he received the same response: silence.

At length they led him to the rear of the widest vehicle where, to his shock, two doors stood open, revealing a hollow interior with benches on either side.

"Get in," somebody said, giving him a gentle push.

"Please listen to me," he said. "Please. Take me to my family! Let us go into slavery together. I'm begging you. It won't make any difference to you, you'll still have me to trade for fuel, but my children must be terrified. For the sake of God, please take me to them."

The man he had spoken to just stared back without blinking. After several seconds he called out, "Hey, Ghost, come here a second."

A lean man about six feet tall crunched over the gravel toward them. He wore a different uniform, a darker one. Parfist could tell immediately this one was in command. He acted as if the desert was his private property.

"What?" Ghost said.

"This IP wants us to take him to his family. If I read this right, he thinks we're collecting slaves or something."

"Yeah? What makes him think that?"

"How should I know?"

The man called Ghost stared at him. Parfist felt naked, but returned an unblinking gaze into the man's bright blue eyes. At length, Ghost turned his head. "Captain Sully, can you come over here?"

Yet another man joined them. This one had two silver bars on his collar.

Ghost said, "This man's not a soldier. You talk to him while I make sure my team is good to go, but make it fast. We've gotta get on the road home."

The captain seemed annoyed. "Whatever you say. I'll take it from here." Sully leaned forward on one knee, halfway into the armored personnel carrier. "I'm Captain Sully. What's your name?"

"Richard," he said. "Richard Parfist. Captain, please take me to my family. Please?"

"Richard, I have to ask if you're one of the soldiers of the man they call General Patton. If you are, then say so now and it will go much easier on you."

"What? No, I'm not one of the General's men. They're the ones who took my family, the ones who are going to sell them into slavery. Aren't you the General's men?"

"No, sir, not that general. Look, I don't have much time right now. We've got to be out of here by sunup. I'm not going to restrain you, but don't try to escape. Otherwise I won't have a choice. Fair enough?"

"But my family! My wife Lisa and my children are back there!"

"Listen, Richard, if what you say is true, you might not have to rescue your family alone. Do you understand? We're here to help people, not hurt them. So if you're telling us the truth, you might have help getting your family back. But for now, I need you to sit down so we can finish loading up."

"Then at least tell me this," Parfist said, his long blonde hair matted to his face. "If you're not General Patton's men, then who are you?"

Sully smiled. "Everybody's asking me that these days. We work for a general, Richard, but the general we work for doesn't like seeing civilians mistreated. I have a feeling this General Patton isn't going to like the shit sandwich that's heading his way. Now sit down. We've got to get moving."

Confused, but seeing no choice, Parfist sat at the far end of one bench, while other men came in and sat down around him. All bore the same letters above the left breast pocket of their uniforms. Parfist knew how to read, so he knew what they said, but that just confused him more. Stenciled in block letters, it read *Marines.* Exactly like General Patton's uniforms said *LifeGuards.*

<hr />

Green Ghost found Vapor standing by himself.

"Everything copa?"

Vapor jumped. Ghost had a way of moving unseen even when he wasn't trying to. "Damn, would you stop doing that? We've got prisoners."

"I know. Are we ready to roll?"

"Yeah, but we've got more prisoners."

"I heard you the first time. Put 'em in the Havoc and let's getfooh. Are they zip tied?"

"Of course, and blindfolded."

"So what's the problem?"

"They're wearing Marine uniforms."

"What?" Green Ghost said.

"I know, right? They're over there."

"Shit, we don't have time for this. Where are they?"

Green Ghost found the two hooded prisoners standing beside a Havoc, flanked by two Marines. He inspected them for a few seconds, noting the ratty dungarees, mismatched belts, and worn-out boots. The men themselves were skinny.

"Why are you men wearing United States Marine uniforms?" Ghost said.

The question took them by surprise, since they could not see him. "Because we're LifeGuards, dumb fuck," the bigger of the two said. "That's what LifeGuards wear. Just wait until the General finds out you grabbed us like this. You'll really be fucked."

The prisoners stood with their backs to the AFVs. Green Ghost reached over and pulled the bigger man's hood off. He blinked, even in the light of pre-dawn. Green Ghost slapped him on the cheek, as one might an errant friend.

"Hey, shithead, over here," Green Ghost said. When the man focused on him, he continued. "Did you say you're a Marine? Name and rank?"

"Can't you hear? I'm a LifeGuard, but I don't have to tell you shit."

"You do if you're a Marine. So, are you a Marine or not?"

"LifeGuards wear these uniforms, so you figure it out, fuckhead."

"I'll assume you think you're a Marine, since you're wearing the uniform. And if you are, I outrank you..." Despite his statement, Green Ghost wore no rank insignia. "See these men all around us? They're Marines. Real Marines. But I don't believe you're a Marine, or even in the U.S. military. You're a maggot, nothing more."

"Fuck you," the man said, and spit on Ghost's shirt.

Within a heartbeat, two rifles pressed into the man's back. Green Ghost shook his head, meaning *Don't shoot*. He reached down and picked up a handful of dirt in his right hand, then pinched his prisoner's nose with his left. Soon enough the pseudo Marine gasped for breath and Green Ghost stuffed dirt into his mouth. Coughing, spitting, the man fell to his knees and started rolling on the ground.

Green Ghost let this go on for almost a minute before he nodded for a PFC to help the gagging man. The Marine filled the prisoner's mouth with water and he spat out the mouthful of mud. They repeated the process until he could breathe again, then the PFC jerked him to his feet.

"Big man," the prisoner said. "When I'm tied up. Lemme loose and we'll see how tough you are."

Green Ghost sneered. "You're tied up for your own protection. You're not a real Marine. See, LifeGuards, whatever they are, aren't Marines. Only Marines are Marines. And you're not, so you're tied up. When we get where we're going, I suggest you be cooperative. Otherwise you'll get to meet a special person, one who likes to stick sharp objects into the bodies of prisoners."

He gave orders to gag and re-hood the man, and throw him in the Havoc.

"Captain Sully," he called, cupping hands around his mouth. "Get-fooh time."

CHAPTER 12

It is essential to understand that battles are primarily won in the hearts of men. Men respond to leadership in a most remarkable way and once you have won his heart, he will follow you anywhere.
       Vince Lombardi

0523 hours, July 27

Nick Angriff spent every spare moment brooding on ways of turning his command from a fragmented hodgepodge into a killing machine. He knew that from earliest times, traditions had been important for military units. They instilled esprit de corps and cemented cohesion. Formalized rituals and behaviors created the group pride necessary for individuals to subsume personal welfare to the greater good of their unit.

The Seventh Cavalry Regiment had a history stretching back to Custer and the conquest of the Old West. Formed in 1866, it had served with distinction until the debacle at the Little Big Horn in 1876. The unit did not die with Custer, though. It won battle honors in both World Wars, Korea, Vietnam, and in Operations Desert Storm, Iraqi Freedom, and Enduring Freedom. When Angriff went cold, it had been on the ground in Syria. The unit's official nickname was *Garryowen*, the catchy song in the 1940 Errol Flynn movie *They Died With Their Boots On*.

The Seventh Cavalry Regiment was gone, but Angriff declared his brigade a continuation of its famous namesake. Although he commanded components from all five branches of the armed forces, he needed the traditions of the old Seventh Cavalry. Its officers did not know each other and had not yet established ties of trust. Noncoms had not yet figured out the talents and flaws of their officers, and vice versa. By now the rank and file knew the name of the person next to them, but had no idea how they would react under fire. Nor did the intrinsic inter-service rivalries help matters any. The Seventh Cavalry Brigade consisted of small groups and cliques, and was not yet a cohesive fighting force.

While they were discussing that over coffee in his office, Norm Fleming recited a story that was funny because it was true. "If you had to explain why the four major services could never work together," Fleming said, "it's because they all speak a different language. For example, if you needed to secure a building, the Navy would turn off the lights and lock the doors. The Air Force would sign a long-term lease or buy it outright. The Army would occupy the building and forbid entry to anyone else. And the Marines would assault the building and defend it to the death with suppressing fire and artillery support."

Angriff chuckled. "That's so true."

"So what's the matter, Nick? Cohesion's already better than it was. These things take time."

"Nothing's the matter. I'm fine."

"And I'm your fairy godmother."

"Sometimes I hate how well you know me. All right, have it your way. Something's bothering me, but I don't know what. I've had this sadness all day, this depression, but I can't explain why. Maybe it's because I know I'll soon have to order combat elements under my command to assault an American city. And there's a high likelihood Americans will die as a result."

"You can't think that way, Nick. You knew this day was coming when you agreed to go cold. We can't resurrect America without getting rid of the bad guys."

"Of course not. You're one hundred percent right. But there's still that other thing nagging at me."

"Which other thing? I can think of a few dozen."

"You know, that feeling that's been bothering me since before I talked to Steeple, the feeling I missed something? Sometimes I forget it completely. Other times, such as today, it's like someone's banging on my front door but I can't find the doorknob to let them in."

"I thought that ended when we confronted Bettison."

"I thought so, too. But I'm having those same thoughts again. My mind keeps telling me I'm still missing something, and it's bugging the shit out of me."

"Go to bed, get some sleep. You're not twenty-five any more. You can't keep pushing yourself forever. We need you fresh and healthy."

"Sleep," Angriff said, glancing upward. "Don't I wish... but I'll sleep when I'm dead."

"Which might be sooner than you think, unless you start taking care of yourself."

"The Seventh Cavalry Brigade has no traditions of its own, and I'm determined to establish some. The first will be the commanding officer greeting task forces when they return from a mission."

"I thought you worked on those logistics projections with Colonel Schiller all night last night."

"Who told you that?"

"You did."

"Oh. I exaggerated."

And so, despite heavy eyelids, he stood in the open southwest portal as Task Force Kicker rumbled into view. With no jacket and rolled-up shirt sleeves, the implication was clear. If the arriving troops needed help, he would get his hands dirty. He strapped his famed twin Desert Eagle pistols tight around his waist, although in combat he wore them in shoulder holsters. Like Patton, he considered them a vital part of his persona. Beside him, as always, was Colonel Walling.

The mission had been dangerous in the extreme. Not only had it been the first time the SEALs had operated in their platoons, but it was also the first cooperative mission with the recon Marines. And it had been a spectacular success. The SEALs had not been spotted and they had grabbed prisoners. The Marine transport and mission security had been flawless. Not only would they now have full knowledge of what awaited them in Prescott, they'd suffered no losses. Angriff knew that would not last.

When the lead Humvee crossed into the mountain, the driver held out his left hand and Angriff slapped it. Around him were an assortment of technicians, officers, engineers, maintenance crew, and onlookers. The report of prisoners in Marine uniforms had spread throughout the base and anybody who could step away from duties came to get a look at them. The rest of the Marine battalion stood glaring and with arms folded.

Humvees led the convoy, then half of the LAV-25s, with the Havocs in the middle and the rest of the LAVs bringing up the rear. Once all were within the enormous western parking garage, the great double doors slid closed with a clang.

Angriff once again mingled with the returning Marines and slapped the backs of the SEALs, helping several out of their gear, asking questions and spreading praise. Captain Sully walked over and saluted, which Angriff returned. Green Ghost followed.

"Task Force Kicker all present and accounted for, sir," Sully said.

"Excellent work, Captain. Report to your CO; I'm not here to disrupt chain of command. When you've done that, come see me, unless Colonel Berger needs you for something else."

"Aye, sir."

"He's a good man," Green Ghost said once Sully was out of earshot. "It was a good op, boss."

"No problems?"

Green Ghost shrugged. "Little stuff, no big deal, about like a training exercise. The SEALs are good, Sully's got his recon company combat ready, and we got prisoners."

"So I heard. Any intel yet?"

"Two are wearing Marine uniforms and are decidedly hostile. They call themselves LifeGuards, whatever the fuck that is. The other appears to be a civilian. Keeps yelling about his family and becoming a slave."

"Slave?"

"That's what he keeps saying."

"I want to meet these prisoners."

Norm Fleming said nothing, but smirked. Angriff noticed, waited a few seconds, and turned on his exec. "What?"

"Isn't interrogating prisoners the job of S-2?" Fleming said. "You know, chain of command and all."

"Kordibowsky will get his crack at them. I just want to see what these *Guards* look like, and why they're wearing Marine uniforms."

"Uh-huh."

Green Ghost left and Angriff, Fleming, and Walling watched the organized chaos of the task force disembarking. Various maintenance and supply crews immediately began servicing the vehicles.

A few minutes later, Green Ghost returned with a man of medium height, wearing brushed animal-hide pants and a long, simple shirt dyed black. He wore Marine issue boots and had trouble walking in them. Soot smeared his face, while sweat left streaks at his temples and cheeks.

"Saint Nick," Green Ghost said, "this is Richard Parfist. We found him prowling around outside an old high school gym. A lot of people are being held captive inside, but he wasn't one of the guards. Mr. Parfist tried sneaking up on us, but all he found was Neil—"

"Neil?" Angriff said.

"He's a dummy we use as a diversion. Neil did his job."

"Maybe I should give him a medal."

"He would appreciate that," Green Ghost said. "He asks for so little. Mr. Parfist wisely gave up when his situation was made clear to him. But like I told you, he's been repeating the same story over and over. He's pretty worked up about it. According to him, his family is about to be sold into slavery."

At the mention of the word *slavery*, all smiles vanished. As an involuntary reflex, Angriff rested his left hand on the butt of a pistol. He turned to Parfist and leaned forward.

"Mr. Parfist, I'm General Nicholas Angriff." He extended his right hand. "Do I understand this correctly, that your family is being held captive? How did this happen?"

Parfist had been told in no uncertain terms not to say anything until directed by Green Ghost. Combined with his shock at seeing so many armed men in such an intimidating setting, the warning had left him too scared to do or say anything for fear of jeopardizing his last chance to save his family. Tentatively, he shook Angriff's hand. He looked at Green Ghost for permission to speak. "You're the general they told me about? Like the one in Prescott?"

Angriff cut a quick glance at Fleming. "Not exactly, Richard. May I call you Richard?" Parfist nodded. "Thank you. My appointment comes from the United States Congress, before the Collapse. As you can see, we are a real American military unit. Whoever this so-called General Patton is, if he was once a part of the armed forces of this country, then he answers to me. If he's a fraud, then he's a criminal and that makes him my enemy. Does that help?"

Parfist cocked his head. "What do you mean, before the Collapse? That was before I was born. Do you mean you all are left over from when there was a United States?"

"That's correct, Richard. How that happened will have to wait until we have more time; it's complicated. At the moment, I need you to tell me about this slavery thing. What did Green Ghost mean when he said your family is about to sold as slaves? Is that true?"

"Yes!" Parfist said, excited that somebody was finally listening. His entire demeanor changed, despite Green Ghost's warnings to stay calm. He began gesturing and licking his lips. "They're all going to be sold to the Chinese! You've got to help me save them!"

Angriff held up both hands in a *slow down* gesture. "Did you say the Chinese?"

"Yes, the Chinese. They've got the fuel; who else would the General trade with?"

"Richard, just so I'm clear, are you telling me this General Patton is going to trade human captives to some Chinese in return for fuel? Gasoline?"

"Yes, of course." Parfist wondered why Angriff asked about something so obvious. "That's what always happens. It's how they get their fuel. Everybody knows that."

Angriff ignored the last comment. "Do you know when this trade is supposed to take place?"

"Not exactly, but soon. They can't keep all those people penned up for too long or they'll get sick, and then the Chinese won't take them."

"How many captives are there?" Angriff said.

"I don't know for sure," Parfist answered. "A lot."

"Have you learned your numbers, Mr. Parfist?" said another voice. They turned. Rip Kordibowski stood to the side.

"Who are you?"

"This is Colonel Kordibowski," Angriff said. "He works with me, asking questions and helping me decide what to do. If he thinks we should help you, that will go a long way toward helping me make up my mind, so please answer any of his questions."

Parfist hesitated for a moment, but then gave up resisting. If these men did not help him, nobody would. "I don't have much choice but to trust you. Yes, Colonel Kor... Kor...duhbosskey?"

"Colonel K will do fine, Richard. So, have you learned your numbers?"

"You mean, can I count? Yes, and I can read and spell, too. My father made sure that I could; he said it was important."

"Excellent, Richard. Your father is a wise man."

"He's dead."

"I'm sorry. He *was* a wise man. Now think. These captives you told us about; how many are there? Guess if you have to."

"Like I said, a lot. When the General's men attacked our village, they took about five hundred people, all those who couldn't run away. But there were already a lot in the gym. I would guess there's at least four or five thousand people gonna be traded to the Chinese."

The American officers went rigid.

"Four or five *thousand*?" Angriff said. "Are you sure?"

"No, General, I'm just guessing. It could be more." Parfist's eyes watered with tears and he fell to his knees, sobbing. "Please save my family, please! They aren't big and important like you, General, but they're all I've got! Please save them!"

Angriff squatted in front of the man then lifted him by the arms. "Richard, you're a citizen of the United States of America. You don't need to beg for my help. That's my job, protecting and liberating citizens of our country. No American will be sold into slavery while I'm around. I serve you, sir, not the other way around."

Parfist raked hair away from his face and tried to understand what Angriff had said. "General, I hear your words, but they don't make sense to me. My dad told me I was a citizen of America, even made me learn to spell it, but I never figured out what it meant. The United States seemed like a children's story."

Angriff gripped his shoulders and held his gaze. "The best way I can explain it, Richard, is that being an American citizen means you kneel for no one. Never... and if somebody tries to make you, that's where we come in."

Chapter 13

Let your blood flow without regret.
    Psalms of the New Prophet, Chapter 11, Verse 14

New Khorasan (formerly Tucson, AZ)
0637 hours, July 27

Morning sunlight poured through windows ringing the upper deck of the old gymnasium, behind the last row of bleacher seats. Several shafts slanted downward through cracks in the ceiling. Torches and braziers lit the hallways and corridors, creating a hanging smoke pall below the rafters.

Men filled the stands, most of them brandishing a rifle. Others ringed the upper walkway while the floor was standing room only. More than ten thousand men stood silent, listening to every word spoken by the man on the makeshift stage.

"Life is pain!" yelled the Emir of New Khorasan. His audience, of course, knew him as Abdul Qudoos el Mofty, Superior Imam and Servant of the Most Holy Who Holds the Fatwa, the New Prophet. Atop the creaky platform in the decrepit high school gym, he swept his hand over the crowd. They stood where a shiny basketball court had once hosted a state championship game, but the plank flooring had long since dried out and warped.

"While you live, you bleed. As you breathe, you ache. Misery is your daily companion, but you are blessed, my children! For the infidels, only death brings relief. But for you, my faithful warriors of the New Prophet sent by Allah, while you bend to the will of the Prophet, your life will be sweet. For you carry the new word of Allah in your hearts. You will still know pain, for that is the price Allah demands for living in his world. But for you, pain is an offering to Allah, because death is but a doorway to paradise. And while you are on Earth, Allah wants you, the believer, to hold dominion over his world and use its creatures to your best advantage! Only then will the world be cleansed of the stink of the infidels."

He paused and raised his arms. The congregation knelt and bent forward for the required ten seconds. His audience seemed hypnotized, or entranced, completely within the spell of his words. He was their leader, their Superior Imam, and their expressions were those of men who looked upon something divine. They would do anything he asked, including die for him.

"Today we leave for the west, where we will avenge our fallen brothers, killed by the infidels who fight for this General Patton. For years, in our mercy, we have allowed them to live in peace, because ours is a religion of peace, and the words of our blessed Caliph dictated that it be so. But no more! When they attacked our brothers, Paco Mohammad and his men, who were on a holy mission, they forfeited any right to peace and instead sowed the seeds of war! And if it's war they seek, it is war they will get!"

As one, thousands of men leapt to their feet and cheered, pumping their fists and jumping up and down. The Emir let them go on for half a minute, then quieted them.

"We leave today for *our* holy mission. Not only to spread the glory of Allah's newest prophet to new lands and new peoples, but to extend our Caliphate. Thousands of your brothers left days ago, walking through the burning desert because the fire in their hearts burned hotter than the sun. You have been chosen to ride. This privilege is yours because you have proven yourselves loyal servants of your Emir and your god. On this journey you must be a shining example with your bravery and your willingness to obey unto death. Go now into the unknown, and find your glory!"

As he stepped down from the stage, the audience chanted his name.

Chapter 14

Thus says the LORD:
See! I rouse against Babylon,
and the inhabitants of Chaldea,
a destroyer wind.
         Jeremiah 51:1

1649 hours, July 27

Rip Kordibowsky was grim as he entered the Crystal Closet. After nodding to each officer sitting around the rectangular table, he took the remaining seat. Angriff sat at the far end, facing the large flat-screen monitor on the wall. To his right was Norm Fleming, then Walling, Kordibowsky, and, on his left, Bill Schiller and Dennis Tompkins.

Angriff started the meeting. "It goes without saying we are going to rescue those people in Prescott or die trying. That means we're going to attack, and we're going to do it soon. The planning starts now. Rip, the floor is yours."

"Gentlemen," Kordibowsky said, "we now have a good idea of this so-called General Patton's rifle strength and weaponry. We also have a date for this exchange of prisoners for fuel, and none of it is good news. Our two prisoners are part of his best troops, the ones he calls Life-Guards, or just Guards. By our standards they are poor soldiers, but they have had some military training and are loyal to this Patton character.

"For planning purposes, you may assume each one has an automatic weapon in the category of an M16 or AK-47. Some of them also have sidearms, and they have a variety of grenade-type explosives. They wear surplus Marine uniforms because there was a warehouse full of them in Prescott. Based on our prisoners, these guys will be tougher than we might have thought. They genuinely believe they are in the United States military and are carrying out legal orders from a legitimate general. Put another way, they think they're us."

"Son of a bitch," Angriff said.

"Exactly, sir. And unless we can convince them otherwise, they're going to see us as an enemy."

"Are you suggesting we try to convince them we are not the enemy?" Fleming said.

"No, General, nor do I think that would work. They believe anyone who defies the authority of this Patton person is an *outsider*. Outsiders do not deserve protection and should either be destroyed or enslaved. Fuel, guns, ammo, there are a wide variety of commodities supplied by the Chinese in exchange for human slaves. The Guards see it as helping America as they know it. Patton claims the New Republic of Arizona is the rightful successor to the United States. To them, everything beyond the immediate Prescott area is foreign territory.

"Moving on to his order of battle, besides his Guards, Patton—"

Angriff interrupted him. "We have got to find something else to call him. It's a disgrace to the memory of George Patton to have this clown mentioned in the same breath. Call him... I don't know..."

"That's what his people call him," Fleming said.

"Yeah, but I don't like it. Somebody think of something."

In the silence, Colonel Schiller cleared his throat.

"Yes, Colonel?" Angriff said.

"General, as your S-4 I took it upon myself to do a deep search for potential supply or equipment depots in this region. I was searching for anything that could be useful for the brigade. As it turns out, there was an Army National Guard depot in Prescott, as well as a Marine storage warehouse. That unit kept its records updated, even after the Collapse began. We have an inventory of what was on hand there months after other units quit reporting to Washington—"

"Thank you, Colonel, that's useful," Angriff said. "Excellent work. Please make copies of that inventory list and give them to Colonel Kordibowsky and General Fleming—"

"Yes, sir, I will, but I discovered something else, too."

Kordibowsky cringed for the colonel. Interrupting Angriff never ended well.

"I may have discovered the identity of this General Patton person."

Angriff's face turned red and he opened his mouth, but then closed it. Kordibowsky knew his commander had worked hard on restraining his impulsive temper.

"Colonel," he said, "I want my subordinates to tell me the truth, the whole truth, and nothing but the truth. But please don't interrupt me again."

"Yes, sir," Schiller said, unpertubed.

"Now, do you mean his real name, not this Patton bullshit?"

"That's correct, General. The data storage for Overtime Prime goes way beyond anything needed for our operations. We literally have every report ever digitized in the history of the United States armed forces, right up until the end. Apparently we are a repository for the archives of all five branches of the armed forces.

"While searching for lost depots, I found reports of every conceivable nature, from OERs to ammunition expenditure at Fort Bragg in 1987," Schiller continued. "There's so much, it's nearly impossible to sort through it all, even with advanced search functions. But one of the last reports ever received by the Pentagon is a change in command at the Prescott National Guard Armory. It seems the colonel in command was relieved for cause by a lieutenant named Lester Hull. What that cause was is not specified. I scanned Hull's personnel file and he was twenty-two at the time. Moreover, his OERs showed he was insubordinate, hard to get along with, and thought he should be in charge of every situation. If this is our man, he would be in his early seventies, but trained by the pre-Collapse Army."

With that, Schiller passed out copies of a one-page synopsis he had written of Hull.

"Colonel, that is one damned fine piece of research and initiative. Is there anything else I should know?"

Schiller hesitated, his blue eyes looking everywhere except at Angriff. "On their last inventory list, the Prescott Armory listed a number of artillery tubes and heavy machine guns, some Bradleys and Humvees, and six M1A1s, retired from active service."

"Six Abrams," Angriff said. "They had armor?"

"Yes, sir. I can't say whether they still do or not, but they did."

"Rip, what are the chances Schiller is onto something here?"

"With Patton's real name or the tanks?" Kordibowsky said.

"Both."

"I do not know offhand," Kordibowski said. "But during our interrogation of Busson, he certainly believed they had tanks. If you recall, he said he felt them through the ground. As for the name, I'll move it to the front burner in case there is anything we might glean from his OERs."

"Damn fine work," Angriff said. "Damned fine. All right, Rip, you said this... Lieutenant Hull, was it?" He turned back to Schiller.

"Yes, General, if he's our man."

"Doesn't matter. I prefer calling him Hull instead of Patton. So Lieutenant Hull has about a thousand of these Guards. Tell me again what else he has."

"He's got a second class of... soldier is not the right word... follower. They are not trained like his Guards, and not as dedicated, but he still trusts them with weapons. They are called Security Police. Busson was one of these."

"These are the ones we likened to the SA in Nazi Germany?" Angriff said.

"That's right, sir. In a firefight, they might or might not stand and fight. I doubt they would stand long against armor or artillery. After that, he has militia, but *mob* is probably a better word. For the most part, I would expect those people to scram at the first opportunity."

"So the bottom line is that we're facing urban combat against at least a full battalion of heavily armed men who are highly motivated and willing to die fighting?" Angriff said. "And they are supported by irregulars who might or might not stand and fight? Plus, we can expect thousands of militia getting in the way? Right so far?"

"That sounds about right, sir," Kordibowsky said.

"On top of that, they probably have anywhere from one to six M1A1s, an unknown number of Bradleys, and we can assume the usual assortment of IEDs and Molotov cocktails, correct?"

Kordibowsky nodded. "Artillery is unknown, General. I would not be surprised if they had mortars, but ammunition could be a problem. After this long, it may have degraded too much to use."

"So that's our enemy in Prescott, gentlemen. Let's remember our primary mission is not liberating this town. We're attacking to free those captives before they can be turned over to the Chinese. And I want to make this very clear to you, so you can make it very clear to every person under your command: that is not going to happen. Those people are going to be rescued, by us, and under no circumstances is even one of them going to wind up in the hands of the fucking Chinese. Not. One."

Scowling, he searched every face at the table. "Very well. Is there anything else you'd like to add, Rip? No? Then you have your marching orders. We attack day after tomorrow. The exact time is up to General Fleming, but I would assume a push-off time of 0100 or thereabouts."

"General," Fleming said, alarmed, "that only gives us thirty-eight hours to draw a battle plan, gear up, distribute ammo, food, and fuel, establish call signs... We can't be ready that quick, not with this command. They simply haven't trained together enough."

Angriff heard him out, then stood and turned to Kordibowski. "What about it, Colonel? Do we have more time than that? Can you guarantee the Chinese won't be here sooner?"

"General, I can't guarantee the Chinese won't be here *before* that."

"Day after tomorrow, 0100 or sooner," Angriff said, leaning forward on his knuckles. "I want those people saved, and if the Chinese show up, we're going to blow them back to Hell. Get to work."

CHAPTER 15

Believe that you can whip the enemy, and you have won half the battle.
        General J.E.B. Stuart

0631 hours, July 28

Schiller brewed the coffee extra strong. Neither Angriff or Fleming had slept, and the effects of sleep deprivation left their faces slack. The clear morning found them yawning and rubbing their eyes. Both smelled of dried sweat. Adjourning to the Crystal Closet, the two old warriors slumped into their respective chairs.

"Lay it out for me, Norm."

"It's pretty complex, Nick," Fleming said, slurring his words. "But it has to be."

He sipped the steaming coffee, but it tasted burnt. A dozen cups throughout the night had left his palate numb to the flavor.

"Just give me the basics," Angriff said. "Then we can get into details."

"I'm using the whole brigade. Everything we've got will at least be in ready reserve. I'm putting the Marines on our left flank, the whole battalion, spread out in a line about twenty miles long. They'll have water barriers on either flank, Horseshoe Reservoir on the left and Lake Pleasant on the right."

"A battalion stretched for twenty miles?"

"Granted that will only allow for hedgehog positions, but we're not expecting trouble from the east. And if need be, we can redeploy them

100

elsewhere. I'm using First Infantry Regiment in the main assault on Prescott and the Second Infantry to cover the Chinese, since we have no idea of their strength. For all we know, they're sending an armored division."

"I hope it's not that bad," Angriff said.

"I hope not, too, but we don't know. If it really is the PLA, then all bets are off. The First Infantry Regiment will send its First Battalion to flank the city from the east, cutting off enemy units trying to escape, while Second Battalion moves into the city from the north. We don't have enough MARSOC Marines to make up a company; we've got about two platoons, eighty-one men. I'm sending them ahead with two SEAL platoons and a Force Recon platoon. And maybe our Nameless squad."

"Green Ghost, too?"

"That's up to him. Mr. Parfist has volunteered to lead them into Prescott."

"I don't like involving civilians."

"We don't have much choice. There are three highways leading into the city that we need to worry about. Second Infantry will send its First Battalion northwest of the city to block any junction with the Chinese down Highway Five. They'll be squarely in the target zone, so they get first priority for artillery and air support.

"Second Battalion will move northeast of the town, on the left flank of the assumed Chinese line of march down Highway 89. I'm giving First Regiment all of Seventh Artillery Battalion and one battery from Eighth. Second Regiment gets the other two batteries.

"The tanks I'm splitting up. First Company is going into Prescott right behind the infiltrators. Second and Third Companies are with Second Infantry's Third Battalion, in the hot zone north of Prescott. Fourth Armored Company is with Fourth Battalion near Highway 89. Highway 10 enters the city from the west, but there's no good road for the Chinese to use to get there, so I think that's an unlikely route."

"You're loading up for the Chinese," Angriff said. "Just in case."

"They're the wild card in this. I can't see any choice. They're also the only real potential danger. The Ranger Company I'm sending to the far right flank, up here..." He pointed to a junction on the map. "...near the old Interstate 40, as tripwires. Our reserves are the SEALS who aren't in the assault and the independent mortar squads, as well as the specialists, such as the Air Force pilots. I propose the headquarters company move to this peak overlooking Prescott. It's called Badger Mountain. Oh, and the Air Force anti-aircraft squads I'm keeping with HQ."

"What about Third Recon Battalion? Are they in reserve?"

"No, they're screening Flagstaff."

"Why, what do we know about Flagstaff?"

"Nothing, Nick. No intel at all," Fleming said. "That's why I want to screen that flank in force before we move west. Once we've secured Prescott, then we can see what's in Flagstaff."

"Is a whole battalion necessary? That's a huge percentage of our combat power, Norm."

"That's exactly why I want to use a full battalion. If they run into trouble, I want enough force so they can hold their own. With just one or two companies, we run a much higher risk of losing them. If there's nobody home in Flagstaff, at least that battalion will have gotten in some badly needed training."

"You're the S-3, so it's your call. I'm not going to override you."

"Air support is where I'm holding back the punch of our reserves. I'm using all the Apaches in the assault on Prescott and against the Chinese, if they show up, and half the Comanches. If anything goes wrong or comes up unexpectedly…"

"If?" Angriff said.

"Excuse me, *when* something goes wrong or comes up unexpectedly," Fleming corrected, "it's nice to have some Comanches in the bank."

Tracing his finger across the map, Fleming outlined the routes through the mountains and foothills. "Thanks to the recons, we know which routes to take. I'm sending three columns. That's not optimal, coordinating all those movements will be tough, but we don't have much choice.

"The first column will set up in a blocking position here," he said, indicating a position on the map south of the city and straddling Interstate 17. "That's the Marines. We've got to guard our eastern flank, but if we need them elsewhere, they can get anywhere on the battlefield in just a few hours."

"You can tell this is your plan, Norm."

"I'll take that as a compliment."

"What about putting them on our far right as a flanking force?" Angriff said.

"I would love to have a flanking force on the right, but we don't have enough troops to do that and screen the left flank. I'd rather chance letting the Chinese escape than get flanked by some enemy column we didn't know existed."

"Caution over aggression. Haven't we had this conversation before?"

"We damned sure have," Fleming said. "You were right in Syria and I was right in Yemen, and if you want to plan your own operations, that's your right. You're the commanding officer."

Angriff patted the air. "Caution is what's needed, Norm, so calm down. We're on the same page."

Fleming rubbed his eyes then downed cold coffee. "Sorry, Nick. I'm tired and I'm worried. This is the only brigade we've got and if we lose it because I overlooked something in the planning, I couldn't live with that."

"We aren't going to lose this brigade, but if we did, it would be my fault, not yours. I'm the boss. I'm the one who accepts or rejects whatever plan you come up with, which means if it fails, I get the blame."

"Thanks for saying that. Okay, if you approve of the plans, then I need to start issuing orders. We need to be on the move in..." Fleming looked at the clock on the wall, then at his watch. "Damn, it's already 0845? We need to be on the move in four hours. Five, tops."

"Looks solid, Norm. I like it. What are you going to call it?"

Fleming had given this some thought. Operational names were important for morale. He'd rejected Operations Liberation, Freedom, and First Step. They were all accurate, but dull, with nothing to fire up the troops. "Operation Kickass," he said.

CHAPTER 16

And I have felt the sudden blow of a nameless wind's cold breath,
And watched the grisly pilgrims go that walk the roads of Death,
And I have seen black valleys gape, abysses in the gloom,
And I have fought the deathless Ape that guards the Doors of Doom.
  Robert E. Howard, from "Recompense"

1129 hours, July 28

"What's that thing do?" Joe Randall asked, reaching back and touching what looked like another periscope.

It was hot in the tank turret with the hatch closed. Sweat soaked his wife's shirt and he could feel her warm heat on the tops of his thighs, stomach, and chest.

"That's the CITV," Morgan Randall said, and nibbled his ear. "The Commander's Independent Thermal Viewer. That gives me a three hundred sixty degree view, night or day." Randall felt her front teeth slide down his neck. "With automatic sector scanning and automatic target cueing of the gunner's sight, so we don't need to communicate." She bit the back of his neck in the sensitive spot just above the spine. "And it's a backup fire control. A lot like your FLIR."

"My FLIR... you make that sound sexy. If we had more room, I'd show you just how sexy."

"I told you it was cozy in here."

"Cozy is a snowed-in chalet with a ski-up door. This is an iron lung."

"Don't like being this close to me?"

He smelled her musk as she sat across his lap, arms wrapped around him. "You're not close enough, baby." He kissed her behind the ear, right where he knew she loved it most. She gave a quick, gasping inhale that meant he had found the right spot.

"If I was any closer, I'd be inside you," she said in a low voice.

"I think that's backward."

"I know how to fix that." She started fumbling with the zipper of her jump suit, already open from her throat to her crotch. Joe tried to help her slip out of it, not the easiest job inside an Abrams. Then, just as his hand slid toward her thigh, somebody knocked on the outside of the tank with a clang.

"Shit," she said, trying to zip up. "There's no fucking privacy in this place."

"I don't think privacy for fucking was a priority." Joe smiled despite the pain in his groin. "Could have been worse; could have been *coitus interruptus.*"

"Hey, boss," said a man's voice outside the tank. "You in there?"

"I'm in here, Toy. Wait a minute and I'll be up." More or less back in uniform, she kissed her husband on the cheek, climbed into the commander's seat on the right side of the turret—her battle station—and opened the hatch. She climbed onto the hatch ring and looked down at her gunner, Staff Sergeant Hank Ootoi. "What's up?"

"Colonel Ricci wants all platoon commanders and seconds at his CP at 1420 hours."

"Did he say why?"

"Word is we've caught an op."

At that moment, Joe Randall stuck his head out of the hatch. "Anything about air support?"

Startled, Ootoi stepped back and saluted. "Captain Randall. Don't know, sir. I didn't hear anything."

"I was showing Captain Randall where we work," Morgan Randall said.

"Sure, Lieutenant, whatever you say. About the meeting—word is we're breaking out TUSK."

"Well, shit," she said. "I did not want to hear that. How reliable is this word?"

Ootoi shrugged. "Straight up, no ice. I've already got Eddie and Tanya prepping for the install. We're in the first slot with the maintenance and repair dogs, but only if we're ready on time."

"What's TUSK?" asked Joe.

"Tank Urban Survival Kit," his wife said. "Second generation stuff. It means we'll be operating in a built-up environment. TUSK adds reactive armor to the sides and rear, which increases protection from RPGs. Toy is our gunner, and he gets a shield and thermal sight added for his 7.62mm machine gun. And the hatch for my fifty gets modified, too, so I can fire from inside the turret. That way your beautiful wife not only gets to stay beautiful, but also keeps her brains inside her head."

"And that's a good thing," he said. "Your brains are beautiful, too, and I'd hate to see you lose them."

"Me, too." She kissed him on top of his head. "But we can only do so much ourselves. The M and R gang have to do the heavy lifting. Sorry, Joe; duty calls. Wish me luck; maybe I'll get to blow something up."

"Damn, if you were a guy I'd think you had a hard on."

Nobody had argued when Lara Snowtiger wanted the top bunk. Not even on Day One, before anybody knew anybody. An aura surrounded the beautiful girl with the lean but defined muscle tone of a natural athlete. Some primitive instinct made her bunk mates wary.

She had not demanded the top bunk, nor been unpleasant about it. Snowtiger had asked, in a quiet voice, if anyone objected to her taking the top. Only Dora, the stout LAV mechanic in the bottom bunk, even dared ask her why she wanted the top.

"When I was a girl in Tennessee," Snowtiger had said, with a soft Southern accent, "my grandmother took me outside one night, when the stars shone brightest and the moon was new. She pointed at the *Fichik Watalhpi* in the clear sky. *That's where Choctaw people come from*, she told me. *We are children of the stars that white men call the Pleiades.* I like being on top because it puts me closer to my ancestors."

"I like the guy to be on top," Dora had said, but Lara had not answered.

Unlike their male counterparts, who bunked with their own squad or crew, the female Marines were all in one barracks. With less than one hundred women in the whole battalion, it made sense. Discussions about bunking them with their male unit comrades went nowhere.

Almost half of them had combat duties. The rest were either administrative or in a maintenance crew. Lara Snowtiger was the only female sniper, same as she had been in the Old Days. Many snipers preferred solitude, it being in the nature of their job, and so it was with Snowtiger. But in the barracks social system, her reticent personality left her isolated and friendless. Some even mocked the classic beauty of her high cheekbones and dark eyes, although never to her face. Despite a growing dislike of the woman they labeled *Ice Bitch*, they instinctively feared her. Lara Snowtiger was an assassin.

At night she spoke to her long-gone identical twin sister, Sara. Words never passed her lips; she spoke with her mind, and believed her sister heard her.

They hate me because they fear me. I want their friendship, Sara, but I've been an outsider for so long I don't know how. Do you remember what Grandmama told us, that true friends bonded the instant they met, because the Great Spirit had ordained it? I want to believe this, but many years have passed now. And yet... I have my comrades; I feel at home among them. And there is one who... but we should not talk of such things.

In the barracks, the situation set up a vicious cycle. The more she was alone, the less she valued human interactions. The resulting separation insulated her even more, which, in turn, further devalued the human experience. But everything had changed on the day of the shootout.

Every Marine without mandatory duty had gathered in the desert to watch the battalion's twelve snipers shoot it out. Nobody had expected Snowtiger to challenge for top honors. Piccaldi had been the favorite, with most people predicting Jenkins second and Menendez third. But when it was over, Piccaldi had beaten Snowtiger by a single point, and some said he'd had an unfair advantage because of the difference in scopes. Snowtiger had congratulated him, seething but showing a calm face to the world.

From that moment, Snowtiger never lacked friends. Opinion within the barracks changed from her being *the* Ice Bitch to being *their* Ice Bitch. For the first time in her life, she had the friendship of other women, and she enjoyed being one of a group. She was still quiet and reserved, but now she would join in barracks chatter, even if only by listening.

Then came the first lurp and the rescue of the Grubb family. Word got around fast that Snowtiger had nailed some hostile manning a chain gun from four hundred yards. One shot, one kill. The distance was not the impressive part. Snowtiger had had the hardest target. She'd needed a head shot to stop the gunner from squeezing his trigger and wiping out her lieutenant, his driver, and the IPs. The sun's glare and whipping desert breezes grew in the telling until the story had her shooting through a tornado. With a lot of variables and no margin for error, Snowtiger had put her target down.

She even impressed Piccaldi. After the lurp, she found herself an outsider in the barracks again, and for a different reason. She had seen the elephant. She had killed a man, with all the attendant baggage. The combat veterans understood and slapped her on the back. The non-combat types went back to avoiding her.

Snowtiger was a meat eater. In the language of her people, she was a *nan abi*—a killer. The other women in combat roles were also trained to kill, and some had, but snipers were different. Snipers did not flank the enemy, they did not recon enemy positions or overrun rear areas to cut off supplies or capture objectives. Snipers had one mission and only one mission: to kill people. Snipers singled you out for destruction in the most personal way possible. They studied your face and counted your breaths before squeezing the trigger. When their rifle recoiled and the bullet spun through the air and smacked you in the side of the head, it took away everything you had, everything you ever would have. All your dreams, plans, and hopes were extinguished forever because the sniper chose you to die. They killed in a way that few people could, and it elicited a primal fear in those who could not.

She became aware her mere presence made some of the women nervous. Some of the men, too, and after a while Snowtiger went back to being Snowtiger.

Without realizing it, she once again began walking on the balls of her feet. Her subconscious began reading other people's body movements and gestures. Her eyes missed nothing, and her brain processed images as threat assessments again. Her new friends feared her for the killer she was. Like all those who are not themselves afraid, Snowtiger instinctively mistrusted them for their fear.

Her immediate superiors had worried she might hesitate when it next came time to pull the trigger. When she regained her swagger, they stopped worrying.

She was in her bunk staring at the ceiling when the call-out came.

"Ears and rears, ladies!" Sergeant Norma Spears yelled from the main doorway. "Fall in at your racks and listen up!" Snowtiger swung her legs over the rail and landed on her toes as women scurried to find their bunks. Within ten seconds everyone stood at attention.

"The battalion will assemble at 1430 hours in full gear in Motor Bay C. For those of you who haven't been paying attention, that's where we have been training. We are exiting this underground playpen for prolonged operations. For those of you in the field force, draw five days' rations and maximum ammo. You have ten minutes to gear up, Marines, so get your fat asses moving!"

Chapter 17

If you're going through Hell, keep going.
    Winston Churchill

1451 hours, July 28

Morgan Randall knew the company CO hated half-assed planning. Captain Robert Malkinovich, commander of Alpha Company, First Armored Battalion, had told her and her platoon leader that less than five minutes earlier. He'd confided his long-held belief that poor battle plans got people killed unnecessarily, and she had to admit Operation Kickass felt thrown together. But orders were orders and their company would be Oscar Mike on time, ready or not.

"Listen up, CDATs—" *computerized dumb-ass tankers* "—I know the big question is *Will we be operating as a battalion?*" Malkinovich said, shouting to be heard. Their fourteen M1A3 Abrams were at the far end of Motor Bay C, well away from where the Marine Recon Battalion had begun to assemble. "And the answer is no, we will not. You're wearing TUSK for a reason. We will be on the heels of the SEALs for this operation, as will the MARSOCs. We will be operating in an urban environment filled with hostiles, neutrals, and friendlies. The ROE is simple: no angels. Got that? The safety of you, your comrades, and your weapons systems is more important than anything else. I want every tank, and every person in that tank, to get home in one piece. Our code name is Task Force Bulldozer. Your platoon leaders are Bulldozer One, Bulldozer Two, and Bulldozer Three. If you're the fourth tank in the first squad, first platoon, you're

Bulldozer One One Four. I am Bulldozer Prime; Lieutenant Embry is Prime Two. Any questions?"

Morgan Randall had a lot of questions, but one in particular bothered her. Sitting in the hatch of Bulldozer One One Two, as executive officer of First Platoon she wanted to ask why the mix of shells included extra armor piercing rounds—M829s—if they were going into urban combat. The M1028 canister rounds she understood, but why the kinetic energy ones? She started to raise her hand when Malkinovich dismissed them.

Toy could tell something was eating at her, though. When she told him what, he told her to ask the platoon commander, Lieutenant Tensikaya, in the tank next to hers. Tensikaya had no idea about the AP, though. He told her to go ask the captain if she was that worried about it. Jumping to the ground, Randall approached Malkinovich while he spoke with the company executive officer, Lieutenant Embry.

"Captain?" she said. "A word, sir?"

"Go ahead, Lieutenant, but make it quick. What's on your mind?"

"Sir, I couldn't help noticing we're carrying more M829s than usual. KE isn't much good against buildings, and I'm wondering if I should be looking for something in particular that might call for KE rounds."

"Nice catch, Lieutenant. I should have mentioned it. That's what happens when you throw an op together at the last minute. Intel says there might be hostile armor in the city, Bradleys and maybe M1s. You never know when you'll need one last KE round to finish them off. But even if you don't need them in the city, it's what they say is coming at us from the west that's a problem."

"The west, Captain? I don't follow."

"Word I get is, there's supposed to be an enemy column closing on Prescott from the west. An armored column. Specifically, a Chinese armored column."

"Chinese?"

"As in People's Liberation Army. Yes, Lieutenant, those Chinese."

—

Joe Randall didn't wait for the Emvee to stop before he jumped off and ran for the hangar bay. He sprinted through the open double doors and down the metal mesh stairs. Synchronized chaos danced to the music of power tools as hundreds of ground crew readied the helicopter gunships for battle. Led by Sergeant Rossi, his own crew scurried around *Tank Girl*, arming and fueling the massive helicopter, with Carlos directing traffic and ticking items off his pre-flight checklist.

"Bunny, what's the Mike?"

Carlos turned and gave him the usual *Where have you been?* look. "The mission is getting ready for combat, sir. To that end, I directed Sergeant Rossi to prep the aircraft. I trust that meets with your approval, Captain?"

Randall returned Carlos' expression with his own *Knock it off, dipshit* expression, since he could not say that in front of the enlisted personnel. "Thank you, Lieutenant, for displaying the military courtesy and deference you should always show me. Do we have specific orders, or are we just standing by to stand by?"

Carolos relaxed, having gotten his point across. "Nothing specific. PNN—" *the Private News Network* "—has the entire brigade moving out around 1500 hours, but nothing more. The Apaches were ordered to be combat ready by then, but we were just ordered to fuel and ammo up, and stand by for further orders."

"So we really are standing by to stand by?"

"Looks that way, but whatever we're doing, we're rolling with a lot of ass."

"What's the package?"

"One each on the gun pods, max ammo, max Dragonfires, half HE and half AP."

"We're hauling fifties and thirty millimeters?"

"Grade-A straight. And get this, Joe... the thirties are AP EXACTO rounds."

"AP EXACTOs? What the hell? We're hunting armor?" Randall said.

"How should I know? One thing's sure—somebody's expecting a shit sandwich."

"With a side order of fucked fries. EXACTOs... damn."

Randall turned to change into his flight suit, but stopped when he saw Rossi unpacking two large, steel squares filled with tubes. "Rossi, what's up with the flares?"

Sergeant Rossi brushed hair from her face. Randall had never realized how young she looked.

"Package four double A, Captain, per orders."

"We've got CIRCM—" *common infrared countermeasures* "—already, and we're getting flares, too?" He turned back to Carlos. "Bunny, AP *and* flares? And nobody has said anything about what we're supposed to find out there?"

"Just the usual bullshit. In fact, it doesn't even rise to PNN-level BS. This is more like fantasy bullshit."

"Fine, it's fantasy bullshit. You're absolved."

"Just remember my BS meter's in the red... Chinese. The bullshit highway says we're facing a Chinese column, size and composition unknown."

Randall could think of nothing to say. Finally, after more than five seconds, he said the first thing that had come to his mind: "Damn. What am I going to play?"

"That's what you're worried about, what music to play? C'mon, man, you're starting to piss me off."

"I'm always starting to piss you off."

"You need to stop worrying about that nonsense before you get us both killed. You were born to fly, to put fire on the target, to kill bad guys, not worry about fucking music. It's ridiculous."

Randall started to say something, then stopped and snapped his fingers. "Born to kill bad guys... Bunny, you're a genius."

"Aw, fuck," Carlos said.

"You're not going and that's that," Green Ghost said.

"Why the fuck not?" Nipple said.

"Because I said so. I need you here more than I need you there."

"You're letting Aaron go and he's an idiot."

Ghost's face darkened. He jabbed a finger at her. "His name is Vapor. Always. You know that."

"Have it your way. You're letting that idiot Vapor go. And Wingnut, and he can't even talk."

"Stop it. I need you here and that's that. Glide is staying, too, and One Eye and Razor. When I'm in the field, it's your job to keep the boss alive. We haven't found all the conspirators yet and I'm not risking a coup while we're preoccupied. Whatever happens, you're to stick with him and keep him breathing."

"This sucks, Big Brother. I know why you're doing this. You think I'm gonna start feeling some kind of attachment to him, and I'm not. I'll never forgive him."

"I don't give two shits how you feel about him. Just carry out your orders."

"What if it comes down to him or me? Who do you want to live?"

"Don't let it come to that."

CHAPTER 18

When virtue has slept, it will arise again all the fresher.
Friedrich Nietsche, from Human, All Too Human

Prescott, Arizona
1702 hours, July 28

Lisa Parfist sat and tried not to move. Breathing the hot air seared her lungs and the more she moved, the deeper she had to inhale. The stale atmosphere inside the dilapidated gym tasted like old fish. The air was so fetid it seemed tactile, like an oily mist hanging over an infected landscape.

Despite the hunger twisting her stomach, the stench made it impossible to eat without gagging. Instead she gave her portions to her children, who somehow choked them down.

She tried to count the people crammed into the building, but gave up. She was too tired to concentrate, and in the end it did not matter. A thousand people, two thousand... they were all in the same cage. Every now and then the guards dragged a body out, usually by the ankles. They only carried the corpses of small children.

The Guards had herded her family into Prescott like cattle, prodding them with rifles and cramming them into the school along with hundreds of others. In the early days, Lisa had befriended an old man bleeding from a deep wound in his thigh. She'd stuffed it with dirty rags and did what she could to stop the oozing, but infection had already turned the leg black. As he lay dying, he'd told her stories of having played high school basketball in that very building, of this or that game when he'd done something heroic.

He'd spoken of things she could only imagine, since they were long gone by the time she'd been born. He'd told her about the high school friendships and rivalries you developed, the cheerleaders, soft drinks, the smell of popcorn, and the taste of corn dogs—all unique American experiences, and all long since gone. On the third morning he'd grinned, sat upright, and blurted *Where's the mustard!*, then fell sideways into the pool of his own blood. Flies had swarmed over the corpse.

Lisa Parfist tried to cry, but was too dehydrated for tears.

She had no idea how long his body lay there. Marking time was only possible by observing the daylight seeping through the windows near the ceiling. She only knew it was long enough for the body to bloat and for maggots to infest the dead flesh. When the stench of rotting corpses became unbearable, four Security Policemen had dragged them from the gym. They'd mopped the sticky puddles of blood but only managed to smear it into larger pools.

In the first few days, Lisa's two children had wandered through the huge room. She'd let them, hoping they might burn off the restless energy of adolescents used to living in the wilds of the desert. But with little food or water, their energy levels had dropped, and soon they sat beside her and rarely spoke. Twelve-year-old Rick, Jr., had a friend also held captive, so he would still leave sometimes to be with his friend. Fifteen-year-old Kayla stared into space most of the time, twirling dirty hair in her fingers.

Despite their desperate situation, Lisa Parfist had not given up hope. Her husband Richard had escaped capture, and she had no doubt he would rescue them. As the week wore on, she stroked Kayla's hair and whispered encouragement, promising her father would come for them.

It seemed hopeless if she thought about it, one man against thousands, but she believed it anyway. She prided herself on being a practical woman who faced life's challenges head-on. She made decisions using logic instead of emotion. But as the sweltering hell drained her body and mind, she clung to a belief everybody else would have said was fantasy. Richard would find a way to save his family. She knew it with absolute certainty.

Lester Hull, known to his followers as General George Patton, scowled at the listless mass of prisoners crowding the old gymnasium. His temper was legendary. Arms crossed, his left fist clenched and unclenched, and guards standing nearby took a step back. Lieutenant

Wimber did not. He had no choice but to stand his ground. The captives were his responsibility.

"They're like a herd of dying antelope," Hull mumbled. His eyes narrowed.

He shifted his gaze to the flag hanging on the far wall, the banner he'd designed to represent his fiefdom. Despite his republican rhetoric, he ruled his de facto kingdom as monarch. On taking power, he'd promised free elections once the Republic of Arizona was stable. That had been forty years ago.

According to Hull, Prescott was now the capital of the legitimate government of the United States of America. His new flag featured one large white star in place of the original fifty, against a black background. The thirteen stripes were still there, but the red stripes were now black.

"Still no sign of Tisky or Chu," Lieutenant Wimber said. "Just a lot of boot prints leading up the hill."

Hull's slit-eyed glare shut him up.

"We'll deal with that in a minute," Hull said. "I put you in charge of these captives because I had faith you would obey orders and keep them in good condition. Now, the day before the single most important day in the history of our reborn Republic, I find that you have disobeyed my orders and put the whole deal in jeopardy."

Hull waved one hand toward the gym full of slaves. "Do you have any idea how much it cost to collect these people? To house them here, to feed them? It put a tremendous strain on our resources, but it was all going to be worth it because of the trade agreement we negotiated with the Chinese. We are getting more fuel per prisoner than ever before, but only with the promise that they'll be in excellent physical condition. The Chinese don't want sick slaves, ahd who can blame them? I trusted you, Wimber, and now I find this mess. Thank God I made this inspection. What's your dead loss so far?"

Wimber blinked in fear. Hull recognized it and continued frowning. *Never let your subordinates get too comfortable.*

"Forty-seven, General," Wimber said.

"How many children?" Hull said.

"Twenty-eight."

Hull balled his fist and pulled it back, like he was going to slug Wimber. "How could you let twenty-eight children die? Do you know how much we get for them?"

"No, General. That's above my clearance."

"You're damned straight it is! And this," he waved his arm again, encompassing the entire room, "is why!"

There was nothing Wimber could do except stand there and hope he wouldn't be executed.

"Here's what you're going to do, Lieutenant," Hull said. "You're going to get these people some food and water. Then you're going to clean this building, and you're going to clean them. I don't care how you do it, but when the Chinese get here tomorrow, I want these people as fresh as the day they were caught.

"Consider yourself lucky, Wimber. I'm not going to punish you. In my past lives, I wouldn't have shown this kind of mercy. When I was Hannibal, I tied men between two elephants and had them torn apart for lesser offenses. When I led my army out of the Alps, I had captives fight to the death and set the winners free. If this happened when I was Napoleon, I would have had you guillotined. But I learned a lot in the life before this one, so I'm going to give you a chance to redeem yourself, just as I would have done when I was Nick Angriff. They called me Nick the A, but I was pretty lenient by then, because all those previous lives had taught me patience."

"Thank you, General," Wimber said with evident relief.

"You're getting a second chance." Hull patted Wimber on the shoulder, although his voice remained stern. "Make me glad I gave it to you."

"I'll do it, General!" Wimber said. "I won't let you down again, sir."

"Very good. I believe you."

Strolling through the fetid mass of humanity, Hull avoided the puddles of blood, vomit, and excrement. Halfway around the gym, he used the tip of his boot to prod a young girl with long blonde hair, curled up on the floor. Terror-stricken, she scooted backward into her mother's arms.

"Stay away from her," Lisa Parfist said, cradling her daughter's face against her breast. "If my husband was here, he'd gut you like a trout."

Hull smiled like a genial grandfather. He loved playing that game, with young women in general and mothers in particular. He eyed the girl's torn shirt and exposed skin. "Is he here, madam? No? So where is he? I would so like to meet him."

Lisa Parfist tried to spit on him, but her mouth was too dry. "You'll meet him soon enough."

"I certainly hope so," Hull said. "Although he'd better hurry." He motioned to Wimber. "This one." He pointed to the cowering girl. "Clean her up and take her to my quarters."

"No!" her mother screamed.

Wimber waved two Security Police over. Strong hands grabbed Kayla and pulled her away. Kicking and biting, Lisa Parfist tried to defend her, but a vicious backhand knocked her senseless. Kayla started crying.

"Stop that, you fool!" Hull snapped. "How much do you think we'll get for her if she's dead, or has a broken jaw? The next man who damages a slave gets a knife up his ass!"

"I'm sorry, General," the guard said, chastised.

"Don't do it again." Hull leaned close to Lisa's face. "Listen to me, lady. Your daughter is going where I say she goes, and if you want to go with her, then shut up and stop fighting. Otherwise, I'll have you shot where you stand."

She wiped at a small trickle of blood coming from her left nostril. "If you do that, you can't trade me for your precious fuel."

"And that's the only thing keeping you alive right now. But if you want to stay that way, you'll go with these men and help make yourself and your daughter pretty for your new owners. And I suggest you be nice to them; the Chinese aren't as generous as I am. In the meantime, if you give me any more trouble, your daughter will need a new mother. So pick your poison."

"I'll go," she said. "And I won't cause trouble. But I'd just as soon be in Hell with my feet on fire than be somebody's slave."

"Once you're paid for, I really don't care what you do."

"I was born in this country, you bastard. I'm an American citizen, my daddy taught me that, and someday you're gonna pay for what you're doing."

Despite his best effort to keep a grim face, Hull couldn't help chuckling. "And who's going to make me pay, hmmm? Your husband? Lady, I *am* America. I'm the president, the Congress, and the military governor. You're only a citizen if I say you're a citizen. You chose to live outside of my protection, to turn your back on your country by living somewhere else, which means you gave up your citizenship. Once you did that, you lost all your rights."

With a shove, Lisa Parfist and her daughter were led away and out of the building. Patton watched them go and then turned back to Wimber.

"Let that be a lesson. That's what happens when you don't see to a slave's basic needs," he said. "They get hungry and thirsty, then they can't sleep, and then they become hard to control. Think of them as a herd of cows." He again waved an arm at the entire room.

"These people are a natural resource that has to be used carefully. You have to *nurture* them."

CHAPTER 19

Study the past if you would define the future.
    Confucius

1719 hours, July 29

"General?"

Lost in thought, Angriff had not heard his visitor enter the office. "Colonel Schiller," he said, turning away from the desert view. "What can I do for you?"

"Sir, I did more digging on Lieutenant Hull and it turns out there was quite a bit more in his records. I put together a dossier in case you wanted inside the mind of your opponent."

"You did that? Colonel, that information could be invaluable."

"I'm glad I could help, General. I'll leave it on your desk."

"No need for that. We don't pull out for a little while. Please, sit down and read it to me."

When Schiller sat in one of the two chairs facing his desk, Angriff noted his stiff posture and ramrod-straight back.

"The style is a bit informal. I was trying to portray more than just hard facts, but this is out of my usual comfort zone." He cleared his throat. "The man who calls himself General George S. Patton was born Lester Earl Hull in a hardscrabble neighborhood in Phoenix. It was the sort of area where *having a working air conditioner, flat screen TV, and car not on blocks in the front yard made you better off than your neighbors.* That's a quote from a report written by his company commander."

"He was lower middle class," Angriff said. "Nothing unusual there."

"I believe Hull saw it differently. From childhood, Hull felt himself driven to dominate whatever situation he was in. He told people that the spirits of great warriors of the past lived within him. Nobody seems to have known if he really believed this or not. He rarely spoke about it, since when he did people thought he was insane.

"Although not physically imposing, Hull was athletic. He made up in persistence what he lacked in talent. He wore down his coaches to become the captain of whatever team he was on, including the chess team. Throughout school most of his peers avoided him, but few people ever picked on him, and the ones who did only did it once. His high school counselor noted that Lester did not understand boundaries. Once, in ninth grade, a larger boy made fun of Hull's tendency toward being chubby. No matter how hard he worked out, it seems he could not get rid of a roll of fat around his hips.

"But Hull did not attack the boy himself. Instead, a police report says he found some old steaks in the dumpster behind a grocery store and inserted finishing nails into a ribeye. He then threw it over the fence for the boy's dog."

"The one who insulted him?"

"Yes, sir. The dog wolfed down the meat, then died a slow and painful death while the boy cradled him and cried. Lester bragged about it the next day and that's how he got caught. A lot of people wanted to hurt him, but nobody did anything. He terrified them. And if he was as crazy as his behavior suggested, then you could never hurt him as bad as he would hurt you in return. To Lester that was a win."

"How did this whack job get into the army?"

"His IQ's pretty high, sir, and from what I can tell, he's relentless when he wants something. Once in the Army, he rose to first lieutenant pretty fast. He always obeyed orders to the letter, but regardless of the situation Hull saw himself as the leader. Multiple evaluators made it clear that what Hull saw as leadership was irritating persistence to everyone else.

"I can only guess, of course, but it sounds to me like Hull might actually believe he is the reincarnation of some famous general from history."

"You gleaned all that from the records?"

The question surprised Schiller. He thought he'd made that clear on the front end. "Yes, sir. I can't guarantee it's one hundred percent accurate, but I think it's close."

"Colonel, you have materially helped me in this operation. Your initiative is a credit to the army. I'm impressed, and that's not easy to do."

"Thank you, sir. I just want to do my part."

"Call me Nick." Angriff stood and extended his hand.

1738 hours

"Tell me about the missing men," Hull said.

Wimber braced himself again. "Two men stationed outside are gone, General, and we found boot prints, really clear ones."

"Be specific, Wimber. What were their names again?"

"Tisky and Chu."

"Tisky? I know him pretty well. He's a good man. Are you telling me they deserted? Were they in trouble?"

"No, General," Wimber said. "They were two of my best men. But I wasn't talking about seeing *their* bootprints; I meant there's other prints. Lots of others. And they're different. The tread on the bottom of these boots ain't worn down like ours. The lines in the dirt are sharp. But Chu and Tisky's prints are there, too. You can tell if you look close."

Hull stopped and rubbed his left jowl. "Where do they lead?"

"Over the hill out back, then off northeast into the desert," Wimber said. "And there are barefoot tracks up there, too."

"How many barefoot?"

"Just one set."

"Are we looking at a kidnapping?" Hull said, disbelief in his voice. "Who would be stupid enough to try something like that?"

"Maybe some men from that last village we raided? Some did get away."

"It couldn't have been. You only found one set of barefoot tracks. None of them would have boots; where would they get them?" Hull stood silent for more than a minute and then headed outside. The hot air refreshed him after the stale fumes inside.

"That's two incidents we can't explain," he said. Wimber still stood beside him, but Hull was talking more to himself than the lieutenant. "This must be connected with those old trucks we found out in the desert. Our vehicles didn't just disappear into thin air, or our men. What was the leader's name again?"

"Busson. Sergeant Slick Busson."

"Yeah, Busson. He was a loyal SP. You told me that and I believe you. So where are he, his men, and most importantly, his vehicles, especially the Bradley? They didn't just vanish. No, there's something else going on here, and we need to find out what it is. We've now lost eight men and three vehicles, and we don't know why."

Hull frowned, thinking. "We found tracks heading north from where those old trucks were found, and that one shell casing. What if Busson did not lead his men into the mountains? What if he's dead, or a prisoner?"

"But who would do that? Who *could* do that? The Bradley had a chain gun. I can't think of anything in the desert that could fight with it."

"The Chinese could," Hull said. "What if the Chinese took them as bargaining chips?"

"You mean Chu and Tisky?"

"I mean all of them, the Bradley, too. What if they're looking to bargain for a better deal? Well, screw them. The fuel is more important than a few men or vehicles." Realizing he had spoken out loud, he added, "Except for the Guards, of course. They're the most important thing."

Wimber nodded. "You're the only man smart enough to figure all that out, General."

"That's why I'm leading this Republic. And we're going to get them all back, just you watch. Detail one of your men to find Colonel Cranston and tell him to meet me at headquarters, then start cleaning those people. I want them pretty for their new owners."

1822 hours

Norbert Cranston rubbed his neck. Preparing for the Chinese meant preparing for anything—a peaceful trade, a tense negotiation, or open war.

Never before had they come to Prescott to pick up such a huge shipment of slaves. In the past the number had never exceeded one or two hundred. Transferring five thousand human beings took a tremendous amount of planning, and readying for potential combat left no room for error. He only had so many men, after all, and in his heart Cranston did not trust the Chinese. Why would they burn so much fuel driving to Prescott when the Republic would have met them halfway?

Regardless, it was Cranston's job to make their route passable for a convoy of heavy vehicles. In the past they had used the western route, following old Interstate 40 to Arizona State Highway 93, then turning southeast until it intersected with SH 96. Taking 96 to SH 89 led them to enter Prescott from the southwest. But several sections of Highway 96 had collapsed, requiring long overland detours for a convoy of trucks and heavy vehicles. This time the Chinese would continue on I-40 until it met SH 89, which led straight into Prescott from the north.

Scouting the routes and coordinating with the advance Chinese patrols had taken all morning and most of the afternoon. The work of clearing the roads and filling holes had been going on for weeks, and

Cranston wanted nothing more than to collapse. Instead, he was heading to confer with his boss, General Patton. He could think of nothing more exhausting.

The sun waned by the time he got there. Shadows from the elm trees in Courthouse Square cooled his face as he approached the broad steps leading inside. The water bucket near the front double doors was full, for once, and he drank cups before moving into the old building.

He found Patton in his office, leaning back in his creaky office chair, bare feet on his desk, lost in thought. When Cranston knocked, Patton waved him in.

"Sit down, Bert. Are we ready to move the prisoners and greet our Chinese friends?" He put emphasis on the word *friends.*

Cranston noticed. "Straight to business," he said. "Got anything to drink?"

Patton pointed to a table against the wall, where a pitcher and some glasses were shaded from the late afternoon sun. Cranston drank yet more water and slumped into a wooden chair. "This heat's hard to take sometimes."

"We're getting old, Bert. After this is over, we can kick back and do some trout fishing, but until then we've got to push on. So, are we ready?"

"If we're not, I don't know what else we can do. This is the worst possible time of year for trading in humans, as I've told you a hundred times. My biggest issue is moving the cargo to the loading zones before the day heats up. I'm sure it's going to be another scorcher tomorrow, so we have to move and load them before the sun kills off the weaker ones. We've consolidated the prisoners as planned in the old community center, the school, and the gym. I heard you inspected them."

Patton nodded. "Briefly. Put the fear of God in a few people, but it wasn't any worse than I expected. We can't keep human beings locked up in this kind of weather for long without incurring dead loss."

"I issued instructions to every citizen that it was their duty to help us get the merchandise to the Chinese transports, even if we have to carry them. The plan is for the prisoners to walk to the reservoir. The Chinese can assemble their trucks there instead of driving into town. I don't like the idea of them in the heart of the city. It smacks of a Trojan horse-type betrayal."

"I had the same thought," Hull said. "They drive in, but instead of empty trucks, they're loaded with troops. They know we have to guard the perimeter and can't spare too much to keep an eye on them."

Cranston nodded. "So we take the merchandise to them, instead of the other way around. If they're planning to fuck us over, we'll screw it up. If they're not, it won't matter where they pick them up.

"My main concern is security along the route of march and having enough water stations set up to keep the prisoners moving. The distance will be about three miles, which shouldn't be a problem for the young and healthy ones, but the children and older adults are a different story. We could have a high attrition rate.

"All storage tanks are ready to accept fuel. We've checked the valves and sealed any leaks, but the one problem we can't solve is capacity. We barely have enough for the amount of gas we've contracted for. We shouldn't need any for a long while after this, maybe as long as three years. The tanker trucks will use the direct route, the one that avoids the transport park and heads directly for the tank storage farm.

"The men are deployed in strongpoints. If the chinks try to double-cross us, we'll make them pay. I've ordered all of the RPGs handed out, and all of the machine guns, too."

"Including the M2s?" Hull said.

Cranston nodded. "And every round of ammo we've got, including training rounds. I think you know I don't trust those slants as far as I can throw them, General, so I'm deploying all available forces. The tanks are positioned near the hospital, and the Bradley, Humvees, and civilian vehicles are ready to transport reserves wherever we need them. If they try something, we're gonna bleed them bad. Honestly, I hope they do. I'm in the mood for a fight."

Hull glared from under bushy brows. "None of that, do you hear me? This republic needs fuel. More importantly, we need the Chinese to keep trading with us. They're our only source of gas. I don't trust the little bastards either, I think they're behind that patrol that disappeared a few weeks ago, and just last night two guards turned up missing. But even if they're behind both of those, that's no reason to start a war."

"What if they shoot first?"

"If the Chinese come here looking for a fight, we'll give it to them, but only if they fire first. I mean it, Bert—only if they start it."

Chapter 20

The lofty pine is oftenest shaken by the winds; High towers fall with a heavier crash; And the lightning strikes the highest mountain.
    Qunitus Horatius Flaccus, a/k/a Horace

1930 hours, July 28

"Attention, all hands."

Throughout the mountain activity stopped.

In Motor Bay C, Marine Battalion Commander Colonel Berger nodded and the battalion's XO, Major Harold 'Harry the Hat' Strickland, ordered "Atten-hut!"

At the other end of the bay, Lt. Col. Bishop T. Hines ordered First Armored Battalion to stop work and cut engines.

In the hangar bay, Frances Rossi shut down her crew.

In the hospital, Colonel Friedenthall stepped away from an MRI console into the hallway.

Everywhere tools were put on work benches, running vehicles were set to low idle, conversations ebbed, machinery was laid aside, as every member of Overtime Prime who could turned to the nearest loudspeaker.

A moment later the voice of Colonel Walling, adjutant to the CO, echoed through the mountain. "Seventh Cavalry Brigade and civilians of Overtime Prime, attention for the commanding officer."

All remaining noise ceased. There was a short pause before Angriff's voice came through, loud, clear, grim, and gruff.

"Ladies and gentlemen of the Seventh Cavalry, today we leave the safety of our mountain fortress for the unknown dangers of the battle-field. We are moving on the city of Prescott, to liberate that place from those who are oppressing its people, and we are going to free thousands of men, women, and children who otherwise are doomed to a life of slavery at the hands of the Chinese.

"My fellow Americans, once upon a time this nation was stained with the blight of slavery, but we long ago flung aside that barbaric practice. However, in Prescott, thousands of our fellow citizens face that cruel fate unless we can save them. And let me make one thing crystal clear—we *are* going to save them.

"I do not know exactly what awaits us on the battlefield, but I have supreme confidence we will prevail, regardless of whatever adversity we face.

"You should know that your foe may well look like you. Reliable intelligence indicates that some of them wear old Marine BDUs. They use American weapons and speak American English. But do not be fooled into thinking they will welcome you. They will not. They will try to kill you. If you can safely take them prisoner, do so, but do not put yourself, your buddies, or your equipment in danger. Rules of Engagement are to protect yourself and your unit first, to rescue hostages second, and then, if possible, to capture unfriendlies.

"And I cannot emphasize this last part enough. There will be no looting or unnecessary destruction. We are not conquerors attacking a foreign city. We are Americans liberating an American city occupied by American citizens who are under the heel of a tyrant. Violations of this directive will have dire consequences.

"So as you move to meet your enemy, know that your cause is just and God is with you. Vengeance is mine, sayeth the Lord, and I pray that God has mercy upon my enemies, because I sure as hell won't. But while the vengeance is His, we're the instruments of that vengeance, and we've got our orders... it's time to start taking our country back."

There were a few scattered cheers among the Marines. But battle was in the offing, real combat with the real likelihood of somebody not coming home. Most of them were combat veterans. They knew the horrors of the battlefield, of holding a shot-up buddy's hand while a corpsman fought to keep him alive long enough to reach a field hospital. Death was coming and that was no cause for celebration.

Standing atop a moveable stairway, Colonel Berger looked over his assembled battalion. With other units also assembled in Motor Bay C, he could not use a megaphone, so he shouted and hoped they heard him.

"First Marine Recon Battalion will not be involved in the attack on Prescott. Our mission is to block the left flank. To that end, we will occupy a line twenty miles long... yes, you heard correctly, twenty miles. There is no known threat to the left flank, so we are a tripwire in case an unknown threat develops, but be ready to move out fast if we're needed elsewhere. Obviously we'll be in hedgehog positions, so dig deep and make sure you have overlapping fields of fire.

"Companies will be in order from left to right, Alpha on the left, Echo on the right, with Bravo, Charlie, and Dog between. We will keep task force names and call signs. So in order—Tailback on the left, then Cornerback, Tackle, Kicker, and finally Safety on the right. Tailback and Safety, you will be responsible for denying your flank, if it comes to that, so leave yourselves a reserve. Headquarters is still Head Coach, service company is Trainer. You company commanders, make sure your platoon and squad leaders have the call signs down cold.

"The snipers will be divvied up two per company, except for Cornerback, who will center the line and have less need for them. There's no arty on call for this operation, it's all going to the attack on Prescott, so place your mortars wisely. Ladies and gentlemen, the bottom line is that if this goes bad, we are just going to have to embrace the suck," and he paused and flashed a big smile, turning so his entire command could see it. "But if this was a piece of cake, they'd give it to the Army! Gear up, jarheads; Oscar Mike in ten."

There was a last minute flurry of activity as crews crammed ammo into any empty niche in their already overloaded vehicles. Friends patted each other on the shoulder and vowed to buy a round of drinks afterward, as soon as drinks were available. Individuals found a spare pocket for one more energy bar, or an extra canteen of water, or another magazine.

But Captain Sully was on a mission. He knew which snipers he wanted and he was not going to let the other platoon commanders get to them first. Spying them off to one side, he pushed through milling Marines and trotted over, pointed first at Piccaldi and then at Snowtiger. "You two on me. Let's go."

He took two steps and stopped. "We found a case of M110s and I requisitioned two for the company. I want them back after this op."

The M110 was an Army semi-automatic sniper system, later replaced by a more compact Heckler & Koch unit, designed for the spotter member of a scout/sniper team. With a higher rate of fire, it made a more effective short-range weapon.

"M110s?" Piccaldi said. "With ammo?"

"Couldn't do much without it. Two hundred rounds per gun."

"Damn, Captain, where did you find M110s?"

"Supply found them and gave them to us. I don't know why they didn't give them to the Army, and I didn't ask."

"Because they Ain't Ready to be Marines Yet, Captain," Piccaldi said.

CHAPTER 21

Plans are established by seeking advice; so if you wage war, obtain guidance.
     Proverbs 20:18

2008 hours, July 28

Dennis Tompkins and John Thibodeaux stood outside the southwest gate and marveled at the procession of titanic vehicles rumbling past. Watching the armored infantry was impressive enough, but then came the battalion of Abrams, followed by the Paladins and MLRSs (multiple launch rocket system) of the self-propelled artillery batteries. Clouds of dust drifted in the light breeze. They wore earplugs because of the engine noise. After a while the vibrations in the ground weakened their legs, as aging muscles became fatigued. Yet neither man made any effort to sit down. After so many years of counting bullets and fighting to survive, the sight of so much American military might seemed like a fantasy.

"I pray them boys watch out," Thibodeaux said during a lull, when it was quiet enough to speak. "Those beans are hot with fire."

Tompkins removed his earplug and asked his friend to repeat what he had said, and Thibodeuax did. Tompkins thought about it for a few seconds.

"You know, John, we've known each other a lot of years now, and there's been a lot of times you've said things I didn't understand right off, but sooner or later I'd figure out what you meant."

"Sure," Thibodeaux said, nodding. "An' you saw I was always right."

"I don't know about *always*," Tompkins said. "But this time I don't want to think about it, so I'm just gonna ask. What the hell are you talking about?"

"That's an expression, Skip. *Beans hot with fire* means you better be careful eatin' your meal, 'cause there might be somethin' in it burns after you swallow it, somethin' that tears up your stomach."

"Oh." Tompkins thought about that as a line of LAV-25s drove out the gate and away to the west. "Now I get it. We might be biting off more than we can chew. John, if there's anybody who can eat this, it's Nick Angriff. Let's get saddled up. We're movin' out when he does."

Thibodeaux grabbed him by the arm. "You mean we're in on this?"

Tompkins smiled. "I knew you'd be excited. We're part of General Angriff's field headquarters company."

"The boys, too?"

"The boys, too. We even get our own LAV, assuming you can drive it. You've been practicing, right? Now, let's go. It's time to get dressed and go to war."

"Hot damn, Skip, it's way past time. We gonna shoot people?"

Tompkins laughed. "More like watch and stay out of the way."

Hands clasped behind his back, Angriff stood at the far end of the Crystal Palace, staring through the glass at the desert beyond. With planning finished, the only thing left was to join his troops. But not yet. The roads were already crowded and since the headquarters company would move fast, they'd wait so as not to hinder the combat forces' movement. Which left him with nothing to do.

The cigar gripped in his teeth was unlit. He was saving it for the drive through open country, when the sight of their general puffing on a cigar would project confidence to the brigade. Then he noticed Sergeant Schiller's reflection in the glass, and spoke before the sergeant announced his presence.

"Can we do this, Schiller? Or is this going to be our first and last battle?"

"That's not for me to say, General." For once Schiller allowed his voice to betray disappointment, because he was staying behind while others went to war. It was risky to chance angering Nick the A, but Schiller was pretty angry himself.

"Your day will come, J.C. And if this op goes south, it might come sooner than you think. Until then, I need you with me."

"Of course, sir. I understand," he said, and they both knew he lied. "And for what it's worth, General, the troops are with you. Morale is through the roof."

"I appreciate that, J.C. I really do. Now, did you have a reason for coming into my office?"

"Yes, sir. Sorry, sir," Schiller said.

"Not your fault. I distracted you."

"Sir, Dr. Goldstone would like to see you for a moment."

"Dr. Goldstone? By all means, show her in." He removed the cigar and slipped it into the inside pocket of his jacket, then straightened his clothes and brushed his hair with his fingers.

She came in smiling, carrying something covered by a white cloth.

"Hello, Dr. Goldstone," he said. "What have we here?"

"Please, General, call me Sharon. I know you have to leave soon, so I wanted to send you off with something special." She set the tray on his desk, moving a few papers in the process, and removed the cloth. Underneath was a tall glass filled with a thick white liquid, condensation running down the sides.

Amazed, Angriff stared at the glass for a moment before he looked up at her. "That looks like milk."

She smiled. "And very cold milk, at that, courtesy of the Grubbs' cow. They wanted you to have the first glass, General."

"Call me Nick," he said, aware his mouth watered. "I didn't know the cow was pregnant."

"Neither did they. It's a good thing we found her when we did; she almost lost her calf. Well, don't just look at it. Drink up before it gets warm."

Angriff hesitated, lifted the glass, and took a sip. "Dear God Almighty, that's amazing." He took a bigger drink and milk residue clung to the inside of the glass in a creamy film. He finished it in one more gulp. "I can't ever remember tasting anything that good."

Goldstone smiled. "It still had the cream."

"Now I feel guilty. You and your people nursed her back to health and you should have gotten the milk."

"Don't feel guilty, General... I mean Nick. Cows give five to seven gallons per day. We'll get our share, but we wanted you to have the first glass."

"After an endless diet of PSBs, Sharon, that was the perfect way to send an old soldier off to war."

"Then make sure you come back." Her smile became something more like a smirk, and Angriff wondered if she was flirting with him. "A few more weeks and I might have a fresh tomato for you." Then her expression changed again. Her eyes narrowed and her expression became stern. "But for now, go do what you were born to do, Nick."

Chapter 22

I hurt with cruelty those who would damage me.
        Archilocus, 650 B.C.

0147 hours, July 29

The world was a fuzzy montage of greens and darker greens. At first Rick Parfist found it disorienting, but after two hours of practice he was getting used to it.

"We're about to move out, Mr. Parfist," Green Ghost said. "Are you good to go?"

"My family's lives depend on it. I'm ready."

"Remember everything we told you. Your mission is to get us to the prisoners without being seen. We do not engage anyone unless it is mandatory, and if that happens, you stay back and let us handle it. We're going to be peeling off assets along the way to secure the road."

"Assets?"

"People. As we move forward, people are going to leave the column at regular intervals. They will stay behind to make sure nobody attacks us from the rear. Once we secure the premises, transport for the prisoners will move into town, load them up, and get them out. Our job is to do all this without firing our weapons, if possible. If not, we are to protect the prisoners at all costs.

"Your job will be to help organize the prisoners and get them on the trucks fast. You will leave Prescott with your family, where you will stand down and stay out of the way. Are we good?"

"Yes, but shouldn't I have a weapon?"

"No can do. You've got your knife back, right? If there's a firefight, get out of the way, keep your head down, and let us handle it."

"And what happens if you don't handle it?"

"Take off those night vision goggles, Mr. Parfist, and then tell me what you see."

Parfist slid them up. "I can't see anything."

"These are fourth-generation night vision goggles, some of the most sophisticated gear our country ever produced. We rule the night. We are the best soldiers in the world. Our enemy is blind, and we are not. Now, as Saint Nick says, you can lead, follow, or get out of the way."

Parfist refitted the goggles on his face. He endured a few seconds of disorientation caused by the green world that appeared around him.

"Follow me," he said, and took a long step forward.

0218 hours

Unseen below them in the black night of the new moon, the valley meandered west. Somewhere in the vast swath of darkness, amid the hollow shells of a broken city, deadly figures picked their way forward. As night vision goggles lit their world in shades of green, they glided forward with the stealth of panthers.

Watching from high above, Nick Angriff swiveled his own night vision binocular on its tripod. Every so often he caught a glimpse of a distant figure darting among the ruins on the outskirts of Prescott.

Along with nearby Chino Valley and Prescott Valley, Prescott was part of an area once known as the Tri-Cities. Some had even called them the Quad Cities by adding the town of Dewey Humboldt. All these small cities were in the Bradshaw Mountains, bordered on the west by North America's largest ponderosa pine forest. In the nineteenth century, the region had been overrun with gold and silver miners. By the twentieth century the mines had run out of precious metals. People left for new strikes elsewhere.

But living was pleasant in the Tri-Cities. The climate was mild, with good rainfall and three distinct variations in topography close by. From the dense mountain forests to the cactus-strewn desert, people again flocked to Prescott. By the year 2000, the area was popular and growing fast.

Dominating the eastern end of the valley, overlooking the towns of Prescott and Prescott Valley, loomed Badger Mountain. More than 6,200 feet high, the peak provided the ideal place from which to direct the coming battle. The brigade's headquarters company lay scattered on the reverse slope. Parked at the crest were two LAV-AD air defense vehicles, with the other vehicles stair-stepped below.

Angriff backed away from the binocular.

"May God help me," he said. "These are the moments I love so much that I hate myself."

Norm Fleming lowered his own binoculars. "You're at your best when I don't know what you're talking about."

"On my orders, a lot of people are likely going to die today. I am sending thousands of America's finest young men and women into combat, including my own daughter. I'm doing it in pursuit of something I believe is worth whatever sacrifice we are called upon to make. If need be, that includes my life, as well. That's a lot of responsibility for any one man, or woman. But I'm willing to take it because somebody has to, and I'm arrogant enough to think I'm the best man for the job."

"We all think you're the best man for the job, Nick."

"Without the faith of my command, I would be nothing. But to be honest with you, Norm, there's a part of me that loves all this. The planning, the smells, the anticipation, the adrenaline... it's like God has laid all of this out just for me, because He knows how much I crave it."

"Are you channeling George Patton again?" Fleming said. "The real George Patton, I mean... you know, 'God help me, I love it so'?"

"I'm not sure George Patton ever said that, but maybe I'm channeling George C. Scott playing Patton. Or Robert E. Lee on Marye's Heights above Fredricksburg. I don't know. I only know I'm ready to get this show on the road. The waiting is killing me."

"SEALs moved out nineteen minutes ago. The MARSOCs should be following in two minutes."

Angriff turned, even though the night was so dark he could barely make out Fleming's outline. "Did you order the Marines back?"

"Yes, three companies, plus the headquarters and service companies. I'm leaving two combat companies on the line. I couldn't stop thinking about what you said yesterday about me being too cautious, and I decided I might have put too much on the left flank. There's no known threat to the east and deploying the entire Marine battalion there was a waste. So I withdrew them and I'm sending them south of the city as a flanking force."

"It's a calculated risk," Angriff said. "That only leaves two recon companies to screen a twenty-mile line. That's what, fifty vehicles, give or take? That's not many, but I back your decision and I think it's the right move. It's all about overrunning that town before they can react."

Behind them they heard the crunch of footsteps and fell silent.

"Nick?" said a voice from the dark.

"We're over here, Dennis. Watch your step, there's some loose rocks."

Dennis Tompkins stepped up beside them, followed closely by Colonel Walling. Despite his eighty-plus years, Tompkins had made the climb from the camp below without getting winded. But the night vision gear took some getting used to.

"Appreciate you letting me come along."

"You're third in the chain of command. You need to be here. You also need to know that Norm pulled most of the Marine battalion back as a mobile force circling the city to the south. That gives us the other two companies as a screen on the left flank."

"All right," Tompkins said, but there was hesitance in his tone.

"What is it?"

"Don't mind me, General. I've never commanded more than a company, and the fights I've been in were close quarters compared to this operation."

"Dennis, I know we don't know each other very well, so let me tell you something about me... I'm a cocky bastard, and I can be downright arrogant at times, which means I sometimes make decisions without asking anybody, because I think I'm the only one smart enough to make the right ones. But not always. Sometimes, when I get out of my own way, I'm smart enough to ask people I respect what they think about something, and when they are my subordinate I expect them to give me a straight answer."

Tompkins nodded, even though nobody could see him do it. "Well, if I've learned anything, it's to expect trouble where I least expect it."

"You mean the left flank? You think it's a mistake? So far there is no sign of anything in Phoenix, and you're the one who told us this Caliphate was well to the east."

"I know, and you're right. I can't think of anything out there to worry about, and that's what worries me. I never got bit by the snake I saw."

Chapter 23

When you let go of what you were, you become what you might be.
    Lao Tzu

0220 hours, July 29

"So that's Phoenix," Piccaldi said, adjusting the infrared binoculars. The starlit desert shimmered with heat signatures, including outlines of distant buildings. Since he'd learned their line of deployment, Piccaldi had told everybody they would be in sight of Phoenix, and nobody could dissuade him. With the signatures nothing more than indistinct images on the horizon, he wasted no time in declaring himself correct.

"I don't think that's Phoenix, Zo," Sergeant Meyers said. "Maybe the northern suburbs. I think we're too far out to see Phoenix in broad daylight, much less now... the map says it might be New River."

"Phoenix, New River, who gives a shit?" Piccaldi said. "I see buildings out there. You know how long it's been since I've seen buildings?"

Meyers shrugged. "It's probably just a strip mall, but yeah, I get your point."

"It's a reminder, you know? About how things used to be. About how maybe they will be again someday."

"Not in our lifetime."

"What do you think, Lara? You think we'll see people living in cities again, going to football games and drinking beer?"

Snowtiger stood facing southeast, where the rising sun would soon shine on her face. "There are mountains, far off on the horizon, whose

135

peaks turn orange with the dawn. Do you see them, Zo? Sergeant Meyers?"

Piccaldi and Meyers exchanged glances. Despite her lithe figure and classic beauty, Piccaldi both feared and adored Snowtiger. He and Meyers had had long discussions about whether she would be worth having as a girlfriend. It wasn't her deadly skills—all Marines could kill—but something about her seemed unnatural. Sometimes she could be a swaggering Marine right out of a recruiting video, foul-mouthed and ready for a fight. But most of the time she was quiet and introspective, and quite spiritual. She also seemed ethereal, somehow.

She'd once told Piccaldi she embodied the spirit of a Choctaw warrior come back to Earth. Piccaldi had no clue whether she was serious. But fear or not, he had the serious hots for her. He thought she didn't know it. He was wrong.

Turning his binoculars to follow where she pointed, Piccaldi did see something orange, but it was far away, a faint speck on the horizon.

"Damn, Lara, how the fuck can you see that without binoculars?"

She smiled. "These mountains are sacred to the Apache. Some believe the entrance to Hell is located close to here. Can you feel the spirits of their ancestors watching us? They guard the mountains, and they are suspicious of why we are here."

"How do you know that? You're not Apache; you're Choctaw," Piccaldi said.

Snowtiger turned away so they could not see her face. *So! Piccaldi does listen to me.*

"We are all one," she said. "The Great Spirit unites us all."

"Uh-huh," Piccaldi said. "I don't know about that Indian mystic bullshit, but you've sure as hell got the best eyesight I ever saw. Not to mention a top ten best ass."

"If you think you've seen nine asses better than mine," she said, "then you're too blind to be a sniper."

Meyers laughed and slapped Piccaldi on the back. Piccaldi blushed. They both walked off toward the coffee. Snowtiger kept staring east until they were gone, then she quietly slid the 25x100mm astronomical binoculars back into her pack, content to let them think she had superhuman eyesight.

They heard the Humvee long before they saw it. First Platoon of Dog Company had deployed hull-down on a long, low ridge, spread out to the west. The company screened seven thousand yards of front. Dog Company was responsible for eighteen hundreds yards all by itself. Instead of even spacing, First Platoon's leader, Lt. Embekwe, had grouped them into hedgehog positions. This opened gaps in the line, but provided greater survivability. The company's mission was to be a tripwire in case of a surprise attack, not hold a line to the death. So when Captain Sully pulled up in his command Humvee, it didn't take long to assemble the squad leaders.

"Good morning, jarheads," Sully said, prompting knowing glances among the Marines standing around him in a teaching circle. They knew he disliked informality and slang. He disliked the sobriquet *Loot*, then *Cap* after his promotion, and he particularly hated the term *jarhead*. He never said anything to stop it, and his men loved him for tolerating it. But when he used the term himself, it was a bad sign.

"I hope you haven't gotten used to the view, because we're redeploying. Prime is pulling out Tackle, Tailback, and Corner, and both Head Coach and Trainer are going with them. Apparently we're in the vacation spot. We are moving to the left flank and Safety will fill in on the right. There's a lot of high ground there and we will move into Tackle's positions.

"There's a big lake over that way to anchor our flank. First squad will be nearest the lake. I can't tell you exactly where to deploy since I haven't scouted the ground; just make sure you can lay down fire all the way to the water. You'll know what to look for; you're good Marines. We move at 0500 hours. It should be light enough by then. Any questions?"

Lieutenant Randolph Embekwe raised a finger. "Cap, I'm no math whiz, but isn't that fifty-two AFVs for twenty miles of front, about one every six hundred yards? Are we sure there are no burps out there?"

"If Prime says we're copa, we're copa," Sully said. "But to answer your first question, yes, we're thin on the line. That confirms we're the tripwire in case an unknown threat materializes. Prime would never spread us out like this if they expected trouble. It's up to you how to deploy your platoon; it really depends on the terrain."

"And if burps do appear out of nowhere?"

"Make preparations to move out fast," Sully said. "You'll hold your positions, report to me, and I will relay to Head Coach. I would expect to get a pull-back order post haste."

"Aye sir, but..."

"But what?"

"It wouldn't take much to flank us, Cap. What if we can't hold until we hear back from Head Coach?"

"In that case, Embekwe, you pull a Basilone. You hold your position anyway, and kill every enemy in sight."

CHAPTER 24

We stand and defend the land of the Free,
For it to stay free, it's up to you and me;
As hard as fighting and dying may be,
It's better than living on bended knee.
　　　　Sergio Velazquez, from "Yoke"

0227 hours, July 29

The street widened as it entered Prescott from the east. It sloped downhill, and rose again as it headed toward Thumb Butte and Granite Mountain, which overlooked the city on the west. In the moonless night, the two mountains were indistinct smears of blackness on the horizon. Once, when the city had been thriving early in the twenty-first century, four lanes of traffic had flowed down the road. This left more than enough room for parking spaces in front of the trendy fusion restaurants and the gift stores selling Chinese-made American Indian artifacts. Nor was the city abandoned now. Thousands still lived in Prescott, but it was no longer alive.

Parfist led the Americans past the shells of ruined buildings. With the night vision goggles, he noticed details never seen during his nocturnal raids. As usual the only sound came from the droning buzz of palo verde beetles and desert cicadas. His sensitive nostrils picked out the faint scent of pine and creosote trees, overlaid by the reek of rotting garbage.

Not all the outlying buildings were empty. But those within slept undisturbed by the wraiths moving past their boarded-up windows. As the tail of the column came abreast the ruins of a mall, they moved into the buildings on the south side of the road. The sprawling parking lot made for an excellent field of fire. A wall surrounded the parking lot, but a heavy machine-gun squad climbed a hill across the street and deployed in an abandoned motel. This set up a deadly fifty-caliber crossfire on the road below. The plan was to repeat this process through the city, thus securing the evacuation route.

He loved his new boots. A supply sergeant had found some that fit, along with a pair of thick hiking socks. He no longer had to avoid broken glass or rusty nails. They were waterproof, snake proof, and almost puncture proof, which to him seemed miraculous.

Two days before he hadn't known such things still existed. Had someone told him, he would have scoffed at such a fantasy. Now he wore them while moving from one pool of shadow to the next, leading more than a hundred men to rescue his family. For him not to see the hand of God at work, Parfist thought he would have to be either blind or stupid.

Parfist chose their route because of the cover it offered. Prescott had once been a city of big trees. Elms, junipers, pines, firs, and dozens of other species had grown tall in ideal growing conditions. But when the power had gone out and the weather had turned cold, the trees burned. Not even stumps remained in most places, replaced by crops and fruit trees. Only at the courthouse did the stately elms still stand.

The old golf courses on the south side were sown with corn and cotton. An apple orchard provided cover on the north side. Large buildings interspersed with the flora made ideal firing positions, on both the roofs and at ground level. Securing the armor's route into the city was a top priority. The most direct route bypassed the city center by a right turn just past an old hotel on the outskirts. Following that road north led straight to the ruined high school housing the prisoners. But that road had open ground and fewer buildings for cover, leaving the tanks vulnerable to anti-tank weapons.

Parfist was trotting when he dropped into a squat so fast that Green Ghost almost tripped over him. They had stopped in front of a cluster of commercial buildings, most with empty windows and broken glass. Green Ghost tapped him on the shoulder and made the pre-arranged signal meaning *What's the problem?*

Parfist leaned close to Ghost's ear, the one without an earpiece, and gestured across the street. His whisper could not be heard over the buzz of the insects. "Two guards are always in the shadows of that big building, the one with five windows across the top."

Green Ghost spelled *OK* with his fingers. In seconds he located the two guards, leaning against the brick wall of a defunct antique store. He signaled to Wingnut behind him, flashing two fingers and pointing across the street. Wingnut relayed the order and four men moved off without making a sound. Ghost then put his mouth to Parfist's ear and cupped a hand over it.

"We'll take care of them," he said. "But remember, they aren't wearing night vision gear. They can't see you, but you can see them."

We own the night.

Parfist nodded.

Within a minute the two guards were gone, although Parfist didn't see what happened to them. Calculating time in his head, he moved off again, picking his cover and staying in the darkest shadows. Desperation drove him to hurry.

In a world where streetlights did not exist, night was the time of the hunter. Predators with superior night vision and heightened senses of smell and hearing had replaced Man at the top of the food chain. Humans who ventured into the dark did so at the risk of sudden and horrifying death. The man who survived in such an environment developed skills beyond those of his fellows.

Richard Parfist had been to Prescott many times, but never in daylight. Instead, he'd crept through the dark streets, stealing supplies or tools his village needed. Over the years he'd mapped every foot of Prescott in his mind, and could have navigated its warrens blind. He knew the guards' general routines, their hiding spots, and even some of their names. Having seen his new allies in action, he also knew they stood no chance against Green Ghost and his men. With Parfist pointing out every sentry and guardhouse, the SEALs took them out without disturbing the tranquility of the night.

A rusty green signpost marked the intersection with Montezuma Street, Prescott's main crossroads. To their left was Courthouse Square, the main headquarters for Patton and his LifeGuards. They moved past with extreme caution. The stately American elms towered in Court Square like sentinels.

On two other corners rose multi-story buildings. A three-story hotel stood on the southwest corner, with laundry hanging from windows. Green Ghost asked about sentries and Parfist shook his head: never. As pre-arranged, they brought four fifty-caliber machine guns forward to cover the courthouse, its green space, and its avenues of approach. This would be their forward base of fire, and a squad of MARSOCs took up defensive positions around the machine guns.

An FAO, *forward artillery observer,* and another squad of MARSOCs moved to the roof of a two-story building to the north. It was a perfect spot to direct the on-call artillery battery. If need be, a few salvos from

155mm guns could reduce the whole area to rubble.

The entire deployment process took less than two minutes.

Parfist motioned for a right turn. But there was a guard shack across the street on the northwest corner, near a ruined Mexican restaurant. Pointing with his hand, Parfist indicated it usually had four guards assigned to it. The shack was a heap of bricks and corrugated metal taken from the crumbling restaurant. A faint light shone through cracks in the walls and around the doorway, a rare thing in Prescott. Candles were scarce.

SEALs glided across the street, coming in from behind. They heard snoring but no talking, and found all four men asleep at their posts. The door was not hinged but only propped in place, open to the cool of the night. Four SEALs moved through and the only noise was the faint scrape of a scuffle.

With that threat neutralized, the column turned north, toward the high school and the thousands of prisoners. Parfist had to force himself not to be in too big of a hurry to rescue his family. He was not used to being part of a team, except on occasional hunting expeditions. Green Ghost had a lot of men to coordinate. The thought of his family suffering tortured him, but he waited until Green Ghost signaled to proceed. From there on they had to avoid alerting the Guards watching the prisoners, so he measured his steps and moved as he did when stalking a gazelle.

Peeking around the corner of an abandoned bank, he saw the dark outline of the high school.

Chapter 25

Till I saw the temples topple, till I saw the idols reel,
Till my brain had turned to iron, and my heart had turned to steel.
    Robert E. Howard, "Always Comes Evening"

0239 hours, July 29

White and green light spilled from a dozen monitors. In front of each one sat a man or woman wearing a headset, faces luminescent in the glow of their video displays. Few spoke, and when they did it was in hushed tones. Everybody listened and stared and waited for the shooting to start. In the meantime there was static and silence and a pervasive tension that charged the air like an approaching electrical storm.

While most headquarters personnel waited for events, Schiller stayed in constant motion. A hundred details needed attention. He hustled down the narrow aisles between banks of electronics, dodging chairs and talking to multiple people at once. Like good NCOs have done since the first army sallied onto the field of battle, Schiller was the backbone of the headquarters company's preparations for battle. He made sure everyone knew their job, had what they needed to perform that duty, and was mentally sharp. He was a blur of chaos in the otherwise quiet interior of the mobile headquarters.

Pausing for a deep breath, he glanced around to see if he had forgotten anything. That was when he realized a key headquarters component was missing: its commander. Exiting the trailer's side door, he stepped into the night and found Angriff on the mountain's edge, puffing a cigar and sipping coffee. Below him to the southwest, the land tailed off into desert, while due west and just over a mile away lay the darkened city of Prescott.

"General, are you all right?" Schiller picked his steps with care.

"Over here, Schiller. I'm watching my people at work."

"You've got better eyes than me, sir."

"Hah," Angriff said, "We both know better than that. Everything ready? Anything I need to do?"

"Grab a quick nap? It's going to be a long day."

"And we also both know that's not going to happen." He pointed toward Prescott, even though in the pitch blackness Schiller could not see him doing it. "I couldn't sleep if you shot me full of elephant tranquilizer. Because of human greed, I have ordered thousands of fine young men and women into harm's way, including my own daughter and son-in-law. And it's inevitable that some of them won't survive the day. As we speak, Mister Parfist is leading the advance team through those streets. They should be about there right now, and we could get the *go* signal any time. After that, if everything goes according to plan, we should have those people safely behind our lines within an hour. Then we can surround the city, capture the defenders, and deal with any Chinese who show up."

"Yes, sir. I'm sure that's what's going to happen."

Angriff raised a skeptical eyebrow, even if Schiller could not see it. "Because plans always survive contact with the enemy, right?"

0244 hours

Green Ghost knew that some human experiences are so instinctive they are instantly recognizable. When the yawning guard at the old high school's main entrance felt coolness on his throat, he went rigid, knowing what the sharp metal edge meant. By reflex he swallowed. The expansion of his throat pushed the blade into his skin, but that light kiss was enough to draw blood. He did not move.

"Good boy," Ghost whispered in his ear. "If you do what I tell you, you'll live to see the sunrise. Is it a deal? If it is, extend your rifle using both hands."

With the guard at the doors neutralized, Ghost's team moved on to the rest of them. One by one the SEALs disarmed, gagged, and zip-tied them all, making so little noise nobody raised an alert. Wingnut found an officer asleep on a table in an office and sent for Green Ghost. The snoring lieutenant awoke to the touch of a silenced pistol barrel between his eyes. He raised his hand to block a blinding light.

"Get that out of my face!" He swiped at the flashlight but missed.

"Ssshhh!" said a faint voice. Ghost moved the gun barrel to the man's forehead and pressed harder. "Be very quiet, unless you're tired of living. Do you understand?"

With sparkles filling his vision, the officer nodded.

"Good. As long as you cooperate, you might live. The people in the building, they're being traded today, right?"

Again the man agreed with a nod.

"You can talk, just not loud. What's your name?"

"Lieutenant Wimber."

"All right, Lieutenant, are these all the prisoners you've got?"

There was the slightest hesitation, then Wimber said, "Yes, this is all of them."

"That's the one and only lie you get to tell me," Ghost said. "Do it again, and I put a bullet in your brain. Last warning. Now, where are the others?"

Richard Parfist stepped back out of the gym. Upon opening the double doors leading to the old basketball court, he'd gagged and almost vomited. One of the SEALs noticed and gave him a small towel to hold over his face. Urine, feces, blood, sweat, unwashed bodies, infection, death... the stench was overwhelming. But he forced himself back inside. The air felt thick, like walking underwater. He stepped over and around the thousands of bodies sprawled in the overcrowded gymnasium. Somewhere in the mass of suffering humanity was his family.

The blackness was absolute. It was darker than outside, where faint starlight had let their night vision goggles turn night into green-tinted day. People lay on every square inch of floor space. Some were already dead. He placed each step with care, knowing that a startled scream could be catastrophic. Yet he had to hurry, because shooting could break out at any time. If anybody noticed him moving among them, they did not react.

Precious minutes passed. Recognizing anybody in the eerie green world was almost impossible, even his family. There were people on top of people, heaps of them everywhere.

Then, like a miracle, he saw the face of his son. Rick was asleep and using someone's leg as a pillow, but there was no mistaking the long mop of hair and the shape of the face. He felt a rush of panic at how gaunt the boy's fleshy face had become, stepped over people, and knelt beside him.

The boy did not wake when Parfist shook him. Stress and the lack of fresh air, food, and water had all drained him of energy. When he did finally open his eyes, all he saw was a distorted shadow with tubes where the eyes should have been. With a yelp he tried to scoot away, but a hand grabbed his ankle and held him in place.

"Rick," whispered the bizarre face. "Rick it's me, Dad."

It took a few seconds for the words to make sense. "Dad, is it really you?"

"Ssshhh," Richard Parfist said. "It's me, son, but we've got to be quiet, okay? We can't make any noise. We need to find your mom and sister. Do you know where they are in here?"

"What's that on your face?"

"They let me see in the dark. It's a long story; I'll tell you later. Your mom?"

"They took her, Dad, her and Kayla both. That old man they call the General, he made them go with him, he said they were going to be a present for somebody. What did he mean?"

If someone had rammed a long knife into his belly, it would not have hurt worse. Parfist sat back on his haunches and said nothing. His son's words confirmed his greatest fear—his wife and daughter were going to be somebody's sex slaves, condemned to a life of unending rape.

"Dad? Are you okay?"

"Son, I want you to think very carefully before answering this. Did the General say where he wanted your mom and sister taken?"

"I don't have to think about it. I remember pretty good—"

"Well," Parfist said, as a reflex. "You remember well." When the words left his mouth, he wondered what that had to do with anything.

"Sorry, I remember *well*. He told them to clean Kayla up and take her to his quarters. Mom tried to fight back and they took her, too. She told him that if you were around, you'd gut him like a trout. Then the General laughed and said he hoped he got to meet you."

"Oh, he did, did he?" Parfist said. "Then I'll see that he gets his wish."

Chapter 26

Every moment lost is worth the life of a thousand men.
Nathan Bedford Forrest

0258 hours, July 29

"Green Ghost reports first objective taken. No shots fired. Prisoners are dispersed in two additional locations. They estimate thirty minutes to secure the new objectives. Request evacuation of liberated personnel begin immediately, and confirmation of same."

"Damn," Angriff said. The end of his cigar flared in the dim lighting of his headquarters. "That's a lot of moving parts... Norm?"

"I think we trust the man on the spot and go. It *is* Green Ghost, after all."

Scowling, with the cigar sticking out from the side of his jaw, Nick Angriff looked for all the world like Winston Churchill.

"Go," he said.

0258 hours

The steel bulk of *Joe's Junk* cooled on the shoulder of the highway that led into Prescott. The night was quiet but an M1A3 Abrams was not. Operating the tank combined a loud growl with a high-pitched whine. Worse, the turbine engine drank so much fuel that idling might have drained the tanks before the coming day's combat. The long column of tanks, AFVs, and trucks stretching behind Morgan Randall's lead vehicle waited for the order to come back to life.

She stood with her platoon commander, Lieutenant Akio Tensikaya, whose tank was behind hers. First Platoon would lead the way for the rest of Alpha Company, but ROE stated the command vehicle should never take the lead if it was possible to avoid it. So the number two tank, *Joe's Junk,* took the point, with Tensikaya following in *Eat A Big One.*

Morgan would decide the column's pace, and whether to keep going or stop, given conditions at the moment. But the critical phrase from her written orders was foremost in her mind: *time is of the essence.* Once the operation began, speed was critical to the survival of the hostages, and any delay could mean death and disaster.

Neither of the officers had spoken for several minutes, as there was nothing left to say. Tensikaya stared at the sky, admiring the clear night's display of stars. Randall imagined forms moving among the houses and buildings ahead, praying they'd secured the route. She did not consider herself paranoid, but in an urban area at night, with enemies around, she was not about to drive into an ambush if she could help it.

"Lieutenant?" Hank Ootoi leaned out of the gunner's hatch. "Word up."

"Roger that, Toy." Making a fist, she bumped it with Tensikaya's.

"Everybody comes home, Morgan," he said. "Let's get this party started."

Chapter 27

Every new beginning comes from some other beginning's end.
    Marcus Annaeus Seneca

0259 hours, July 29

Kayla was snoring, but despite having bathed and eaten, Lisa Parfist couldn't sleep. She knew what *being a gift for a Chinese official* meant, and she vowed neither of them would ever be somebody's sex slave. Her captors were in for a nasty surprise if they tried to take her daughter again. She wasn't sure what she would do or how she would do it, but she was going to hurt anybody who tried.

0300 hours

Richard Parfist knew his family was in the courthouse, and had a good idea where. He had penetrated the General's lair twice over the years, both times looking for guns or ammunition. He knew where Patton's quarters were and the overall layout of the building. Taking Rick, Jr., by the hand, he led him outside. Green Ghost stood beside the main entrance, huddled with several soldiers.

"I found my son," Parfist said, interrupting Green Ghost, who turned.

"That's great, Mr. Parfist, but we've got more prisoners to rescue. Do you know where the old YMCA is? Also, there's supposed to be an old elementary school nearby."

"The YMCA is just down this street over here," he said, stepping out and pointing east. "There's a couple of fields, I think they used to be for baseball, but now there's peppers and pumpkins planted there. It's right behind those. There are a few different buildings that used to be schools, but the closest one is down that way and a little bit west. It's close. But look, any of these guards can show you where it is. I need you to watch my son for me. My wife and daughter were taken somewhere else, I think to the courthouse we passed. I've got to go get them."

"Not possible, sir. The trucks are already rolling and before long that whole area may be under fire. I can't let civilians into a free fire zone. We have multiple weapons systems zeroed on the courthouse, including heavy artillery, and trust me, you don't want to be anywhere near there if we call in arty. You and your son are on the first truck out of here, just like we promised."

"The deal was for my family."

"And your son is your family, Mr. Parfist. I'm sorry, but that's how it's gotta be."

"And I'm sorry, too, Lieutenant, but you're going to have to shoot me to stop me."

He darted into the night and headed for the crumbling football stadium just to the south. Rick started to follow, but a strong hand on his shoulder stopped him. With every step, Parfist expected to hear a shot. When he reached the ruined stands and ducked behind a jagged sheet of metal, he paused to gulp a few breaths. In a low voice he said, "Take care of my son for me, Green G. I've got to do this. I hope you understand."

Standing in the doorway, Green Ghost watched him go without raising his rifle. He had said what he had to say, and Parfist did what he had to do. It was exactly what the Ghost himself would have done.

Lester Hull inspected himself in the large mirror beside his bed. He was the only person in the Republic of Arizona who could use electric lamps for his own purposes. Of three working generators in the Republic, two powered his headquarters and one his personal rooms. Worn out and balky, with lightbulbs scarce, Hull rationalized their use on a day like today, when he had to look his best for the Chinese.

His personal weapon was a replica Colt Peacemaker which he wore on his right hip, just like the man he imitated. Ivory grips weren't available anywhere in the Republic, despite a rigorous and systematic search. But his uniform was clean and pressed. Although made from mismatched pieces, he still wore his officer's hat from fifty years ago. The five stars across the front he had crafted from the bottom of a coffee can decades before. It looked sharp.

Satisfied, he nodded to his reflection and stepped into the hallway. There were guards on either side of his door and he spoke to the one on the left.

"Bring me the girl and her mother."

CHAPTER 28

A wraith in the wind, a wisp in the night,
The trace of a dream, a whisper of fright.
        Scrap from an incomplete Viking epic

0311 hours, July 29

Within minutes, Parfist neared the courthouse. Despite it being Patton's headquarters, and the barracks for his LifeGuards, he knew of a way in. At the back was a window with a busted lock. Once inside, he knew where to find Patton's rooms.

A few had suspected an intruder's presence in Prescott, but although he'd roamed the streets for years, nobody had ever spotted him. No one dreamed that somebody would try to break into the fortified courthouse, so nobody noticed him cross the street. He crawled through the overgrown greenery at its rear and raised the broken window. Candles and lanterns lit the building, but the ambient lighting remained dim. Few people seemed to be awake at that hour.

Parfist had once overheard a conversation between some guards that told him Patton lived on the ground floor. The General worried about getting out in the event of a fire, they'd said. So he moved through the corridors like a shadow, with the stealth of someone who'd crept among his enemies for decades without their knowing it. When he saw two guards flanking a door at the far end of a long hallway, he knew it had to be Patton's room. But what could he do now that he'd found it? How could he get there with those two in the way? Time was passing and the sounds of the first vehicles moving into town could not be far away.

Movement at the door. Parfist pressed into a dark corner. The door to Patton's room opened and the General himself stepped out. He spoke to one of the guards and went back inside. The guard immediately headed down the hall toward him. Parfist clutched his knife and wondered if he could kill the man without the other noticing. But two doors from where Parfist stood, the guard went into a room on the left. For a moment there was silence, then came the sound of voices, one a man's, and the other a woman's. Lisa's.

He slipped in behind the guard. He passed through a large empty room, but the voices came through a door on his right. Parfist saw the guard standing in the doorway, his rifle pointing at Kayla, who sat in a chair crying. Lisa Parfist stepped in front of her daughter, and now the gun pointed at her chest.

"You're not taking her anywhere," she said. In her hand was a shard of jagged wood wrenched from a chair that lay shattered in the corner. "Not until you kill me first."

"Lady," the guard said, raising his rifle and aiming at her face, "nothing would make me happier than to blow your fucking head off. And if you and your daughter don't come with me right now, maybe I'll get to do just that."

"You're a tough man when you're holding a gun on a girl and her mother. If my husband was here, you wouldn't be smiling like that."

"Yeah, somebody heard you say that earlier. We all got a laugh out of it," he said. "So where is he? Why isn't he here? I'll bet he's hiding in a cave, pissing all over himself."

The guard heard a whisper in his right ear and felt something sharp at the base of his neck.

"Or maybe he's right behind you," Richard Parfist said. Before the guard could react, he shoved the blade hilt deep into his throat, severing the vocal chords. The man fell to his knees, gasping and thrashing. Parfist finished him with a second thrust through the eye. Covered in blood, he knelt and grabbed the man's rifle, yanking the belt with extra ammo from around his waist. When he stood up, his wife seemed stunned by the gory apparition in the doorway.

"I never thought I'd see or hear you again." She buried her cheek in his chest despite the blood. Kayla ran over and hugged them both.

"We've got to go, right now," he said. "There's a fight coming and we don't want to be around when it gets here."

"A fight? With who, the Chinese? And what is that around your neck? And those clothes?"

Parfist shook his head. "No time for questions, baby. It's a long story, and you won't believe it until you see it with your own eyes. But the good guys are back."

0323 hours

Lester Hull ticked off details with his fingers. Had he forgotten anything? It was the day of days for his republic. Instead of bartering for enough fuel to get by for a few months, they would secure their energy needs for years, long enough to finally begin rebuilding society according to his vision. True, the price was high. Replacing four thousand workers, with their attendant skills and talents, would be difficult. Maybe impossible. But without gasoline, the Republic of Arizona could never rise above a primitive subsistence level, and the price per slave was better than he'd dared hope. The Chinese must either be awash in gasoline, or desperate for workers, to pay what they were paying.

He would never admit that he felt twinges of empathy with the slaves, but it wasn't like they had ever been citizens. They had all lived in far-flung villages outside the authority of the ROA, so there was no actual loss as such, just lost potential. Assuming, of course, it was not some elaborate Chinese trap.

It was time to leave for the field headquarters. Hull took a last glance at his mirror and turned off the small electric lamp. Stepping into the hallway again, he saw only one guard. "Where's Lehandro? Why isn't he back with those women?"

"I don't know, General," the second guard said. "He should've been back by now."

"Go find him, dammit!"

Hull glanced at his watch and paced in a small circle. From the other direction, he heard footsteps on the tile floor and saw someone approaching, holding a candle. As the figure drew near, he recognized the sagging jowls of Norbert Cranston, the man in charge of the day's operation.

"What are you doing here, Bert? Shouldn't you be in the field?"

"Can't you hear it?" Cranston pointed to his right.

"Hear what?"

"Engines! Lots of them, getting closer, and some of them sound like tanks."

"Tanks? What the hell?"

"It's an unmistakeable sound," Cranston said. "That's assuming theirs sound like ours."

"I don't understand. Who is *theirs*?"

"The Chinese! Who else could it be?"

At that moment the guard ran back down the hall. "General Patton, Lehandro's dead and those women are gone!"

"Dead how?"

"Somebody knifed him right here." The guard gestured to the side of his throat. "There's blood everywhere."

"Son of a bitch," Hull said. "It's got to be the chinks. Somehow they found out that girl and her mother were here, and the little bastards snuck into my headquarters! They've got the women and now they're moving into town before we're ready. Shit! Bert, get the men organized. If they know I'm here, then this is where they're headed. Get somebody on the sirens. And find those women. They can't have gotten far!"

CHAPTER 29

The gods conceal from men the happiness of death, that they may endure life.
Marcus Anneaus Lucanus

0336 hours, July 29

Thanks to his night vision goggles, they had avoided milling guards while navigating the maze of halls and rooms. In less than three minutes, they found the unsecured window. Parfist turned to his wife and slid the goggles down. Starlight filtered through the grimy window glass and he saw the faint outline of her familiar face.

"Once you're outside, take Kayla and run directly across the street. Once you're in the hotel, you should be okay. There's soldiers over there, but they are not the General's; they're on our side."

"Richard, what are you talking about? Aren't you coming with us?"

"Listen to me, Lisa. We only have a few seconds. I'm staying here until you are across the street, then I'm following you. But you can't wait for me, do you understand? You have to get Kayla to the high school. These soldiers have already released the prisoners there, and they are watching Rick for me. Run as fast as you can and don't wait for me. I'll probably catch up before you get there, but if I don't, you can't stop. You have to keep going. There are trucks on the way to take you and the kids to safety and you've got to be on them. Can you do this?"

"I don't understand any of this!"

"I know you don't, but for now you've got to do what I tell you. Can you do that?"

She hesitated. "I can do that."

"You're an amazing woman. I'd be stupid not to love you. Now, get out of here."

At that moment they heard distant yelling and the muffled sounds of people running in the halls. A siren began to wail.

"Go!" He almost pushed his wife out the window. Once outside, she helped her daughter through, blew her husband a kiss, and took off running, hand in hand with Kayla. Parfist could not breathe as they ran. He pulled up the night vision goggles and watched them, and his temples pounded with the real possibility that somebody might shoot them. Once they disappeared into the hotel across the street and turned right toward the high school, he let out his breath.

The siren echoed over the city. He had only heard it once before, a long time ago when there had been some unknown emergency in Prescott. Now it was nearby, loud and grating on the nerves. *Oo-wah. Oo-wah.*

Instead of following his wife and daughter, he turned back to the interior of the courthouse. Fighting could break out at any time, but he was hoping for that. The chaos of combat was his best chance to finish his mission. General Patton said he'd wanted to meet Lisa's husband. Richard Parfist was going to introduce himself.

0336 hours

"Bulldozer One One Two, this is Copperhead. You're cleared to the courthouse, over."

"Roger that, Copperhead. Any burps with tubes along my route?"

"We're spread thin, One One Two. You should be good, but eyes up anyway. Look for friendlies every few hundred yards. They'll pass you along. Flash code is two short, one long, two short. If you don't see that, shoot to kill."

Corporal Tanya Marscal put *Joe's Junk* in gear and the Abrams lurched forward at a moderate pace. Fast, but not too fast. Despite the need for speed, Morgan Randall was taking no unnecessary chances. She ordered *Joe's Junk* buttoned up. It restricted their ability to see enemy infantry, but also negated the danger from snipers.

Leading the long column of vehicles through an urban landscape was the hardest possible mission. A tank's greatest advantage was its ability to kill at long distances. The biggest danger of fighting in a city was the buildings, where a single man with a rocket-propelled grenade could hide in ambush. A well-placed RPG round could kill an Abrams and its crew. Randall's crew was her extended family and losing one of them would break her heart.

"I'm feeling blind, boss," Joe Ootoi said on the intercom.

"Me, too," Randall said. "So work your periscopes like your life depends on it."

It was a hard call. Staying buttoned up risked ambush. And while it was true the commander's station had six periscopes, providing a 360 degree view, even when using night vision gear she couldn't see everywhere at once. Yet if they opened the hatch for a better look, a sniper could be waiting on the roof of any building they passed. So the hatches stayed closed. Their lives depended on the SEALs and MARSOCs having cleared the route.

Prescott had an inner core of homes and businesses that had stood for generations. But as the city had spread to the suburbs, profit had trumped permanence. Moving west into the old town, the column rumbled past the remains of crumbling strip malls and fast food restaurants. Looters had long since stripped them of knives, metal cookware, and anything else of value. A stand of southwestern ponderosa pines had grown through the collapsed roof of a mall on the edge of town. Cacti and flowers pushed through cracks in the asphalt parking lot. Randall scanned this through the surreal prism of night vision lenses.

The highway widened from two lanes to four. Their speed increased. They came to the fork where the broad highway veered right. Going straight led through a more congested area, but the highway on the right was a chimera. The briefing intel indicated that road had a wide trench caused by a sinkhole years before. It was a dead end. Morgan Randall kept going straight.

A MARSOC team on the right flashed the recognition code using an infrared flashlight, passing *Joe's Junk* on to the next team a few hundred yards west. Randall was turning to scan the left side of the road when the world exploded around her. There was a loud *whang!* The Abrams rocked to the right, stunning the crew. Her vision sparkled red, but within seconds Randall had recovered and scanned the shadows, where she saw a figure running down a side road. She aimed the fifty-caliber machine gun using the controls installed with the TUSK package. A stream of tracers pursued the retreating shape. She missed to the left but corrected fire until bullets poured into the man who had fired the RPG. His green shape flew sideways, then he rolled to a stop.

"Anybody hurt?" she said into the intercom mike.

"Tanya's got a headache," Toy said. "Otherwise we're good."

"Hey, Morgan," Tanya said. When she got excited, her slight Ukrainian accent became more noticeable. "Looks like the TUSK armor took most of it, but she seems to be pulling to the left a little. We might have a bent sprocket."

Within the confines of their tank, Randall's crew called her by her name, although Ootoi called her *boss*. None of them ever questioned her authority, so she saw no need for formalities.

"Shit," Randall said. "Can you tell how bad?"

"I can hold her. Just don't ask for anything fancy."

"No promises. Do the best you can. Let me know if it gets worse."

"You hear that, boss?" Toy said. "Sounds like a siren."

Randall pushed back the tactical headset and paused to listen. The whine and rumble of the Abrams drowned out almost everything else. She concentrated on filtering out the familiar sounds of her tank in motion. And then she heard something else, faint but unmistakable.

"I hear it, Toy," she said. "You're right. It sounds like a tornado siren. Shit."

What to do? They were approaching Montezuma Street, the intersection where they would turn right and head to the school. But if the enemy was already alerted, there was a good chance they would have to fight their way out. Which meant that every minute they hesitated gave the enemy more time to deploy to stop them. Without orders to the contrary, as the lead tank it was her job to keep moving.

The next MARSOC team waved her to a stop. Randall hesitated. Stopping the entire column in what was clearly unsecured territory put the entire mission at risk. But the Marines would not have told her to pull up unless there was danger ahead.

"Tanya, the jarheads want us to pull over," she said.

"I see 'em, boss. Do I do it?"

"Slow down but don't stop." Despite possible snipers, she opened the hatch and motioned a Marine closer to the Abrams. "I'm cleared all the way through!" She shouted over the engine noise.

"Enemy occupies a big building ahead on the left. Wait here until we assess the situation."

"No can do. We're going through."

"Can't allow that, ma'am."

"I didn't ask you, Corporal." She disappeared back into the tank. "Move out, Tanya."

"Boss, they're waving us down. Do I stop?"

There was no hesitation this time. "Negative. Speed up and get ready for a right-hand turn on my signal. We're going through, come hell or high water. Load up. Toy, shoot first and apologize later. Marty, HEAT until I tell you different, but have KE at the ready."

"You sure you wanna do this, boss?" Toy said.

"Time is of the essence. Our orders are to rescue people, and we can't do that sitting on our asses. Copperhead cleared us to the courthouse, so let's go see what's there. If this goes south, I promise not to tell your new commander how much you all suck."

———∞———

0341 hours

"Sir, Bulldozer One One Two just blew through a stop signal, hauling ass," Sergeant Schiller said.

"Bulldozer One One Two?" Angriff said.

"Yes, General."

He shook his head. "She takes after her mother."

———∞———

0341 hours

"Bulldozer One One Two, this is Bulldozer One One. You ignored a stop. Explain."

"We were cleared by Copperhead all the way through, One One. We've already taken one hit and stopping now could expose the entire convoy to attack. Our orders are to keep moving no matter what."

"All right, Morgan, I've got your back, but I think it's about to get hot."

CHAPTER 30

Twilight gathers and none can save me,
Well and well, for I would not stay...
        Robert E. Howard, from *"Lines Written in the Realization That I Must
        Die"*

0343 hours, July 29

If Hell existed, a real place where tormented souls spent the after-life, Norbert Cranston knew it would sound like this. The screeching wail of hand-cranked emergency sirens bothered him more than any other noise. He didn't know why. He had vague memories of a movie that had scared him as a child, but he could no longer recall the details. He only endured the noise because he had to.

The design of the Yavapai County Courthouse in Prescott had been the result of a national contest. The intent behind building the court-house was for it to last forever. The walls were granite over reinforced concrete. Its neo-Classical design was so stout and intimidating, it stood like a giant mausoleum. By its nature it made an excellent bunker, which was the chief reason Lester Hull had chosen it as the headquarters for the Republic of Arizona.

Hull had also ordered a sprawling underground warehouse dug in the adjoining park, connected to the courthouse. Escape tunnels led in all four directions; Lester Hull was nothing if not careful.

The original roof sloped too much for standing on, so Hull had built an observation platform that wrapped around all four edges. Stairs to the platform led up to a trap door in the ceiling of the floor below.

Standing on the east side of the wooden platform, Hull and Cranston tried to pick out approaching vehicles. Hearing them was impossible over the sirens. Finally, Hull had had enough of the noise and waved for them to stop.

"I don't see anything," he said once the sirens' echo faded. His binoculars were not designed for night use.

"There, General!" said a man near the northeast corner of the platform. "Down around the cornfield. I see something moving."

Hull focused in the direction indicated and picked out... something. Like a subtle ripple on a black backdrop, something moved their way. As he tried to focus the binoculars, there was a bright flash, then the *boom* of an explosion. He turned away and squinted. Colors sparkled in his vision for a few seconds and then faded.

"RPG," Cranston said. "Whoever they are, we hit one of the bastards."

Below them, men slid into defensive positions around the courthouse. The city was alive with Guards and Security Police moving to assigned positions, while the populace scrambled for a safe place to hide. As the dark shapes came into focus as definitely being tanks, squads of LifeGuards ran for the other side of the street to lay down crossfire.

But halfway across, machine gun and rifle fire ripped into their ranks, knocking several men backward while others lurched and fell. Survivors knelt in the middle of the street and returned fire. Sparks flew as bullets ricocheted off the asphalt. Then, out of the darkness to their right, a column of Abrams tanks sped toward them with machine guns blazing. The remaining Guards flung down their weapons and fled.

"Son of a bitch," Hull said. "Those are our tanks."

In the light of gun flashes, Norbert Cranston picked out details as the first tank turned right onto Montezuma Street.

"No, they're not," he said, unable to comprehend what he saw. "Those are American tanks, but they're not ours."

One of their M249 light machine gun opened fire from the roof of the old brewery across the street. Wood splinters cut Cranston's cheek as an enemy gunner returned the fire. Guards on the ground used the elm trees for cover and joined the firefight. Another machine gun blazed away from behind the bronze statue honoring Buckey O'Neill, which stood on a marble pedestal in the park.

O'Neill had once been mayor of Prescott. He'd ridden up San Juan Hill with Teddy Roosevelt's Rough Riders, and died there. Hull admired O'Neill and had resisted suggestions to melt his statue down for its bronze. The sturdy statue and its enormous square base also provided excellent cover.

An RPG round screamed from Court Square, glancing off the turret of the second tank in the column before exploding across the street. The turrets of the second and third Abrams had already been traversing, but now they had a hard target.

Bullets began striking the platform near Hull and Cranston. Seeing the M1s preparing to fire, Cranston grabbed Hull's shoulder and pulled him close. Yelling over the gunfire, he said, "We've got to get below!"

Sighting down Cranston's pointing arm, Hull saw the third tank's cannon barrel elevating. He nodded and they ran for the stairs. Seconds later the building shook as a 120mm shell vaporized the machine gun and its crew.

0346 hours

When he discovered Patton wasn't in his quarters, Richard Parfist moved from doorway to doorway searching for him. Twice he avoided men hurrying somewhere. He felt encumbered by the rifle but was unwilling to give up its firepower.

At each room, he put his ear to the door and listened for anyone inside, but hearing anything was impossible over the wail of the siren. Halfway through the first floor, he had not opened any doors and desperation was setting in. The longer it took, the more likely he was to get caught. When the sirens tailed off and ended, he froze. What had happened?

Then the shooting started.

The chatter of machine guns came from above. Rifle fire from Court Square came through the open front doors. He crouched in a doorway near the central stairwell, wondering what to do next, when there was a muffled explosion. Seconds later the entire building shook and a much louder blast echoed down the stairs.

Once, a long time ago, Parfist had watched from a distance as Patton's tanks had attacked a village near his home in the mountains. They had fired a few cannon shells and he remembered the sound, and it was just like this explosion. He knew immediately what it meant—the Americans had arrived and opened fire, and he was out of time.

0348 hours

Ceiling plaster fell around Hull and Cranston in chunks. The weak beams of their flashlights reflected off the pulverized plaster that filled the air with a fine white powder. It clogged their noses and made them cough. Then there was another, much stronger explosion. It lifted the heavy building from its foundations and slammed it back down.

Following a Security Policeman down the stairs, Cranston turned to Hull behind him. "That's artillery!"

"Where the hell did that come from?" Hull yelled back. "Who are these people?"

At the first floor, they turned left toward Hull's office. There was the loud *crack* of a rifle and the SP man staggered, clutched his chest, and fell. Cranston whirled back up the stairs, but before Hull could follow a hand grabbed his collar and jerked him backward. He felt the barrel of a rifle press against his spine and stopped struggling.

"Whoever you are, General Patton is up those stairs but you're letting him get away," Hull said. "I'm his assistant."

Parfist knew that voice too well to fall for such a trick. He had eavesdropped on the leader of the New Republic of Arizona many times over the years. "Oh, no, General Patton. I know exactly who you are. I'm here because you said you wanted to meet me, and now we're going somewhere to have a nice talk."

Still with his back to the man, Hull was not about to give up so easily. "If I yell, you'll never get out of here alive."

"Nobody lives forever," Parfist said. "I'm ready to die, as long as you do, too."

"Who are you?"

"Remember that beautiful woman and her sweet daughter you were giving to the Chinese commander as a gift?"

Hull did not answer, so Parfist poked him with the gun to prompt him. "I asked you a question."

"Yes."

"The woman told you that you would have to deal with her husband. Do you remember that, too?"

"I'll be rescued any minute now," Hull said. "Surrender and I'll spare your life."

"You'd better hope that doesn't happen," Parfist said. "I'm just looking for an excuse to kill you. Now answer my question or I'll drop you like a bighorn sheep. Do you remember she said her husband would gut you like a trout?"

"Yes."

"And you said you looked forward to meeting him?"

"Yes."

"Then you should be happy, because her husband is me."

CHAPTER 31

Line them up, big and small,
Line them up, we'll fight them all.
    Sergio Velazquez, from "Yoke"

0349 hours, July 29

Using her Common Remotely Operated Weapon Station, Morgan Randall sprayed the street ahead with her M2HB fifty-caliber machine gun. Hostiles engaged in a firefight with the SEALs scattered when her rounds cut into their ranks. She cleared the area of living enemies, but just in case any survived, *Joe's Junk* ran over them without slowing down. As part of the Tank Urban Survival Kit, the TUSK, she thought CROWS was a great idea.

Ting-ting-ting.

Speeding through the firefight, *Joe's Junk* took hits from both sides. The echo of ricocheting bullets rang through the hull. They all leaned left as Tanya made the sharp right-hand turn that led to their destination. Seconds later they heard a 120mm gun firing behind them, and knew the rest of the column would have to fight its way through.

Flashes outside lit the staircase with a strobe effect, but Cranston didn't slow down. Whoever shot the Security man might be chasing him. Two more guards were running downstairs and he grabbed one by the arm, ordering him to go down and rescue the General. Then he headed for the radio room on the third floor.

The radios at the courthouse ran on one of the working gas-powered generators. The most crucial military units had handsets with rechargeable batteries. The sets had limited range, but within the Prescott area reception was generally good.

Panting after sprinting up two flights of stairs, Cranston held onto the radio room doorframe as another shell landed in Court Square. An elm tilted to one side, pulling a root ball from the ground.

To his astonishment, two men still sat in the room, waiting for orders.

"To all commands," he shouted. "Enemy inside the city. Headquarters under attack. Secure prisoners—"

A large shell exploded outside the window, shattering the remaining glass. The blast knocked everyone to the floor and toppled the radio gear, smashing it. Cranston touched his forehead and came away with a bloody hand, while the two radio men did not move. One groaned, but the other had a jagged glass shard in his neck and was bleeding out. Groggy, Cranston crawled for the door.

The courthouse was not defensible, that much was obvious; he had to get out of there. He took one of the dead radio operators' M16s. Hull had had escape tunnels dug from the basement for just such a situation. Stumbling, bleeding, Cranston headed back down the stairs.

0351 hours

Green Ghost heard gunfire and explosions to the south, from the courthouse area. Flashes of exploding shells lit the night sky like lightning. He recognized the sound of every weapon, from the M16s to the incoming artillery rounds.

The instant the first small arms fire erupted, his men had gone into full defense mode. Their mission was to protect the prisoners until the evacuation trucks arrived.

"Green Ghost, this is Copperhead Nine," a voice said in his earphone. "Friendly armor headed your way."

Over the din of combat, he heard the unmistakable rumble of an M1A3 Abrams growing louder in the darkness. Seconds later, the familiar outline materialized and pulled up next to the doors of the gym. The tank's front left showed blast marks. The commander's hatch opened and a head popped up.

"Enemy positions?" a female voice shouted down.

"Negative, Lieutenant," Green Ghost said, recognizing Morgan Randall. "I've got LPs out, and you passed the second and third holding stations. What's going on back there?"

"Firefight by the courthouse; burps are trying to stop us. Until they're suppressed, the convoy can't get through." She stood higher in the turret and scanned the area for a few seconds. "I'm setting up over there." Pointing, she indicated the northern end of the old football stadium.

Green Ghost approved of her setup spot and gave her thumbs-up. "From there you can dominate the approaches to the buildings," he yelled, cupping hands around his mouth. "But watch out for enemy infantry."

"Are we expecting any?"

"I don't know, but until the convoy gets here, we're on our own."

Randall nodded and dropped back into *Joe's Junk*.

0358 hours

"General, Bulldozer One One Two has made contact with Green Ghost," the radio technician said. "They've taken up defensive position. No enemy activity yet."

"Where's the rest of Bulldozer?" Angriff asked Norm Fleming.

Fleming held one cup of a headset to his ear and raised a finger, meaning *Give me a second.* Then he smiled and lowered the headset. "Bulldozer One One reports the garrison at the courthouse is surrendering. Apparently the artillery didn't agree with them."

Angriff could not help smiling. "Shrapnel's hard to digest."

0408 hours

Morgan Randall happened to be looking right at a pile of debris when the hot outline of a man popped into her night vision goggles. Before she could fire the M2HB, there was a flash. Something smashed into the right side of *Joe's Junk,* rocking the Abrams like a lizard shaking a rat.

Although stunned, her crew's training took over and all became reflex. The turret rotated and the barrel depressed, aiming at the heap of rubble. The Abrams rocked backward with recoil as a 120mm round fired at the target less than thirty yards away, blowing man and debris to smithereens. Shrapnel and clods of rubbish clanged off the top of the tank.

"Damage?" Morgan Randall called into her mike.

"My sanity," Toy said. "Everything else checks."

"I'm good here," Marty said.

"Tanya?"

"Not sure. Display's rebooting, but I can't guarantee anything until we start moving. I think we're good, though."

"If we ever meet the guy who designed TUSK, somebody should give him a blowjob," Toy said.

"Be my guest," Tanya said.

0411 hours

The activity resembled the organized purpose of an anthill. Tanks and APCs deployed around the perimeter of the high school campus, while the following trucks lined up at the entrance. MARSOC teams directed traffic and helped the liberated prisoners into the transports. There was no stampede, since most of the prisoners were so weak even standing was difficult. Some cried but most stood silent, unsure of what was happening. Many thought it was time for transfer to the Chinese. There was a constant stream of shouted orders and the roar of powerful engines. At the center of it all was the lean figure of Green Ghost.

He and Wingnut were deep in conversation when somebody tapped on his shoulder. They were in a puddle of darkness fifty feet from the entrance to the gym, and it took him a second to recognize Richard Parfist.

"Mr. Parfist, now's not the time," he said, and turned back to Wingnut. He issued an order and Wingnut trotted off. When he turned, he found Parfist still there, pointing an M16 at a heavy-set man.

"I'm very busy, Mr. Parfist. I don't know where your family is," he said. "But I'm sure they're over there somewhere."

"Thanks, Ghost. Could you take this guy off my hands?"

"Who is he?"

"He's General Patton, the leader of this place."

0413 hours

"Say again, Green Ghost. I repeat, say again."

The radio operator switched to speaker. The voice sounded clear but compressed.

"Prime, this is Green Ghost. We have enemy commander in custody. Need instructions A-sap."

Ten feet away, Nick Angriff turned and pushed down the crowded aisle to the station. Keying the mike, he took over the call. "Green Ghost, this is Saint Nick. How do you know he's the right guy?"

There was a short pause and some inaudible background chatter. Then Green Ghost was back. "No doubt, sir. It's him. Requesting orders."

"Great work. All right, tell him this—he's to order an immediate stand-down for all forces under his command. Do whatever is necessary to help him accomplish this. Whatever it takes, do you understand? This is your top priority after the safety of the hostages. If he refuses, tell him his only other option is to be shot on the spot, but don't actually do that. Do you understand these orders?"

"Aye, sir."

"Nipple's not with you, is she?"

"No, she's attached to your headquarters security team."

"Good. And again, great work. I don't know how you did it, but you just saved a lot of lives."

"It wasn't me, Saint, or anybody under my command. It was Mr. Parfist."

"Parfist? The guy who was your guide?"

"Roger that. He's very resourceful."

"Give him my thanks. We need all the men like him we can get."

CHAPTER 32

We pray for one last landing, on the globe that gave us birth,
Let us rest our eyes on the fleecy skies, and the cool, green hills of Earth.
Robert A. Heinlein, from "The Green Hills of Earth"

0414 hours, July 29

Creeping through the dark streets, Norbert Cranston wondered why the shelling had stopped. But his primary concern was not getting shot by his own men, so he focused on his immediate surroundings. The trip, normally five minutes in daylight, took much longer, but within half an hour, when he emerged from the tunnel, he found General Patton's tanks still on the west side of the hospital, within sight of the high school. Not one of the six even had its engine running. Holding them as a reserve had been the right move, but they should have already counter-attacked.

The tank crews, though, were confused, scared, and unsure what to do next. Cranston did not hesitate. After a brief pep talk, he ordered an immediate attack to retake the high school and secure the hostages. The crews cheered, but it sounded forced to Cranston's ears. They had heard the artillery barrage and the sounds of large vehicles, and he could read the fear in their eyes.

No matter. As long as they obeyed, he didn't care what they thought about the situation. Engine cranking, the first tank clanked past the hospital and turned right at a street that led straight to the high school.

0418 hours

"Tank signature at ten o'clock," Toy said over the intercom. "It's an M1, boss. One of ours?"

Morgan Randall saw it move from the cover of a building and turn directly for *Joe's Junk*.

"Shit! I don't know. Marty, what's in the chamber?"

"HEAT, boss. Switch 'em out?"

"No, KE next." Behind the first tank, she saw others following. "Bulldozer One One, I've got unidentified Abrams tanks headed toward my position west of the high school, range two hundred and closing fast. Urgently need ID. Are they friendly?"

"Boss," Toy said, "the gun. Look at the gun."

Randall focused on the screen. As she watched, the oncoming tank rotated its turret from side to side, as if seeking a target. At first glance the gun appeared identical to theirs, but then she picked up the small differences in length and width. "That's a 105, not a 120! Enemy in sight! Toy, you locked in?"

"I've got him, boss."

"Fire!"

Joe's Junk rocked backward as the HEAT round left the barrel and struck the oncoming M1 at the turret seam, just below the main gun. At point-blank range, the round penetrated the tank's armor, releasing its jet of volcanic fire into the crew compartment and killing everyone inside. The exploding shell set off the ready ammunition. Secondary explosions were visible more than a mile away. They ripped out the sides and blew the turret fifty feet into the air.

The following M1s panicked, but the glare of the explosions revealed a tank under some trees at the end of the street. Without precise firing data, but at a range of less than a hundred yards, the second M1 fired one round and then turned. The rest of the line all swerved and turned at once, with the fourth and fifth tanks ramming each other, disabling both and blocking the street. In the light of their burning comrades, the crews bailed out and ran away. Seeing their friends racing past them, the last M1 crew climbed out and joined the fleeing group, leaving their tank running.

Norbert Cranston tried to stop them. He waved his arms and shouted and threatened, but nothing could stop their headlong flight. He would have shot them if he'd had a sidearm. Finally, as they disappeared into the night, he knew there was no choice except to join them.

To Morgan Randall's mind, the muzzle flash was simultaneous with a loud *crack* as the 105mm round struck a massive pine tree three feet to the left of *Joe's Junk*. Wood splinters showered the hull. Then the Abrams was shaken and collapsed on its shock absorbers as the tree fell on top of them. The weight tilted the huge tank backward at more than a ten degree angle.

"Fuck!" Toy said. "Did we get stepped on by a giant?"

Stunned, Morgan Randall shook her head hard and sought a new target. She assumed the enemy was lining up for a kill shot. Instead, she saw the receding shapes of the enemy tankers running away. "Sound off," she said.

"I'm good," Tanya said.

"Me, too," Marty said.

"I need a drink," Toy said.

"Boss, I'm spiking hot," Tanya said. "I think something's blocking the air intakes."

"I'm going topside." But when Randall tried, the commander's hatch would not open. "Damn, something's blocking it. Tanya, move us up but be careful. I think that's a tree up there."

The radio crackled. "Bulldozer One One Two, gimme a sitrep."

Scanning her display for new threats, Randall spoke into the headset as she multi-tasked. "One enemy tank destroyed, four or five others abandoned by hostiles. I'm damaged, extent currently unknown. Request immediate support."

"Bulldozer One Two One and One Two Two are on the way."

"One One Two out."

Tanya inched *Joe's Junk* forward. As the tank moved, they heard screeching as the tree scraped against the hull. It pressed down further and further on the hull's rear until it rolled off and the whole tank sprang up, then down, and finally settled on an even keel. Morgan Randall shoved her hatch open and climbed out. After checking for enemies, she inspected the damage.

Needles and branches lay all over the top, and there was the strong scent of pine. The CROWS tilted left and the fifty-caliber machine gun angled backward, its barrel bent downward by some massive weight. Behind them was the hulk of a huge pine tree, at least 36 inches in diameter.

"Shit," she said. "What next?"

0420 hours

Flame jetted high into the air; Green Ghost could see it above the ruined football stadium grandstands. A series of explosions followed that he recognized as ammunition cooking off.

"Looks like your friend didn't make it," Hull said, smiling. "Too bad."

They had been standing in the darkness, watching trucks loading up with Hull's former prisoners. Green Ghost watched the flames for a moment, then turned. He reached down to his ankle holster and drew his personal weapon, a 9mm Kimber Solo Crimson Carry. He jammed the barrel of the little pistol into Hull's lower jaw, just behind his chin.

Two SEALs stood with Hull, more for his safety than for any real need. If the hostages recognized him, they might tear him to pieces. But neither SEAL reacted to Green Ghost threatening him.

"In the next minute, one of two things is going to happen," Green Ghost said. "Either you're going to use one of our radios and issue a surrender order, or I'm going to pull this trigger. And honestly, I'd just as soon blow your fucking head off."

"What's your rank, soldier? I want your name and rank, and I want them now!"

Green Ghost leaned in close. "I'm not a soldier," he said in a low voice that was almost a growl. "I'm a SEAL. Fifty seconds."

"Do you know who I am?" Hull continued. "Do you? I'm a five-star general in the American Army. I outrank every one of you, and I will have you court-martialed for this!"

"Forty seconds."

Hull stood with his mouth half open for at least ten more seconds. Green Ghost saw the disbelief in his eyes. It had been years since anyone had questioned his authority, and he could not believe it was happening now. But Hull's face tightened as reality sank in.

"Twenty seconds."

"You're going to regret this," Hull said.

"Only if I don't get to kill you. Fifteen seconds."

"Give me the fucking radio."

0426 hours

"Bulldozer One One Two reports enemy abandoned their armor and are fleeing west. One enemy M1 destroyed," Schiller said, emphasizing *Bulldozer One One Two.* They had all heard the report of a tank exploding in Morgan Randall's operating area and it was his way of telling Angriff that she was safe.

"Thanks, J.C," Angriff said.

"General Fleming," one of the radio operators said, "General Angriff, the enemy commander is about to broadcast a stand-down order. Would you like it on speaker?"

Fleming pointed, meaning *yes*.

A few moments later—"To all members of the military services of the Republic of Arizona, this is your commander, General George Patton. You know me and you know my voice, so listen up. This is an order: you are to stand down immediately. Do you hear me? Surrender and hand over your weapons. These are not enemies. They are the legitimate armed forces of the United States of America. These are your country-men, not your enemies. Stand down right now."

Angriff grinned and stuck an unlit cigar in his jaw. "Green Ghost can be very persuasive. But we can't count on all those people rolling over for us. Some might not have radios. Signal all units to accept surrenders but to be on alert for tricks."

"More good news, Nick," Fleming said, reading from a sheet of paper just handed to him. "Lead elements of the Marines report no enemy contact on the south side of the city. They are turning north to cut Highway 10 on the west side. ETA thirty minutes. Pulling those Marine companies out of the east paid off."

"They put everything on the north to keep the Chinese honest, just like we thought."

"Looks that way," Fleming said. "So far, so good. Now if the Chinese just cooperate, our dispositions will be perfect."

"That's what worries me."

CHAPTER 33

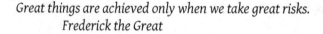

Great things are achieved only when we take great risks.
       Frederick the Great

0430 hours, July 29

Throughout Prescott, LifeGuards and Security Police came forward, hands raised and calling out not to shoot. Despite the lack of radios in the various sub-units, word traveled fast. Most of them were glad to surrender, especially when they heard American voices responding to them out of the darkness.

But some fled west along with Norbert Cranston, and before long more than two hundred men gathered with him in the Prescott National Forest. He considered a counter-attack but that seemed futile. Instead, he led them deeper into the pine forest to plan their next move.

0437 hours

The coffee was fresh and hot. In the pre-dawn cool on top of Badger Mountain, it tasted better than anything Nick Angriff could remember drinking. Stepping out for fresh air before the arrival of the Chinese, he could almost feel the various components of his command moving around him. From the infantry regiments blocking the northern approaches and covered by the artillery, to the Marines sweeping north to cut off the city on the west, Angriff could see them all in his mind's eye.

He visualized the helicopter gunship squadrons going over last-minute checklists, and the medical services re-checking inventories. And he was right where he wanted to be, at the center of it all.

0439 hours

Morgan Randall ran fingers through her hair, feeling the dampness of her sweat. The air had a slight chill that felt good after the confines of her tank, and they all felt better with the rest of the company present. Lights had been set up at the evacuation points to help load the hostages, and her crew used the artificial daylight to inspect the damage to *Joe's Junk.*

"Two RPGs and a tree," Lieutenant Tensikaya said. "Not bad, Morgan. I've never heard of anybody getting hit by a tree before."

"We're trend-setters, Akio," she said. "Pretty soon everybody will be doing it."

0440 hours

The fires in Prescott had died down and only the Klieg lights competed with starlight to illuminate the city. The eastern horizon did not yet hint at the coming dawn. Standing atop Badger Mountain, with a chilly breeze whipping at his shirt and the ash of his cigar glowing, Angriff remembered another time and place, when he'd stood atop a castle looking down at another city, wondering what the future held. For a moment he wondered what had become of Salzburg and whether anyone still played Mozart, or even remembered who Mozart was. It was all so long ago and far away.

"General?" Schiller said, crunching over the mountain gravel toward him. "Ranger LP on the north has the Chinese in sight."

The momentary lapse into memory vanished. "On my way." He took a long draw and then pinched the ash end from his cigar, saving the rest for later.

Activity in the Mobile Command Center had tapered to a low buzz when he'd left a few minutes before, but now it was loud again. "What have we got?" he asked.

Norm Fleming answered. "Ranger Team Three has eyes on the intersection of Interstate 40 and Highway 89, a hamlet named Ash Fork. That's about eighty klicks from Prescott, seventy-two from our forward dispositions. The Chinese column is moving slowly and is screened by light recon vehicles. It's followed by a long line of transports and tanker trucks. No armor yet, but the column is only now turning onto 89."

"No tanks? No APCs?"

"Not yet."

"That's odd. Why would the Chinese commander do that, send out what has to be major assets with minimal protection? We're missing something."

"Is that intuition, or jumping to a conclusion? Could be they trust their trading partner," Fleming said. "From what we know, they've been doing business for a long time. Why be suspicious now?"

"Because they're Chinese Communists, that's why. When have you ever known a Chicom to trust anybody, Norm? Hell, they don't trust their own mothers; why would they trust some outsider warlord? I know you're playing devil's advocate, but this doesn't make any sense. Either the Chinese got stupid after we went cold, or there's something we don't know... or we missed something. Help me see this, Norm. Help me see what I'm missing or if I'm being paranoid."

"Go back to zero, before the Chinese set this operation in motion," Fleming said. "There are no plans, no actions, nobody is on the move, nobody has done anything. You're the Chinese commander. The Americans need fuel, you need slaves. You have been trading with them for years and have never had any problems. You trust them as much as you trust anybody. What now?"

"You trust them as much as you trust anybody..." Angriff mused. "Damn... all right, you trust them. You put a huge convoy on the road, with trucks and fuel and manpower. This represents a major commitment of resources. You screen it with recon vehicles because... because why? That's all you've got?"

"Or maybe the only threat you see is guerillas," Fleming said. "And they're fast enough to hunt them down."

"No, I don't see that. Nobody would attack a military convoy that big unless they wanted to destroy it, even if they don't have heavy protection. Even guerillas would have to weigh the cost-benefit side of things—"

"Am I interrupting?" Dennis Tompkins walked up rubbing his neck and stretching it.

"Not at all," Angriff said. "I thought you were asleep."

"That's one of the joys of getting old. You can only sleep when you don't want to. How are things below?"

Walling briefed him.

"Huh," Tompkins said.

"Huh, what?" Angriff said. "What are you thinking?"

"Don't mind me, Nick. I've been living in the wilderness so long I see traps everywhere. Even when they don't exist."

"Traps?" Fleming said. "Nick here feels there's something wrong with this set-up and you think it's a trap?"

"Yeah, help us figure this out," Angriff said. "What are we missing, Dennis?"

"Is there a map I can look at?" Tompkins said. "And maybe some coffee?"

Sergeant Schiller brought the coffee and pointed at a monitor showing a topographical map of the Prescott region.

Tompkins scratched his chin. "I can't make heads or tails out of those digital things. Is there a paper map?"

"It's pretty old, sir," Schiller said.

"So am I."

As part of the brigade's archives, hard-copy maps of the entire country backed up the digital ones. It took a few minutes to locate and roll out the right sheet. Once spread on a table, with a high intensity lamp picking out every detail, Tompkins took a moment to inspect it and then stood up, still massaging his neck and shoulder.

"Let me ask you this, Nick, because I'm not used to thinking on such a big scale. If this convoy is what it looks like, then we have plenty of firepower to deal with it, don't we?"

"Hell, yes," Angriff said. "Especially with Prescott in our hands. It's not even a fight at this point."

"That's what I thought. So the way I see it, and remember, I'm not used to these big operations—"

"A big operation is just a small operation with more men and machines."

"—then think of it this way. What are we all standing here talking about?"

The knot of officers looked at each other, wondering what he was getting at. "About this Chinese convoy," Fleming finally said. "And its intentions, and whether our dispositions are correct to deal with it."

"Right," Tompkins said, pointing at him.

Angriff touched his forehead, seeing where Tompkins was heading. "The convoy is dangling in front of us like a cow begging to be ground into hamburger. We're busy figuring out the best way to cook it, and meanwhile... Dennis, you're a tactical genius. It's a decoy. Where's that map?"

Tompkins shrugged. "I may be dead wrong, sir."

"I don't think so."

Poring over the map, Angriff demanded a magnifying glass, but it was in the intelligence tent for photo and video interpretation. Instead, one of the techs handed over his prescription glasses which, held at the correct distance, had a similar effect.

"Son of a bitch," Angriff said. "That's got to be it, right there." He pointed to a thin white ribbon, running through the desert from its junction with Interstate 40 at a place called Seligman. "This highway, Highway 5, it's probably no more than a two-lane strip of asphalt. But it runs almost due south through some pretty desolate-looking country. Nobody would ever expect a large armored force to use such a road. But we have to assume the Chinese did their homework. They may have used this road before, or at least scouted it."

"We could ask our prisoner," Fleming said.

"You mean the slave-trader? There's no time and we couldn't believe anything he told us, anyway."

"Even if they are using that highway, Nick, by the time it reaches Prescott it's only, what, three miles from Highway 89? We're already covering it with our current dispositions."

"You're right, Norm, but I think there's more to it. If I'm right, the Chinese would want their enemy stretched to the breaking point. So what if they split again and leave Highway 5? Another force could come through here, through... what does that say? Skull Valley? What if they come through Skull Valley and then pick up Highway 10, due west of the city?"

"That's a big if," Fleming said. "How do we know if that country is suitable for tanks or not?"

"How soon can we get an air asset there?"

"They're all scheduled to sortie at dawn against the convoy."

"I didn't ask that."

"If they take off immediately, flying at night, a Comanche could be there in under an hour. An Apache would take longer."

"Dennis, you're awfully quiet."

"Well, since you asked my opinion," Tompkins said, "I think you're right. I think the convoy is a trick. If the Chinese have tanks, then I reckon you're gonna find them out yonder somewhere. And since you said we've already got plenty of assets to deal with this convoy. I don't see much harm in poking around some."

"You nailed it, Dennis. Here are my orders," Angriff said. "First, send one of the Marine recon companies down this Highway 10 to right here, where it crosses this valley. Have them deploy there and await further orders. Second, get something in the air to scout that valley. Third, get those tanks in Prescott ready to re-deploy to the west, if the situation warrants. Fourth, alert the artillery we may be re-deploying assets and to find suitable setup areas to the west. Fifth, do the same with the other tank companies, and find roads that will get them to the combat area fast. Sixth, speed up the evacuation of the hostages. Seventh, if I'm right and the Chinese are pulling a fast one, I want the Army regiments to attack that convoy immediately. The idea is to seize as many of those fuel and transport trucks as possible. I've got a feeling they're not all loaded with gas. Last, find that local, the man who guided the infiltration teams to the prisoners. See what he knows about this valley and whether it's good tank country."

"Parfist?" Fleming said. "The evacuation has started and he was supposed to be on the first truck out."

"I don't care how you do it. Just find him."

0454 hours

Someone pulled aside the canvas flap. A man wearing night vision goggles pushed up on his helmet stuck his head inside the back of the truck. In the dim light he looked like a giant insect.

"Richard Parfist, are you in here?" he said. "I need Richard Parfist. If you're in here, it's urgent."

Seated on the bench near the cab of the crowded truck, Lisa Parfist dug her nails into her husband's left arm. She put a finger to his lips. Parfist patted her knee and pulled her finger away, kissing it. Even under all the gear, he recognized that man, especially his raspy voice. "I'm right here, Ghost."

"Could we speak for a moment, Mr. Parfist?"

"Richard, don't," his wife said. "You don't owe these people anything."

He smiled and kissed her cheek. "Sweetheart, if it wasn't for them, you'd be learning to speak Chinese."

Once outside the truck, Green Ghost sketched the situation. "Have you ever heard of Skull Valley?"

"Of course," Parfist said. "I lived there for a few years, until Patton started raiding settlements west of Prescott. My dad was a forest ranger in the Bradshaw District... that's the name of a mountain range. He taught me every rock and trail, and he even named all the cougars."

"There's a road that leads into Prescott from the northwest. Old maps label it Highway 5. Do you know that road?"

"I know every road in this area, including that one. The signs are still up."

"Good. I know you're not an expert," Green Ghost said. "But you see what our tanks are like. Do you think a large force of tanks could leave that highway and move through Skull Valley to come at Prescott from the west? Would that be doable?"

"Skull Valley? The town? You wouldn't have to go that far south;

you could just cut across country, then pick up Highway 10 and follow it into Prescott. There's some pretty thick woods through there, but there's plenty of places to get through."

"Even with tanks?"

"Sure."

"I'm sorry to ask this, Mr. Parfist, and you are free to say no. But could you guide us one more time and help us block those trails? If the Chinese are coming through there, in force, we need to put something in their way to slow them down. We need you. Your country needs you."

"My country," Parfist said. "That doesn't even make sense to me. I've never had a country before, but so far you've done what you said you'd do, and my family is safe because of you. So yeah. Yeah, I'll guide you."

CHAPTER 34

Every soldier must know, before he goes into battle, how the little battle he is to fight fits into the larger picture, and how the success of his fighting will influence the battle as a whole.
     Field Marshal Sir Bernard Law Montgomery

0512 hours, July 29

Rather than using the radio, Lieutenant Tensikaya walked fifty yards to the clearing where the crew of Bulldozer One One Two were inspecting the damage to their tank. The number designation painted on the turret was 1-1-2, although the pine tree had scraped most of the 2 off the left side. He entered the pool of light thrown by the portable LED lamps connected to the battery. Squatting for a closer look at the scorch marks from the RPGs, he scooted down and knelt beside Corporal Marscal, checking out the damaged sprocket. It was obvious *Joe's Junk* had been through a battle.

"How's it looking?" he said.

"You don't have a replacement sprocket, do you, Akio?" answered Morgan Randall. She lay on her back inspecting the torsion bars. Wiggling out from under the tank, she climbed to her feet. "The sprocket has some bent teeth and two treads are damaged. A couple of the wheels are going to need replacing. Some of the electronics are screwed up. Marty is running diagnostics to see if it's just loose connections or actual damage. The weapons systems and engine are fine."

"Are you combat capable?"

"We can fight, but mobility is a problem. We can move well enough, but I don't want to throw a tread, so we need to keep it slow. What do you have in mind?"

"Prime thinks the Chinese might be coming in force from the west, with tanks, using Highway 10. That's the road over there, the one you turned off of to get to the high school. Follow it straight out of town and that's where they think the Chicoms are coming. I'm taking the company out about ten miles and we're doing to deploy there, but I can't have a cripple if it comes to a fight. You'd be a sitting duck, so I want you to be a final block in case something gets through. There's a big bend in the road. You set up there and stay there. I'll leave glowsticks to mark the spot."

"What are my orders?"

"If they come through, stop them."

0513 hours

The coffee was hot, black, and bitter, just the way Joe Randall liked it. He blew on the steaming liquid and slurped, smacking his lips the way Bunny Carlos hated. It was his second cup of the morning, and there would be at least a third before he and Carlos took off on the day's first sortie. The Comanche had an in-flight urinary disposal system, so he wasn't worried about a full bladder.

Both men sat on the bench by their lockers, pulling on their flight gear. They heard a knock.

"Change in plans, sirs," Sergeant Rossi said from around the corner.

"Come in, Rossi, we're dressed," Carlos said.

"Sortie time, sirs. Immediate liftoff. You're to do a seek-and-destroy recon of a valley west of Prescott. Coordinates are locked in and orders pulled up on the display."

"Seek and destroy?" Randall said, wide awake. "What are we looking for?"

"Don't know, sir, but guess would be Chinese tanks."

"Just us, or is Ripsaw Two going along for the fun?"

"Both of you, Captain."

"Good," he said. "Alisa's cranky in the morning, puts her in the mood to blow something up."

"If they're committing two Comanches to this," Carlos said, "our Fuck Meter has got to be pegged on max."

"Yeah," Randall said. "No kidding."

"Please be careful, sirs," she said, indicating both of them, but staring only at Carlos.

0513 hours

Remembering the half-smoked cigar in his front pocket, Angriff stepped outside and soon had it relit. Once you had done everything you could, when the pieces were in motion and beyond your control, the hardest part was waiting. He instinctively looked far to the west, trying to visualize where Skull Valley was and imagining he could see it.

"You're out there," he said to the night. "I know it as sure as I'm standing here."

He didn't know why he was so positive, but on certain occasions in his life he'd seen things others had not. He had always been right, too, and this was one of those times. Some said he knew the enemy's moves before the enemy did. For the moment, however, he could only wait and smoke. Until someone laid eyes on that strip of land, he was powerless.

The night-draped city three thousand feet below was alive with heat signatures. Joe Randall and Bunny Carlos could see almost the entire brigade below their racing gunship, and the sight was impressive. They passed the artillery batteries spread to the northeast of Prescott, then overflew the two infantry regiments deployed to the north and northwest. The long line of trucks evacuating the hostages to a holding field on Prescott's eastern boundary sped forward. Their headlights lit the way.

"That can't be good," Joe Randall said. "Either it's over on the ground or they're in a big hurry."

"They remind me of ants running from a flood," Carlos said.

Banking west, within the city they saw the signatures of tanks, trucks, APCs, fires, hot craters, people, artificial lights, torches, and, on the western fringe, a line of tanks heading out of the city. One tank lagged behind but Randall had no way of knowing his wife was its commander. From positions to the north, they saw more tanks moving west.

"I wonder where everybody's going," Alisa Plotz said. Randall was not a stickler for radio discipline, and radio silence was pointless since the ground units were chattering away.

"Reminds me of Syria," Randall said.

"The advance or the retreat?"

As they flew west, the dead town of Chino Valley slipped away on their right. Soon enough the heat signatures disappeared and they saw nothing but the dark of a forest. Here and there a dot appeared and then vanished, a mule deer or cougar.

The half-light of dawn crept over the land. Details became distinguishable. They turned southwest and large hills appeared dead ahead. Those gave way to rugged desert as they approached their objective, and then they saw it.

"Oh, fuck," Alisa Plotz said. "Now I know where those tanks are headed."

"Shit," Carlos said into the intercom.

Randall took *Tank Girl* up to five thousand feet for a more panoramic view, and also to process what he saw. Moreover, he needed line of sight to headquarters.

"Prime, this is Ripsaw Real," he said. "Urgent! We are over target area bearing two twenty, altitude five thousand, heading two two five, speed one forty. Stand by for video feed."

0526 hours

Over the large map table at the end of the Mobile Command Center was a sixty-inch super-high definition monitor. It was difficult to back up far enough to get a good perspective, but the resolution was so good it made studying the picture much easier. When the video began, it was the big picture that mattered and the details seemed unimportant.

"Son of a bitch," Norm Fleming said. "I should have known."

From the height of the helicopter, they all saw what looked like a river of hot metal flowing south. There were too many heat signatures of tanks to count, interspersed with armored personnel carriers and some trucks. The line of vehicles stretched out of sight toward the town of Skull Valley to the south. When the Comanche swung around to fly north, they saw that it ran to Highway 5, and north on that road for more than a mile.

"I was praying that I was wrong," Angriff said. "Damn. That's at least a full armored division, if not a whole corps."

"I don't see any artillery," Kordibowski said. "Or mobile triple-A, although some could be Type 95s. It's hard to tell."

"Type 95?" Angriff said. "I'm not up to speed on the PLA."

"Tracked triple-A. Four 25mm cannon in a turret. Sometimes have missiles, too."

"Like the old German Wirbelwind."

"If you say so."

"Am I wrong, Rip, or is that an armored corps I'm looking at?" Angriff said.

"It could be a reinforced division, but yes, General, it's probably a whole corps."

"Time is of the essence, people," Angriff said. "Deploy the rest of the tank battalion here, as far north of Skull Valley the town as possible. Tell them to step on it; there's just one company there now. Re-deploy the First Infantry Regiment along this line here, and the Second is to attack the column on Highway 89 immediately.

"I want as much artillery on this valley as possible, as fast as possible. That means both battalions will need to move their gun tubes west, and I do not want a clusterfuck of them advancing in front of the infantry. Work it out on the front end. Get the MLRSs firing A-sap.

"All air assets are to concentrate on this tank corps. Block Highway 5 north of the city with one Marine company, then position the rest of the battalion to back up Bulldozer. One company can't hold for long. Let's move, hit 'em hard, and make 'em think."

"Do we withdraw the other two Marine companies off the left flank?"

"No, not yet. We have to have something out there."

"What about Ripsaw, General? Attack now or wait for reinforcements?"

"Ripsaw? That's Randall, isn't it?"

"It is, sir," said Walling.

Angriff hesitated for only a moment. "Doesn't matter. Attack immediately."

0531 hours

"Ripsaw Two, wait two minutes, then hit the rear of the column. I'm heading south to its head. When you finish your pass, I'll make mine the other way. After that, fire on targets of opportunity."

"Roger that, Ripsaw Real. You're buying the first round."

"I'll buy the first two rounds. Be on guard for triple-A and missiles; you can bet they're down there. Good luck, Alisa, and good hunting." Into the intercom mike, he said, "You shoot, I'll fly. Make it count, Bunny. We might not get a second pass."

"Just don't get us hit by our own ordnance."

The head of the column was five miles south. Randall pushed his speed up to 170 knots, losing altitude as *Tank Girl* thundered through the growing morning light. After bringing the nose around to the right, he was half a mile from the convoy when something exploded in the distance. Ripsaw Two had started her run. He continued banking and dropped to less than one hundred feet.

"Damn, Joe," Carlos said. "I mean, damn! They're lined up for miles. I've never seen anything like this before."

"And you'll never see it again. I hope."

As *Tank Girl* straightened out for her initial attack run, Carlos targeted an APC that was in the lead. At three hundred yards, he opened fire and watched his explosive rounds tear it apart.

0532 hours

The pine tree had damaged her hatch, fifty-caliber machine gun, and periscopes. Morgan Randall had no choice but to expose herself to see what was happening around her. *Joe's Junk* lurched for the spot marked by Lieutenant Tensikaya, a shoulder of Highway 10 covering a wide bend where it turned toward Skull Valley. The Marine recon companies had rolled past and her own tank company was long gone, and it pissed her off that *Joe's Junk* had to sit this one out. Her place was beside her comrades in the thick of the fighting.

High above, she heard the unmistakable sound of an AH-72 Comanche, flying fast and heading south. Her breath caught for just a moment... could that be Joe? Within two minutes of the gunship passing overhead, she heard the zipping buzz of a Gatling gun followed by a large explosion. Then more explosions, and the distant tree line was backlit by a red glow. Something streaked through the sky and blew up, without doubt a surface-to-air missile. The action was close, no more than two miles away.

Joe Ootoi stood in the gunner's hatch, took in the sights and sounds, then whistled. "Somebody's mad at somebody."

"Yeah," she said. "They're close, Joe. If we could just move a mile, we'd be in it."

"Look at the bright side, boss," he said. "If the Chicoms break through, we'll have all the targets we want."

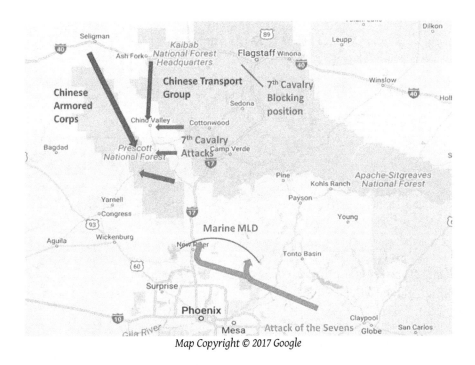

Map Copyright © 2017 Google

CHAPTER 35

If any of you cry at my funeral, I'll never speak to you again.
  Stan Laurel

As dawn lightened the eastern sky, the 7th Cavalry was in motion. Gunships raced for Skull Valley and swarmed the Chinese armored column like red wasps defending their nest against a centipede. At first stunned by the air attacks, the Chinese recovered and fought back. The Chinese were veterans of a hundred fights in California and Mexico. Their weapons were modern and they knew how to use them.

Sunlight crept over the treetops and brightened the valley. The battle became a duel between the helicopters and the mobile Chinese anti-aircraft vehicles. All were Type 95s SPAAAs, self-propelled anti-aircraft artillery. Fully tracked, like a tank, the Type 95 was a deadly vehicle. They mounted dual 25mm cannon on each side of the turret, with two QW-2 infrared homing missiles above each cannon, for a total of four missiles. Unfortunately for the Chinese, years of fighting had reduced the supply of QW-2s to a minimum. Since they hadn't been expecting air attacks, few were actually on hand that morning.

With ridges, mountains, hills, and dense stands of trees to hide behind, the gunships had a huge advantage. Once they targeted a particular vehicle, the pilot ducked behind cover and re-emerged to strike from a different spot. This didn't give the Type 95s a chance to track their new position.

By the time the first gunship sortie ran low on ammunition, most of the SPAAAs were flaming wreckage. Burning vehicles littered the valley, but compared to the numbers of the Chinese juggernaut, the losses were minimal.

As the climbing sun brightened the day, details of the battlefield became clear. It was ideal tank country. Most of the valley itself was flat, with some low hills and scrub vegetation. Some lines of sight were long and clear, but the rolling topography obscured other approaches. Danger could come from any angle. The possibility of cresting a hill and finding an enemy tank, waiting on the other side for a point-blank kill shot, was real.

The Chinese rolled forward and their objective became clear. They weren't heading for Skull Valley but Highway 10, which led to Prescott from the west. Lieutenant Tensikaya and the rest of First Platoon deployed forward to defend the highway. A small road crossed a ridgeline and bypassed the need to enter the town of Skull Valley itself. Without *Joe's Junk*, he only had 13 Abrams to cover a mile of ground.

But they had a secret weapon: each tank carried five EXACTO rounds. There had been a hot debate about issuing the precious can't-miss shells so early in the brigade's operational history. They were irreplaceable, but the unknown scope of the crisis overrode all other concerns.

The three Marine recon companies provided cover against Chinese infantry and light vehicles. But they were nothing more than targets against the Chinese Type 98 and 99 main battle tanks filling the valley.

With the coming of daylight, targets became clearer. The din of battle vibrated the cool early morning air. The crack of cannons, screech of shells, and the reverberating explosions from tanks that had taken mortal hits, all drowned out the screams of wounded men. Chinese infantry poured from armored personnel carriers and moved over the hills and gulleys.

Guided by Richard Parfist's knowledge of the terrain, the Americans deployed far forward to prevent the Chinese from flanking them on the east. In the process they blocked Highway 10 as it headed for Prescott. The town of Skull Valley had no tactical importance, except the highway passed through it and ran northeast toward Prescott.

Chinese pressure forced the Americans back to the west, uncovering the cross-country route to the highway. Task Force Bulldozer had no choice but to retreat, being both outnumbered and outgunned. This prevented them from stopping the Chinese advance down Highway 10. That left two Marine companies, deployed along a low ridge on the east side of the valley, as the last blocking force until reinforcements arrived. They had no choice but to hold as long as possible. Hull-down on the opposite side, with only the small turret exposed, the Marine LAV-25s were a difficult target to hit with the 125mm main gun of a Type 98 tank. The Marines fielded 50 LAVs of all types lined up in less than a mile, or one about every 35 feet.

But Marine light reconnaissance units were not intended for pitched battles. Their greatest asset was mobility, with a strong punch from the 25mm chain gun giving them a deadly edge. Standing and fighting was a last ditch resort, especially against scores of main battle tanks, where chain guns had limited effect.

0658 hours

Morgan Randall stood on the turret of *Joe's Junk.* She braced her right foot against the twisted hatch and scanned the area to the south and west. The sounds of heavy combat were clear and close. Dense palls of smoke spiraled above the trees, with an occasional tongue of flame spewing into the black columns rising to the sky. For the past two hours the sounds of battle had been coming closer. In the gunner's hatch next to her, Joe Ootoi stood guard with an M16, watching the underbrush for infiltrators.

"Where the hell is the rest of the battalion?" he said. "I feel like the staked goat in *Jurassic Park*, with velociraptors running around in the bushes."

"It was a T-Rex," she said. "The velociraptors got a cow."

"Well, that makes me feel better."

"They'll be here when they're here. Just keep a sharp lookout."

Several explosions threw dirt in the air less than four hundred yards away. Rifle and chain-gun fire followed immediately.

"Crank us up, Tanya," she said. "I think we're about to go on stage."

0730 hours

Angriff was a pacer. During times of stress and decision, and in particular during the heat of combat, he would stalk and smoke and rub his chin. This ritual helped him visualize the battlefield, where his assets were in relation to the enemy. He talked to himself, sometimes lapsing into the German his father had spoken during his boyhood.

He had an uncanny knack for feeling how much his troops could take before breaking. He also knew when to launch counter-attacks for maximum effect. But his normal method of operation was to scout the ground first, except this time he couldn't do that. The few drones available to the engaged units hadn't lasted long, so he only had a vague idea of the topography and roads.

He was still outside pacing when Schiller stepped out with the latest reports.

"Bulldozer has been forced back into the town of Skull Valley, sir. The Marines are holding the line, but barely. They're going to have to move soon or be overrun."

"Status of the tank battalion?"

"Apparently somebody blew up part of the road just west of the city, creating a bottleneck. They're repairing it as fast as they can, but there's no ETA yet."

"Damn." Angriff tossed the butt of his cigar into the dirt. He followed Schiller back into the MCC and got a quick recap from Fleming. "If the tanks are caught strung out on that road, it could get ugly," Angriff said.

"Very," Fleming said.

"If they do break through, is there anything to slow them down until we can deploy the tanks?"

"Just one." Fleming pointed to the map, and a bend in the road that led toward Prescott. Looking up, he met Angriff's eyes. "Bulldozer One One Two is in a blocking position right here."

"There? I thought she... they... were closer to the city."

Fleming shook his head. "No, they're here. If the Chinese get that far, and get past them, they can hit the rest of the battalion while it's in road march order."

"Then Bulldozer One One Two has to hold at all costs," Angriff said.

Fleming nodded.

"Send the order."

CHAPTER 36

Stranger, Go tell the Spartans
We died here obedient to their commands.
    Inscription at Thermopylae

0733 hours, July 29

"I guess that's it, then," Morgan Randall said after reading the stand-fast order to her crew. "We're here to stay."

"They can't mean *no matter what,* boss," Toy said.

"*At all costs* seems pretty clear to me," she said. "Tanya, EXACTO rounds ready?"

"Locked and loaded, boss," Tanya said.

"Main gun for AFVs only, unless I order otherwise."

"We don't have the fifty, boss," Toy said. "There's not much to keep infantry off our ass."

"The other two machine guns will be enough. The rest of the battalion is just down the road and they'll be here any minute. We'll be fine."

"And if we're not?"

"Then we're not," she said.

"Ripsaw Real, this is Prime. What is your fuel and ammo status?"

"Low on both, Prime, but we've got enough for a few more runs."

"Be advised of change in mission parameters. Coordinates being sent now. At western edge of the city, there is a highway leading to the

Chinese position. You are to assist Bulldozer One One Two if needed. Bulldozer is in blocking position. It is believed Chinese are closing on their position. Do you copy?"

"Roger that, Prime. On my way."

"Bulldozer One One Two," Carlos said. "Isn't that Morgan?"

"Yeah." Randall shoved the throttle to the wall.

0739 hours

While she sat in the commander's seat with her head exposed, a bullet ricocheted off the ruined hatch inches from Morgan Randall's right ear. Toy turned and fired the M16, then ducked inside the turret as small arms fire broke out in return.

"Shit," he said. It took a few seconds to aim and fire the coaxial 7.62mm machine gun in reply. Then he found the range. Heads disappeared behind a hill several hundred yards away as bullets kicked up the dirt. Toy began tracking the 120mm gun in their direction.

"Forget that, Toy. I said main gun for armor only," Randall said. "Expect enemy armor to come over that hill any minute."

Four hundred yards down a straight patch of the highway rose a slight hill that obscured whatever lay beyond. Almost on cue, the barrel of a tank's main gun rumbled into sight, followed by the bottom of a Type 98 main battle tank.

"Ready to fire," Toy said.

"Fire!"

Joe's Junk recoiled as the 120mm smoothbore cannon fired its massive shell. The EXACTO round struck the underside of the target about a quarter of the way back. Penetrating the thin metal bottom, it exploded in the crew compartment with a huge roar and a tower of flame and smoke. The turret flew upward and crashed back on top of the stricken tank, then the ammunition began cooking off, ripping holes in the hull.

"Repeat EXACTO," Randall said. "New target should be to one side of the first tank."

"We've got infantry at two and ten o'clock, boss," said Tanya. "Two hundred yards and closing."

"Roger that. Marty, next round is EXACTO."

"We've only got four left," Marty said.

"EXACTO, damn it," Randall said.

Out of the smoke boiling from their first kill, another Type 98 raced over the hill so fast that for just an instant it went airborne. Slamming back to Earth, the Chinese tank did not wait to stabilize before shooting. Both the American and the Chinese tank fired simultaneously. At a hy-

STANDING IN THE STORM

personic closing rate, the two shells passed within six feet of each other as they sped toward their intended targets.

The American EXACTO round penetrated the turret junction with the hull, a lethal hit that set off another massive explosion. The Chinese round was off target because of its bouncing firing platform, the Type 98 itself. Instead of hitting the front glacis plate, it struck the left front tread, where it touched with the ground. The resulting detonation lifted the front of *Joe's Junk* five feet in the air and then slammed it back down. Seventy-ton tanks were not meant to absorb such a shock.

"Report," Randall said. Her head had smacked into the hull with the shell's impact and there were sparkles in her vision. She did not feel the blood running past her right ear and down her back.

"I'm here," Tanya said in a weak voice. "Marty's wounded. I can't tell how bad. I think the left tracks are destroyed."

"Reporting for duty," Toy said. "Fire control is up, all systems operable, except my brain."

"Marty, report your status. Marty? Marty, can you hear me? Damn... Tanya, can you load an M1028? We've got enemy infantry all over the place. Need it quick."

"Can do, boss."

"Toy, get on the MG. Keep 'em back!"

Bullets sprayed the tank, bouncing off but making a loud *clang* with every hit. Randall grabbed her M16 and tried to pin down the closest Chinese, but a machine gun fire-hosed her position. She slumped back inside.

"Tanya, we're out of time!"

"Almost there, boss. Marty's in the way... locked and loaded!"

The M1028 warhead contained eleven hundred 10mm tungsten balls. When fired, they spread in a shotgun pattern and beyond five hundred yards could rip a man to pieces. A platoon of Chinese infantry had just topped a small rise a hundred yards to their right front, at the one o'clock position. Several carried RPGs. Toy rotated the turret; it seemed to take forever, although it was less than two seconds. He fired without waiting for the order and the blast effect was devastating. All but two of the Chinese flew backward in the storm of metal, body parts flying. The rest of the Chinese dove for cover.

Tanya immediately loaded another M1028. Toy was looking for another group of infantry when, without warning, a Type 98 roared out of the blazing conflagration in front of them. The turret rotated until the barrel of its main gun pointed right at them.

Nobody said anything because there was nothing to say. Toy brought the gun to bear in less than two seconds, but they had no time to switch out the anti-infantry round. The tungsten balls would bounce off the Chinese tank without even making a dent. Re-loading would take at least four seconds, which in the real time of combat was forever. All they could do was watch, in horror, as the Chinese tank fired while on the move.

Completely as a reflex, Toy pushed FIRE milliseconds after the Chinese tank's cannon roared. *Joe's Junk* recoiled again as the M1028 left the barrel. Thirty feet from the mouth of the gun, the cluster of metal balls was perhaps three feet in width when they struck the Chinese round and detonated it. The result wasn't as catastrophic as the shell actually hitting, but it was close.

The force of the explosion bent the cannon barrel, rendering the main gun useless. Shrapnel sprayed the turret and front half of the tank. Several splinters of white-hot steel penetrated the thinner top armor. One such struck Tanya in the foot. For the second time in minutes, *Joe's Junk* got thrown in the air by the force of the blast, and then slammed back down hard enough to stun the crew. Armored tiles from the TUSK kit fell off the sides. All electronics went dark, including the displays, although the engine kept running. The interior smelled like burning wire.

"Get out!" Randall said. Then, realizing the intercom was dead, she took off her helmet and shouted. "Get out! Abandon the tank! Let's go!"

"I'm hit, boss," Tanya said. "I can't move my foot!"

"Toy, go, get out. I'm gonna help Tanya!"

"Boss!" Toy grabbed her shoulder and pointed out the view slit.

The Type 98 had advanced another twenty yards and stopped. This time they didn't hurry. They were aiming for the kill shot.

"Oh, no," she said, knowing there was nothing any of them could do to stave off a sudden and fiery death. "Dear God..."

Then fountains of dirt sprang up all around the Chinese tank. Flashes spread over the hull, like white Christmas lights winking on a tree. Except she recognized the impact of 30mm cannon shells tipped with depleted uranium. The shells penetrated the tank's armor and exploded inside, filling the interior with red hot shrapnel. The shells kept hitting the hull for more than four seconds. Given the twin Gatling guns' high rate of fire, that meant hundreds of the lethal rounds shredded the Chinese tank. Flames licked out of holes in the hull. Seconds later the main gun ammo started cooking off, ripping it apart.

As Toy and Randall watched, hypnotized, an AH-72 Comanche flew past. Painted on its side was a half-naked blonde sitting spread-legged on a cannon barrel. The caption below it read *Tank Girl*. Without slowing down, it fired a salvo of Dragonfire missiles at some Chinese infantry closing on their position. Most of the Chinese dove for cover but others never had a chance as detonations tore up the hill.

"Zippity damn do dah!" Toy said. "Wonder how the fuckers like that?"

"Toy, we've got to get out of here. You help Tanya. I'll get Marty."

Randall tried bracing herself with her right hand, but the blood on her palm made everything slippery. She hadn't noticed it before, but there was no time to investigate where it came from. The distinctive smell of an electric fire was strong.

The turret's rotation allowed Tanya to escape through the gunner's hatch. Toy grabbed her under her armpits and, pushing off with her good leg, she was able to get a handhold on the outside of the turret. Toy then pushed her and she tumbled out. She almost rolled off the tank but caught herself on the mangled shields surrounding the pindle-mounted machine gun. Toy followed her out, but he crawled to the front. Randall would need help getting Marty out.

Except that Marty wasn't getting out.

Randall opened the hatch in front of the turret and shook her head. "She's gone."

"She can't be," he said, not understanding. "Where did she go?"

"No, she's dead."

The whine of a ricocheting bullet broke the pause. Morgan felt a searing burn in her right shoulder but kept moving as more bullets pinged around her. They were immediately followed by the sound of a Dragonfire missile vaporizing the shooter.

Randall's right shoulder throbbed and she had trouble lifting the arm to climb out. Toy reached in and grabbed the back of her jacket, and felt something warm and wet.

"Aw, shit, boss," he said. "Come on, let's get you out of there."

Between the two of them, they got her out of the hatch. She slid off the left side, away from the Chinese. Tanya crawled over and joined them, and they all leaned against the armored tiles hanging over the side. Toy drew his sidearm.

"Where's Marty?" Tanya said.

"She didn't make it," Randall said, holding Tanya's gaze until she understood. Seeing her eyes water, Randall shook her head. "No time for that. We've got to get out of here while we've got air cover."

Tanya nodded and wiped her eyes. Randall found it hard to think and felt cold, and somewhere in her mind she knew it was the result of blood loss. Blood soaked Tanya's left pant leg, too. There was a shallow ditch on the far side of the road and they ran for it as fast as they could, with rifle shots skipping off the pavement behind them. They jumped into the ditch and ducked, trying to keep their heads below the top.

Morgan felt the world spinning around her. Prop wash blew across the highway, throwing dust and small stones around like a small tornado. Fifty feet to their right, *Tank Girl* hovered ten feet off the ground. As Morgan Randall stared at the cockpit, Joe Randall pushed up his visor and locked eyes with his wife. Then she passed out.

CHAPTER 37

The deepest wounds happen to those we love.
   Unknown Athenian playwright, circa 410 B.C.

0757 hours, July 29
   "I'm putting her down," Joe Randall said. He could still see his wife's bloody back.
   "There's Chicoms all over the place!" Carlos said.
   "I don't care."
   "Getting us killed won't help Morgan!"
   To his right, Carlos' peripheral vision sensed movement. Four hundred yards down the highway advanced a column of M1A3s, led by a Humvee; the rest of the tanks had arrived at last. He touched Randall's shoulder and pointed at the oncoming armor, hoping it would dissuade him from making *Tank Girl* a better target than she already was. It didn't. When the landing gear touched down, Randall flung off his helmet, ducked, and leapt out the cockpit door, running for the ditch. Carlos crossed himself, hoping the oncoming tanks did not mistake them for Chinese. *Shoot first and ask questions later* was never a bad idea in the chaos of combat.
   Randall slid into the ditch beside his wife. "How bad is she?" he asked Toy.
   "I don't know, Captain. She's lost a lot of blood."
   The right side of Morgan's face was streaked with blood from a long, shallow gash at her temple, but it was the right shoulder that worried her husband. Her blouse had been torn by something, probably a bullet, and blood soaked her side.

The lead Humvee sped up and approached fast.

Randall pointed at Tanya. "Can you carry her?" Not waiting for an answer, he slid his arms under his limp wife and fast-walked toward the approaching Humvee.

Although he didn't see it, a Chinese soldier made the poor decision to take aim at him while standing fifty yards in front of *Tank Girl*. Carlos touched the trigger and 30mm cannon shells vaporized the man before he could fire.

The Humvee screeched to a stop just as Randall circled behind it, holding his wife in his arms. An angry major got out and stomped over. The name stenciled over his left breast pocket read CLARINGDON.

"What the hell do you think you're doing?" he said, yelling to be heard over the whine of the Comanche's engine. "Get that damned helicopter out of my way!"

"Sir, this lieutenant is my wife. She's bleeding out. I need you to take her to your medics right now, or she will die."

Claringdon was the battalion XO and knew Morgan Randall as the executive officer of First Platoon, Alpha Company. In the frenzy of the moment he did not ask how a husband and wife had become part of the brigade. "If I don't get those tanks down this road, a lot of people are going to die! Now get out of my way!"

"She's one of yours, Major," Randall said. "I need you to take her and her crewman to your medics!"

"Put her down over there and I'll have the medics get to her when they can."

"Not good enough, sir. She'll be dead by then."

"Captain, you're disobeying a direct order under combat conditions. Do you know what that means? Now put her down and move that Comanche!"

"She's General Angriff's daughter," Randall said.

Claringdon blinked. "She's what?"

"She is General Angriff's only surviving child," Randall said forcefully. Without waiting, he laid her in the passenger seat where Claringdon had sat. He motioned Toy to help Tanya into a back seat. Claringdon trailed behind them without knowing quite what to do.

"If you want her out, sir, you're going to have to take her out yourself," Randall said. "I'm getting back into the fight. If I survive, you can press charges later."

"This isn't the end of it," Claringdon said.

0822 hours

"The Chinese have taken the ridge from the Marines," Fleming said as Angriff looked on. "They've screened and pinned down Bulldozer in Skull Valley the town and are trying to cut Highway 10 here, here, and here. The Marines are still trying to hold them off but are getting chewed up. We need to pull them out. And they've reached the highway here."

"That's Bulldozer One One Two?"

"Yes. Ripsaw and Buzzsaw were re-routed for air support, and they report at least two mechanized battalions in the area, but so far the highway is still open. One One Two sent video before..."

"Before what?" Angriff said.

"Before we lost the feed."

"Don't play games with me, Norm. If she's dead..." he forced the words out, "just tell me."

"We don't know anything yet. They took out two Chinese tanks and a bunch of infantry. Then something knocked out the feed."

From several stations down the long center table, Colonel Walling straightened. "General Angriff, First Armored reports they are at Bulldozer One One Two's position. Lieutenant Randall's tank is badly damaged and she is wounded, but the medics are with her now. They've called for medevac, but the LZ is hot. Apparently..."

"Apparently what?"

Walling looked uncomfortable. "General, it appears Captain Randall blocked the highway with his helicopter until the medics would attend to Lieutenant Randall. The tank battalion executive officer, Major Claringdon, used the word *extortion*."

"That is completely unacceptable," Angriff said. Faces turned at his reaction, as he knew they would. He tried to keep his relief from being too obvious.

He considered all the young men and women he sent into battle to be his children, and he wanted them to know it. In a unit where nobody's parents still lived, he was a father figure to them all. But at a fundamental level, there was something different about ordering your own flesh and blood into harm's way. He could not condone a court-martial offense, but the father in him wanted to shake his son-in-law's hand. Any doubts he might have had about Joe Randall vanished.

"Have the tanks spread out as far as is practicable in the direction of Skull Valley. Let's pull the Marines back to here, but bring their infantry and heavy weapons forward to support the tanks. If we can hold here until the First Infantry comes on line, we've got them. I doubt they were expecting a pitched battle on this scale, or air attacks. Their fuel situation has to be critical. We cannot let them rejoin with the other column."

"I just hope we have the firepower to contain them."

"There's no hoping to it."

North of Prescott, the 2nd Infantry Regiment moved out of their defensive positions just after sunup. When the first air strikes had gone in before dawn, the eastern Chinese column had stopped north of the tiny settlement of Paulden. As dawn broke, it spread onto the grounds of an abandoned firearms training compound. The ground was either flat or rolling, with excellent lines of sight. Confusion reigned but canceling the operation seemed unthinkable. The Chinese could not imagine they faced a new and much more dangerous enemy than expected.

The two American infantry battalions advanced on the Chinese force, but the Chinese blocked this with a nasty surprise. Infantry filled the trucks brought along to haul slaves, and half the tankers held heavy weapons instead of fuel. The sprawling battlefield meant the Americans kept trying to turn a flank, while Chinese moved to block them while holding open the road to Interstate 40. Late in the morning, the Army reconnaissance battalion made a drive to cut the Chinese off and surround them.

The Chinese position was precarious. They had the men and firepower to hold the Americans back, but the American artillery devastated their ranks. Wherever a defense coalesced for too long, it was soon engulfed by a metal storm of artillery. By early afternoon, the Chinese position was critical. Facing annihilation, the Chinese executed a fighting withdrawal. The exhausted Americans followed at a safe distance.

As afternoon shadows stretched over the battlefield, the ravaged Chinese fled west on Interstate 40, with a rear guard to stop pursuit. But the Americans had to worry about their own left flank. The further they chased the beaten column, the more exposed they became to Chinese tank formations in Skull Valley, a mere eight miles away. Stopping at the settlement of Drake, they faced the Chinese rear guard at Hell Canyon, where the retreating enemy had blown the bridges. Angriff called off the pursuit and shifted the 1st Infantry Battalion west, to cut off the Chinese armor in Skull Valley.

The Chinese armored corps tried to cut Highway 10 until noon. Fighting along the ridge near the highway swirled back and forth. For a few brief seconds a Chinese infantry squad used *Joe's Junk* for cover, but they were soon driven back.

Air strikes turned the tide. Knowing Patton had no air power, the Chinese had only brought vehicles useful in ground attack mode. The few SPAAAs carried a heavier ammunition load and left most of their SAMs at home. Moreover, it had been twenty-plus years since they'd last engaged enemy aircraft. With no practical way to practice anti-aircraft gunnery, all they could do was fire a lot of rounds and hope for the best.

They were sitting ducks.

The Americans targeted the SPAAAs first, destroying them early in the fight. By 1230 hours the Chinese commander realized he faced a professional military. And as impossible as it seemed, it was a professional *American* military force. He'd expected an easy victory and instead suffered heavy losses against an enemy of unknown strength. With no way of knowing he still outnumbered the Americans almost two to one, he ordered his scattered force to withdraw.

If the Chinese had attacked any spot on the ridge by Highway 10 in strength, they would have broken through. The entire American position would have crumbled. But they did not launch such an attack. The afternoon became a battle of fire and movement, as the Chinese withdrew and the Americans tried to trap them.

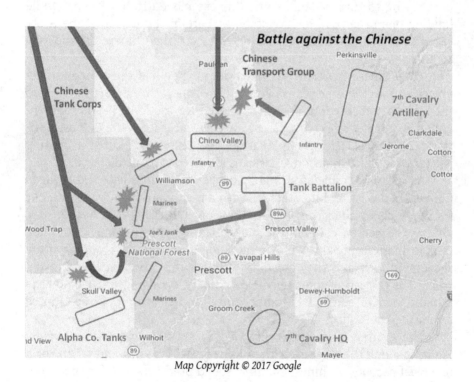

Map Copyright © 2017 Google

Chapter 38

The bastards tried to come over me last night. I guess they didn't know I was a Marine.

PFC Edward H. Ahrens, Tulagi, 1942

1423 hours, July 29

Standing watch was Lara Snowtiger's least favorite duty. But she knew its importance and was never distracted. And that watchfulness paid off.

She saw something in the far distance. But what? All she caught was a glimpse of a dust cloud, but it was miles away and she couldn't be sure before it vanished. Binoculars couldn't see through dirt. The Sonoran Desert was like an ocean chopped by wind and then flash-frozen where the swells became rolling hills. Besides the hills there were trees, cacti, bushes, dry river valleys, and arroyos. Any of them could hide an approaching enemy.

It might have been nothing more than a dust devil, spun up like a tornado by the rising thermals and gone as fast as it appeared. Or a herd of antelope chased by a predator. Yet Snowtiger's instincts told her it was neither of those things.

"Muthah fucker," Piccaldi said. "Who set the thermostat on Hell?"

"Poor baby, did the nasty heat wake you up? Wanna trade places?" she said.

"Fuck, no. I did my watch."

"At dawn," she said. "So SITFU and stop whining."

He rolled out from under the LAV-25. Sweat soaked his back and armpits, and he drank as much water as he could. Snowtiger glanced his way and snickered. Like her, Piccaldi was a killer. She also thought he could act like a little boy. He complained nonstop about the incessant swarming flies, ants, wasps, beetles, and mosquitoes. But the real threats, scorpions, centipedes, and rattlesnakes, didn't seem to worry him.

"Anything new from Prescott?" Piccaldi said, turning to their platoon leader, Lieutenant Embekwe, who sat on the shady side of the LAV. "Sounded like grim city over there earlier."

"Captain Sully might know, but I don't. Last I heard, the situation was pretty confused."

"By *pretty confused*," Piccaldi said, "you mean a clusterfuck, right?"

"The last I got was the Chinese had at least one reinforced armored division, but no air cover or artillery. I have no idea if that's accurate. It's just what Cap told us."

"Fighting a fucking armored division." Piccaldi shook his head. "With LAVs... damn."

"Yeah," Embekwe said. "We may be doing an about face before this is over."

"Let the good times roll."

Embekwe had spread the platoon over a series of low hills. The vehicles were hull-down, and only those Marines on watch were in the open. The rest hid from the burning sunlight, either under their vehicles or in the shade. Nobody sat inside them. With the engines off, it was like sitting in a convection oven.

Snowtiger resumed making slow sweeps across the desert to their front. She felt the sun and heat like anyone else, but her dark skin did not burn easily and the wide-brimmed Boonie hat protected her face. She could have crawled under a LAV as others did, but the vantage was better standing on the hill; the higher the elevation, the further she could see. Moreover, Piccaldi could not understand how she withstood the scorching sunlight and he couldn't.

Then she lowered the binoculars and cocked her head to one side. She'd started doing that as a little girl, and her grandmother had joked she was part German Shepherd. She felt something in the ground. Faint vibrations whispered in her feet as a slight tickle. There was no sound, just the least movement in the loose desert soil. She knelt, laying her palm on the ground. She paused like that, then turned from the east to the northwest. There, topping a small hill and moving their way at a dead gallop, were three men on horseback.

"Company coming," she said.

Without a word, the squad scrambled to battle stations. Piccaldi knelt with rifle in hand, ready to fire. "Where?" he said, scope to his eye.

"On our seven," she said. "Three men on horseback. They're armed and... they're wearing feathers in their hats."

Within a second he had acquired the target and focused on the middle rider. "Dope the wind, Lara." *Is there any wind?*

She raised her left index finger. "Two-two-five at five." *Winds out of the southwest at five miles an hour.*

"Engagement sequence completed. I'm losing the ballistic advantage, Loot."

"Don't shoot yet," Embekwe said. "Radetsky, get the Cap over here, pronto."

The two flanking riders peeled off, vanishing into the rolling hills, and the last rider slowed to a canter. Moments later the other two reappeared on small hills to either side, with only their heads and rifles visible. The guns pointed skyward.

"Skipper on the way," the LAV chain gunner, Ivan Radetsky, called down. "ETA five minutes."

"He's Apache," Snowtiger said as the rider drew near. "I think he's a chief."

"Hot shit, it's about fucking time something happened," Piccaldi said. "I hope he's a real Indian. How cool would that be?"

"Yeah," Snowtiger said. "Imagine meeting a real Indian."

"You know what I mean."

High overhead a prairie falcon screeched as it circled. It sounded like a battle cry.

Less than a minute later, the rider slowed his mount and stopped about thirty feet from the group. He ignored the weapons pointed at him and studied each of them in turn. His dark eyes seemed able to strip them naked and see into their hearts. He said nothing until he came to Snowtiger, when his expression softened.

"How is this possible?" he said in a deep voice. "How are you here?" Gray streaked his shoulder-length hair. Underneath brushed leather pants and a dirt-stained white cotton shirt, it was obvious there was hard muscle with little fat.

"I'm Choctaw," Snowtiger said, unsure what he meant.

"Of course you are." He nodded, as if she'd confirmed something he already knew. "I have little time for this mystery today, though. Who's in charge here? Is it you?"

"It's not me," Snowtiger said.

"Our company commander will be here in a minute," Embekwe said. "Until then, I am."

The rider inspected each of them again. He stopped when he came

205

to Piccaldi and regarded him for a moment, untroubled by the rifle pointed at his chest. "You are a deadly warrior, but you will never be the one in command. You are a tool used by the one who is. You," he continued, pointing to Embekwe. "You are too young. I will wait to speak with your commander."

"Yeah?" Piccaldi said, forgetting that Embekwe was the ranking man on the spot. "And how do you know I'll never be in command?"

"I watched you shoot a man who stood next to your captain. He knew the shot was coming yet he did not flinch, which means that he knew, without a doubt, that you would not miss. You are a perfect killing machine, and he used you to best advantage. But machines need others to operate them."

It took them all a moment to realize what he was talking about. "You were there when we rescued the family," Snowtiger said.

"You are his equal," the Apache said to her. "But there are two of you and only one of him."

"What do you mean, two of me?"

Before he could answer, the dust cloud from a Humvee announced the arrival of Captain Sully. Climbing from the passenger seat, Sully wiped his face with his forearm and eyed the stranger on the horse.

For his part, the Apache studied him back. "It was you I saw rescue that family. You were in charge. You are a man of courage, but to what end?"

"Somebody get me up to speed," Sully said. "Lieutenant?"

"This guy came riding up, Captain, said he would only talk to you. He's got covering fire on that hill over there, and that one."

Sully turned to the horseman. "I'm Captain Sully. Mind telling me who you are?"

"I am Govind, of the Western Apache. You are the one who took that family a few weeks ago. You stood like a statue while that man and the Indian woman shot the men pointing guns at you, and you did not flinch. I respect your courage, Captain, which is why I am here."

"Thank you. May I ask exactly what that means, and why you have men pointing guns at us?"

"The guns are not pointed at you; they are pointed at me. Those are my brothers. You wear uniforms like those men called Guards who serve the General named Patton, in the Republic of Arizona. You have the same white star on your vehicles, and you take people as captives like they do, but I am not a man who makes assumptions. We have watched you from afar for many weeks. I am here to find out who you serve, but I will not be made a prisoner. If you try to take me, my brothers will kill me. It is a fate preferable to a life of slavery."

"Then you'll be happy to know your brothers don't have to shoot you, because we don't serve this General Patton. Our general is named Angriff, we are Marines, and we serve only the United States of America."

Govind leaned back in his saddle. "There is no United States. America died decades ago."

"Reports of our death were greatly exaggerated. We're back. And we have no quarrel with the Apache, you're as American as I am, and I'm sure my general would like to meet you. But only at your request. We will not force you to do anything."

"What you say makes no sense, Captain. You saved that family, and then took them against their will. You even used a helicopter to help you do it. I was not aware there were any helicopters left that could fly. Yet we have seen others around your mountain."

"I don't know who *we* is, but if you saw the medevac helicopter, then you also saw the big red cross painted on its side. And I think you know exactly what that means... Govind? Did I say that right? The grandmother had been shot and was bleeding to death, so we flew her to our base for medical attention. None of those people is a prisoner, and none is a slave. Right this minute, as we speak, others of us are fighting in the city of Prescott to rescue thousands of people who were about to be sold as slaves. We're the good guys."

"Yes, we saw that and wondered about it. Some of my people think you wanted the slaves for yourself."

"We are there to save those people and free that city from the control of this so-called general."

Govind studied him but Sully matched his stare. "I do not see treachery in your eyes," the Apache finally said. "I hear no lies in your voice. If time were not short, I would think about this, but time *is* short and I must make a fast decision. So I will trust you, even though I don't understand what you mean."

"Thank you. Would you care to join us for some coffee? We could whip some up post haste."

"Thank you, coffee would be welcome, but there is no time. You must act now or be destroyed."

"Destroyed? By what?"

"She knows," he said, pointing to Snowtiger. "She has seen it."

Sully raised both eyebrows when he looked at Snowtiger.

"Right before he rode up, sir, I thought I saw a dust cloud, but it was far away and I wasn't sure. I don't know how he knew that. It could have been a dust devil. "

"Oh, no," Govind said. "Devils, yes, but not of dust. Those are men."

"Please just tell me what you mean," Sully said.

"Captain, about ten miles away is the army of the Caliphate, those that call themselves Sevens, followers of the New Prophet. They have moved from the place they call New Khorasan, but you may know it as Tucson. What this woman saw was the cloud raised by their vehicles."

"Army?" Sully said, stunned. "How big of an army are we talking about here?"

"No less than thirty thousand men, perhaps more, and more than five hundred vehicles."

"What's their heading? Where are they going?"

"Going? Captain, they're heading right for you."

CHAPTER 39

Boys, do you hear that musketry and that artillery? It means that our friends are falling by the hundreds at the hands of the enemy... let's go and help them. What do you say?

   Nathan Bedford Forrest

1453 hours, July 29

   "We've got 'em, Norm," Angriff said. "By God, I think we've got 'em."

   "We've still got to finish the job," Fleming said.

   "We just turned back an entire armored corps. I'll take that for our first fight."

   "General," Sergeant Major Schiller said, tapping Angriff on the shoulder.

   Angriff was watching a live feed over a corporal's shoulder as mortar rounds impacted near some Americans. The Chinese might have been retreating, but their rear guard was fighting hard. He pulled off the right cup of his headphones and Schiller spoke into his ear.

   "It's Captain Sully of Task Force Kicker. He asked for you personally, sir."

   "Tell him I'm busy, dammit."

   "Sir, he says the safety of the brigade is at stake."

   Annoyed, Angriff yanked off his headphones and took the radio mike from Schiller. "Angriff here. What is it, Captain? I'm up to my eyeballs in Chinese."

   "General," Sully said, his voice affected by a slight tremor that he could not suppress, "we have another army within seven miles of our position."

Angriff turned completely away from the video monitor and rubbed his chin. He paused long enough to make sure he had control of his voice. "Slow down and take it from the top, Captain. What are you talking about? What army?"

"Sir," Sully said, and now Angriff heard him suppressing his fear, "we were alerted to a major enemy presence closing on our position. We sent out two recon drones. They showed hundreds of military and civilian vehicles before they were shot down. The vehicles are flying Islamic flags, and intel from some local Apaches say they're from this Caliphate. The Apaches estimate their number north of thirty thousand. I repeat, that's three zero thousand. I need orders, sir. My company is strung out for miles. I've only got Safety on my right flank and they're spread out like we are."

"Captain, are you certain of your information? Can we trust these Indians, whoever they are?"

"One hundred percent certain, General. I'm not taking their word for it. I've sent you the video from our drones for confirmation. I've got to tell you, sir, that outside of the Liberty Bowl, I've never seen so many people in my life."

"What is your estimated time until engagement?"

"Unknown, sir, but not long. I think they're deploying to hit the whole line at once."

"We don't have enough men," Angriff said to himself, then turned his attention back to the call. "What was your name again, Captain?"

"Sully, sir, Martin S."

"That's right, I remember you now. You brought in that family during the first recon. All right, listen to me, Sully. You have to hold, do you hear me? I have no assets to send you right now, I've got to detach some from contact with the enemy and that will take time. All reserves are committed. You are our flank and you have to buy time. If you give way the whole brigade is in danger. Stand your ground. God bless you, Captain."

"Thank you, sir," Sully said. "But instead, would you ask God to pick up an M16 and bring some angels down here with Him?"

1505 hours

Bare of trees and flat at the peak, the slopes of Badger Mountain dominated the valley below like some enormous stone toad. The 7th Cavalry Headquarters Company was strewn on the crown. The view from its heights afforded clear observation of old Highway 169, which ran straight into Prescott from the east. It skirted north of the mountain before intersecting Interstate 17 well to the east. West of Badger Mountain, Highway 69 ran south toward Phoenix.

Dennis Tompkins had felt like the third wheel on a bicycle since the beginning of the attack. In theory he was third in command, and *God bless 'em!*, Generals Angriff and Fleming tried to keep him in the loop. But the truth was he had nothing to do except stand around and watch.

He'd given input early that morning, it was true. But his other warning, about the left flank, had gone unheeded and, as it turned out, ignoring him seemed to be the right call. That should not have been a surprise to anybody. His experience was in small unit actions, not major battles or coordinating combined arms attacks.

He was not asked for his advice again, and in the cramped confines of the command vehicle he was in the way. Nobody said anything, but nobody had to. So as the day wore on, he slipped out, joined his men in the shade of a tent, and speculated about the battle's progress.

They heard distant explosions, small arms fire, the shriek of artillery rounds, and the roar of helicopters diving in to the attack. From their high vantage point, they saw smoke and flames spread over a wide swath, but it was impossible to know who was doing what where.

"Kinda like watchin' a football game without knowin' who's playin'," Thibodeaux said. "But somebody down there is gettin' his ass kicked."

Two towering explosions on the far horizon brought all six men to the edge of the crest facing the long western slope. They were still there when a flurry of activity started in the MCC. Aides ran inside, while others left in a hurry. Sergeant Major Schiller sprinted out and headed for General Fleming's M1130, the eight-wheeled specialized control and command vehicle separate from Angriff's Mobile Command Center. Tompkins watched as Schiller pointed and gestured with General Fleming, then they both started running back to Angriff's trailer.

Tompkins called to him. "Sergeant Schiller, what's going on?"

Schiller stopped and took a moment to focus on who'd spoken. " General Tompkins, there you are. Would you please join Generals Angriff and Fleming in the MCC?"

"Something wrong?"

"You might say that, sir."

"On my way."

The MCC was a modified mobile home pulled by a tractor trailer. The original design had been for use in the Washington, D.C. area during a national security crisis. Tompkins entered through a side door.

Inside was bedlam.

The noise overwhelmed him. A dozen radio operators spoke to formations in the field. Officers stared at screens and shouted orders. At the far end, Nick Angriff and Norm Fleming were in a deep discussion. Their faces reflected obvious worry.

Tompkins noted a tangible scent permeating the narrow trailer, one he knew only too well. He had smelled it when hiding from enemies who'd stalked his command for fifty years. It was the smell of fear, a mixture of sweat and pheromones that hung in the air like an invisible fog. His brain translated the scent into thoughts, and he knew that something had gone disastrously wrong.

Schiller looked up and noticed him. "Back here, General."

Tompkins scooted along the narrow aisle on the right side of the trailer. In the small cleared area in the back stood, shoulder to shoulder, Angriff, Walling, Fleming, and himself, with Schiller at Angriff's elbow. Tompkins noticed they all wore sidearms, and Angriff wore two massive pistols in shoulder holsters crossed on his chest. The guns looked familiar, but Tompkins had not seen one in half a century and it took him a few seconds to remember it: a fifty-caliber Desert Eagle. Once, long before, a buddy had let him fire off a few rounds during target practice.

He also remembered they weren't decorative. Angriff used them in combat. Tompkins wondered how. The gun's power had hurt his wrist and shoulder for days. It was like firing a small cannon.

"Gentlemen, we have a dire situation," Angriff said without preamble. "Dennis, you were right for the second time and we should have listened to you. We stripped the left flank, leaving only a thin screen, and now we have no assets left in reserve. Two companies screening a twenty-mile line was a calculated risk, and it's backfired. Now they're facing an army of at least thirty thousand men, hundreds of vehicles of various types, both civilian and military. That's one hundred to one odds, people. One hundred to one.

"Task Force Kicker used two of its drones to scout this new force, but both were shot down. But before the video shut off, we got a pretty good look at what we're facing. It's that Caliphate we keep hearing about. They appear to be irregulars, but with plenty of RPGs and automatic weapons, like a huge mob. We are reliably informed they came from Tucson, which means they crossed the desert and so are disciplined, motivated, and tough. They fly Islamic flags, but unlike anything in our database. They are within five miles of Kicker and Safety," he said, pausing to glance at his watch, "and may already be in contact.

"I have ordered the rest of the Marine battalion back to their old positions, but it will take them at least two hours to disengage and move through Prescott. Redirecting artillery might take longer than that. Air assets should be available sooner.

"But here's the biggest problem, gentlemen. Not having ground reserves means that within an hour, either one of those highways below this mountain could be crawling with jimbangs. And they'll be climbing these slopes like ants, or hitting our rear areas in Prescott, including the evacuation camp. If we don't do something right now, it's *Remember the Alamo* time. And by *right now,* I mean in the next five minutes.

"At this moment, I see no choice but to prepare the entire brigade to disengage and retreat, but I'm praying for alternatives. Nothing is off the table. Every man and woman is expendable. Talk to me, boys."

Fleming spoke first. "Based on the position of the highway and the deployments, Kicker is in the crosshairs more than Safety. We could pull out a platoon and shift them to Kicker."

"It's already just a picket line. If we spread them out further, the enemy might slip through without us knowing it. We could lose the line and both companies. Then the whole brigade is flanked and we're caught between the Chinese and the jimbangs. We can't risk that. What about the battalion screening Flagstaff?"

"They're dug in and spread out. With the highway in the condition it's in, they're at least six hours away."

"And we've already been flanked once," Angriff said. "Leave them in place. Come on people, think."

"This is all my fault," Fleming said.

"No, it's not, and there's no time for that now," Angriff said. "Everything that happens is my responsibility. And just so you know, I've ordered Colonel Coghlan of First Artillery Battalion to prepare for the use of special ordnance."

There were six people who knew *special ordnance* meant tactical nuclear shells—the five men standing there and the S-4, Colonel Schiller. The implications of using nuclear weapons hammered home to Tompkins the desperation of the situation.

Angriff looked at each man in turn, but nobody said anything. "Surely there's something we can do."

Tompkins spoke up. "The headquarters company isn't committed. We've got seven LAVs, counting mine, including two mortars. That's a platoon right there. Arm everybody you can spare and let us plug the gap. I'll bet we can whip up half a company."

Angriff snapped his fingers. "Dennis, you're a damned smart man. I should have thought of that. Schiller, comb out supply, repair, as many bodies as you can find. Get those LAVs cranked up and running. Tell them they've got ten minutes to gear up and then they're on the road. Take all the ammo you can carry."

"Yes, sir," Schiller said. "Preference given to combat veterans?"

"Of course, but hurry," Angriff said, then paused, realizing what Schiller had meant. "Wait a minute..." There was a long silence, during which he studied the man he considered the most valuable soldier in the brigade. Then he pointed at the door. "Go."

Schiller grinned and headed down the line of radio operators, collecting those he wanted.

"With your permission, General, I'm gonna get my men and draw weapons and ammo," Tompkins said.

"Negative, Dennis. Major generals don't get into firefights, and your men..." Realizing what he was about to say, Angriff stopped.

"My men are what, sir? Too old? If that's what you mean, just say so."

"All right, your men are too old. Besides, if we don't stop them on the flank, you and your men will have all the fighting you want."

"With all due respect, General Angriff, my men and I have more combat experience than anybody else in this brigade. Hell, maybe in the whole country, and it's recent, too."

"Doesn't matter," Angriff said. "The answer is no."

"You just finished saying you should have listened to me in the first place, and that you would do so in the future. And here you are ignoring my advice again just a couple of minutes later," Tompkins said.

Norm Fleming glanced at Angriff, his expression shocked. Then Fleming spoke up, deflecting Angriff's rising anger. "I seem to remember a lieutenant general getting into a firefight against direct orders."

Angriff's glance seemed murderous, but Fleming had seen it many times and grinned. It meant Angriff knew he was right.

"General," Tompkins said. "Nick... I'm eighty-one years old. Whatever happens today, I don't have many years left. I'm third in command of this brigade, but I've never commanded anything bigger than a company. The truth is there are plenty of officers more qualified to lead it than I am. We need every man on that line, God knows, and especially men who won't fold and run. At the end of the day, I'm just a soldier like everybody else. I've shot it out with these bastards before, and I think you should let me do it again."

"You did say everybody was expendable," Fleming said.

Angriff studied Tompkins' watery blue eyes in their wrinkled sockets. His skin was a leathery brown, with dark spots on his forehead and deep creases in his cheeks, but there was a vitality in Dennis Tompkins that was lacking in others half his age.

The two men held each other's gaze for more than ten seconds, which seemed like an hour.

"Get your men and go," Angriff finally said. "But!" He pointed a finger and poked Tompkins in the chest. "Please don't get killed."

214

1508 hours

As *Tank Girl* settled to the hangar floor and Carlos shut down the engine, Joe Randall leaned back in his seat, took off his helmet, and rubbed his eyes.

"Son of a bitch," he said over the whine of the slowing engine. Morgan's dried blood covered his chest and arms. "What a day. Those fuckers aren't fuckin' around."

"That last triple A, honest to God, Joe, I don't know how you avoided it. This thing's not supposed to pull those kinds of Gs."

Randall shrugged. "I don't know, man. I just did it and prayed she wouldn't fly apart."

As the rotor slowed to a stop, Sergeant Rossi opened the pilot-side door and motioned Randall out of the cockpit.

Exhausted after his third sortie of the day, Randall did not move. "Give me a minute," he said, feeling sweat running down his back. "Any word on my wife? They oughta know something by now."

"Nothing, Captain, but this is turn and burn time. You've got fresh orders. We're to get you back in the air in ten minutes or less. Piss it out and drink it in. Coffee, energy bars, and Go-Juice on the table." When Randall sat unmoving, stunned, Rossi frowned. "Let's go, sir. We've gotta change the ordnance package, so I need to get the diagnostics check over with."

Finally climbing out, Randall wiped his forehead with a towel and headed for the table with the drinks. "Why are we changing the package? There's plenty of Chinese armor left out there."

Carlos handed him a cherry-flavored energy bar and a bottle of lemon Go-Juice. He didn't know how Randall could stomach the combination, much less like it.

"Not Chinese this time," Rossi called from inside the cockpit. "You're to head southwest, near Phoenix. I'm uploading the intel right now, but the short version is an army of jimbangs showed up out of nowhere. Tens of thousands of them, hundreds of vehicles, probably got Stingers. The Marines are holding the line with two light recon companies."

Already chewing, he couldn't say anything until he swallowed and washed it down with a long pull from the Go-Juice squeezer. In the meantime, he exchanged glances with Carlos.

"What the hell?" he finally managed to ask. "Is that PNN?"

"No, sir, that's confirmed, and right now you're the only air asset available."

"Where the fuck did some new army come from?"

Rossi put up her hands. "That's above my pay grade, Captain. Sir, I need to finish in the cockpit."

"Shit. Has anybody heard from Plotz?"

"As far as I know, she's still out there. I asked her chief right before you landed and he said she's okay." Rossi's tone made it clear that she didn't have time to answer any more questions. Her fingers moved over the helicopter's controls like a savant playing a grand piano.

As she and her team swarmed over the massive helicopter like a NASCAR pit crew, Randall and Carlos peed, zipped down their flight suits to cool off, re-zipped, grabbed some more Go-Juice, and were back in their chairs within five minutes.

"Flares reloaded," Rossi said. "Back to max ammo, but watch your engine temp, Captain; there's a couple of things we didn't have time to check."

Starting the engine, Randall stuck his arm out the side window and gave Rossi a thumbs-up, then lifted off to go fight an entire army. Once outside the mountain, *Tank Girl* banked south in search of prey.

CHAPTER 40

The enemy fought with savage fury, and met death with all its horrors, without shrinking or complaining. Not one asked to be spared, but fought as long as they could stand or sit.
     Davy Crockett

1452 hours, July 29
     Captain Sully noted the incongruity of it all. Blasting heat distorted vision and sucked the life out of any man foolish enough to stand for long in direct sunlight. The daytime belonged to snakes, scorpions, and lizards. Tufts of grass sprang from the powdery mustard soil, so much like the moon dust in Afghanistan. Rocks lay in piles of red and brown and black.
     Yet flowers of all sizes and shapes also carpeted the scorched landscape. From delicate blues to bloodiest reds, they painted the desert floor, reminding him of his favorite Impressionist painters. Majestic saguaro cacti peppered the boulder-strewn hills like sentinels watching for intruders. Mesquite and riparian trees grew tall along shallow stream beds. At another time, he would have found the panorama breathtaking.
     But not now. Now the enemy was coming. They were almost within mortar range, but he would not give the order to open fire until they were too close to miss. Between the rolling nature of the terrain, the boulders, and the cactus, visibility in places was less than a hundred yards. A mass of humanity headed right for them like a swarm of army ants, relentless and voracious. And while they looked like a mob, they

moved like an army. If they wanted to even delay the attackers, every shot had to count. The Marines had to wait until they couldn't miss before opening fire, and then pour it on.

Sully surveyed his re-deployments yet again. The odds against his command were hopeless, yet he tried to spot a miracle defensive trick he might have overlooked. They had dug in at the top of the tallest hills in the area, no more than seventy-five feet high, but with long slopes and excellent fields of fire. Some three hundred yards to his left was the shoreline of Horseshoe Reservoir. It made a solid anchor, as far as it went.

His far right was less vulnerable. Jagged mountains and foothills made for rough country. Beyond those mountains to the west was a broad, flat valley, cut by a few deep arroyos. Even further west were more mountains and impassable rough country. Getting through there would take hours, even without opposition.

Then came the wide flat country bordering Interstate 17. That freeway had once hummed with traffic moving north from Phoenix. Sully had placed an entire platoon there, at the junction with Echo Company, a/k/a Task Force Safety. Echo had responsibility for Interstate 17 itself. The sun-bleached asphalt had cracks choked with weeds and flowers, but it was still navigable at speeds up to thirty or more miles per hour. A vehicle moving north could turn west at Highway 69 and be in Prescott within sixty minutes.

Ruined buildings bordered the freeway and lay scattered about the landscape. By stretching his own line further, Sully had allowed Safety to concentrate firepower at the interstate, with their right flank anchored on Lake Pleasant less than four miles to the west. Both company commanders had assumed the enemy would hit the interstate hardest, so they put the bulk of their forces there. But Sully knew there was another weak spot to worry about: his extreme left flank.

The reservoir protected his left flank, but everything else worried him. To his immediate left were several deep ravines. Beyond those was a hill, perhaps thirty feet high, near the shoreline of the reservoir, a small knob of rock he'd tagged, with grim humor, Last Stand Hill. When he'd been a teenager and faced a dilemma, his mom used to ask him, *Is this the hill you want to die on?* Such was the question now. Was that chunk of useless desert worth the lives of his Marines?

If the enemy took that hill, they would turn his left flank. The entire Marine position might then crumble, all the way to Lake Pleasant, with tens of thousands of Islamists pouring into the brigade's unprotected rear. He couldn't let that happen, so the grim answer was yes; holding the hill was worth the lives of his Marines. Just like Custer's 7th Cavalry, his men would live or die on Last Stand Hill.

He had placed a precious LAV-25 there, hull-down, but there had been no time to dig a proper revetment. This left a lot of the armored fighting vehicle exposed as a target for RPGs. They were fortunate because all their LAV-25s were the upgraded A2 variant, with additional armor and a fire suppression system, which enhanced their survivability in combat. Speed gave them a battlefield advantage as reconnaissance vehicles. And if fighting was unavoidable, they carried a nasty punch. But LAVs were not designed for static defensive roles.

Also on Last Stand Hill, he'd put a heavy machine gun squad and six infantrymen. Piccaldi was there with both of his rifles. Snowtiger was on the same hill as Sully and Embekwe, but placed to cover both their front and Last Stand Hill. She had her M110 lying on a towel, with fifteen magazines arranged for quick reloads and her M40 ready in her arms.

The enemy was within range. Sully had deployed his Marines in the best way he knew, to both block the enemy and give his people a chance to survive. He was not fooling himself that they could last long against such numbers, though. He knew that, unless reinforcements showed up soon, his company would be overrun. No matter how many they killed, more were behind them, and there weren't enough Marines to kill them all.

But it was time to start trying.

1515 hours

Snowtiger was fastidious when preparing to shoot. First, she did a quick cleaning of both rifles. It wasn't necessary. She cleaned the M40 every day without fail, like a religious ritual, but the condition of her weapon was a part of her environment she could control, a risk she could mitigate, and she never took unnecessary chances.

Next, she examined the magazines for both of her rifles, reloading one because it might have gotten dirty. Finally, she went through the motions of feeling every magazine on her shooting vest. Her fingertips moved over them and memorized their differences. In the heat of combat, losing even one second while reloading could be fatal.

Chapter 41

Then out spake brave Horatius,
The Captain of the Gate:
"To every man upon this earth
Death cometh soon or late.
And how can man die better
Than facing fearful odds,
For the ashes of his fathers,
And the temples of his Gods."
       Thomas Babington Macaulay, *"Horatius at the Bridge"*

1532 hours, July 29

Dirt spattered his boot as a bullet smacked the desert near his left foot. Sully didn't move. Another round hit two feet to his right, but he kept the binoculars to his eyes.

"Cap, they've got you zeroed in," said Company Sergeant Meyer.

"Damn." Sully scanned to his right. "Whoever these people are, they're not a mob. There's discipline out there."

"Please, Captain, take cover."

"Captain, I've got the shooter locked in. Permission to fire?" Lara Snowtiger said.

"Permission granted."

Five hundred yards away, shrouded by dust: Snowtiger watched the man with dark hair sighting on Sully. The rifle had flashed twice with two misses, and she wasn't going to let him get a third chance.

Slowing her breathing, she squeezed the trigger. She didn't hear the *crack* of the bullet; she only felt the recoil into her right shoulder. She kept the scope on her target and saw the distant man's head explode in a haze of red.

"Target down," she said.

"Nice shot." Sully finally dropped behind the crest of the hill and slid a few feet on his back. He motioned for the radio. Taking a deep breath, he keyed the mike. "Kicker All, this is Kicker Real. Heads up, boys and girls. They've split into four columns, and most of the vehicles appear to be heading for the interstate. Today is why you get the big bucks. Remember your orders. No retreat. No fall back. We stand or die on this line. The entire brigade is counting on us, which is why General Angriff put Marines here instead of Army. Good luck and good shooting."

He'd no sooner finished than Meyers handed him another radio. "It's Prime, sir."

"Kicker Real here."

"Captain Sully, this is General Fleming. The cavalry's on the way, son, we're sending you everything we've got, but you've got to hold on until they get there. Can you think of anything else we can do?"

Crawling to the crest, Sully glanced at the tidal wave of humanity heading his way. "Yes, sir. Send more burps."

1537 hours

Nick Angriff paced the cramped headquarters trailer like a caged panther. He stopped when a corporal manning one of the radios leaned back and addressed him.

"General, Silver Fox asked Kicker Real if they needed anything and Kicker's response doesn't make sense."

"What was it?" Angriff said.

"He just said, 'Send more burps.' Why would he want more of the enemy, sir?"

A thin smile creased Angriff's face as he thought of the mythic bravado from the Battle of Wake Island in 1941, where the Marines had been surrounded and without hope of rescue. The legend said the American command at Pearl Harbor had asked if they needed anything . Lt. Commander Cunningham, the CO, had radioed back, "Send more Japs."

"That man's getting the biggest medal I can find."

General Muhdin was not sure about the exact strength of the forces opposing him, nor of their exact nature. But he had no illusions about his own army. He knew them to be a fanatical mob more afraid of their own leaders than their enemy. In military terms, they were good only for mass attacks. Anything requiring subtlety or creative thinking on the battlefield was beyond their capabilities.

Having no other choice, he launched his men at what he saw as the weak points in his enemy's defense. He expected to overwhelm what he thought was a small number of Patton's half-trained and ill-equipped troops, like his own. He believed he faced men called LifeGuards. He didn't know that he was actually up against real warriors.

He watched his regiments move into position to attack. It was he who'd formed the Sevens into regiments of roughly one thousand men, each one named for something sacred to the Caliphate. They were not regiments in the American sense of the word, because such organization required a large number of qualified officers. Yet mob or not, Muhdin was proud of them. There was discipline in the ranks, too. The men knew how to use their weapons and they obeyed orders. For those who hesitated or disobeyed, punishment was swift and severe. After all, if your actions guaranteed your place in Heaven, what fear could death hold?

The plan was simple because it had to be. Muhdin intended to attack down three main axes, while infiltrating in the areas between. The first column was also the weakest, with no more than three thousand men. They would try to turn the far right flank of the American position, the one anchored on Lake Pleasant.

The middle column, less than two miles away, would drive straight north on old Interstate 17. This force was by far the strongest. Led by five rebuilt Bradleys and three working Abrams tanks, behind those crowded hundreds of civilian trucks, SUVs, and cars. All carried as many riders as could fit inside or hang on. No less than fifteen thousand men followed on foot.

Once through the defenses, they would drive at maximum speed to seize Prescott. A large contingent he ordered to take the big mountain in the distance, the one his map labeled Badger Mountain.

That left ten thousand men to assault his enemy's far left flank. From what Muhdin could see, only a scattering of LifeGuards stood in his way. His only concern was all of the enemy vehicles. What were they, and where had they all come from?

—❧—

1547 hours

They lay on the opposite slope of the hill, below the crest. Sully knew they still had two or three minutes before opening fire, so he turned to Sergeant Meyer lying next to him. "How are you holding up?"

"I'm good, sir." But Meyer's hand trembled as he smoked a cigarette.

"You ever killed anybody, Meyer?"

"Not sure, Cap. I shot at a lot of burps in Afghanistan and Syria, and I think I hit some of them, but I can't say for sure I killed any. No time to count bodies."

"Yeah," Sully said. "Right. You're a good Marine, Meyers."

On his right, Lara Snowtiger lay at the crest, sighting through her scope. Bullets kicked up dirt here and there, but with her Ghillie suit pulled over her head, she was invisible.

"What's the range, Lara?" he said.

"Three-two-zero, Cap."

Sully signaled *open fire* to the mortar squad and both tubes coughed. The first shells arced toward the enemy. The nature of the terrain meant the Sevens would only expose themselves as they crested the rolling hills. Once in the lee of the next hill, they would be safe from direct fire. To prevent the enemy gathering there to get organized, Sully had directed his mortars to lay their shells in those hidey holes.

The *whump* of exploding mortar rounds prompted a yell, and a few brave souls charged the Marine positions. As thousands more joined in, it changed from a primal scream to something both old and new. *Nabi Akbar! Nabi Akbar!* The army of the Caliphate jumped to its feet and sprinted at the Americans, like a massive Japanese banzai charge.

"Cap..." Snowtiger said in a calm voice. She centered her crosshairs on a man who appeared to be giving orders. "...guess who's coming for dinner."

Motioning for the radio, Sully keyed the mike. "Kicker All, this is Kicker Real. Time to earn your pay. Fire at will."

Snowtiger squeezed the trigger and a red patch blossomed on her target's left breast. He toppled backward, but she had already moved to another man. Then the rest of the squad opened up.

The LAV-25 nearest her blasted away with both its coaxial M240 machine gun and the second machine gun mounted on the turret top. The chain gun was silent for the moment. All along the lines, Marines poured fire into their attackers. Shell casings piled up around them. An explosion below the crest of the hill sent dirt raining on Sully and Snowtiger. Bullets zipped past their heads.

The Sevens' tactics were simple—each man ran as fast as he could toward the Americans. Some fired as they moved and some stopped to aim. A lot had RPGs. While changing magazines, Sully noted with alarm how close they already were.

Then the chain guns opened fire.

The M242 Bushmaster was an externally powered, chain-driven, single-barrel weapon. It could fire in semi-automatic, burst, or automatic modes. The feed was a metallic link belt with dual-feed capability. The term *chain gun* derived from the use of a roller chain that drove the bolt back and forth.

The massive 25mm shells could destroy anything up to, and sometimes including, a tank. At point-blank range, high explosive shells tore into the charging infantry, ripping them to shreds and blowing huge gaps in their lines. Like a chainsaw hacking through a grove of saplings, the Sevens fell in heaps. Limbs spun away and blood sprayed the air with a red mist. Men flew backwards while others rolled down the hill, some screaming, some not.

But others returned fire. An RPG round exploded on the reverse slope just below the LAV, then another went high, flying past the turret at 295 feet per second. Sully heard a wet *thunk* sound to his left and saw PFC Brutonski roll down the hill, trailing blood.

Turning back, he fired at a man in jeans and a ragged shirt who knelt on a knoll, aiming an RPG. The bullet struck the man in the forehead, snapping his head back. By reflex, he pulled the trigger. The grenade launcher swiveled downward as he fell and the explosive charge rocketed into the ground between two of his fellow Sevens. The blast blew them sideways.

Beside him, Snowtiger fired like a machine. Load, aim, fire; load, aim, fire; and with every squeeze of the trigger another Seven toppled.

Not every Seven carried a rifle or RPG. Like Soviet troops early in World War Two, they picked up weapons from men who fell. Also like the Red Army, hand-picked men aimed machine guns at their backs with orders to shoot anyone who retreated. They fell by the score, but in their frenzy of kill-or-be-shot madness, the volume of fire aimed at the few Marines lying prone behind the hill was like a hurricane.

Snowtiger pushed the last loaded magazine into her M40. With the back of her left hand, she wiped sweat and dirt from her eyes. She glanced at Last Stand Hill just in time to see something slam into the right front tire of the LAV parked there. The blast blew off the tire and lifted the twelve-ton vehicle several feet in the air. The commander flew out of the turret, rolled to a stop, and didn't move.

When the LAV slammed back down, it leaned to the right like a listing ship. Seconds later another explosion blew the machine gun crew backward.

The only Marine left fighting on Last Stand Hill was Piccaldi.

For several seconds she watched him sight and aim, as though on the target shooting range. And with every squeeze of the trigger, another Seven fell. But there were hundreds charging him, and he could not kill them all before being overrun.

"Cap!" she yelled. "Captain Sully!"

Sully ducked below the crest, his face red and streaked with sweat. "What?"

"Sir, Zo's all alone. If they take that hill, we're fucked. I'm going to help."

Before Sully could say anything, she grabbed the M110 and five 20-round magazines, gathered herself, and took off at a sprint to cover the two hundred yards to Last Stand Hill. She had only gone twenty yards before the enemy spotted her, but Snowtiger was quick on her feet. Despite bullets whizzing past her ears, she zig-zagged through no-man's land and made it across. She hit the dirt beside Piccaldi.

"Couldn't stay away, huh?" He sighted on yet another burp.

"This position is too important to leave in your hands," she said, panting from the run.

Piccaldi looked her in the eyes for one brief moment. "Thanks for coming, Lara, but I think we're the only ones left."

"I think you're right. I'm moving to the other side." She nodded at the LAV.

Before she could move, Piccaldi reached out and stopped her. Confused, she met his eyes.

"Don't you dare get killed," he said, then released her.

"You either," she said.

Scooting downhill first, she moved behind the knocked-out LAV and dug into hard-packed soil on its left side, lying prone at the crest. She leveled the gun on its bipod. To her left, three Marines lay groaning from wounds. Two gave her a thumbs-up and went back to giving themselves first aid. All she could do to help was keep the Sevens at bay, so she laid the magazines out for fast reload and took aim. There were targets everywhere.

Between her and Piccaldi, they had no more than two hundred rounds. The math was easy. Even if every shot they fired struck home and was fatal, they were still going to die. They needed more firepower.

1604 hours

It was all happening exactly as Sully had known it would. His Marines were slaughtering the onrushing enemy, but there weren't enough of them. Soon it would be hand to hand, and that would be the end. Emptying his magazine into a knot of burps only thirty yards away, he reached over Meyer's prone form and grabbed the radio. He spoke in open language on the common frequency.

"Overtime Prime, this is Kicker Real. Pressure all along my line. I have heavy casualties and at least four LAVs out of action. My extreme left flank is held by two Marine snipers. I repeat, two Marines are holding my left flank. If they're overrun, this line is lost. Mortars are out of ammo; crews are on the line. If you're coming, for God's sake, hurry."

1605 hours

They all heard Sully's mayday.

"John, can you get us there?" Tompkins said.

"I can if ya tell me the way," John Thibodeaux answered. "An' a road might be nice, too."

Behind them followed the rest of the headquarters company vehicles, crammed with clerks, computer technicians, supply specialists, and every surplus man or woman who could carry a rifle. Tompkins studied the map as they bounced down the broken pavement of what had once been I-17, tracing the route with his finger. Finally he stabbed at the map. "On your left, John. There should be a turnoff coming up soon."

A few seconds later, Thibodeaux nodded. "I see it."

"Take that road for about three miles, then we've gotta go cross country. And for Christ's sake, floor it."

The danger was not only on the left flank, where Piccaldi and Snowtiger fought all alone on their hill. Interstate 17 ran almost due north through a flat valley more than a mile wide. The ruins of gas stations and strip malls dotted the landscape. There were a few low hills, but it was ideal country for fast-moving vehicles.

The two Marine companies, Dog and Echo, had done what they could to fortify the area in a short time. They blew holes in the roadbed and rolled boulders onto the pavement. Placement of the LAVs concentrated on the highway instead of the desert. Their chain guns could chew up anything that came their way, including Abrams tanks if they found a sensitive spot. Three teams using FGM-148 Javelin anti-tank missiles fortified their positions overlooking the interstate. And then they waited.

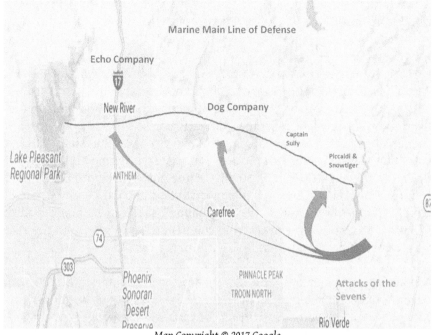

Map Copyright © 2017 Google

1617 hours

When *Tank Girl* first lifted out of the hangar, Joe Randall had felt nauseous at the memory of his wife bleeding in his arms. The metallic smell of her blood on his flight suit dragged him back to that horrible moment he'd looked into her slack face, white from blood loss. But then, forcing the memories from his mind, he re-focused on his mission. He firewalled the throttle and *Tank Girl* thundered south at a height of one hundred feet.

His fatigue vanished in a wash of adrenaline. News of the fight along I-17 made navigation easy; he just followed the road. Smoke on the horizon pinpointed the exact location of the fighting as wildfires added to the palls from burning vehicles. He glanced at the air speed indicator, which registered more than 200 knots. The giant helicopter vibrated as the turboshaft engines strained for every last ounce of horsepower.

Shapes grew in the forward targeting sight. Vehicles of every size, color, and purpose filled the display. He saw everything from huge delivery trucks and tractor trailers to... Randall could not believe what he saw. Tanks! After a morning spent hunting Chinese Type 98s, here were yet more tanks, and Abrams, no less. *Tank Girl* was again hunting her natural prey.

227

As the range decreased, Randall made his musical selection. The distinctive opening guitar riff filled the cockpit.

Carlos nodded; even he knew that one. "Good choice. I like this song."

"We're comin' in low and hot," Randall said, aiming at an Abrams. "If that's not flirtin' with disaster, I don't know what is."

A dozen streams of bright blobs floated toward *Tank Girl*. Tracers from a dozen different machine guns crisscrossed the sky, all firing at them. The M1A1 dead ahead poured out fire with its main battery, smashing Marine positions as it drove north. Carlos armed four Dragonfire anti-tank missiles and the 30mm Gatling gun armed with EXACTO AP rounds. From the right came an explosive flash and Carlos saw it immediately. From the corner of his eye, Randall saw him launch a pod of flares to lure the Stinger away from the helicopter. A glance in the rear view camera showed the missile explode in their wake.

The hardest part for Randall was waiting to press the trigger. The Comanche screamed over the bleached asphalt of Interstate I-17, with dozens of people trying to shoot them out of the sky, but he knew firing too soon would be pointless. Hitting the tank wasn't enough; the Dragonfire missiles also had to penetrate its armor.

Finally came the exact right instant to start the killing. In his mind's eye Randall could see the devastation he was about to unleash. Then he motioned to Carlos, who pressed the trigger.

Chapter 42

And when he gets to heaven,
To Saint Peter he will tell;
"One more Marine reporting, sir.
I've served my time in Hell!"
>   PFC James A. Donahue, USMC, 1st Marine Division, H Company, 2nd Bat-
>   talion, 1st Regiment

1618 hours, July 29

The Sevens were less than fifty yards away, so close Snowtiger couldn't miss if she tried. The 7.62mm rounds ripped through flesh and vital organs. She was killing dozens, but they numbered in the hundreds.

She paused, wiped sweat from her right eye, and glanced between the tires of the damaged LAV on her right. Piccaldi had been matching her shot for shot. To her horror he was on his back, rolling from side to side and slapping the ground with his left hand. Blood soaked his right shoulder.

Without a thought, she scrambled around the LAV and fell to her knees beside Piccaldi. Bullets whined past her ears and smacked the ground.

"Shit," she said, unbuttoning his shirt to inspect the wound.

"Lara, stop!" Piccaldi said.

"Shut up, Zo. I've got to stop the bleeding."

"No." Piccaldi reached across his body and grabbed her arm with his left hand. "Listen to me, Lara! Don't pet a burning dog!"

"I'm not going anywhere, so hold still."

Piccaldi pulled her close until his mouth was inches from hers. "If you don't leave, we're both dead. Go!"

She cut a strip away from his pants leg with her knife, wrapped it around his shoulder, and pulled it tight, knotting it. Her chiseled features had taken on a determined look. "Orders are orders, Zo. Stand or die, go tell the Spartans, and all that shit."

"Get the fuck out of here," he said in a weaker voice.

"I'm not leaving you."

She stared at him for two seconds and looked up. Four men, less than ten yards away, raised their rifles. In one smooth motion, she hefted the M110 and put bullets through all four of them, one after the other in the space of three seconds.

But hundreds more followed those.

What to do? Her mind processed the situation in nanoseconds. Piccaldi would be dead in minutes, but if she tried to stop his bleeding, they would all be overrun.

The choice was clear. She had to stop the Sevens, but how? The M110 was a precision weapon and she needed something with mass killing power. The fifty-caliber machine gun was upside down at the bottom of the hill. What else was there?

The LAV.

The missing front right tire left it leaning, but the machine gun and chain gun looked undamaged. Snowtiger scrambed up the side. Bullets ricocheted off the metal around her. One round creased her left wrist, leaving a streak of burned flesh.

LAVs had two hatches in the turret, one for the gunner and the other for the commander. In the right hatch, she found the vehicle commander, dead from a jagged neck wound. Sticky blood puddled in his seat and dripped to the floor. Flies swarmed over the warm feast. Using every bit of her strength, Snowtiger manhandled the body out of the seat.

Then, as she was about to climb in, something slammed into her left shoulder and knocked her to her knees. Searing pain shot through her body, like somebody had shoved a white-hot knife into her flesh. Panting at the pain, she saw her shirt turn dark with blood. But with a huge effort, she pulled herself through the hatch.

After sliding into the seat, she called out. A faint voice answered; someone was still alive below.

"Can you fight?" she called down.

"No," the man said. "I don't think so."

Like many Marines, Snowtiger had been cross-trained and had actually operated a LAV turret before. She knew how to shoot both the chain gun and the coaxial 7.62mm machine gun. The computer display verified the gun was already set to shoot HEI-T rounds, high explosive incindiary, at a low rate of fire. Her breath came in gulps, yet somehow she aimed the gun.

A group of three Sevens had stopped ten yards from the LAV, wearing loose white pants and long-sleeved tunics. They sprayed the hill with bullets. She laid the aiming reticle on the center of mass of the one on the left and fired.

At point-blank range, the 25mm rounds blew them apart. The first shell struck its target above the groin and did not explode until it had penetrated his spine, blowing him in two. His head and shoulders landed twenty feet away while his hips and legs vanished. The second man had his left shoulder shot away, and the third flew backward minus his head.

When the chain gun opened fire again, most of the Sevens dove to the ground. The horror of seeing their friends blown to bits stunned them. A few stayed on their feet and were cut down by the next burst. But they did not stay down long. Bullets tore up the dirt as machine guns fired *behind* them. In knots they sprinted from one hill to another, going to ground as the turret rotated their way, jumping up when it moved on.

Snowtiger kept up a continuous fire, slowing the attack to a crawl, but not stopping it. She didn't think about her situation, or her pain, or even saving Piccaldi. Her mission was to hold the hill long enough for help to come, and every minute she bought was a minute more for the brigade to react and strike back.

More Sevens went down. One lost an arm and wandered backward, screaming for his mother. Snowtiger felt faint as pain, fatigue, and blood loss sapped her strength. She blinked at the shimmering stars clouding her vision and focused on the display. For several long minutes, the threat of decapitation by a 25mm shell held back the swarm of Sevens, even as their own comrades shot at them to make them move.

Two things happened at once. First was the dreaded *click* of an empty magazine. She hadn't noticed the low ammunition warning on her computer display, but before she could look for more, a second RPG round slammed into the LAV. There was a flash as the rocket-propelled grenade penetrated the hull low on the left side. Snowtiger's right shoulder slammed into the hard metal of the hatch.

She screamed as agony overwhelmed her. Her right arm went limp as pain shot through her neck, shoulders, and torso. Her brain told her to tilt her head back and keep screaming.

But the most basic of animal instincts, survival, cut through the haze in her mind, warning of a new and deadly danger: smoke. A spark of consciousness begged her to wake up and get out, but she was too groggy and injured to respond. When she tried to move, her head lolled from side to side.

Get out!

The warning came in the voice of her lost twin sister, Sara. It screamed through the murk in her mind, connecting at some primal level with her physical brain. It felt like someone shook her, trying to wake her up.

Get up and get out, now!

Her body's last reserves of energy poured through her. For a moment her mind cleared and the pain subsided enough to think. She had to get out of the smoldering LAV before the stored ammo cooked off. Her left arm hung useless and though her right arm was numb, she lifted it far enough to hook on the hatch rim. Before she stood, she called down to the man she'd spoken to earlier. He didn't respond and she was in no shape to try and drag him out.

Using her right elbow, and then her arm as sensation returned, she push-clawed her way onto the turret top. When the Sevens realized the LAV wasn't firing any more, they filled the air around her with bullets. Lying behind the turret for several seconds, she saw Piccaldi lying motionless in the dirt, his M110 beside him. Twenty yards away, a skirmish line of Sevens rose and moved forward, squeezing off shots as they came. In a minute, they would find Piccaldi helpless at their feet and she was not going to let that happen.

"Zo," she said, slurring the word. Pulling with her right hand, leaving a smear of blood, she swung her legs around and slid off head first. She hit the hull, bounced off, and slammed into the dust.

The powdery topsoil matted her face and hands. Her eyes teared up and made the world appear as if she were underwater. Piccaldi lay ten feet away and she crawled toward him. Once beside him, she checked the pulse at his neck—shallow, but steady. Then a bullet struck the hillcrest two feet from his head and, without thinking, she lay on top of him.

Using her right arm, she pulled over his M110, got the butt into her armpit, and hefted the rifle onto its bipod. Immediately she saw the Sevens moving forward ten yards away, rifles swiveling as they looked for her. She dropped three of them before the rest could shoot. She ducked and buried her face in Piccaldi's back, where she could smell his sweat and his blood. Clods of dirt spattered her as bullets chewed up the terrain.

A bullet grazed her left temple and felt like somebody'd hit her with a hammer. She heard something to her right. Her head wobbled and everything was a blur, but she saw someone standing there. He seemed translucent, as if she could see through him to the desert beyond. He was holding something, a weapon, in both hands and near his waist. As she watched, stupefied, he lifted the weapon. Was it a sword? A hatchet, an axe? Her mind couldn't process the images any more. Whatever it was, he stepped forward and lifted it over his head, preparing for the killing stroke. Snow-tiger knew she was about to die, but she was too weak to move.

1633 hours

Four hundred yards behind Last Stand Hill, they heard the sounds of gunfire dead ahead. John Thibodeaux drove like a wild man, bouncing and skidding cross country at max speed. Dennis Tompkins had his binoculars focused on the LAV ahead when something struck it and exploded. Smoke began curling skyward. Seconds later, someone crawled from the top hatch and jumped to the ground, but there were no signs of anyone still fighting. Were they too late?

"Head's up, Dugout," he said into his helmet mike, using the code name for his little force. "On my command we advance to that hill on the extreme left and hold it come hell or high water. Mortars stay here and support; put your rounds fifty yards east of our position. We will correct fire once we're there. No retreat, folks; that's where we stand or die! Move out!"

"Target identified," Schiller said from behind the chain gun. "Permission to fire?"

"Hell, yes," Tompkins said. He saw what Schiller saw.

A man in a long white robe had crested the hill and aimed his rifle at two Marines prone on the reverse slope. Tompkins couldn't tell if they were still alive, but something must have gone wrong, because the burp raised the rifle over his head as if to club them to death. Then, just as he was swinging down, the chain gun over Tompkins' shoulder fired a three-round burst that blew the burp out of sight.

"Damn, son!" Tompkins said. "Nice shootin'."

"Target destroyed," Schiller said, every bit as surprised—and pleased—as Tompkins.

The other LAVs took off when he told them to and were only seconds away from reaching Last Stand Hill.

"Let's go, John!" Tompkins said. "We're holding up the rear."

1633 hours

General Ahmednur Muhdin valued nothing more than his Leica binoculars. The post-Collapse world no longer made such precise instruments. But rank had its privileges, and as the top-ranking general in New

Khorasan, it was his prerogative to keep such rare treasures for himself.

With the Leica mounted on a tripod, Muhdin could see the entire battlefield from his position five hundred yards east of the Marine lines. He watched his men advance through heavy fire, and had to admit the infidels could fight. He hadn't realized Patton commanded such a strong force. It didn't look like more than a handful of enemies held the little hill on his right.

But every time he thought the enemy were all killed, they started shooting again. Hundreds of his men lay dead and dying all over the desert. When the armored vehicle started firing its chain gun again, he regretted sending all his own combat vehicles to break through at the highway. Fortunately, somebody hit it with another RPG round, which seemed to kill it once and for all.

Stepping back from the binoculars, he allowed a servant to wipe the dirty sweat from his face. He motioned to another man, who handed him a wooden cup filled with water. Blinking and rubbing his eyes, Muhdin bent and looked through the Leica again.

His men were like waves in a stormy sea, washing ashore and sweeping all before them. Dozens of them had finally reached the little hill on the shore of the lake. They charged up its side and disappeared over the crest. The battle was over and won. Now they could wheel left and attack the enemy on the next hill from the flank and rear, roll over them, and continue to the next hill, and the next, until the road to Prescott was open. It was time for him to move forward and direct the next attack.

But before he could move, the first man over the crest flew backward in a spray of red. A second wave reached the crest and he saw them raise their rifles and start shooting at something on the other side. Then something ripped through them, too. Many rolled backward, dead. Yet more men poured over the crest and disappeared down the other side.

1639 hours

Hundreds of men wearing white robes poured over the hill waving guns. Some knelt to loot the Marine bodies lying in the dirt, while others kept running until they spotted the five LAVs speeding right for them. Dennis Tompkins saw a few of the weapons he dreaded most, the rocket-propelled grenade. But for the sake of the Marines scattered over the hillside, they couldn't stop.

"RPGs, watch it, watch it!" he yelled into the mike, forgetting radio discipline. "Open fire, but don't hit the Marines!"

Swiveling the pindle-mounted 7.62mm machine gun, Tompkins heard Schiller start blasting away with the Bushmaster. The other four

LAVs joined in. Bullets clanged off the turret, but he squeezed the trigger and watched tracers arc toward the mob running at him. The firefight was quick and one-sided. The combined firepower of five chain guns and ten machine guns mowed down the Sevens by the dozen. Only one man fired an RPG round, and it missed. The other survivors broke and ran.

1641 hours

Muhdin heard the staccato chatter of chain guns beyond the hill. Within seconds, the ugly snouts of more of those damned AFVs moved into view atop the hill. Their chain guns and machine guns cut wide swaths in his men.

Where had those come from?

It was too much to expect men who were not trained infantry to continue an assault in the face of automatic cannon and machine gun fire. The enemy gunnery was accurate, efficient, and deadly. No man dared show himself. A few men began crawling backward. Then others joined them, and then still more. Soon they all were crawling, duck-walking, or outright running back the way they had come.

"No!" Muhdin screamed, standing straight. "No! Go forward, you cowards. Forward, forward!"

It was no use. Against the deafening din of battle, his voice was like the flapping of a bird's wings high overhead. Panic spread through the ranks and a retreat turned into a run-for-your-life rout. The turnaround stunned him.

The Superior Imam would not understand this. He would ask what measures Muhdin had taken to reverse the situation. It was his life on the line now. The Emir often told him he was too soft on his men. His enemies could use the failure of this attack as clear evidence of that accusation as truth. Unless, of course, he could prove otherwise.

Four machine-gun crews had been firing at his men to remind them of what awaited cowards. But they had been shooting to threaten, not to kill. That was about to change.

"Get ready to fire!" he yelled to the machine gunners. "If they're running, kill them! No mercy to cowards!"

"My brother is out there," one of the gunners yelled. "I cannot kill my brother!"

"Do as I tell you!"

But it was too late. The other machine gunners refused to kill their friends and family. One threw down his gun, then another. Fleeing men ran past without a shot being fired, and then the gunners joined in the general flight. Disgusted, Muhdin debated whether to draw his pistol and charge the enemy himself, or take his chances with the Emir. The pistol remained in its holster as he whirled and stalked from the battlefield.

1652 hours

"Hold your positions," Tompkins said into his helmet mike.

The sudden silence seemed ominous. Hundreds of bodies littered the desert before the Marine positions and the air reeked of gore, but nowhere did he see a living enemy. After two minutes without a threat, he knew the danger had passed.

"I think that's what you call close," Thibodeaux said.

"If that's not in the nick of time," Tompkins said, "I don't know what is. C'mon, let's dismount and help the wounded."

Once on the ground, Tompkins glanced at a mesquite tree not far from the hill. A prairie falcon met his gaze. After a loud *scree!* it flapped away north.

Chapter 43

They shall not pass!
General Robert Nivelle at the Battle of Verdun, 1916

The fighting at the Marines' main line of defense was brief but violent. Burning wrecks littered the old interstate, including all three M1A1 Abrams. The Sevens kept their tactics simple—drive as fast as possible right at the defenders, shoot at them with everything you had, and keep going until you died or got through. Dozens of cars, trucks, tractor-trailer cabs, and SUVs went up in flames. Some careened out of control, some rolled over and over, flinging bodies in all directions, and others exploded. One flaming man ran from a burning Ford truck, screaming for help, until his RPG blew up and scattered him all over the desert.

1707 hours, July 29
"Missile at two o'clock!" Bunny Carlos said in a loud but businesslike tone. "All flares expended."

Racing over the desert at more than 200 knots, Joe Randall saw the flash eight hundred yards away and knew it was a Stinger. Working in microseconds, his brain reviewed the problem, listed his options, and calculated the odds. With the missile coming in from his right front, and counter-rotating rotors that moved left faster than right, the only possible evasive action was a left turn as hard as they could stand. Even with a G-suit, it was risky. They might surpass six Gs of gravitational force. In theory their suits could handle nine Gs, but at such low altitude, even a momentary blackout could be fatal.

Randall had to time it to the second. He could not make the move too soon. A homing missile going the opposite direction would first have to pass its target to pick up the heat signature. It would have already accelerated past nineteen hundred miles per hour. Once past the Comanche, the missile would then execute a one-hundred-eighty degree turn before locking onto the heat source. The turn would slow it down and cause it to loop around, both of which would buy time. If the missile traveled one hundred yards past its target before beginning a turnaround, and the target flew at two hundred miles per hour, Randall calculated he might have two seconds to shake it off.

"Hang on, hard left," was all he said, but Carlos understood. So far that day the Stingers had all been older models, homing on infrared signatures only and not UV, so their flares had worked. But the flares were all gone.

The small missile raced past them on the right and Randall jammed the stick hard left. He strained to keep the massive gunship from nosing straight into the ground. *Tank Girl* was agile for such a massive aircraft, but momentum in helicopters was never easy to control. And when they were as large as a Comanche, it was especially hard.

Tilting at a thirty degree angle, both men felt the gunship skidding, which would be fatal if they couldn't stop it. Blood drained from their brains as the G-forces increased. Straining every muscle to hold *Tank Girl* steady against the forces ripping at the airframe, Randall had an instant's glimpse of men firing up at him with small arms. They seemed close enough that he could have reached out and snatched them up like some huge raptor. Then the rotors bit the air again and *Tank Girl* straightened out like a car on a roller coaster. The missile corrected course a second time and kept coming.

Randall held the rocketing helicopter ten feet off the ground. The backwash created a dust cloud, but did nothing to stop the Stinger. The desert around them was flat, but he needed some irregularity in the terrain or they were dead. Then he saw his chance. A big truck passed in front of a hill, with a wide ditch beyond them both. It wasn't much, but it was all he had.

"It's gaining fast." Carlos's voice took on an urgent edge.

Both knew they had three seconds left. No time to think, just to react. Randall's calculations didn't register as a conscious thought.

Carlos understood the plan as if he shared a mind with Randall. Centering the truck in his gunsight, Randall pressed the 30mm trigger and Carlos fired off the last ten Dragonfire missiles. In the next three seconds many things happened, too fast to follow.

Hundreds of exploding cannon shells obliterated the truck, blowing pieces of it all over the desert. It began to roll, and then the Dragonfires hit. The missile detonations ignited the fuel tanks and the whole thing became a giant tumbling fireball. Flames mushroomed skyward and *Tank Girl* headed straight for them.

Once again Randall had to wait until the exact microsecond to avoid hitting the flaming wreckage. He and Carlos yanked *Tank Girl* straight up. Smaller helicopters could execute such a maneuver with little forward skid, because their momentum versus lift capacity and thrust was more favorable. But enormous gunships carrying the massive firepower of a Comanche were, by definition, heavy. That, combined with the forward momentum generated by traveling at 200-plus knots, meant *Tank Girl* lacked the crisp response of a lighter aircraft.

Tank Girl responded by skidding right at the boiling flames. Almost perpendicular to the ground, she gained altitude but it seemed to take forever, although in reality it was microseconds. The Stinger had closed to within one hundred yards when the rotors regained lift and the helicopter screamed skyward at an eighty-degree angle. The tail dragged through the top of the flames, scorching the paint.

But the danger wasn't over. If the Stinger was an older model, it would hit the flaming hell below. But if it locked onto their ultra-violet signature, the fire would have no effect. They couldn't wait to find out if it hit the truck, because it would be too late. They had to immediately hide their UV signature and force it to make another target selection. Worse, as a helicopter bleeds off upward speed, the motion of the rotors that provide lift when the aircraft is in level flight begin to pull it sideways. Then, as the aircraft tilts backward, it flips it upside down and drags it toward the ground. The danger wasn't only behind them, but in their very motions.

In three seconds of real time, *Tank Girl* roared straight up and stood on her tail, with the flames from the burning truck licking up at her. Then, as her speed bled away, Randall and Carlos fought to bring her nose down before she flipped over. As stall speed approached, the huge helicopter pivoted forward and fell. The nose plunged down. They had to level out or slam into the desert. Randall realized they weren't going to make it. But just beyond the truck, the hill shielded a dry riverbed. The extra twenty feet of depth was just enough to avoid disaster as Randall fought her into straight and level flight at an altitude of five feet.

The Stinger followed *Tank Girl's* path upward until she fell behind the hill, which blocked her UV signature. With no target to follow, the missile's dual IR/UV sensor homing system searched for a new target and found the roaring fire two hundred feet below. Two seconds later, it became one more explosion in the mass of fire.

When *Tank Girl* regained lift, her powerful engines drove her forward, away from the battlefield. Joe Randall shook as he navigated down the riverbed.

"Everything looks good." Carlos's quavered.

"Does it? Good... good."

"Damn, Joe," Carlos said. "I mean, damn!"

"I know. Fuck. I can't believe we did that."

Both men fell quiet, content to let their helicopter speed north. Finally Randall eased them back into open sky and up to three thousand feet. They were just west of I-17. They flew over the ruins of a small city in the valley below, including an airport.

"Black Canyon City," Carlos said, pointing down.

"Dead Canyon City is more like it," Randall said.

Palls of smoke stretched across the I-17 corridor to the south. Each column marked the pyre of another vehicle, and there were hundreds of them. They had accounted for fifteen by themselves. But where were the other helicopter gunships? Somebody else had to be available by that point.

But the Sevens had broken through the Marine line and a veritable flood of trucks, cars, and assorted vehicles moved north through the valley. Randall tried to count them, but it was hopeless. There were too many.

"Prime, this is Ripsaw Real, do you copy?" Carlos said.

"Go ahead, Ripsaw."

"Urgent! We are approximately ten miles south of the crossroads of I-17 and Highway 169, altitude three thousand. A large number of enemy vehicles are heading north, speed thirty-five. We are low on fuel, but can monitor to verify they turn toward Prescott."

"Ripsaw, can you give an estimate on numbers?"

"Wild guess only, Prime; visibility is obscured by their dust cloud. Probably no less than three hundred vehicles, but could be double that. Strongly advise air strikes immediately."

They could do nothing more than watch the tidal wave of steel and chrome drive on beneath them and wish they had ammo. When the lead vehicles turned onto Highway 169, they had a definitive answer to the enemy's destination.

"Prime, this is Ripsaw. It's load and lock time. You're about to have company."

Chapter 44

I have never, on the field of battle, sent you where I was unwilling to go myself; nor would I advise to go a course which I myself was unwilling to pursue.
     Nathan Bedford Forrest

1739 hours, July 29

Over the years, Nick Angriff had practiced with his weapons on a regular basis. He hadn't had time since Overtime Prime went active, but he was confident he could put the Desert Eagles' rounds on target every time. Since the first time he'd fired a weapon, he'd been a crack shot, just like his father. Both of his girls had inherited not only his accuracy but his reflexes.

He also cleaned his own weapons and knew his Desert Eagles were combat ready. One was missing its optic sight, lost during his last action in the Congo and never replaced. He preferred loading his own ammo, but there had not been time. Boxes of non-practice ammunition were part of his personal belongings, three hundred grain action express rounds designed for accuracy and lethality, so he loaded those. Despite the Desert Eagle's recoil, Angriff's strong wrists and forearms allowed for their easy use. Once, he had fired the full seven rounds of a Desert Eagle in under three seconds, hitting the target at forty-five feet with all seven.

Inside the Mobile Command Center, soldiers ran down the aisles, trying to find their combat gear. Angriff ordered Norm Fleming to stay behind with four communications specialists. Every other man and woman were to find a gun and assemble outside the MCC in ten minutes. No exceptions.

As he buckled on the shoulder holsters that held his twin Desert Ea-

241

gles, Colonel Walling stood by.

"Artillery is forty-five minutes from being in range, give or take," Walling said. "For air support, three Apaches and two Comanches are either in the hangar or almost back. Counting flight time, their ETA is thirty-five to forty minutes. Three Marine companies have disengaged and should be in position to cover the approaches to Prescott from the east within an hour."

Angriff sighted down the barrel of one of his Desert Eagles. Satisfied with the sights' alignment, he slid the big gun into its holster. "And the enemy will be in the refugee staging area when?"

"Twenty minutes, twenty-five tops," Walling said.

"So you're saying it's up to us to buy at least half an hour." It was not a question.

"That's what I'm saying."

Angriff pushed a .32 revolver into its ankle holster and put on his helmet. It still had three stars, not five. "Good. I hate to let everybody else have all the fun."

He strode for the rear entrance, followed by every person in the command center. The remaining headquarters company personnel assembled in the small clearing, about fifty men and women. None were combat veterans. They were clerks, radio operators, computer techs, and staff officers. But everybody had an M16 and most wore helmets, and they held their weapons with confidence. Angriff had insisted from day one of activation that every person on the base knew how to field strip and clean an M16, and take weekly target practice.

Walling started to call them to attention but Angriff waved him off. Almost by instinct, they formed a semi-circle. He started to speak, but saw four people standing to his right that he didn't expect: his Zombies. He recognized Nipple, Wingnut, and Glide.

"What are you doing here?" He addressed the question to Nipple.

But Glide answered. "It's our mission, Saint. We're your security detail."

"I..." He started to protest, but realized he could use four dangerous killers right about now. "I'm glad to see you. Bring plenty of ammo." He turned back to the rest of them. "Here's the sitrep." He pointed northeast, indicating the ribbon of highway at the mountain's foot. The volume and gruffness of his voice conveyed strength and inspired confidence. "Two hundred enemy vehicles will be here any minute. They are probably loaded with troops. If they continue toward Prescott, they will overrun the area where thousands of sick refugees are receiving emergency medical treatment. Then they can hit the rear of our forces and this entire brigade will face destruction. That is not going to happen."

He moved among them, looking each man and woman in the eye, patting a shoulder here and shaking a hand there. When he came to Nipple, she kept her arms crossed and her expression dared him to touch her.

"We are going to engage the enemy and force him to fight us. We are going to stop him and we are going to kill him. We are going to keep on killing him until either we are dead or somebody saves our asses, but we are not going to let him into Prescott. We're Americans, by God! Every damned one of you is an American patriot with a gun! And there is nobody on the face of this Earth more dangerous to the enemies of freedom than an American patriot with a gun!"

Cheering, they split up and ran to the vehicles. After Tompkins had left with the headquarters company's combat elements and veteran personnel, only three M4 Bradley command and control vehicles remained that had guns. Those had been retro-fitted to augment the brigade's C and C capabilities, but in doing so gave up their TOW missiles.

The rest were emptied supply trucks, their contents strewn on the ground. A total of seventeen trucks and Bradleys followed Angriff's Humvee down the mountain.

The stretch of desert on the north and northeastern sides of Badger Mountain offered no natural defensive obstacles. There was nothing to do except lager the trucks to block the highway and fight for as long as possible. Angriff positioned his Humvee at the center of the circle. It mounted the GAU-19/A fifty-caliber Gatling gun with a rate of fire of 1300 rounds per minute and 1500 rounds of ammunition. Any Seven who broke through the lager would see the face of Satan dealing multi-barreled death.

Standing in the Humvee, hands on hips, Angriff inspected the improvised defensive position. He saw plenty of weak spots, but was out of time to fix them. From the east, a shining river of metal sped straight for the lager.

"Enemy in sight, General." The driver of his Humvee stood on the hood, pointing east. She was young and scared to death. "Looks like a lot of them."

Manning the Gatling gun was a skinny corporal. His dark skin shone with sweat. A rod fixed to the windshield flew the guidon Angriff had ordered, a duplicate of the one Custer had carried at the Little Big Horn. The irony did not escape him.

"Get me General Fleming on the horn," he said. She climbed back into the driver's seat, and a few seconds later handed him the radio.

"Norm, I need a favor. Tell Bulldozer One One Two that Nicholas is a helluva good name for a boy. Can you do that?"

"You're coming back, Nick," Fleming said.

Angriff took a cigar out of his pocket and stuck it in his mouth. "Yeah, I know. But just in case."

"Nicholas is a great name."

"Thanks." He handed the radio back to the driver. "What's your name, Private?"

"Julianna Santos, General," she said.

"Supply?"

"Yes sir, ordnance and ammunition."

"What about you, Corporal? What's your name?"

"Imboden, sir, Donald H."

"You ever shot one of those before?" Angriff pointed at the Gatling gun.

Designed for occasions when a cannon was impractical, or the mission called for a smaller round with a higher rate of fire, the rotating gun barrels fired the NATO standard 12.7mm round. In U.S. parlance, it was a fifty-caliber. The Humvee version fired 1300 rounds per minute, a devastating blizzard of steel against man or machine.

"Not before I went cold, General. Sergeant Major Schiller insisted somebody cross-train on the Gatling and he picked me to volunteer. I'm usually a Comm Spec."

"Either one of you ever fired your weapon in anger?"

"No, sir," Imboden said.

"Private Santos?"

"No, General."

Angriff reached over and stroked the top barrel of the Gatling. "This guy is a monster, Corporal. When you press that trigger, it will lay down the hate. I want you to remember those sonsabitches wanna kill me, you, Santos, and every decent thing left in this world. You are the last thing preventing that from happening; you are the last Spartan standing. If you don't stop them, nobody will. Can you do that, Imboden?"

"Aye, sir!" the corporal said, feeling a rush of adrenaline.

"Good man. I know you can do it."

A light breeze swirled over the desert. Angriff lit a match and cupped his hands to light the Cubana. The rich smoke tasted better than ever. Once he had a nice ash going, he drew a Desert Eagle from its holster, gripped it in both hands, and pretended to draw a bead. It was a nervous habit before he went into combat; he might draw and re-holster the guns twenty times or more.

Imboden seemed confident in his ability to handle the Gatling, but Santos couldn't stop shaking. Angriff lowered the gun and looked at the worried soldier. Her rifle seemed as big as she was.

He winked and grinned. "Private Santos, I want you to remember everything you can about this day. You see, today is a day you're gonna tell your grandkids about, when you and Nick the A kicked Islamic ass side by side in the Arizona desert."

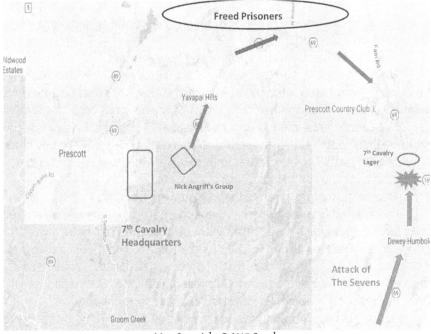

Map Copyright © 2017 Google

1805 hours

A once-yellow Z-28 led the pack, when the driver spotted something five hundred yards ahead—a bunch of trucks blocking the highway. Not knowing what to do, he rolled to a stop. More cars pulled over, and then some trucks, and soon Highway 169 became a parking lot that spilled into the adjoining desert. The afternoon was passing and night wasn't too far away. If they were going to get into Prescott before darkness fell, they had to keep moving.

Sati Bashara couldn't believe what he saw. After the vicious fight to break through Patton's defenses to the south, here were even more of the cursed infidels. How could it be? Where had they all come from?

He climbed on the roof of the Z-28 and inspected the heap of trucks in the middle of the highway. The angle of the sun interfered with his focus, but he saw an older man standing on a vehicle and wondered if that was the infamous General Patton.

He called for a volunteer. Dozens of young men stepped forward. Selecting one of the youngest, he gave the boy instructions to drive one of the larger trucks at the enemy barricade as fast as he could. The boy smiled as if Allah himself had picked him. Bashara ordered a battered Ford F-650 with a bent flatbed brought forward.

"May our beloved Caliph be with you," he said, patting the boy's cheek.

"He is a brave warrior." Haleem reached over and wiped dirty sweat from Bashara's face and neck.

"Yes, he is filled with the spirit of the New Prophet."

"Your eyes are better than mine, Sati, but even I see two Bradleys blocking the road, and after the events of this day, we must assume their weapons work. That boy will never get within one hundred yards of them."

"We cannot presume to know the wisdom of the New Prophet or the will of Allah," Sati said. "But even if you are right, we must know their firepower. He will draw their fire, and then we will know. And if his truck burns, perhaps the smoke will mask our approach."

Haleem gave him a strange look. "You were not always this cruel."

Bashara had learned how to command by studying his uncle, and his tone left no room for dispute. "Did you not hear the Emir before we left? Life is cruel. The New Prophet gives us the tools to complete the work of Allah, but it is up to us to use them. Too many of our men have already died this day. If by his death this young man can save more, then he will have his heavenly rewards. What more could anyone ask for?"

The eager boy climbed into the truck and its previous driver gave him a quick lesson in how to drive it. Then, grinning at Bashara, he gunned the engine and started forward on the uneven pavement. After going a hundred yards, he had the feel of the truck and accelerated. By the time he had gone three hundred yards, he was at close to thirty-five miles per hour, a dangerous speed with so many cracks and holes in the asphalt. Bashara had heard stories of Japanese *kamikaze* pilots, and this seemed identical. The boy was intent on ramming his truck into the Bradley blocking the road. For a brief instant, Bashara thought he might make it.

Then American gunfire raked the truck at two hundred yards from the perimeter. A 25mm shell smashed through the windshield and decapitated the driver. Several others penetrated the engine, and another blew off a tire. Flames spouted as the careening truck flipped over and over again before coming to a fiery finish eighty yards short of the perimeter. But with little wind to diffuse it, the oily black smoke hovered over the highway and obscured the Americans' vision.

"You see?" Bashara said to Haleem, pointing at the burning wreckage. "The boy is with Allah in paradise, and we have a smokescreen to hide our advance. Without his sacrifice, that could have happened to us all. Learn, Haleem. Kindness is often cruel, and cruelty is often kind."

1819 hours

Scattered cheering broke out as the truck blew up, but Nick Angriff had seen this before.

"They were measuring our guns," he said to Colonel Walling. The two men strode among the troops, giving encouragement and patting backs. "The next time they come, it will be in force." He stopped beside a tall, lanky kid who gripped his M16 like a drowning man holding a life preserver. "What's your name, son?"

"Oresco, sir. Corporal Harold B."

"Where are you from?"

"Dublin, Ohio, General."

"Where's that?"

"It's a suburb of Columbus... well, it was."

Angriff's smile was sympathetic. "Well, Oresco, Harold B., this is a good spot, but you might want to move over a little, put the engine block between you and the enemy. And remember, once you start shooting, don't stop until there aren't any more targets, got that? Keep firing no matter what."

"Yes, General. Thank you."

Walling waited to take notes or carry out orders, but the only thing left to do was fight.

"The first thing they're going to do is fan out left and right to put pressure on our flanks." Using his index finger, Angriff traced a flat arc in the air, indicating the ground on either side. "That's the obvious move. Sending that truck in alone was smart, but I don't think the guy over there is a pro. So once they're in place on our flanks, they'll come straight down the highway with big stuff. Trucks, semis, anything that can take a hit and keep going. And that's how we'll hold them."

"I don't follow, General," Walling said.

"The Bradleys will chew them up before they get to the perimeter, then they'll block the highway with their own wreckage. The smaller cars and trucks in the rear won't have anywhere to go. It'll take a while for the infantry to get here and punch a hole in our defense."

"And then?"

"Then we kill the bastards and hope reinforcements get here before we're dead."

CHAPTER 45

Man, man, your time is sand, your days are leaves upon the sea,
I am the eyes of Nostradamus, all your ways are known to me.
    Al Stewart, "Nostradamus"

1824 hours, July 29

It happened exactly as Angriff described, only faster. Each minute brought salvation closer, so he hoped his enemy would delay to consider his next move. But as the sun sank toward the horizon, thirty light vehicles full of men fanned out on either side of the lager. If he commanded those vehicles, he'd coordinate with the main attack and then have them race to the perimeter, disgorge their men, and attack. On Highway 169, he would select a dozen of the largest trucks to smash into the Bradleys. Direct on their heels, he'd send in the infantry, with the first wave carrying any RPGs they still had. Finally, the rest of the vehicles would be in reserve, to exploit an opportunity if one arose.

Angriff cursed the oily black smoke boiling from the shot-up Ford. Hanging low over the highway, it obscured visibility. A Caterpillar dump truck wasn't spotted until it was less than three hundred yards away.

Standing in the passenger seat of his Humvee, Angriff raised the radio mike and spoke to the Bradleys. "Don't fire until you've got a clear shot. Then make it count. You've got to take out the leaders."

Santos stood beside him. She rested her rifle on the top bar of the windshield and licked her lips.

Angriff nudged her. "You good, private?"

"On fleek, sir." Her voice wavered.

He nodded, as though he knew what 'on fleek' meant. She looked up and their eyes met, and Angriff could see she was fighting back tears.

"You're gonna be fine, Santos. I promise."

The first two vehicles were heavy trucks, the Caterpillar and another dump truck, and they sped forward side by side, racing to hit the Americans first. Several times one or the other almost ran off the road. They rammed the burning truck and knocked the wreckage completely off the highway. On either side, the vehicles in the desert spewed dirt from their back tires and sped straight at the perimeter.

The Bradleys opened up and 25mm high explosive rounds smashed into the twin dump trucks. As chunks flew off in their slipstream, they absorbed the damage and kept coming. The hood flipped backward on the right hand one, smashed the windshield, and fell off. Shell impacts shattered glass on both and the engines spewed steam from penetrating hits to the radiators. But the trucks hurtled forward anyway. One hundred fifty yards, then one twenty, one ten, one hundred... finally, at ninety yards, the left-hand truck caught fire and the engine exploded. The dying driver tried to hold it on the road but couldn't. It skidded sideways, flipped, rolled over three times, and slid to stop within fifty yards of the lager.

The other truck weaved to avoid the killing cannon shells. The driver lost control and it ran off the road, smashing into a boulder thirty feet from the highway. The gas tank exploded, spewing flaming gas all over the road.

The Americans shifted fire to the following vehicles. This took a few seconds and the range had closed to less than one hundred twenty yards before the Bradleys lined them up in their targeting sights. The first dump truck blocked part of the highway. The Sevens either had to detour into the desert, or skirt around the massive roadblock in a single line. They did both.

A refrigerator truck got within eighty yards before the 25mm shells did their work and it blew up in a fireball. But while the gunners concentrated on it, a fire truck picked up speed and burst out of a smoke cloud. It crashed less than twenty yards from the Bradley on the left. Two tractor trailers that skirted the shoulder of the road roared forward. A Bushmaster ripped the lead one into bits. The largest fragments slid to a stop ten yards from the perimeter, but the second one slammed into a truck and pushed it backward thirty feet. As the tractor trailer hissed steam from a ruptured radiator, the driver fell out. Bleeding from a cut scalp, he shouldered a rifle and aimed at a wiry soldier. But as his finger moved to the trigger, a bullet smashed into his back and left a hole the size of walnut. It severed his spinal cord, cut through his chest, and exited below the sternum. The impact knocked him five feet backward.

Standing in his Humvee twenty yards away, Nick Angriff still had his sights on the man when the body fell face down in the dirt.

"That's one," he said.

"Good shot, General," Santos said, although her face said she wanted to throw up.

As the main attack down the highway penetrated the lager, the wave of cars and light trucks reached it on the flanks. A few took hits from small arms fire and spun out of control, but most got within ten yards of the perimeter and unloaded their cargoes of screaming men. Climbing over, under, and through the trucks, the Sevens shot it out with the Americans at close range. Six of them wriggled under one truck and came out inside the perimeter. Angriff saw them and tapped Imboden on the arm. The corporal swiveled the gun and pressed the trigger. A burst of fifty-caliber shells spattered the trucks with their bodies.

Meanwhile, other vehicles had run the gauntlet of gunfire and smashed into the Bradleys. Enemy troops began coming through the lager. Angriff picked off targets all around the perimeter. He was methodical and deadly; Nick Angriff rarely missed. Spotting a man scooting over the hood of a truck, he waited for him to land on his feet and put one round between his eyes. Another Seven climbed through a truck cab, peered out the driver's window into the lager's interior, and got a bullet in the eye for his trouble. Santos fired, too, while Imboden swung the GAU this way and that.

Colonel Walling had been with the Bradleys and ran back to Angriff's Humvee, dirty and bleeding. His rifle still smoked from firing its last burst.

"We can't hold, General. There's too many of them!" he shouted over the din of explosions and rifle reports.

"No, we can't," Angriff said. Hits ripped into the Humvee all around him, but he ignored them. He pulled the trigger and the Desert Eagle recoiled in his hands. A stocky man in a red shirt and jeans flipped onto his back from the impact of a fifty-caliber round smashing into his chest.

Standing in defiance of danger, with the standard of the 7th Cavalry beside him, Angriff took aim and fired, again and again and again. When both pistols were empty, he leaned close to Walling's ear and said, "Our mission is to buy time, and that's what we're going to do. Pull everybody back to here and this is where we'll make our stand." He began reloading one of the Eagles.

"How are you holding up, private?" he said to Santos.

But the young woman was crumpled in the seat, although she tried to mumble in response.

Angriff went to his knees and saw the wound immediately. He slid one arm under her and put his other hand over the hole in her throat. Her blood soaked his uniform. "Medic!" he screamed. "Medic! You're gonna be fine, private, you hear me? Medic!"

Glide and Nipple were on the perimeter and heard his call. Both had trained as field medics.

Angriff saw them running his way and locked eyes with Glide. "She's got a throat wound. There's a first aid kit in the back."

Glide grabbed the kit while Nipple leaned in to see the wound.

"I want her doing this," he said, indicating Glide.

But Glide shook her head. "She's a lot better than me."

With obvious reluctance, Angriff let Nipple tend to Santos. He stood and finished reloading.

Walling pulled those soldiers manning the west barricades first. Working as a counterattack squad, they cleared the southern perimeter by killing the Sevens who had broken through. He had eighteen troops and ordered them to rally around Angriff's Humvee and to put suppressing fire on the abandoned perimeter. With Imboden covering him with the GAU, Walling next pulled back the northern troops, and then the eastern. Running through the firefight, by a miracle his only new wound was a graze to his left forearm. Finally, when the living had pulled back, Walling himself ran to join them.

From underneath a burning truck, a Seven who had feigned death raised his lever-action Winchester and fired, striking Walling in the left shoulder. The colonel staggered but did not fall. He continued stumbling toward the knot of friendly troops surrounding the Humvee. Several men rushed to help him. The Seven pushed down on the lever to reload his rifle and Angriff caught the movement in the shadows under the truck. Before the Seven could get off a second shot, a fifty-caliber action express round took off the left side of his face.

For a few seconds, silence fell among the drifting smoke. Angriff took the opportunity to reload the second Desert Eagle and then brought it to port. Surrounding his Humvee were the forty or so surviving men and women of his headquarters company. The wounded lay beside the Humvee, while the rest stood or knelt between them and the Sevens. Colonel Walling propped hmself against a front tire and held an oily rag against his bleeding shoulder. Corporal Imboden moved the GAU back and forth looking for targets. Nipple still worked on Private Santos, who was conscious enough to cry.

As the little band waited for the final attack, above them flapped the double-pointed flag of the 7th Cavalry.

1838 hours

All Sati Bashara could see was smoke and flame, even though they had moved within two hundred yards of the perimeter. Specks of carbon floated in the cloud hanging low over the roadway. Besides the smoldering wreckage strewn on Highway 169, flames also engulfed a truck on the eastern side of the perimeter. The Bradleys were silent but not on fire.

He turned to Haleem. "Go forward and tell them to finish this. Night is coming and we have wasted too much time here already. Tell the men to attack and not to use those vehicles as cover; we need to save as many as we can. Now go!"

As his friend took off running down the scorched pavement, Bashara nodded in satisfaction. He hadn't expected such a bloodbath as the day had brought. There had been no evidence those infidels, whoever they were, would fight so hard or so well. The Emirate's losses had been terrible.

But the loss of life didn't bother him as long as they had won. Spreading the New Prophet's word at the point of a sword meant casualties, and those who survived were now hardened combat veterans. As for the fallen, they were in paradise, and what more could any man ask?

Haleem was back in less than three minutes. Hands on knees, he gulped the hot, dry air. "They're going to attack shortly. I told them that any man who stayed behind cover would be considered a traitor to the Emir and would be executed."

"Excellent!" Bashara said. "You are growing to be a valuable leader within the Emirate, Haleem. I am very proud of you."

1842 hours

"Here they come!" somebody yelled. Angriff and his entire command stiffened and looked for targets.

The crowd of Sevens surged forward over the lagered vehicles. The first men came into view and exchanged shots, but a new sound froze both sides. It was a high, piercing screech that grew louder and louder at it approached.

Angriff recognized it immediately. "Down! Everybody on the ground! Now!"

He helped Imboden unbuckle from the gunner's straps binding him to the GAU, then knelt and covered both Nipple and Santos with his body. Angriff knew the sound of incoming 155mm artillery shells when he heard them.

1842 hours

Sati Bashara didn't know the sound of incoming artillery rounds. The first explosion was fifty yards to their left. The ground shook and he winced when it went off, filling the air with the zipping sound of shrapnel. The second shell hit thirty yards to their rear and drove them to their knees. Another hit was even closer.

There was a meaty *thwip* sound and Haleem staggered forward. He cocked his head, and with a quizzical expression touched his neck. Blood covered his hand.

"Sati?" he said, and then collapsed.

Shells fell in clusters and it seemed the entire world was exploding. Dirt clods rained on him. Bashara took off the scarf tied around his head as a sweat band and wrapped it around his friends' neck. By himself, he manhandled Haleem into the passenger seat of the Z-28. All around him shells ripped into cars, trucks, SUVs, and men. He couldn't see the highway leading back east, the way they had come, for the smoke. More shrapnel struck the Z and cut the back of his right hand.

For a brief moment, Bashara wondered what to do. He couldn't stay there and he couldn't go back. To go forward meant death. So, as the ground quaked and steel splinters peppered the Z-28, he steered the big sports car off the highway and into the desert. Heading south, he floored it.

The psychological effect of a heavy artillery barrage on the Sevens was instantaneous. In the parched desert soil, the 155mm shells left craters four feet deep and ten or twelve feet across, with a shrapnel radius exceeding a hundred yards. Shells rained for more than a minute.

When the barrage started, the Sevens surrounding Angriff and his company panicked and fled. Some headed south on foot. Most scrambled back to their vehicles and fled the shelling to the west, toward Prescott. They hadn't gone far before they ran into the leading elements of the redeploying Marine companies. A few cars tried to turn around, a few tried to fight, but after two pitched battles in one day, the majority of the Sevens had had enough. They poured out of their cars and trucks with their hands in the air.

The backlog of cars on the eastern side of the perimeter tried to withdraw back the way they had come, despite artillery shells chewing up the highway. But a rhythmic roaring indicated the helicopter gunships had arrived overhead, ready to shoot anything that moved. In the fading light many of the Sevens got away, some down I-17, others across the desert. Apaches and Comanches searched for targets long after dark.

———◦———

1851 hours

"She gonna make it?" Angriff asked.

Nipple's eyes cut sideways to meet his. "Maybe."

"It's just you and me right now, so tell me something. Not general to subordinate; person to person. It's obvious I piss you off. Why? What have I ever done to you?"

"That," she said with emphasis. "That right there. The fact that you fucking have to ask."

CHAPTER 46

Now mount we our horses,
Now bare we our brands,
Now haste we hard, maidens,
Hence far, far, away.
　　　　Battle Song of the Valkyries

1859 hours, July 29

Fires burned all around them as the Marines entered the lager and surrounded their commanding general. Corpsmen tended the wounded until the ambulances arrived. Angriff ordered a Dustoff team for Santos. He stayed behind, organizing the pursuit of escaping enemy units. The Humvee wouldn't start, so once night fell, he commandeered a LAV to take him back up Badger Mountain, escorted by a full platoon.

Norm Fleming waited outside headquarters when Angriff climbed down. "Are you hit?"

Angriff's uniform was stiff with dried blood. "That's not mine."

"Well, you did it," Fleming said. "You stopped them."

"I didn't do anything," Angriff said. "They did. Those kids. Those are some brave people. Fill me in on what I've missed."

"Let's go inside so I can show you on the map."

Angriff waved him off and walked over to the edge of the crest, facing Prescott. Black smoke plumes dotted the valley below, both in the city and extending far to the north and west. Fires burned from the suburbs of Phoenix into Prescott and beyond. Night made details hard to distinguish, except where the Klieg lights burned.

Fleming handed him a squeezer of water. "The Chinese were already withdrawing under pressure when you went down the mountain. That continued, but it never became a rout. We followed at a safe distance, but I didn't want to let them know how weak we really are. They left fifty-seven tanks and other armored vehicles behind, not counting most of the tanker trucks.

"The Marines followed up west of Prescott, ensuring the Chinese didn't double back. Then they raced back and blocked the road leading to the refugee camp. Right now all Army units are holding their positions just in case the Chinese haven't had enough.

"As for the army of this Hull character, few of their men were killed or wounded. The updated figure on prisoners is over a thousand."

"Norm, I know we're all beat, but I don't want any unit standing down yet. Nobody rests while there's the slightest chance we've still got wounded out there."

"That order went out half an hour ago."

"Good. That's good." Angriff pulled a half-smoked cigar from his breast pocket and flared a match. Once he had the coal going, he took a moment to enjoy it.

In the camouflaging darkness, Fleming eased three feet further away.

"Remember what it's like, Norm? After a battle? There's happy re-unions going on down there. Friends slapping each other on the back, and grim silence for the faces they'll never see again."

"We've got a happy reunion right here."

"So we do."

The Battle of the Highway, as it became known, might or might not have saved the brigade from destruction. But most members of the 7th Cavalry thought it had. It grew in the telling and was soon ranked beside the Alamo and Thermopylae. Angriff laughed that off as hyperbole, yet there was no doubt that at the least, it saved the brigade from much higher casualties.

The combination of the last-second artillery barrage, counterattack from the west, and the growing swarm of helicopter gunships had crushed the Sevens. Angriff ordered the pursuit cut short two hours after full darkness settled in. He also recalled the gunships. Despite their night-vision gear, there was no profit in having tired crews chasing individual cars all over the desert.

All through the night, the Sevens streamed southeastward. Some even passed through Phoenix and were never seen again. There was no cohesion, nothing like the army that had marched west. They were just a mob scattered over a wide swath of desert. When they tallied their total casualties, they'd lost ten thousand men and two hundred fifty vehicles of various types, including the only three working Abrams and half the Bradleys.

0601 hours, July 30

Angriff left a five A.M. wakeup call for the next morning, but Norm Fleming changed it to six. Too exhausted to care, he slept in the blood-covered uniform.

When he awoke, his head throbbed and every muscle in his body burned like fire, but he acted like he'd slept for twelve hours. He was grateful for the extra hour of sleep, but he didn't mention that, either.

When Sergeant Schiller brought him a breakfast tray with hot coffee, smoked ham, and fresh eggs, however, he said something. "Where the hell did we get this?" He inhaled the intoxicating smell. "Are these actual eggs?"

"That they are, General. And real ham, too. Compliments of General Patton's well-stocked personal pantry."

At the first bite Angriff closed his eyes and enjoyed flavors he hadn't tasted in half a century. "I'll bet the common people didn't eat like this."

"Not even close. Patton had a large herd of pigs, chickens, turkeys, some cattle, goats... you name it, he had it. He and his men ate very well, but the rest of the people, not so much. I hear they ate a lot of corn and pumpkin."

"Dairy cattle?"

"You'll have to ask Colonel Schiller about that, sir. He's taking inventory as we speak."

"Your brother seems like quite an efficient officer."

"That he is."

After finishing his meal, Angriff handed the tray back and wiped his mouth on a rag. "My God, I'd forgotten what real food tasted like. Thanks, J.C., I needed that. Do I have a spare uniform?"

"Not here, General; they're back at Prime. That's my fault."

"Shake it off, J.C. I'll make it. Hey, check on the condition of one of our wounded, will you? A private named Santos; she's in Supply."

Schiller looked down.

"She didn't make it, did she?" Angriff said.

"Still touch and go, but she's not dead. The doctors said your stitches gave her a fighting chance."

"Stitches? I didn't give her stitches. That had to have been Nipple."

"The psycho?... I'm sorry, General, that slipped out."

"It's all right, J.C. I called her that, too." Angriff remembered the vicious look Nipple had given him the day before, and her cryptic words about why she didn't like him. In most ways she acted crazy. And yet she'd stitched up a gushing throat wound in the middle of a firefight. There was something stranger about her than mere insanity. He would have to ask Green Ghost for more info.

Pushing up from his cot in the MCC, Angriff opened the one door in his tiny room and exited out the back into fresh skies and a cool breeze. The charred scent of burning rubbed tainted an otherwise perfect dawn.

Surrounded by the least-damaged Marine company, Bravo, Angriff drove back to the site of the Battle of the Highway. At the center of the charred ring of vehicles stood his Humvee. He counted 38 bullet holes, a few of which had hit the engine. Repairs would require towing back to Prime.

"How did I live through that?" he asked no one in particular.

Despite a huge bandage on his wounded shoulder and his left arm in a sling, Colonel Walling was on the scene supervising the recovery effort. "I asked myself the same question, General. If you find an answer, will you let me know?"

Angriff smiled. "B.F., every survivor of every battle fought since the beginning of time has asked the same question. And whether you're a man of faith or not, the answer is always the same: it just wasn't your time."

Four trucks were write-offs and four more needed extensive repairs. All three Bradleys were salvageable, but would need rebuilding. Eight people from the headquarters company had died defending the highway, with seventeen more wounded. Six of those were critical, including Private Santos.

Black vultures flapped away as Angriff stepped outside the lager's skeleton. Circling overhead, the birds waited for the humans to leave so they could resume feasting on dead Sevens. Hundreds of bodies surrounded the scorched lager, along with dozens of burned-out vehicles. The reek was unbearable. Flies swarmed in thick clouds.

Angriff took an hour inspecting the battle site. No detail escaped his experienced eyes. From the clothing the Sevens wore, to their weapons and even the mixture of fuel in their vehicles, he wanted to know everything. Once finished there, his convoy headed down Highway 169 to its juncture with Interstate 17. Walling accompanied Angriff. They passed abandoned cars and trucks, some shot up, some undamaged. It reminded him of the Highway of Death during Operation Desert Storm, albeit on a smaller scale.

The convoy veered right to tour the Marine positions. Angriff started with the far left flank. Sully, Embekwe, and Task Force Kicker had held the line just long enough for Dennis Tompkins' scratch force to seal the breach. They'd spent the night manning the main line of resistance, minus Sergeant Schiller, in case the enemy came back.

Tompkins joined Angriff and Walling as they exited the Hummer. "Morning, General. I heard you got in on the fun yesterday."

"Who told you that?"

Tompkins shrugged. "News like that gets around. Ain't every day the commanding general stops an army with a pair of pistols."

"Is that what they're saying? Hell..."

"You're a hero, General, whether you like it or not."

"No, not me," Angriff said. "The heroes were on this hill, and all the others like it."

"Amen to that... they named this one Last Stand Hill."

And Angriff found the name too fitting for comment.

By early afternoon Angriff, Tompkins, and Walling were at the courthouse in Prescott. The immediate concerns were to secure the city and protect against counterattacks. Even though Hull was in custody, they knew Norbert Cranston had slipped away with a large contingent of followers and disappeared into the Prescott National Forest. They also had to guard against the Chinese regrouping and coming back. Angriff deemed that unlikely, given the brigade's dominance of the skies, but was taking no chances.

Casualties overwhelmed the medical staff. Besides the brigade's own wounded, they also treated the thousands of released prisoners, many of whom needed immediate medical intervention. All needed water and food.

The citizens of Prescott had no idea what had happened, who the newcomers were, or what would happen next. Rounding up Hull's Life-Guards and their bully-boy partners, the Security Police, was a priority. LAVs with loudspeakers drove the streets and spread the word of Hull's ouster, but it all took time.

After inspecting the damaged courthouse, Angriff and his entourage were preparing to move out when a heavy equipment transport passed in front of them towing a battered Abrams. It had a bulging phallus painted on its side and the name *Joe's Junk* written below it. Black burn marks bubbled the paint in many places. Jagged steel peeled back from the front left corner. A smear of blood trailed down the left side of the hull.

Standing in the tank's hatch, a mechanic recognized him and saluted. Angriff returned the salute, then his daughter's tank disappeared around a bend.

Chapter 47

Through the fogs old Time came striding,
Radiant clouds were 'bout me riding,
As my soul when gliding, gliding,
From the shadow into day.
        Robert E. Howard, "The Tempter"

New Khorasan (formerly Tuscon, AZ)
0702 hours, July 31

Richard Lee Armstrong stood on the stone patio of his villa and wondered if it was time to cut his losses. He had been the Emir of Khorasan for more than thirty years. During that time he and his brother, Larry, better known as the New Prophet of the Seven Prayers, had conned their way to more power than either had ever dreamed possible. Their caliphate covered most of Texas, New Mexico, and southeastern Arizona, and their followers numbered in the hundreds of thousands, maybe millions. Anything they wanted was theirs for the taking, and even in a ruined world, life was good for the men at the top.

Only two people knew their secret. One was their little sister, Evie, but she hadn't even told her son, Sati Bashara, about their true identities. Bashara thought himself an Iraqi.

The other was his only confidant. It was dangerous to allow a man to live who knew their secret. But Armstrong needed his advice more than he needed to tie up a loose end. And so he motioned to the guard.

"Bring me the Wise One."

While waiting, he sipped his morning coffee and enjoyed the fresh-ness of the breeze, chilled as it was with hints of the coming autumn. At length the twisted old man limped onto the patio and plopped into a chair. The attendant poured his coffee, then closed the patio doors and left them alone.

"Coffee's good. I heard things didn't go too well?"

"The expedition to Prescott ended in disaster," Armstrong said without preamble. "I don't know who we fought, but it wasn't that clown who calls himself Patton. Those were real troops. If I didn't know better, I'd say it was the actual United States Army."

"How is that possible?" See note

"I don't know, but we got the shit kicked out of us. I sent thirty thousand men out there. I sent every military vehicle I had into that at-tack, just to make sure it worked. And instead we got our ass handed to us. What other possibilities are there?"

"The Chinese?"

"No, they flew the American flag. The helicopters had white stars. Somehow they were Americans."

The old man frowned. Armstrong was good at reading body lan-guage, and he *thought* the old man knew more than he said. But his advi-sor was also the only man he couldn't really read.

"So what's next?" the old man asked.

"The smart move would be to cut and run, but that would mean giv-ing up the work of a lifetime and starting all over again. You know I'm a realist. As an aging man with no survival skills, I'd last about ten minutes. It's a brutal world out there, and I'm too old to try."

"So what then? I can't do anything but stay here, anyway."

"This afternoon we're stoning cowards who ran during the fight. I ordered one thousand men to draw lots, just like the Romans used to do. One hundred of them will be stoned by the rest."

"Decimation."

"Right. They've had to dig their own burial pit. We'll have them kneel and pray for forgiveness until they're all dead. I need to do this for the disciplinary effect, but I want something to cheer up the survivors."

"The carrot and the stick."

"I've decided what we need is a real military. Tonight's my weekly talk with Larry, and he's not the forgiving sort. When I tell him what happened, he's going to go off. Unless I have a plan, he might order my execution."

"Would he really do that to his own brother?"

"You know he would. Overwhelming numbers are clearly not enough any more. So I'm announcing plans to develop a true army. Then we can go back and teach whoever we fought a lesson. I'm going to tell my brother that the Sword of the New Prophet has grown dull and needs sharpening. For the Caliphate to thrive, we need a professional military, one that can defeat any enemy in open war. I'm announcing that today after the stoning."

CHAPTER 48

All we see, and all we seem is but a dream,
And darkness weaves with many shades.
          Karl Edward Wagner, "Darkness Weaves"

0955 hours, July 31

Her mind swam in darkness.

Some spark within her knew she faced two paths, one of strength and one of weakness. There was nothing else, no right, no wrong, no good or bad. The path of weakness was the easiest, like a river current for those too feeble to resist, bobbing along in the gentle waves, spent, exhausted, carried forever to a place of peace and rest.

For those with strength to fight the current, there was the other path.

Hers was the path of weakness. Swept away in the current, she was too weak and too damaged to save. Her energy dissipated and her strength waned.

But some essence of her spirit cried out for help, for the strength to fight back, to survive, as the river swept her into oblivion.

And someone answered.

Not in words, thoughts, or ideas. Those things did not exist. There was only strength and weakness, and someone gave her strength. She could feel it filling her, reviving her flagging will to survive, giving her the power to fight impending death.

Then thoughts and dreams existed again. A voice came to her, a familiar voice, a voice that was part of her.

You will not die this day, my sister.

0536 hours, August 2

It remained hot, but when fall arrived and colder weather came to the mountains, new challenges would present themselves daily. Angriff knew the urgency of the moment and his energy was infectious. He was awake early every morning. He greeted returning combat units and helped prioritize repairs, read after-action reports and intelligence summaries, and prepared for possible future enemy action.

A big question was how best to incorporate the citizens of Prescott into a viable community. Others were what to do with prisoners and taking stock of food distribution, including the huge cache set aside for Hull and his cronies. The list of things to do seemed endless.

On the third day, Sergeant Schiller brought a glass of (powdered) orange juice and the first cup of coffee of the morning to his office. He also brought the word Angriff had been waiting for. "They're both awake, General. There's an Emvee standing by."

"Thank you, J.C.. Give me a minute to down this," he said, holding up the coffee mug.

0617 hours

"You've been skating," Piccaldi said. "It's about time you woke up."

Lara Snowtiger opened one eye and then closed it again; the light was glaring. She did not see the concern on his face, nor the cast on his right shoulder and arm. Piccaldi had insisted on being at her bedside from the moment she came out of surgery, and nobody had dared say no. For the first twenty-four hours the doctor hadn't been optimistic. But then, like a miracle, she rallied, and throughout the morning she had been waking up and going back to sleep.

"Don't pet a burning dog," she said in a weak voice.

But it made Piccaldi smile. "SITFU, Marine," he said. "Stop slacking off... I'm glad you're back, Lara."

"Can I have your scope?" she whispered, her eyes opening and then closing again.

"Depends on what I get in return," Piccaldi said.

She smiled but did not re-open her eyes.

"Let her sleep, Sergeant." Nick Angriff stood at the foot of her hospital bed, along with Norm Fleming, Dennis Tompkins, and B.F. Walling. In his hand were a Purple Heart and the most prestigious honor America could give a member of its armed forces, the Congressional Medal of Honor. With no Congress to authorize the citation, Angriff had taken the authority on himself.

Snowtiger was heavily bandaged. With her body and shoulder wrapped like a mummy, Angriff pinned the medals to her blanket. Piccaldi's Silver Star hung below the left breast pocket of his pajamas.

"When she wakes up," Angriff said, "please tell her how proud we all are to have such fine Marines as the two of you serving under our command, and that we are praying for her speedy recovery."

"I'll do that, sir," Piccaldi said. "You know... the doctors didn't think she was going to make it."

"I heard that."

"Yes, sir, but here's what's weird. Her vitals were dropping, but then she started talking in her sleep. She kept saying a name, over and over. I thought it was her own name, Lara. You know, like telling yourself to wake up, but that wasn't it. She was saying *Sara*."

"Do we know who Sara is?"

"Sara was her twin sister. It's like she was talking to her, asking her for help. It was only seconds later when her vitals started coming back. You could see it in her body; she had strength again. I've never seen anything like it."

"Remarkable," Angriff said, his hand on the door frame. "Get well soon, Gunny."

"Sir?"

Angriff smiled. "You more than earned it."

Gunny... three up and two down. Piccaldi had always wanted to make gunnery sergeant, but hadn't thought about it since thawing out. As a sniper, he didn't have the specialized experience with company-sized units that was usually a prerequisite for promotion to gunnery sergeant.

Smiling, he propped his chin in his left palm and stared at Snowtiger. "Why do you have to be such a fucking motard?" he whispered.

Angriff tried to visit every wounded soldier and Marine, but after Morgan there was one person he wanted to check on in person. He found her unconscious, with a tube down her throat and several PICC lines. Heavy bandages wrapped around her throat.

Doctor Freidenthall hadn't left the hospital since the battle and looked worse for the wear. "At this point, General, I think she'll make it. I can't guarantee a full recovery, she lost a lot of blood before we got to her, but she should live."

"Thank you, Colonel. She's a good soldier. I'd like to get her back if I can."

"Didn't one of Green Ghost's men treat her?"

"Not a man, a female. But yeah, she pushed me out of the way."

"No offense, sir, but it's a good thing she did."

1200 hours

"Sit down, Major Claringdon," Angriff said in a friendly tone. "Thank you for coming."

"My pleasure, General." Claringdon maintained the pretense that he'd had a choice in the matter. He knew the purpose of the meeting, and Angriff knew that he knew, so neither pretended otherwise.

"Cigar?"

"No, thank you, sir."

"Good for you. Wish I'd never gotten the habit." In deference to the major, Angriff put down his own cigar, unlit. "Let me get right to the point. In the heat of battle, Major, men often display both their best and worst characteristics. The prudent officer weighs a subordinate's value to his unit against any slips in judgment that might occur during the stress of combat. Discipline comes first, of course. But discipline needs to be tempered by good judgment and the individual's value to his or her unit. Don't you agree?"

Claringdon squirmed. Angriff had left him no out. "Of course, sir. May I take it this is about Captain Randall's actions last week?"

"You may and it is. As I'm sure you know, Lieutenant Randall is my daughter. So the father in me is eternally grateful to the man who saved her life. The doctors tell me another five minutes without medical attention and she would have died. Additionally, Captain Randall is far and away our best gunship pilot. He does things with a Comanche that my aviation experts tell me are impossible.

"However, my larger responsibility is to this brigade. I cannot have officers hindering movements I have ordered during combat, and that includes Captain Randall. What he did is a court-martial infraction. But for a court-martial to occur, you must press charges. If you don't, you must rely on me to handle the matter discreetly and in the manner I think best fits the situation. Which do you think is best for the brigade, Major?"

Fitzhugh Howarth Claringdon was a well-educated man. He had attended prep school and an expensive private college. During his time at the Pentagon, he'd learned the language of compromise. He was not the smartest officer in the brigade, nor the youngest, tallest, shortest, fittest, or oldest. More to the point, while he was no genius, he also wasn't stupid.

"General, I can think of no one I would trust more to uphold the finest traditions and disciplines of the United States Army than you," he said. "I leave the matter entirely to your discretion."

Angriff leaned back and grinned. "I think you've made a wise decision." He then picked up a pen and signed two sheets of paper. "Would you please stand?"

Confused, Claringdon stood and, when Angriff rounded his desk and walked toward him, he stiffened to attention. Reaching into his left breast pocket, Angriff pulled out two silver oak leaves and pinned one to each of Claringdon's collars. After this, he stepped back and saluted. Claringdon returned the salute, and then Angriff shook his hand.

"Congratulations, Colonel."

1435 hours

"Mr. and Mrs. Parfist, thank you for agreeing to meet me here," Angriff said. "I apologize for the inconvenience of asking you to travel so far, but as you might expect, I've been busy in the aftermath of the battle."

"Uh, sure, General," Richard Parfist said. "I mean, it's all pretty overwhelming. We've never seen anything like this before."

Schiller brought a pot of coffee with three cups, served everyone, and left.

"Mr. Parfist, during the liberation of Prescott you showed great courage, wisdom, and resourcefulness. My command is a military unit; our mission is primarily oriented to combat. In rebuilding cities like Prescott, we need help from the locals, help from people like you. Would you be willing to help us rebuild your city and the surrounding areas, Mr.Parfist?"

"Me? You want me?"

"I can't think of anybody better to be mayor of Prescott. Will you do it?"

"I don't know anything about being a mayor. Are you sure it's me you want?"

Angriff smiled. "Does anybody know Prescott better? Somebody I can trust?"

"Prescott is my home," he said. "And I owe you my family's life. If that's what you need me to do, and you're sure you want me, then yes, I'll do it."

"There's nobody we want more."

1722 hours

Angriff, Fleming, Tompkins, and Walling toured the entire hangar. They spoke with every crew, including the ground crew for the one Apache shot down. Although mourning the loss of their pilot and co-pilot, they were bound and determined to scavenge every part they could and, if possible, rebuild a combat-ready aircraft.

Every helicopter had battle damage, even the medical and transport ones, and Angriff found it miraculous only one had gone down.

As they completed the circuit of the hangar, the officers reached *Tank Girl*. Rossi's crew had timed their advance and cleaned the bay, because they had their bird combat ready again. There were still holes in the fuselage, and scorch marks, but nothing that affected air-worthiness or fighting capabilities.

When the knot of officers rounded into view, Rossi called *"Ten-hut!"* and both crew and officers snapped to attention. Bunny Carlos and Joe Randall stood particularly straight, their salutes sharp.

Angriff stopped in front of them and gave his best salute. "At ease." He raised his voice, because Alisa Plotz's crew were using air tools in the next bay. "It looks like you gentlemen have quite the story to tell your grandchildren." He spent a few seconds inspecting the giant helicopter, his gaze lingering several seconds on the semi-obscene picture under her name. "Is *Tank Girl* ready if we need her again?"

"Thanks to Sergeant Rossi and her crew, she's ready to fight, General," Randall said. "I've got the best ground crew on the base."

Angriff nodded; Randall said what all good leaders would say. "In my experience, a superior team inspires superior performance. And the results you achieved over the battlefield speak for themselves. I read your account of escaping that last Stinger and have seen the video. I'm reliably informed that what you did is impossible, that an AH-72 cannot do those things. How do you respond to that?"

"With all due respect, sir, I'm standing here, and that's all the proof I need. When I'm in combat I react. My brain and my reflexes sync up and I just do things. Maybe someday I'll try a maneuver that's beyond her capabilities. Maybe I'll die that day, but if I start thinking about what I'm doing when people shoot at me, then I'll die for certain."

"How does that make you feel, Lieutenant?" Angriff turned to Carlos.

"I'm alive because Joe... Captain Randall knows things by instinct that others don't and never will. You can't teach what he can do with a Comanche, General; you can either do it or you can't. It's a privilege to be his co-pilot."

"More than commanding your own aircraft?"

That took Carlos by surprise. "I... I would have to think about that, General."

"Do that, Lieutenant. By the way, was it you who gave Captain Randall's wife the nickname Tank Girl?"

Carlos refused to squirm. "It was done with great affection, General."

Angriff scowled and said nothing. Then, with a wink, he patted Carlos' shoulder. "It's a good nickname, Lieutenant. And to all of you, I want to formally convey the gratitude of the entire brigade for your heroic actions during the fighting. And by all of you, I mean Captain Randall and Lieutenant Carlos, and you, too, Sergeant Rossi. You and your entire crew.

"The records show you turned *Tank Girl* around nearly twice as fast as any other crew, including the Apaches. Had you taken ten more minutes during that final turnaround, the enemy would have been scattered all over the desert before Captain Randall got there, and that would have been that. As it was, they were still bunched up when Captain Randall and Lieutenant Carlos arrived, and the damage they inflicted slowed down the enemy long enough for us to organize a defense further down the road. That's damned fine teamwork.

"I hereby award you, Sergeant Rossi, and your entire crew the Bronze Star for meritorious service during combat operations. You are each promoted one grade. As for you, Captain Randall and Lieutenant Carlos, you are both awarded the Silver Star for performance above and beyond the call of duty."

After shaking hands, Angriff motioned Randall aside. Out of earshot, Angriff put his mouth close to Randall's ear. "I'm damned proud to have you as my son-in-law," he said. "You obviously care about Morgan as much as I do, and that's all I can ask. But if you ever again put me in the position you did by stopping that tank column, I may shoot you myself. Is that clear?"

Randall just nodded, knowing it was not a bluff.

"Good," Angriff said. "Welcome to the family."

———— ∞ ————

"Sergeant Arnold?"

Sitting on a bench in the bay next to *Tank Girl*, Andy Arnold leaned forward and peered around. A skinny private stood in the doorway above that into the main base, holding a covered stainless steel bowl.

"Down here," Arnold said.

The private saw him and eased down the stairs, carefully balancing the bowl.

Alisa Plotz joined Arnold and spread her hands in a *What gives?* gesture. He shrugged.

"With General Angriff's compliments, Sergeant," the private said.

Arnold took the bowl and sniffed it. The metal was cold. Condensation ran down the sides. After uncovering it, he couldn't believe what it held—a big mound of ambrosia, filled with apples and grapes the way his grandmother had made it, topped with orange slices, whipped cream, and shredded coconut.

He had no idea where they had gotten the ingredients, nor did he care. He called the ground crew over, and without further ado, they ate the whole thing. Arnold saved the final pleasure of licking the bowl for himself.

CHAPTER 49

After a victory, sharpen your sword.
Admiral Togo, after his victory at The Battle of Tsushima in 1905

August 3

Most of the brigade remained in the field, so Angriff scheduled award ceremonies during a general tour of the liberated areas. The last stop was with the tank battalion, which had pulled back into reserve at Prescott Valley city. While there, he awarded four Silver Stars, including one to his own daughter. The old hospital in Prescott had been in use even during the years of the Republic of Arizona. Although primitive, it was shelter, and the medical teams put it to good use. Morgan Randall was recovering there.

By early afternoon, the three generals were back in the Crystal Closet, along with Colonel Walling and Lt. Colonel Kordibowski. Lunch was a soup made from dried navy beans found in Prescott, with reconstituted onions and tomatoes. Tasty as it was, Kordibowski's preliminary intelligence summaries were the reason for their gathering.

"Let us start with this Islamic entity. We now know it is officially called the Caliphate of the Seven Prayers of the New Prophet," Kordibowski said.

"Pretentious bastard, isn't he?" Angriff said.

Kordibowski smiled. "You don't know the half of it. We have approximately five hundred fifty prisoners from what was their army. If it's pretentiousness you want, try this: it's called the Sword of the New Prophet."

"What?" Angriff said, sitting up. "Say that again, Rip."

Kordibowski glanced at Fleming. "Their army is called the Sword of the New Prophet."

"I've heard that before," Angriff said. "I'm sure of it."

"I don't remember fighting such an army in the old days," Fleming said.

"No, not that. It's something else. Go on, Rip; I didn't mean to hijack your briefing. It'll come to me if I quit thinking about it."

"Ummm, yes. We have a lot of prisoners, most of whom were more than willing to talk. It's an excellent sample size, so we can be pretty confident about our conclusions."

"So what's the story with this new prophet nonsense?" Angriff said.

"This is not traditional Islam. We thought they were Muslims, and in a sense they are, but honestly, gentlemen, I'm not exactly sure what this movement is. The Koran is venerated, but it's treated something like how Christians treat the Old Testament. More important are the teachings of their leader, the Caliph, also known as the New Prophet. He lives somewhere in Texas and his brother runs the show in Tucson."

"I thought the Koran was supposed to be Allah's final word on the subject," Angriff said. "I don't remember anything about another prophet."

"That's true, although some scholars could argue that Jesus is coming back at the end of days and that he would, therefore, be the last prophet. But for the sake of our discussion, the answer is yes, Mohammad was the last prophet. We really don't know much about the new teachings at all, except they are especially brutal. And we can assume they endorse Naskh, which others call abrogation. It would not surprise me if this new prophet was just another strongman using Islam as a front, framing orders as religious dogma."

"A con artist?"

"Something like that, yes. As I said, these are not Muslims as we know them. As to their capabilities, they are well-armed and have some leftover National Guard assets."

"Minus three tanks," Angriff said.

Kordibowski allowed a moment for laughter. "The quantities of fuel needed for so many vehicles is high, so it may be surmised they have access to a steady source of gasoline and diesel. That makes sense when considering the Texas connection, if we also assume wells and refineries are still operational there. If this is true, and I would say that it almost has to be, then our enemies to the east and west have access to almost unlimited fuel supplies, while we do not. This puts us at a distinct disadvantage over a long period. Other than these factors, the chief threat from the Caliphate is the manpower pool available."

"Lots of mobile light infantry," Angriff said.

"Exactly. Their decision to move west was prompted by our initial engagement on Activation Day. When General Tompkins rescued those women, the Caliphate sent a force in pursuit that was much larger than necessary, the idea being to gain those men field experience. They never expected that force to be destroyed; it was outside the scope of their thinking that such power still existed. But as we feared, at least one of them survived to report being attacked from the air.

"They knew the remnant of some American military force was in Prescott, and made the assumption it was this organization that attacked them. Such a challenge could not go unpunished. Thus they mobilized an army to take Prescott and wipe out this threat. Here's the amazing part—the timing of their attack was completely coincidental."

"There are no coincidences," Angriff said.

Kordibowski shrugged. "However it happened, they had no idea the Seventh Cavalry existed. They had promised a lot of these men farms in Prescott Valley, and the slaves to work them."

"Slavery," Angriff said. "The world worked for centuries eliminating it, and the minute the power went off, it came back like cancer."

When he said nothing more, Kordibowski continued. "We wiped out about a third of them, including hundreds of vehicles of all types. But the worst loss for them was the specialized trucks, the heavy ones they brought to get Prescott back up and running quickly. The good news for us is that some of them can be salvaged and others were abandoned undamaged. For example, we have a street roller in nearly pristine condition.

"Moving on to Prescott itself, the situation there is stable and our intel is based on hundreds of interviews with a cross-section of the population. We are still compiling data, but it's clear the Prescott community was well organized.

"As you might expect, a disproportionate percentage of the food supply went to the ruling junta, for lack of a better word. Nevertheless, and to Hull's credit, the people themselves were not starving. They grow quite a variety of crops and the ones who did the work were allowed to keep enough to survive. As long as they did what they were told, I should add.

"The only potential danger now is the escape of Hull's number two man, a Norbert Cranston, with between one hundred and three hundred followers. Their likely hiding spot is the Prescott National Forest, west of the city. We do not believe they got away with any heavy weapons, and unless they've got caches of food somewhere, he will have a hard time holding that group together. Nevertheless, it is a loose end."

"Norm, make sure the sentries are alert for food raids," Angriff said. "Let's put some round-the-clock patrols around some of the nearer farms, too. These guys can't go guerilla for long."

"Our intel on the Chinese, unfortunately, isn't nearly as complete. We only took five prisoners and one of those is seriously wounded. The other four either don't know much or won't talk. So here's what we do know: we faced the Ninth Armored Division of the People's Liberation Army, reinforced by elements of the One Thirty-Fourth Infantry Division, both of which are Class A units—"

"Excuse me," Tompkins said, "but is that like being first class?"

The question took them all by surprise. It was the first time Tompkins had ever interrupted a speaker in a meeting.

"It is, General. Class A units are full-time, intensely trained, and fully equipped with the most modern weapons."

"Thank you," Tompkins said.

"The Chinese had specialized sub-units attached. They brought more than two hundred tanks for the attack, so they were definitely planning to stay. They landed in California many years after the initial Collapse, when there was no functioning central authority or military to stop them. China itself later underwent massive upheavals of some kind, and so the expeditionary force wound up stranded in America when its lifeline dwindled. They control the Pacific Coast from Baja to about Monterrey, and inland to the mountains. Total strength is only a reinforced corps of four divisions, not enough to seize more territory and control it. Apparently there are a number of guerilla groups in that area.

"The oil pumps and refineries they revived, which gives them unlimited fuel, too. What they do not have enough of is workers. For decades they have been trading fuel for people, but this time they made the decision to seize Prescott and expand their footprint into Arizona."

Angriff held up a hand, then paused before speaking, as if he did not believe what he'd heard. "Let me make sure I understand the big picture, Rip. On the very day that we decided to move in and liberate the hostages and the city, two completely different armies also chose that day to attack? Completely unknown to each other, and from two opposing directions? This was all just some huge coincidence?"

"Let's call it synchronicity, General. The Caliphate was set in motion by General Tompkins' actions and ours. But the Chinese..." Rip's voice trailed off.

"Incredible. So if we'd waited one more day to attack, the Chinese would have overrun Prescott, and the Sevens then would have attacked the Chinese?"

"That sounds right."

"The whole city would have gone up in flames and we would have walked right into that. My God, even if we'd won that fight, there would not have been anything, or anybody, left to save."

"I can't argue with any of that, General," Kordibowski said.

"Truth is always stranger than fiction. Go ahead and finish, Rip. I promise not to interrupt again."

"The CO can interrupt whenever he wants, sir. The Chinese left fifty-seven AFVs on the field, along with ten self-propelled triple-As. I believe we can put some of those back in service. We also captured seventeen trucks of various types and twenty-three tanker trucks. Six of those are still filled with high-grade fuel. I believe this represents one-third of the total Chinese armor in North America, about a quarter of the tanker trucks, and ten percent of their other vehicles. We killed upwards of fourteen hundred enemy soldiers. Since the Chinese evacuated their wounded, we have no idea of those numbers.

"But the most noticeable thing about the Chinese soldiers is their age. These are the original men who invaded California thirty-plus years ago. That puts them in their fifties, at least. There's a second generation coming up, but the Chinese were forbidden to intermarry with the locals until recently."

"Any update on the prisoners we rescued?" Angriff said, ignoring his promise not to ask another question.

"Beyond the numbers, General, no. We've been stretched pretty thin. I made the call to interrogate enemy prisoners first and debrief liberated IPs later. All I can tell you is they are from dozens of small but functioning towns and villages scattered all over the place."

"Anything else we should know?"

"Lots and nothing, General."

"Good." Angriff stood and stretched his aching lower back. "Gentlemen, I'm adjourning to the observation deck to have a smoke. You are more than welcome to join me, or not."

1537 hours

Corporal Dupree couldn't stop licking his teeth, a nervous habit his mother had tried, and failed, to break. Angriff stepped out of his office toward the ramp. Watching him, Dupree waited at Schiller's desk. Angriff exchanged salutes but kept walking.

Dupree called after him. "I did as you ordered, General," he said, hoping he wouldn't anger Angriff by speaking first. "I've allocated the mainframe and we're scrubbing it of important data."

Angriff paused. His furrowed brow showed Dupree he had completely forgotten about it. A second later he snapped his fingers and grinned. "The trap for our hacker friends?"

"They weren't exactly hackers, General, but that's close enough. The engineers are working on rerouting the tapline and selecting the data to upload, but it's going to be a while. The mainframe won't be ready for weeks, at least. We're short-handed on techs. It could be months, but when it's done, we'll turn it back on and see what happens."

"Fine work, son. Come to me as soon as you know something."

CHAPTER 50

They hauled him to the crossroads
As day was at its close;
They hung him to the gallows
And left him for the crows.
    Robert E. Howard, "The Moor Ghost"

1620 hours, August 3

"Unlock this door!" Lester Hull yelled again. "I order you to let me out!"

By then he was certain that, in some unknown way, an American military unit was still in existence. The uniforms, equipment, markings, insignia, even the slang, were all genuine U.S. Army. How that could be, he didn't know, but the one thing he did know was that he outranked everybody he would meet. When that colonel had tried to question him, he'd played the rank card and said nothing. And that was exactly how he intended to act until he knew what was going on and how he could turn it to his advantage.

Lester Hull wanted to pace the square room, but without a belt his pants fell down, so instead he sat on the hard bunk in the corner and screamed. They'd taken his shoelaces, too, and despite the heat outside there was a chill in his cell. They'd let him keep his uniform and insignia, but the outright contempt shown to him was beyond imagining.

They'd blindfolded him in Prescott before transporting him to wherever he was. By using his other senses, Hull had gotten a good idea that he was in the mountains to the north or northeast. He'd felt the sun on the back and left side of his neck, and based on the time of day, it had started out overhead and then moved west.

Once he'd arrived, things had become more confusing. The echoes around him had indicated interior spaces, a large building, or maybe a tunnel of some sort, with lots of twists and turns. He could tell there was light everywhere, bright light, and it had to be artificial. Where did the energy necessary for so much lighting come from? What were the strange noises, the clangs and hums and other unidentified sounds?

His room had also surprised him. He'd expected it to be dark, perhaps with restraints or torture devices. Instead, while it was small, perhaps ten feet by ten feet, the room was clean and well lit by some type of recessed lighting. It had a sturdy cot with clean sheets and a blanket, and a small table with two chairs in the center of the room. An actual steel toilet took up the far corner. The door was metal with a small window.

Time was hard to measure. He thought three days had passed, but couldn't be sure. The food was strange, with odd flavors and a stringy texture. The worst part was the boredom. About all he could do was sit and yell.

The door opened and he figured it was another meal, which was good because he was hungry. The man who entered, however, did not carry a tray.

He was large, about six feet or so, with wide shoulders and a deep chest, drooping jowls, and light grey hair cut short. His eyebrows were shaggy. His dominant feature were the bright blue eyes, which burned with internal fire Hull had never encountered before. Behind the stranger's scowl was a tangible *gravitas* Hull felt immediately, like a physical force pushing into his cell. The man wore no insignia, had no signs of rank, yet Hull knew by instinct he was the man in charge.

"So," Hull said. "You would be my number two, then." He would play this out and see how it went.

The man sat in the nearest chair and crossed his legs, saying nothing.

"I did not give you permission to sit down!" Hull rose, and grabbed his pants when they started sliding to his knees. "You will stand at attention until I tell you otherwise."

His visitor raised his eyebrows and smiled, withdrew a trimmed cigar that was ready to toast, and with obvious relish lit it. At the first draw he closed his eyes, enjoying the flavor while ignoring Hull.

Hull's face flushed with rage. "I did not give you permission to smoke! If you don't put that out right now, I'll put it out for you!"

"Don't I wish you would try," the man said.

Hull realized indignation would not work on this man. He began to feel desperate and tapped his lips with his index finger, thinking. "Got another one?"

"That depends. If you give me what I want, I'll give you a cigar."

"There it is. You want something from me."

"Of course I do. That's why you're still alive."

"You can't simply execute me."

"Well, you'd have a trial first, but I doubt a court-martial would be inclined to leniency."

"So what is it you want from me?"

The man spread his arms, like the answer was obvious. "I want everything you know."

"About?"

"About everything."

"You want me to answer all your questions in exchange for a cigar?"

"I'm sorry, I haven't made myself clear. I want you to cooperate fully with anyone and everyone who talks to you. I want you to answer their questions to the best of your knowledge. And I want you to discontinue this inane posturing."

"What posturing?"

"This Patton masquerade. Give it up."

"So if I do all of this, I get a cigar?"

"No. You get to keep breathing, and you don't get to meet a young lady named Nipple. Think of the cigar as a bonus for good behavior."

"You're threatening a superior officer?"

"No, I'm threatening you... Lieutenant."

Hull almost leaped at him, but controlled himself. "Do you see these stars on my collar? There's five of them, and since you are obviously a member of the United States Army, I outrank you and every other member of your command!"

"Whoever made those did a lousy job. Do you want to see what a five-star cluster really looks like?" Reaching into his left breast pocket, the man withdrew his own symbols of rank and laid them on the table. "What do you have to say to that, Lieutenant Lester Earl Hull?"

Hull leaned back as if slapped; for several seconds he didn't respond. His mind tried to rationalize the reality confronting him. "Lester Hull doesn't exist. I am the reincarnated spirit of George Patton."

"Right, George Patton. Are you also all the people Patton was before he was Patton?"

"I am, and one after him."

"After him? You were somebody else, too?"

"*Am* somebody else. I am the accumulation of my past lives."

"Right, right, an accumulation. So who else are you?"

As he replied, Hull leaned forward on the table, getting close to the man's face. His voice dropped to a hiss between clenched teeth. "You mean besides Hannibal, Julius Caesar, and Napoleon? I am also Nicholas T. Angriff, Nick the fucking A. How do you like that?"

The stranger withdrew a .32 revolver from an ankle holster and pushed the muzzle into Hull's mouth.

"What a coincidence," he said. "So am I."

Chapter 51

But if I die a lonely death,
My soul will wander nameless;
I cannot rest while you draw breath,
And I will have my vengeance.

> Anonymous stele found at Tannis, believed to have come from Pi-Ramesses

1937 hours, August 3

Nick Angriff and Norm Fleming stood alone at the top of their mountain, facing the sunset. On their left, arrays of solar panels marched down a gentle slope on the southern face. A large metal shed, shaped like an igloo to counteract the summit's buffeting winds, served as the access elevator's topside terminal. Around the domed shed ran a wide stone walkway and a narrow road large enough for forklifts and Emvees.

Since the solar collectors were functioning as expected, Angriff and Fleming had the mountain peak all to themselves. Neither man had spoken since they'd first stepped out of the elevator half an hour before. The view in all directions was spectacular, and after the travails of the past few months, the tranquility was a blessing.

As usual, Angriff smoked a cigar. "You know, Norm, I'm not always the sharpest knife in the drawer," he said, staring into the distance. "But I can see through a wall in time."

"A cliché, followed by Tolkien. You never cease to amaze me, Nick."

"I forgot you liked Tolkien, too. So let me try one my grandmother used to say all the time: don't spit on my cake and tell me it's icing."

"Quaint. So what does it mean?"

"Now that things have calmed, I've had more time to think about our whole situation, how we got to this point and where we should go from here. As I've told you a hundred times, since I first heard about Project Overtime, there's been something that's bothered me about the whole thing. I couldn't put my finger on it, and I still can't, but I have figured out one thing: somebody lied to me, and that somebody was Thomas Steeple."

"How so?" Fleming moved sideways as the wind shifted and cigar smoke wafted his way.

"Morgan." He paused to let that sink in. "You don't break one of the main protocols for an operation of this size without the permission of the head guy, and that was Steeple. And if you don't bring him in on such a decision, you risk the wrath of God. Who would do that? Angering Steeple was a career-ender.

"But Morgan got married with the knowledge and permission of her Overtime recruiters. She wasn't married first, then followed her husband into Long Sleep. They told Overtime to either take both or neither, and Overtime agreed, and then let them get married. Who had to sign off on that?"

"Steeple. But we've already gone over this. You can't be sure he knew about it. Look how many sleepers weren't on the manifest."

"I'm not buying it, not for two active-duty Army officers. The others were shadowy characters like Bettison."

"What about those geneticists?'

"I'll grant you they're an aberration. But you're missing my point. If Steeple didn't actually give permission for Morgan and Randall to join up, he sure as hell knew about it. He had to. And that was more than a year before he recruited me. All of which adds up to him lying to me by omission. He knew my daughter was alive and part of Overtime, but he didn't tell me.

"Instead, if he didn't engineer the whole charade with her funeral and the ashes and all that shit, he sure as hell signed off on it. That might be the worst thing anybody has ever done to me. He made me think my daughter died in a war I argued was necessary. Who does that? What kind of man could lay such guilt on a brother officer?"

"Come on, Nick. I didn't like Steeple either, but you're jumping to conclusions."

"No, I'm not. Overtime is by far the most well thought out, well planned, and well executed military project I have ever seen or heard of. There was a central mind behind this whole thing, and if it wasn't Steeple, then who was it? Aliens? Bigfoot? It had to be Steeple. And don't say it's a coincidence that Morgan's death was faked and then within a year I was recruited..." His voice trailed off. His expression went from brows-lifted speculation to a staring-at-the-ground glare. "No. No, they would never do that."

"Who would never do what?"

Angriff looked up and there was death in his eyes. He raised a fore-finger, and stood like that for several minutes, thinking the unthinkable. When he spoke again, his voice had dropped an octave.

"Consider this: the Zero Defects Initiative began shortly after Over-time got the green light. We didn't know it then, but we do now. Highly trained men and women found themselves pushed out of the military for no good reason. Many of them had no family other than their branch of service. Suddenly there's a pool of talented recruits for a secret project in need of just such people. Coincidence? You know how I feel about coinci-dences. Then, when the ranks are filling up, they look for a commander.

"When my daughter and her husband made themselves a package deal, that put me one step closer to being available. Only my wife and other daughter stood in the way, and this is where it becomes downright demonic. Maybe they could be turned into an advantage. What if they died? And at the same time, their deaths motivated me to lead Overtime with a passion others wouldn't have."

"That's a lot of maybes. You can't possibly mean any of that."

"No? Why not? Until that meeting I had with Steeple, I thought he was the Devil incarnate. I thought I was a good judge of character and that he was being honest. But as I'm sure you remember, I wasn't think-ing straight. I wanted to avenge my wife and daughter so bad, I would've agreed to cut off my right hand if it meant killing their killers, and Stee-ple knew that. He knew I was vulnerable and he used it. But that's not the worst of it, Norm. What if Steeple was behind the whole thing?"

"Are you seriously suggesting that Tom Steeple, the highest-ranking officer in the United States armed forces, had your family murdered? Just so you would have nothing to hold you back from this assignment?"

"I'm saying it makes as much sense as anything else. And what about Bettison? I've never thought he was some rogue, in it for himself; he wasn't that clever. If he was working with Steeple, then it makes perfect sense that he wouldn't find my family's killers or even try very hard."

"Well, I think you've gone off the deep end, Nick."

"Yeah? Then chew on this. The group who claimed responsibility for Janine and Cynthia's deaths? Do you remember their name?"

Fleming shook his head.

"Well, I do. They called themselves the Sword of the New Prophet."

"The Sevens."

"Yes, the Sevens. They're one and the same."

Fleming walked off a few paces and rubbed his chin, trying to make sense of it all. "I don't know how to explain that. I wish I could. And maybe I'm being naïve here, but I just can't see the senior officer in the U.S. Army sanctioning the murder of a subordinate's family—for any reason, much less for such a risky project as Overtime. But let's say for the sake of argument that I could suspend my disbelief. Why would such a man do that when he would not even be around to benefit from his treachery...?" Then Fleming remembered his own words, not so long ago.

Angriff saw the recognition in his face. "Now you've come to it, Norm. You said it yourself, remember? If one Project Overtime was possible, why not two? Why die in the Collapse when Long Sleep could preserve you until America could be rebuilt in your preferred image and the image of the president you serve?"

"Part of me thinks you've gone insane, Nick."

"But the other part knows it's possible."

Fleming adopted the pose he took when thinking deeply about something. Hands clasped behind his back, he stared into the western sky, where the sun had sunk behind a distant butte. "The president, his closest advisers, and Tom Steeple, all out there somewhere..."

"Maybe waiting for us to clean things up before they move in and take over," Angriff said. "Claiming to be the rightful U.S. government."

"But wouldn't they *be* the rightful government?" Fleming said.

"I doubt it, not after this much time. But I don't know and I don't care. If Steeple was behind the death of my family, and if he's still out there somewhere, then he and I have a score to settle. And since I don't believe they would be the legitimately elected government, I'm not about to let him, his president, or any of his cronies take over this country a second time."

"But if they *were* legitimate, what then?"

"You know I believe the Constitution is second only to the Bible in its importance. If they were eligible, and they were elected, I'd respect it. But I'd have to be sure the election was fair. Anybody who could engineer a project this size is a genius. But to do it with such little regard for his brothers in arms takes a monster, and even more than that—"

Angriff stopped again. In all their years together, Fleming had never seen the expression he now saw on his best friend's face. Beyond shock, with wide eyes and open mouth, for moments all Angriff did was blink and shake his head.

"Oh, my God," he finally mumbled. "Oh, my God, oh, my God."

Fleming touched Angriff's shoulder and turned him so they were face to face. "Nick? Talk to me. Tell me what's going on."

The look on Angriff's face twisted into something more familiar, with jaw set and mouth turned down. "Do you remember when we sat in my office back in Virginia, the first time I said I was missing something about all this? That I knew something was wrong, except I didn't know what?"

"Sure, and you've said it a hundred times since then."

"I finally thought of it. Dear God, Norm, I know what I missed."

"Okay, that's good. Take a deep breath and tell me."

Angriff was so angry he shook. "Do you remember when we were on sub-floor eleven with Bettison?"

Fleming thought, *I got shot twice in the chest. I'm not likely to forget that.* But out loud he said, "Sure, Nick. How could I forget?"

"The little guy, remember him? With the Boston accent?"

"Yeah, Mole Man."

"Right. His voice, I'd heard it before. I knew it as soon as he said something, but I couldn't place it until just now. The video Bettison showed me of the terrorist attack, the one recovered from the tour boat? In the background somebody kept repeating *Allahu Akbar.* He said it very slow and clear."

"I remember you telling me that."

"Not like the ISIS mobs, or Hezbollah, but calmly. He annunciated each word so you couldn't miss it. He wasn't shouting it; he was saying it. Do you see what I mean?"

"I do. Terrorists would be jumping around."

"Exactly! It was his voice on the video. I know you're gonna say a lot of people have that accent, but it's not just that. It was him. I've heard it in my dreams so many times I can't count. Which means it was no terrorist attack. That was targeted at my family, specifically. All those innocent people used as a smokescreen for the murder of my family."

"And you're sure about this?"

"With God as my witness, I'm certain. So connect Mole Man with who took credit. Remember? The Sword of the New Prophet, which has morphed over the years into this Caliphate we just fought. This whole thing was nothing more than a conspiracy to ensure I took command of this brigade. Even Morgan being here... another bargaining chip in case I said no."

Norm Fleming rarely cursed. For this situation, he couldn't help himself. "Son of a bitch! It seems like a nightmare. I don't want to believe it, but all the pieces fit. I think you're right. They might really be out there somewhere and we could be facing more enemies than we thought."

"Yeah," Angriff said. "Maybe so, but if we are, so are they. And if Tom Steeple is out there, I'm gonna track him down. Then we're going to have a discussion he might not like."

Epilogue

Our genius ain't appreciated around here. Let's scram.
   Moe Howard

1357 hours, November 24

Green Ghost stood on the crest of the hill, ignoring the cold winds blowing in from the northwest. Nipple, Vapor, and Wingnut had retreated down the lee slope to avoid the icy breezes. The chill penetrated him as much as it did the others, and the older he got, the more he felt the effects of cold weather. Next time he would bring heavy clothes. It had been a stupid oversight, one he wouldn't usually make. But for the time being, he suppressed the shivering his body demanded and continued looking for skid marks near the river below.

"I'm fucking cold," his sister yelled. "Hey, B.B., let's get out of here."

Green Ghost could only stay underground for so long. With the brigade consolidating their hold on the newly liberated areas, his job as S-5 became tedious. Taking his three closest friends, the Core Four of Task Force Zombie, he'd announced to Angriff they were leaving on a slurp and wouldn't be back for a few weeks. The CO hadn't liked it, but just wished them well.

They'd decided to follow the gorge of the Little Colorado River north until it joined its larger namesake. For two days the sojourn had been a delightful hike through the high country in perfect fall weather. Game animals and predators filled the land, and Green Ghost got a feel for what it must have been like before the coming of white men to Arizona.

But on the third morning, Vapor had found tracks unlike anything he'd seen before. They appeared to be skid marks from some type of sled, only much bigger. There were three distinct sled tracks, each one about twenty-two inches wide. Inboard of the outer tracks were regular tire tracks. The whole mechanical footprint measured eight feet across, and the tracks sank deep into the hard-packed dirt. Whatever made them weighed several tons, at least.

Even stranger was the disruption of topsoil by some sort of wind. For twenty feet on either side of the tracks, something had thrown dirt and rocks out of the sled's way. Green Ghost had no explanation, except some giant type of propeller.

They'd lost the tracks in the hard rocks near the confluence of the two rivers. Instinct told him the secret of the skids was important, but winter had begun to settle over the land. And as much as he hated it, duties awaited back at Prime.

After admiring the view for a few more minutes, he called to his friends. "Let's head west and ford the river. There's a town over there called Cameron. Maybe we can put a roof over our heads tonight."

"That's the first sense you've made in days," Vapor said.

Nipple couldn't help chipping in. "More like years."

The End

About the Author

Native Memphian Bill grew up eating wild blackberries while riding his bicycle on back-country roads, day-dreaming about spaceships and devouring books. He has read *The Lord of the Rings* 32 times so far.

Grooming four acres of land east of Memphis maintains his boyish figure. Bill loves nothing more than reading (and writing!) an enthralling book, while ignoring eight barking dogs and two cranky old cats, four nests of screeching hawks bordering his property, various bobcats and coyotes, and a constant barrage of cartoons aimed at a three year old.

His indulgent wife just shakes her head and smiles.

Also from Dingbat Publishing

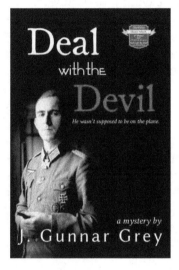

late evening, Saturday, 24 August 1940
over the village of Patchbourne, England

Something soft and annoying whooshed past his face. Faust brushed at it, but it was already gone and he was too damn sleepy to care. He dropped his arm to the bed.

There was no bed.

There wasn't anything. His arm was dangling out in space. So was the rest of him. Faust snapped his eyes open. A strong wind pummeled him, tumbled him arse over head. The ground was a long way down. He was falling and it was real, not some stupid nightmare.

Panic leapt like a predator through his veins. He twisted, fighting against gravity. An icicle of light from the distant ground stabbed at his eyes, swept past him, and far below, several red flashes popped in quick succession. A rumbling vibrated the air around him, something that sounded like an artillery round exploded nearby, and sharp chemical smoke scoured his nostrils.

Then tight cords wrapped about his body, between his legs, jerking him upright and throwing him higher, dangling him across the light-slashed night sky. The rumbling intensified. His head snapped back. Above him, a parachute canopy blazed white in the spotlight from below. Beyond it loomed a huge dark beast, moving past in impossible slow motion. It towered over him. The parachute danced closer, second by drawn-out second; then it bowed, canted, and slid away, laying Faust on his back as it hauled him aside.

He gripped the harness shroudlines, his chest and belly flinching. It was the bomber, the one he'd been riding in. The belly hatch framed Erhard's laughing face, lit from below by a spotlight. With one hand, Erhard clutched the rubber coaming, cupping the other about his mouth. He yelled something—something short—that was overwhelmed by the racket and growing distance.

Maybe the plane was having mechanical problems—but Faust, Erhard, and the mechanics had tuned the Heinkel's twin engines all afternoon. No one else was bailing out.

Erhard had thrown him overboard.

It didn't matter how much schnapps he'd slugged nor how drunk he remained. When Faust hit the ground, Erhard was toast.

The spotlight's cone slid from the front half of the bomber to the tail fin, the glare flashing across the metal and leaving a dark, mysterious line at the tailfin's hinge. The line and the glare slid across the matte metal, twisting and writhing, finally falling off the back edge. The bomber was turning from the light. It pirouetted in a slow, graceful curtsy like a prancing war horse and plowed into the side of the neighboring plane. Metal screeched and crumpled. The two bombers hung motionless, pinned to the night sky by the fingers of light from below. Then Erhard's plane rolled the other one over. Flames spiraled from the mass of cartwheeling metal.

From between the bombers fell a squirming, thrashing human. Another white canopy blossomed above it. But within moments the parachute silk convulsed in scarlet flames, melted to flaring sparks of gold and orange, and crumpled to nothingness. In a clear, bizarre second, Faust again glimpsed Erhard's face, no longer laughing but mouth open in a scream not drowned by the clamor as he fell beyond the spotlight's reach.

The entwined bombers exploded. Faust twisted, wrapping his elbows about his face, hands clutching the shroudlines. Something sharp and hot punched his right shoulder. Heat flared across his back. But when he twisted back around, the night sky was empty. The droning engines ebbed away and the searchlights vanished one by one. A final, embarrassingly late flak round exploded well behind the departing squadron and black smoke drifted through the lone remaining searchlight finger.

The light fastened onto him and his slaloming parachute, tracking his descent. He exhaled, one relieved whoosh. He'd been trained on parachutes before the invasion of Norway, months ago, but this was his first real jump. Okay, it wasn't that bad. But he couldn't wait for the ground crews to find him so he could scramble back to Paris, and if he never flew again, it would be too soon.

His breath caught. German groundfire had no reason to shoot at German planes.

Where the hell was he?

The spotlight vanished, leaving him blind upon his stage. He glanced down just as his feet slammed into something solid. His knees buckled, tumbling him backward into stubbly stalks. The scent of fresh-mown grass was overlaid with the acrid tang of burning metal. Clouds lowered the night sky almost within reach. Shoot, he didn't want to deal with Erhard's mess tonight, no matter where he was. Faust lay on his back and closed his eyes, letting the alcohol fuzz take over again. The klaxon of the air-raid alarm seemed to fade, not to silence but to an incomprehensible distance, like waves creaming over a remote Dover beach. Matthew Arnold wrote that one, about pebbles being drawn back then flung ashore by waves on the Sea of Faith. *Ah, love, let us be true to one another...*

But the unpoetical parachute harness tugged at his torso and groin, jerking him awake and dragging him prone across the field. The canopy billowed about. Sharp stubble poked his shoulders and back. He grunted, eyes jolting open.

There was a quick release snap somewhere. He fumbled with the harness, found something, and pressed it. It clicked and the pressure about his chest released, letting him twist from the harness. Any possibility of carefully gathering the miles of cloth into a manageable bundle was swept away when the rousing breeze yanked the 'chute right out of his hands. Crouched on his knees, he watched the white silk sail away, like some demented specter, toward a distant stand of dark waving trees, and tried to decide if it mattered a damn. Parachutes were reusable, weren't they? Should he try to chase the thing down? He closed his eyes and rubbed his face. Nope, he was still drunk, worrying about a frigging parachute when he should be worrying about himself.

A quivering voice blew with the breeze across the dark void surrounding him. "Jake, you sure he came down out here? I thought he was heading nearer town."

Faust's eyes flew open. The wind gusting over his exposed skin, face and hands, was suddenly chill. He shivered and hugged himself. The twisting in the pit of his stomach was more than just alcohol coming back to haunt him. Some deep part of his soul, something as primeval as the night itself, quaked beneath his skin. But his conscious mind hadn't yet figured out why.

A second voice spoke, more quietly than the first, and steadier. "Be quiet, you daft bugger."

Another gust of cold air splashed across his face, reaching through his skin into his heart and brain and being. Faust heard his breath rasping in the night's quiet and tried to still it. But the beating of his heart was just as loud and would not be calmed.

They spoke in English.

He wanted to be still so his unseen visitors wouldn't detect his presence, but he had to admit he froze because he was too scared to move. It took long moments before he could convince his body to curl over and duck his head down between his shoulders to hide his face. And no matter what he did, his lungs demanded oxygen and sounded like a bellows working it.

"Jake, there's something moving over by the trees."

He was beginning to sympathize with poor Jake: that daft bugger really wouldn't shut up.

"Yeah, I see it. Let's work our way over there, *quietly*, now."

Faust tensed every muscle he possessed, ready to run or fight for it. But he wasn't near any trees. His nerves quivered as the wind danced over his skin. It might be a small animal, shaking the branches at the far end of the field—then he remembered how his parachute had billowed about like a live thing and blown away toward those trees. He stuffed his hand into his mouth, stifling a giggle.

He held himself still, breathing more easily, until the discreet footfalls waned in the night. Then he scrambled up, balanced a moment to make certain he'd stay that way, and staggered in the opposite direction. A hedgerow bordered the field at the foot of a small hill, and a white-painted gate partway along glowed like a beacon. He scuttled toward it. There had to be somewhere he could hide.

Thanks for reading! Dingbat Publishing strives to bring you quality entertainment that doesn't take itself too seriously. I mean honestly, with a name like that, our books have to be good or we're going to be laughed at. Or maybe both.

If you enjoyed this book, the best thing you can do is buy a million more copies and give them to all your friends... erm, leave a review on the readers' website of your preference. All authors love feedback and we take reviews from readers like you seriously.

Oh, and c'mon over to our website:
www.DingbatPublishing.ninja

Who knows what other books you'll find there?

Cheers,

Gunnar Grey,
publisher, author, and Chief Dingbat

CPSIA information can be obtained
at www.ICGtesting.com
Printed in the USA
BVHW081258190819
556217BV00023B/2332/P